Pakistan's National Security Approach and Post-Cold War Security

I0585738

This book analyzes the paradox that despite being a national security state, Pakistan has become even more insecure in the post-Cold War era. It provides an in-depth analysis of Pakistan's foreign and security policies and their implications for the overall state and society.

The book identifies the immediate security challenges to Pakistan and charts the distinctive evolution of Pakistan's national security state in which the military elite became the dominant actor in the political sphere of government during and after the Cold War period. By examining the national security state, militarization, democracy and security, proxy wars, and the hyper-military-industrial complex, the author illustrates how the vanguard role of the military created considerable structural, sociopolitical, economic, and security problems in Pakistan. Furthermore, the author argues that the mismatch between Pakistan's national security stance and the transformed security environment has been facilitated and sustained by the embedded interests of the country's military-industrial complex.

A critical evaluation of the role of the military in the political affairs of the government and how it has created structural problems for Pakistan, this book will be of interest to academics in the field of South Asian Politics and Security, South Asian Foreign and Security Policy, International Relations, Asian Security, and Cold War Studies.

Arshad Ali is an Assistant Professor in the Department of Political Science and International Relations at the University of Management and Technology, Pakistan.

Routledge Studies in South Asian Politics

For more information about this series, please visit: www.routledge.com/asianst udies/series/RSSAP

Pakistan's National Security Approach and Post-Cold War Security

Uneasy Co-existence

Arshad Ali

Routledge
Taylor & Francis Group

LONDON AND NEW YORK

First published 2021
by Routledge
2 Park Square, Milton Park, Abingdon, Oxon OX14 4RN

and by Routledge
52 Vanderbilt Avenue, New York, NY 10017

Routledge is an imprint of the Taylor & Francis Group, an informa business

British Library Cataloguing-in-Publication Data
A catalogue record for this book is available from the British Library

Library of Congress Cataloging-in-Publication Data
Names: Ali, Arshad, author.
Title: Pakistan's national security approach and post-Cold War security :
uneasy co-existence / Arshad Ali.
Description: Abingdon, Oxon ; New York, NY : Routledge, 2021. |
Series: Routledge studies in South Asian politics | Includes bibliographical
references and index.
Identifiers: LCCN 2020047713 | ISBN 9780367709785 (hardback) |
ISBN 9781003152224 (ebook)
Subjects: LCSH: National security--Pakistan. | Pakistan--Foreign relations. |
Jammu and Kashmir (India)--Politics and government. |
Terrorism--Pakistan--Prevention. | War on Terrorism, 2001-2009.
Classification: LCC UA853.P3 A585 2021 | DDC 355/.03355491--dc23
LC record available at https://lccn.loc.gov/2020047713

ISBN: 978-0-367-70978-5 (hbk)
ISBN: 978-0-367-71475-8 (pbk)
ISBN: 978-1-003-15222-4 (ebk)

Typeset in Times New Roman
by Deanta Global Publishing Services, Chennai, India

Dedicated to my wife Shabana Arshad, son Azlan Khan and daughter Zarshal Khan

Contents

Tables

Acknowledgements

As I reflect back on writing this book, it has been very tough but equally reward-ing as I have accomplished something for which I have been striving the last few years. This journey would not have been possible without the constant support and encouragement of many influential people including teachers, colleagues, friends, and family members.

I am deeply grateful to Professor Robert G. Patman for his continuous sup-port and encouragement, insightful advice, critical engagement, and extensive analytical discussions around this monograph. It was Professor Patman who guided me to convert my PhD thesis into a book manuscript for a renowned publisher. I would like to offer special appreciations to Dr. Chris Rudd for his constructive suggestions and valuable feedback and ideas which helped me in producing this piece of study. Special thanks to my department colleagues at the University of Management and Technology, Lahore, especially to Professor Muhammad Shoaib Pervez for his collegial support and leadership, inspiration, and constructive ideas to complete the revisions of this book on time. I would like to extend my gratitude to Dr. Anwar Shah and Dr. Arabinda Acharya for their unconditional support and assistance in my academic progress. Also, I am eternally indebted to my mentors Fazal Subhan and Inaytullah for believing in me and often encouraging me to excel in my academic journey.

I gratefully acknowledge my friends and old colleagues who assisted me in doing my field research in Pakistan. Three people deserve special words of gratitude: Dr. Sadia Sulaiman, Dr. Khuram Iqbal, and Dr. Shahzad Akhtar for their help and support in approaching interviewees. I extend my special thanks to Dr. Khuram and his wife who shared their residence with me during my stay in Islamabad. I am also very grateful to Yahya Maqbool and Assadullah Khan for organizing my visit to the parliament to interview politicians.

I am obligated to my siblings and parents Muhammad Payun and Bacha Bibi whose support are central to my academic success. I extend my appreciations and thanks to my awesome wife Shabana who waited patiently all the way until the completion of my PhD studies in New Zealand. Let me admit, I understand her feelings while leaving her behind with our twins Azlan Khan and Zarshal Khan in a society where patriarchy is the norm. On top of this, when one of our children

(Zarshal) is disabled. Furthermore, I grew up when my father was working abroad so I do understand the feelings of my kids during my absence. I owe them the most especially to Shabana for taking care of our twins and giving me time to follow my intellectual pursuits. I will try to support her and my kids in their future endeavours.

Introduction

Pakistan became an independent country after the partition of British India on 14 August 1947. Since then, the country has perceived serious regional threats to its national sovereignty and territorial integrity. The issue of Kashmir and fears that India may attempt to undo the process of partition were the major security concerns of Pakistan after independence. Since partition, India has been a dominant power in South Asia due to the large size of its territory, population, economy, and military power. Moreover, Indian leaders only reluctantly accepted Pakistan as an independent state, believing that the creation of Pakistan was temporary and eventually it would be reintegrated into a United India (Burke 1973; Paul 2005). Prime Minister Jawaharlal Nehru claimed that "partition would be temporary" and "Indo-Pakistani confederation remains our ultimate end" (Waheed 2017, 284). Consequently, Pakistani leadership perceived India as a real threat to the national sovereignty of the country and considered India to be a permanent enemy in its neighbourhood for the foreseeable future. Muhammad Ali Jinnah, the founder of Pakistan, expressed his concerns (Jaffrelot 2016, 2):

> the Congress has accepted the present settlements with mental reservations. They now proclaim their determination to restore the unity of India as soon as possible. With that determination they will naturally be regarded as avowed enemies of Pakistan State working for its overthrow.

Therefore, the survival of the Pakistani state became a primary concern of the country's leadership immediately after independence in 1947. Subsequently, there was a perceived need for constant military preparedness, given the prospect of war against India. Such a prospect required a strong military force to protect Pakistan's sovereignty and territorial integrity (Cohen 2004). The war in Kashmir already started right after independence. In October 1948, Prime Minister Liaquat Ali Khan declared in a speech to the nation that "the defence of the state is our foremost consideration. We will not grudge any amount on the defence of our country" (Singh and Baily 2013, 113). As a result, Pakistan adopted a military-centred national security state approach to counter local and regional threats to its national security.

Pakistan's concerns about India played a key role in the formulation of Pakistan's foreign and security policy. Consequently, Pakistan's military competition with India was prioritized over nation-building after the country's independence (Singh and Baily 2013). The government allotted a massive portion of its annual budget to defence expenditure. Throughout the Cold War, defence spending remained more than 50 percent of total government expenditure. Pakistan spent 60.69 percent of its total government expenditure on defence in the first 11 years following independence (Rizvi 2000). This provided the foundation for a national security apparatus that emphasized the pivotal role of the nation's military in countering the apparent external threat from India. Nonetheless, it was a very expensive national security approach for a new country to sustain with only limited economic resources.

In addition, the Muslim League, which led Pakistan's independence movement, was unable to transform itself from a nationalist movement into a strong political party after 1947 (Rizvi 2000). The political leadership was also weakened following the deaths of two main leaders, namely, Muhammad Ali Jinnah, the founder of Pakistan, in 1948, and Liaquat Ali Khan, the country's first prime minister, in 1951 (Blom 2011). This created leadership crises in the country soon after its inception. Subsequently, the military leadership took over the role of state administration. Under General Ayub Khan, a strong military institution was formed that gradually established its control over state affairs during the 1950s. The Pakistani military began its formal watchdog role over defence affairs in 1952 and steadily extended its role as the sole guarantor of the state's survival. In 1954, the defence ministry was taken over by the military, and later, General Ayub imposed martial law administration in October 1958, becoming the first of the four chief martial law administrators (Gates and Roy 2011).

Interestingly, the Pakistani military used its political and administrative autonomy to establish its own commercial and welfare enterprises in the country, starting in 1954. Since then, there has been both vertical and horizontal growth in their business conglomerates. They became directly involved in various commercial ventures such as building roads, collecting road tolls, real estate, cement factories, private banks, education, and even grocery stores (Siddiqa 2007). This, in turn, led to a distinctive formation in Pakistan of what US President Dwight Eisenhower subsequently termed "a military-industrial complex" (Eisenhower 1961), which enabled the military to build its own economic base to act autonomously and largely escape civilian control in shaping the national security policies of the country. Thus, the Pakistani military elite also monopolized economic resources during the Cold War period.

In the 1970s, the Inter-Services Intelligence (ISI) became another key actor in Pakistan's state affairs within its military-centred national security state. On the external front, the ISI provided key information about India's armed forces and its operational planning in the 1971 war. During the 1979 Afghan war, the ISI planned to step up support for the Afghan resistance movement and carried out the world's biggest covert operation along with Central Intelligence Agency (CIA) against the Soviet forces in Afghanistan (Haqqani 2005; Datta 2014).

Nonetheless, the ISI formed alliances with religious and far-right groups in order to control domestic politics. Thus, the Pakistan military and the ISI consolidated power in the country during the Cold War.

The end of the Cold War did little to diminish Pakistan's fixation with the Kashmir conflict and its intense rivalry with India continued in South Asia, including in war-torn Afghanistan. Moreover, radical Islam emerged after the collapse of the Soviet Union in 1991, and after the events of 9/11, this threat to Pakistan deepened. Thus, Islamabad has had to deal with both interstate and intra-state security threats in the post-Cold War era. Notwithstanding this, Pakistan has persisted with its military-first national security state approach.

This security approach was relatively successful during the Cold War era. Pakistan responded to the Cold War security environment by taking advantage of the superpower rivalry between the US and the Soviet Union in order to help achieve its own core national security goals. Pakistan aligned with the US mainly to gain economic and military aid to more effectively counter Indian military power. However, the post-Cold War transformation of the regional and international strategic environment – especially after the 9/11 terror attacks – has somewhat exposed the limitations of the focus on Pakistan's strategic rivalry with India. India embarked on a successful process of economic liberalization in the early 1990s that would significantly widen the wealth gap between a rising India and a desperately poor Pakistan. Moreover, the US no longer needed Pakistan after Soviet withdrawal from Afghanistan in the late 1980s and had drastically reduced its military support for Islamabad, shifting the balance of power in favour of India.

Within a national security state framework, the Pakistani military elite showed little willingness to adapt to the realities of a transformed strategic environment in the post-Cold War security environment. Nonetheless, the civilian leadership of Benazir Bhutto and Nawaz Sharif attempted to adjust its foreign and security policies in the new global context of the post-Cold War era and tried to find diplomatic solutions to the outstanding issues with India and Afghanistan. Such initiatives were thwarted by the military on the pretext of national security interests. Consequently, three elected governments were dismissed in the 1990s, twice by President Ghulam Ishaq Khan and once by Farooq Laghari, with support of the Pakistani army (Aziz 2008).

The Pakistani military leadership justified their action under the geostrategic global environment and domestic compulsion to protect the country's national interests. For example, the nuclear programme was used by the military as a good bargaining chip with Prime Minister Bhutto, where she was being charged with freezing Pakistan nuclear programme due to international pressure, mainly from the US under "Pressler Amendment." Bhutto was also kept out of the planning of this strategy to use a "proxy war" in Kashmir against India by the Pakistani military (Nawaz 2009). They justified their Kashmir policy on the pretext of the culture of secrecy in proxy wars and domestic compulsion. Hence, the Pakistani military elite used hybrid module of the geostrategic global environment and domestic compulsion as a leading cause of military ascendency, especially in the decade of 1990s.

There are multiple factors behind this military ascendency. First, the long military rule of General Zia (1977–1988) gave military the economic ascendency over their civilian counterparts; second, the democracy in Pakistan in the 1990s was under the patronage and oversight of military elites who did not leave any stone unturned to belittle it on one pretext or the other; third, the political parties in Pakistan have yet to develop grass root infrastructure and are fairly elitist (feudalist and industrialist) at the time. The military elites instrumentally used the fallacies of their political counterparts to portray themselves as the saviour of the nation. The geostrategic environment in the shape of Kashmir uprising and American new world order in the 1990s also favoured the Pakistani military elite as it was very convenient for the US to focus on one army chief instead of the whole bunch of rowdy political elites.

Thus, Islamabad persisted with its involvement in proxy wars in Kashmir, supporting militant Islamist forces opposing the Indian presence, and in Afghanistan where it supported Taliban militants in a bid to gain strategic depth and counter Indian influence in that country. However, Pakistan's proxy wars have fuelled militancy and radicalization internally as well. Pakistan has gone from a country which was largely preoccupied with external security threats during the Cold War to one that increasingly has to factor in concerns about internal security threats from home-grown terrorism and repercussions from covert involvement in neighbouring external conflicts. According to the Global Peace Index (GPI),[1] the country was among the ten least peaceful countries in 2012–2016 (Appendix 1).

Ironically, Pakistan has faced this increasing security threat despite holding a large military of 919,000 personnel, nuclear weapons, and a substantial intelligence network, while it competes with developed countries with regard to military modernization (Worldatlas 2018). At the same time, the military has continued to command the lion's share of the government's expenditure, and this has left only meagre financial resources to address chronic socio-economic problems in the country. And yet, in 2020, Pakistan was ranked 152 out of 163 countries on the GPI, which means it has largely remained insecure (GPI 2020).

Both the military and civilian leadership in Pakistan have apparently recognized that the internal security threat has become greater than its external threats. In June 2009, then-President Asif Ali Zardari admitted that (Nelson 2009):

> I do not consider India a military threat; the question is that India has the capability. Capability is what matters. [With regard to] intention I think we both have our good intentions. India is a reality, Pakistan is a reality, but Taliban are a threat, an international threat … to our way of life. And at the moment, I'm focused on the Taliban. It's something that has been going on for a long time and of course went unchecked under the dictatorial rule of the last president.

In August 2013, the chief of the Army Staff, General Ashfaq Pervez Kayani, confessed that (BBC 2012):

We realise that the most difficult task for any army is to fight against its own people. But this happens as a last resort. Our real objective is to restore peace in these areas so that people can lead normal lives. No state can afford a parallel system or a militant force. The fight against extremism and terrorism is our own war and we are right in fighting it. Let there be no doubt about it, otherwise we'll be divided and taken towards civil war. Our minds should be clear on this.

Hence, the perpetuation of Pakistan's military-centred national security state approach in the post-Cold War era has done little to curb mounting insecurity within the country and has not solved its external security problems in relation to India. The Kashmir conflict has remained unresolved between the two countries. In fact, India has unilaterally annexed Indian-administrated Kashmir within its union territory by revoking its special status under Article 370 of the Indian constitution in August 2019 (Shakir 2020). Therefore, this study's central research question is: why has Pakistan persisted with a military-centric national security state approach at a time when it has faced intensifying security challenges in the post-Cold War era?

This book aims to explain an important paradox – the Pakistani state has focused disproportionately on strengthening national security but in the process has experienced a very real decline in its overall security position in the post-Cold War era. Pakistan's premier intelligence agency, the ISI has used "proxy war" as a strategic tool of its foreign policy to protect its so-called national security interests. However, such proxy wars have created severe blowback, serving to increase or create internal and external security threats. The internal security threat has become almost an existential one to Pakistan as the militants had established their control over north-western areas in Khyber Pakhtunkhwa (KP) province from 2007 to 2013. Moreover, Pakistan has been blamed as a terror-sponsoring country, being placed on the grey list of the Financial Action Task Force (FATF) on money laundering and terror financing for the second time in the 2010s. In October 2019, the FATF showed serious concerns and warned Islamabad that the country might be blacklisted if it did not take significant steps to curb terror financing and money laundering by February 2020 (FATF 2019).

Domestically, the Pakistani military has been involved directly and indirectly in monitoring internal political matters since the 1950s in order to maintain the military's functional dominance over the civilian leadership in questions of national and international security. As mentioned, the ISI has established close relations with religious political parties and far-right groups that have been used against popular civilian governments. For example, the Islami Jamhoori Ittehad (IJI) worked as a political wing of the military which was used by the ISI to destabilize Benazir Bhutto's government between 1988 and 1990. More recently, the Tehreek-i-Labbaik Pakistan (TLP) was utilized against the Pakistan Muslim League-Nawaz (PMLN) government in 2017 (see Chapter 6). Thus, the military has continued to use the far-right groups against mainstream prominent political parties to maintain its functional dominance in the state affairs, but it has continued to create political instability in the country.

Academic literature on Pakistan's national security state approach in the context of the military-industrial complex is sparse, and seldom have any integrated efforts have been made to adequately (or holistically) explain security, economy, political, and strategic consequences of Pakistan's military-industrial complex within its national security state. Shuja Nawaz provided a comprehensive insight into the ultimate power circles of the Pakistani state in a historical context. He also examines the various wars (within) between the civilian and the military elites as well as wars within each of these institutions. Nawaz drew attention to various key past events such as the Kashmir conflict, fall of Dhaka, and the Kargil War and explained how the Pakistani army had maintained a dominant role in state affairs (Nawaz 2009). Nevertheless, his book does not critically evaluate the role of the military in establishing political and economic control in state affairs which has created more insecurity in the country. Aqil Shah explores the key historical conditions, events, and decisions that offer the process of Pakistan's military intervention in the country's politics. He illustrates that the military institutional thinking has been shaped by geopolitical insecurity, nation-building problems, Cold War dynamics, war on terror, and institutional interests. Shah argues that the Pakistani military has gradually transformed itself from an "apolitical professional military" into the sole guardian of national security, a role which the military elite considers necessary for the very existence of the country (Shah 2014). This book does not explain Pakistan's military industrial complex in which the military has exercised overall control in state affairs.

Ayesha Siddiqa has provided a comprehensive study of Pakistan's military business and its political economy. She explained that there has been vertical and horizontal growth in the military business conglomerates which drives their political ambitions. Siddiqa argues that bourgeoning economic empires establish the interests of the military elite in retaining political control in state affairs (Siddiqa 2007). However, her study does not deeply devolve into Pakistan's national security state which played a key role in building the military-industrial complex during the Cold War. In fact, this military-industrial complex is sustained due to perpetuation of Pakistan's national security state. This study will give an in-depth analysis of the evolution of Pakistan's national security state as well as linkages between Pakistan's military-industrial complex and national security shortfalls. It argues that the incessant involvement of the military elite in state affairs has created more insecurity in Pakistan due to its parochial and vested institutional interests.

Christine Fair has analyzed the strategic culture of the Pakistan army in domestic politics and foreign policy. She explained that the army has presented itself as the guardian and protector of Pakistan's ideological and territorial boundaries under which rivalry with India has been framed as a civilizational one. The army has maintained the upper hand in the state affairs as the state apparatus is at its disposal to protect its institutional interests. Fair argues that the Pakistan army's strategic culture has been remarkably conservative and resistant to change since independence (Fair 2014). Unlike Fair, this study will explain that it is primarily the military-industrial complex which is the most important variable in Pakistan's national security state (military perspective) which does not allow any division in military strategic culture. Nonetheless, this variable is closely tied to the domestic instability on which the military elite in Pakistan has successfully portrayed itself as the saviour of the nation and, with the utilization of public resources, has developed an efficient military economic organization to instrumentally blackmail the political elite. Nevertheless, this variable is linked to internal and external security threats, but the military always took credit for improving the security situation and stability in the country while placing all the blame on the civilians for insecurity. This variable also associated to economic crises of the country as the military has prioritized and protected their commercial interests at the cost of economic and social development.

To sum up, this book briefly traverses the history of Pakistan since its inception in order to see the intransigence of military elites in the body of state politics. It seeks to identify the immediate security challenges to Pakistan and chart the distinctive evolution of the national security state in which the military elite became the dominant actor in the political sphere of government during and after the Cold War period. It explains that Pakistan adopted the American Cold War model of the national security state, but the country has gone much further than its American counterpart in embedding and institutionalizing the leading role of the military in formulating security and foreign policies of the country. In fact, Pakistan has not only complied almost perfectly with the US national security state approach but developed its own unique approach. For instances, the US military has always remained under civilian control in principle, whereas the Pakistani military had the consistent capacity to act in a much more autonomous fashion. Moreover, the Pakistani military directly ran various business conglomerates and intervened in the political sphere of state affairs to produce what could be termed a "hyper-military-industrial complex." This study will provide an in-depth analysis of Pakistan's military-industrial complex and will illuminate how the vanguard role of the military created considerable structural, sociopolitical, economic, and security problems in Pakistan in the post-Cold War security environment and instigated the role of Pakistan's military-industrial complex in this declining national security situation, political instability, and economic insecurity in the country. The book argues that the mismatch between Pakistan's military-centric approach to national security and a transformed security environment has been facilitated and sustained by the embedded and parochial interests of the country's military-industrial complex.

The study covers two key regional conflicts in South Asia: first, the Kashmir dispute (1989–2001), the long-running militarized conflict between two nuclear armed countries, India and Pakistan, and second, the global war on terror (2001–2013), which is the longest war the US has ever been engaged in. Pakistan has always been key to regional security in South Asia and has played a central role during and after the Cold War. Pakistan was a key ally of the US-led Western bloc during the Cold War as well as during the global war on terror. This book will show that Pakistan's evolving national security state took advantage of US-Soviet rivalry but nevertheless maintained its own security agenda during the Cold War era and did the same when Pakistan became a key security partner of Washington during Bush's war on terror after 9/11.

Nevertheless, this study will critically analyze the above two cases of how the military elite has handled the issue of Kashmir and the global war on terror within Pakistan's national security state framework in the post-Cold War era. In most of the prior studies on Kashmir, there is seldom any study which focused on this perennial security dispute from a national security state framework, and this study will highlight those missing links. The primary objective of the two cases is to see the efficacy of the national security state approach in solving major disputes confronted by the country in the post-Cold War era. The two cases argue that Pakistan's national security state has largely failed to protect its national security interests in the post-Cold War era. Despite its failures, Pakistan has persisted with a military-centred national security state in the post-Cold War era.

The study is based on the following assumption:

- The perpetuation of Pakistan's military-centred national security state approach in the post-Cold War era has created domestic and regional insecurity and has caused political instability within the country.
- Pakistan's national security state not only facilitated and protected the military's commercial interests but also ensured a functional dominance over the civilian leadership in the running of state affairs.
- The Pakistani military elites instrumentally belittle their political counterparts as they prefer a "hybrid democracy" and "strong central government" for their own parochial interests in order to have the upper hand in the policymaking of the country.
- The Pakistani military has largely depended on asymmetric warfare to balance a hegemonic India and to protect its strategic interests and used far-right groups to counter anti-military democratic groups and individuals.

Research methodology

This book is a study of the national security state and considers the case of Pakistan. The book uses case study methodology. In qualitative research, the case study method "is used to provide an in-depth understanding of a phenomenon as it occurs in real-time to portray the complexities, interactions, and occurrences that explain how, what, and why" (Frey 2008, 2). A major advantage of the case study approach is that it offers the chance to investigate complex social issues consisting of multiple variables by providing specific and detailed information and insights

(Frey 2008). This study uses the explorative case study method, which allows for an in-depth analysis of Pakistan's foreign and security policies and their implications for the overall state and society. This study examines two cases: the Kashmir dispute between Pakistan and India in 1988–2001 and Pakistan's participation in the global war on terror in 2001–2008. Both the Kashmir conflict and Pakistan's participation in the global war on terror are important factors in Islamabad's foreign and security policy in the post-Cold War era.

This study applies "process tracing" for analyzing the cases. Process tracing can be defined as "the systematic examination of diagnostic evidence selected and analyzed in light of research questions and hypotheses posed by the investigator" (Collier 2011, 823). The study uses descriptive and causal inference for process tracing which are necessary for in-depth analysis of events, situations over time, and stakeholders. For example, process tracing stresses unfolding events and situations such as the 9/11 terror attack, but it requires adequate description to understand at a particular point in time (Collier 2011). In this context, the process tracing method needs a detailed description within a case study by using unfolding events and phenomena to explain the causal mechanism under investigation and analysis.

Numerous secondary sources of information and analysis on Pakistan's national security and foreign policy are available to researchers. Secondary data was obtained for this study from academic journals, books, policy papers in national and international newspapers, occasional papers, internet searches, government reports, and publications by national and international non-governmental organizations (NGOs) and organizations such as Human Rights Watch, Carnegie Endowment, RAND Corporation, Brookings Institution, the US State Department, the World Bank, the International Monetary Fund (IMF), and Pakistan Institute of Legislative Development and Transparency (PILDAT).

Furthermore, indexes such as GPI and Human Development Index (HDI)[2] will be used to see the overall security and economic situation in the country. Beside these indexes, the study will take radicalization and extremism, political instability, and economic insecurity as major indicators of the mounting insecurity within the country.

However, secondary material does not always include the views of practitioners, especially politicians, diplomats, and representatives of the military in Pakistan. The secondary sources are susceptible to becoming outdated and provide sometimes limited insights into political events that often, in the Pakistani context, take place behind closed doors (Lilleker 2003). In order to minimize the impact of these limitations, primary field research was undertaken to fill the research gaps and supplement the secondary research in this area. Prior to conducting field research, I prepared a questionnaire guide (Appendix 2) that was consistent with the major lines of my research inquiry. I listed 28 prospective interviewees from both government and non-government organizations that had detailed knowledge of Pakistan's national security policies and some awareness of the possible implications for national, regional, and international security. The respondents were selected from four groups, including *diplomats* who served as ambassadors to countries such as India, Afghanistan, and the US; former or currently serving senior *military officers* such as generals and brigadiers; *academics* well known for their policy inputs on foreign policy, from different universities such as Quaid-i-Azam University, Peshawar University, the National Defence University, Iqra University, and the National University of Sciences and Technology, as well as think tanks such as the Institute of Strategic Studies Islamabad and the Islamabad Policy Institute; and *politicians* belonging to the Pakistan Muslim League (Nawaz Group), Pakistan Tehreek-e-Insaf, Pakistan's People Party, Awami National Party, and Qaumi Watan Party.

The primary research was conducted in Islamabad and Rawalpindi, Pakistan. The interviews were formally scheduled and were conducted through what is known as the snowball sampling technique. I conducted 28 targeted interviews in which 23 were face-to-face and remaining 5 via Skype. While doing the field research, some consideration was given to the selection of participants in terms of age, gender, world view, and discipline. This provided a diverse opinion on the subject of inquiry.

Limitations of this study

Military businesses in Pakistan are managed through a closed system, and information relating to military conglomerates is not made public. Moreover, there is very limited debate on military expenditure and their businesses in parliament or the media. This study has relied mainly on data available in annual budgets, together with national and international media reports. Furthermore, this study has explained how the military-industrial complex has contributed to the economic crisis in Pakistan. Nonetheless, there is a need for a comprehensive study to specifically analyze how much the military-centric national security state has contributed to human insecurity in the country. Finally, this book has applied the concept of the national security state, which was proposed by some leaders and developed by some scholars in the US after the end of the Second World War. The national security state underpinned realist theory and this book does not consider other paradigms within the subject of international relations such as liberalism and social constructivism.

Structure of the book

The first chapter in this book reviews existing literature on the evolution of national security state that was born out of very extreme security circumstances in the US at the beginning of the Cold War. The realist school of thought in international relations theory underpins the establishment of the national security state, and this chapter identifies some of the key features and ideas characterizing the US national security state model in which military power is perceived as the primary instrument of the state for maintaining its national security interests, and the military and related institutional sectors possess substantial political and economic power. This American model could be deployed in the case of Pakistan, as the book revolves around Pakistan's national security state.

The second chapter explains that Pakistan's national security state was also born in difficult security circumstance like the US. After independence, Pakistan perceived external threats, whether real or not, from neighbouring countries that played a major role in the formulation of this security approach in which military interests were prioritized over nation-building. The military consolidated power in the 1950s and the ISI in 1970s as primary actors in foreign and security policies as well as domestic politics of the country. More importantly, the military established its functional dominance over state affairs through establishing its alliances with religious and far-right groups as well as constitutional amendments introduced during periods of military rule in the Cold War era. This chapter also identifies some of the key features and ideas characterizing Pakistan's national security state model and analyzes the evolution of Pakistan's military-centric national security state approach during the Cold War. Pakistan has not only complied almost perfectly with the US national security state approach but established its own unique approach in which the Pakistani military elite has maintained a dominant position in state affairs. Nonetheless, the Pakistani military presented a range of obstacles to political parties or leaders that wanted reformation Pakistan's national security state.

The third chapter clarifies that Pakistan has continued with its military-centric national security state approach in the changing post-Cold War security environment. In South Asia, the security situation essentially remained the same for Pakistan despite a changing global security environment. However, Islamabad lost the strategic position it once had occupied during the Cold War. Even with civilians in power, the Pakistani military elite excluded the civilian leadership from key strategic decision making with respect to the Kashmir conflict and the country's nuclear programme, and the president dismissed three elected governments with the support of the Pakistani military in the post-Cold War era. After the 9/11 terrorist attacks, General Pervez Musharraf's government reinvigorated its military-centred national security approach by making an alliance with the US in the global war on terror. However, this development has had severe destabilizing consequences for the country.

The fourth chapter considers the case of the Kashmir conflict (1989–2001) between Pakistan and India in order to analyze the efficacy of Pakistan's military-centred national security state approach in the post-Cold War era. The Kashmir conflict has been one of the longest unresolved military conflicts in the contemporary world. During 1989–2001, Islamabad attempted to find military and diplomatic solutions to the conflict but failed. The ISI used Islamic militancy as a strategic tool to counter Indian military power and gain international attention to resolve the Kashmir dispute. In 1999, the Pakistani military instigated a war in Kargil to gain a strategic advantage over India in Kashmir.

The civilian leadership tried to find a political settlement of the outstanding issues including Kashmir through a peace process which was thwarted by the military using the issue of national security. After the 9/11 terror attacks, India successfully linked Kashmiri indigenous movement for the right to self-determination with Islamic terrorism and blamed Pakistan for sponsoring terror groups. The Kashmir case (1989–2001) confirms that Pakistan's national security state approach failed not only to resolve the Kashmir issue but exacerbated security threats.

The fifth chapter examines Pakistan's strategic considerations and regional stability in South Asia by looking at the case of Pakistan's participation in the global war on terror from 2001 to 2013. This is another important case to see the effectiveness of Pakistan's national security state policies in protecting its regional security interests in the post-Cold War era. The 9/11 terror attacks changed the security dynamics of South Asia. Pakistan once again became a key strategic ally in the US-led global war on terror, which provided another opportunity for the Pakistani military to buttress its national security state. While Pakistan and the US forged a new relationship after the 9/11 attacks, both countries maintained diverse objectives and interests in their global war on terror. The US required Pakistan's support to dislodge the Afghan Taliban regime in Kabul and eliminate Al-Qaeda, whereas Pakistan supported the US war on terror to have a friendly regime in Kabul to prevent Indian influence in Afghanistan. Musharraf adopted a dual policy in the war on terror, which was self-defeating as Islamabad supported the Kabul regime but at the same time aided the Afghan Taliban after joining the global war on terror. The study argues that this dual policy has had severe consequences for Pakistan, making it more insecure than before, as well as a pariah state. This case also confirms that Islamabad has largely failed to protect its regional security interests under the national security state in the post-9/11 period. However, Pakistan has persisted with a military-centred national security state in the post-Cold War era.

The sixth chapter directly addresses the central question of this book. In light of the evidence presented here, this chapter argues that Islamabad persisted with its military-centric national security state because it provides a privileged role to the Pakistani military elite in the state affairs. Since Pakistan's 1947, the perceived threat to national survival has enabled the country's military elite to build a hyper-military-industrial complex in which the Pakistani military exercised overall economic and political control of the state. This military-industrial complex has played a major role in preventing any reform of the military's self-serving national security state. However, this security approach has largely failed to adapt to the radically transformed security environment of the post-Cold War era. This failure to adapt has not only exacerbated external threats but also fuelled new internal insecurity problems and created something of an internal-external threat nexus facing Pakistan. Moreover, it has created political instability in Pakistan that led to weak civilian institutions, socio-economic problems, and a fragile democracy in the country.

Notes

1 "The GPI is based on 23 different indicators, including political terror, deaths from internal conflict, and murder rate."
2 "The HDI ranking of a country is measured by combining indicators of life expectancy, educational attainment, gender development, income inequality, countries trade and income."

References

Aziz, M. 2008. *Military Control in Pakistan: A Parallel State*. Routledge.
Blom, E. 2011. *Pakistan: Coercion and Capital in an Insecurity State*. IRSEM, Paris Papers.
Burke, S. M. 1973. *Pakistan's Foreign Policy: An Historical Analysis*. Oxford University Press.
Cohen, S. P. 2004. *The Idea of Pakistan*. Brooking Institute Press.
Collier, D. 2011. "Understanding Process Tracing." *Political Science & Politics* 44 (4): 823–830.
Datta, S. K. 2014. *Inside ISI: The Story and Involvement of the ISI in Afghan Jihad, Taliban, Al-Qaeda, 9/11, Osama Bin Laden, 26/11 and the Future of Al-Qaeda*. Vij Books India Pvt Ltd.
Eisenhower, D. 1961. "Farewell Radio and Television Address to American People." *Public Papers of the Presidents of the United States: Dwight D. Eisenhower, 1960–61* (Washington: GPO): 1035–1040.
Fair, C. C. 2014. *Fighting to the End: The Pakistan Army's Way of War*. Oxford University Press.
FATF Official Report. 2019. "Improving Global AML/CFT Compliance: On-Going Process." October 18, 2019. Retrieved on December 20, 2019, http://www.fatf-gafi.org/countries/d-i/iceland/documents/fatf-compliance-october-2019.html#Pakistan.
Frey, B. B. 2008. *The SAGE Encyclopedia of Educational Research, Measurement, and Evaluation*. SAGE Publications, Inc.
Gates, S. and Roy, K. 2011. *Conventional Warfare in South Asia, 1947 to the Present*. Routledge.
Haqqani, H. 2005. *Pakistan: Between Mosque and Military*. Carnegie. Endowment for International Peace.
Institute for Economics & Peace. 2020. *Global Peace Index 2020: Measuring Peace in a Complex World*. Retrieved on http://visionofhumanity.org/reports.
Jaffrelot, C. 2016. *Pakistan at the Crossroads: Domestic Dynamics and External Pressures*. Columbia University Press.
Lilleker, D. G. 2003. "Interviewing the Political Elite: Navigating a Potential Minefield." *Politics* 23 (3): 207–214.
Nawaz, S. 2009. *Crossed Swords: Pakistan, Its Army, and the Wars Within*. Oxford University Press.
Nelson, D. 2009. "Pakistan: India no Longer a Military Threat." *Telegraph*, South Asia, June 24, 2009. Retrieved on September 5, 2018, https://www.telegraph.co.uk/news/worldnews/asia/pakistan/5625759/Pakistan-India-no-longer-a-military-threat.html.
"Pakistan Army Chief Ashfaq Parvez Kayani in Unity Plea." BBC, Asia, August 14, 2012. Retrieved on November 22, 2018, https://www.bbc.com/news/world-us-canada-19254070

Paul, T. V. 2005. *The India-Pakistan Conflict: An Enduring Rivalry*. Cambridge University Press.

Rizvi, H. A. 2000. *Military State and Society in Pakistan*. Palgrave Macmillan.

Shakir, A. R. 2020. "August 05: Reminiscent of Blatant Indian Aggression." *The Nation*, Pakistan, August 6, 2020, Retrieved on September 2, 2020, https://nation.com.pk/06-Aug-2020/august-05-reminiscent-of-blatant-indian-aggression.

Shah, A. 2014. *The Army and Democracy: Military Politics in Pakistan*. Harvard University Press.

Siddiqa, A. 2007. *Military Inc. Inside Pakistan's Military Economy*. Pluto Press.

Singh, C. and Baily, M. 2013. "Praetorian Democracy, Illiberal but Enduring: Pakistan as Exemplar." *Southeast Review of Asian Studies* 35: 103–126.

Waheed, A. W. 2017. "State Sovereignty and International Relations in Pakistan: Analysing the Realism Stranglehold." *South Asia Research* 37 (3): 277–295.

Worldatlas Report. 2018. "29 Largest Armies in the World." February 12, 2018, Retrieved on September 9, 2018, https://www.worldatlas.com/articles/29-largest-armies-in-the-world.html.

1 A conceptual overview of the national security state

This book focuses on the experience of what became of Pakistan's national security state during and after the Cold War. Nonetheless, the national security state approach emerged in the US at the beginning of the Cold War. Before exploring Pakistan's national security state, this chapter reviews the available literature on the evolution of the US national security state model and then identifies its key features and ideas that could be deployed in the case of Pakistan.

The emergence of the concept of national security[1]

Historically, sovereign states have had a preoccupation with national defence, but the concept of national security only really appeared in the literature after 1945. The term was closely associated with the emergence of the US as a superpower in the post-1945 period and was used to identify elements that were seen to directly and indirectly affect the power and security position of the country (Leffler 1990).

Unlike the idea of national defence, which emphasizes the territorial integrity and physical protection of the nation-state, the concept of national security is linked to various political, cultural, economic, and military factors that potentially impact on the core interests of the nation-state (Patman, ed. 2006). Therefore, national security is more than the physical well-being of the state. According to Walter Lippmann, the concept of national security is much broader than national defence. National security suggests not only resistance to aggression but also may counter any potential danger by reaching outward to anticipate and neutralize it (Lippmann 1943). For instance, in 1948, President Truman said that "the loss of independence by any nation adds directly to the insecurity of the United States and all free nations" (Patman ed. 2006, 6). In other words, Truman's understanding of American national security went well beyond the physical security of the national borders of the US and other states.

In addition, and not unrelated, there appears to be little agreement on the meaning of national security (Baldwin 1997). For instance, states often regard economic, political, and military developments in other states with some suspicion and believe such developments may potentially threaten their own security. Nevertheless, it is important here to clarify the concept of national security. Arnold Wolfers (1952) distinguished between the objective and subjective dimensions of the term: the achievement of "national security objectively means the absence of threats to acquired values and subjectively, the absence of fear that such values will be attacked." This definition illuminates why national security is often a contested concept. State actors often disagree on objective and subjective indicators of national security. Some states may seek to maintain the status quo to protect their acquired values, whereas other states may believe it is necessary to revise the international status quo to protect and extend their values (Ripsman and Paul 2005).

Building on the definition of Wolfers, Morton Berkowitz and P. G. Bock (1965) have defined national security as "the ability of a nation to protect its internal values from external threat" (in Hermann 1977). The core internal values of a state may require the support of various interest groups, including government agencies, influential individuals, and political and religious groups. Trade-offs are made between interest groups to reach a consensus over core values such as liberal democracy, the right to self-determination, religious freedom, and other human rights (Leffler 1990, 145). Policymakers outline national security goals to protect such core values from external threats. It could be argued, for example, that liberal democracy has been the core value of the US and formed part of its foreign policy disposition. Thus, the US saw itself as an international protector of liberal democracy during the Cold War against the perceived Soviet totalitarian threat (Cox and Stokes, Ed. 2008).

In international relations (IR), the concept of national security is conditionally based on two major assumptions: the threats to a state's security principally arise from outside its borders, and such threats are primarily military in nature. Lippmann (1943) outlined these assumptions in his definition of national security:

> A nation is secure to the extent to which it is not in danger of having to sacrifice core values, if it wishes to avoid war, and is able, if challenged, to maintain them by victory in such a war.

Lippmann's definition, as Arnold Wolfers (1952) pointed out, "implies that security rises and falls with the ability of a nation to deter an attack, or to defeat it." Thus, national security has been defined in terms of military strength to protect core values within a sovereign state and sustain its territorial integrity. This perspective had a significant impact during the Cold War. Therefore, the main area of focus for both statesmen and academics during the Cold War was the enhancement of military capabilities to uphold national security.

Unpacking the idea of the national security state

The US maintained its territorial security throughout its history prior to the Second World War. Apart from the War of 1812, the physical security of the US was challenged for the first time when Japan attacked the US naval base and other military installations at Pearl Harbour on 6 December 1941 (Stuart 2000). Additionally, the advent of sophisticated arms such as long-range bombers, atomic bombs, and ballistic missiles had further reduced the invulnerability of the US after 1945. The potential impact of these modern arms was devastating as they could be used not only to target security installations but also population centres, markets, and industrial zones (Stuart 2000, 9). After the decline of the British Empire and the Soviet Union's key role in defeating Nazi Germany during the Second World War, Moscow emerged as a superpower in the post-war period and rival to the US with a competing ideology and philosophy towards international security and the global governance system (Library of Congress, Retrieved: May 2016). Therefore, for the first time in its history, the US leadership felt its security was directly threatened by a state that was geographically removed from the region in which America was located.

In this context, the Truman administration was convinced that there was a need to move from the traditional idea of national defence to one national security in order to safeguard the country in the post-1945 era. The attack on Pearl Harbour, the advent of new long-range sophisticated weaponry, including nuclear arms, and the rise of the Soviet Union in Europe, all helped to transform US foreign and security policy thinking after 1945. It was a turning point in US history with regard to the shaping of its national security policies. Consequently, the US adopted the national security state that was born out of very extreme security circumstances at the beginning of the Cold War.

The US national security state was based on two key ideas: anti-communism and a new security doctrine to uphold US interests such as physical security, the promotion of core values, and economic prosperity (Yergin 1977). The new security concerns briefly coexisted with America's traditional understanding of security based on national defence after 1945 (Hogan 1998). However, the new national security ideology prevailed after many public discussions and debate in Congress. In March 1947, President Truman announced the country's new security doctrine – known as the Truman Doctrine – and said that the US would support free countries or people anywhere in the world in their fight against the spread of communism (Watson 2002). The Truman Doctrine was very important as it showed that the US was prepared to resist and contain the expansion of communism in the world.

Consequently, the Truman administration oversaw the reorganization of the American state so that military, foreign policy, and domestic economic resources could be coordinated and channelled in a more efficient fashion to meet the newly perceived security challenges. This led to the creation of an American national security state in the late 1940s (Yergin 1977). In the next four decades, this fledgeling national security structure consolidated itself to become a powerful actor in the making of US foreign policy and had a profound impact on American governance and society.

The US had emerged as the world's most powerful nation after the Second World War. Most of its Western allies were affected by the war, and they depended on US aid to restore their war-torn social and economic structures. In addition, developing countries were looking towards the US for its support for their national independence movements against their colonial regimes.

Therefore, many nations looked for US support to achieve an economic revival and national renewal after the Second World War (Raskin 1976). On the other hand, the Soviet Union was trying to increase its influence around the world and tried to fill the vacuum left in Europe and northeast Asia. For instance, the Soviet Red Army occupied Eastern Europe and their apparent agenda was to expand their socialist model to the rest of Europe. This led to the beginning of a constant global power struggle between the US and Soviet Union known as the Cold War. The global competition for power between the superpowers included ideological confrontation, an arms race, propaganda, diplomatic outbursts, proxy wars, and economic rivalry (Patman ed. 2006). The confrontation between superpowers resulted in two opposing blocs: the Western Alliance led by the US and the Socialist bloc led by the Soviet Union. Such polarization reinforced the notion of national security in the Cold War era as a majority of states in the developing world were courted by the superpowers to align with the Western or the Socialist blocs.

Meanwhile, the US and the Soviet Union both saw each other as security threats to their core political values (in Walker 2009). The Soviet Union's ideology was based on communism with its one-party political system and closed economy, where the state had full control over the economic system. However, the US political system was based on liberal democracy and capitalism, with private ownership of the economy (Library of Congress, Retrieved: May 2016). According to President Truman, "the US must be willing to help free peoples to maintain their free institutions and their national integrity against aggressive movements that seek to impose upon them totalitarian regimes" (in Watson 2002). That meant that the US after 1945 increasingly felt it had to play a leading role in containing the perceived Soviet totalitarian threat on a global basis.

Against this backdrop, there was initially no clear security template on how the US should fight the Cold War. However, the Deputy Chief of Mission at the US Embassy in Moscow helped to provide the intellectual framework to fill this gap. George F. Kennan advocated the idea of firm containment in his famous article "The Sources of Soviet Conduct" in 1947. Kennan (1947) wrote that "the main element of any US policy toward the Soviet Union must be that of a long-term, patient but firm and vigilant containment of Russian expansive tendencies." Subsequently, the Truman administration adopted a containment strategy to counter the Soviets' expansion and intervene when it was necessary to safeguard Western interests (The Office of the Historian, Retrieved: June 2016). To implement the containment strategy, the US came up with a national security strategy to integrate "foreign, economic and military policies relating to the national security so as to enable the military services and the other departments and agencies of the government to cooperate more closely and effectively in matters involving national security" (Raskin 1976, 194). Throughout the Cold War era, the containment strategy became the major component of US national security policies in which diplomatic, military, economic, cultural, nuclear, and covert initiatives were integrated to counter the Soviet aggression and its expansion (Lucas and Mistry 2009).

The US national security state was formally established after the US Congress enacted several key pieces of legislation. The main objective was to create an organizational framework that was capable of developing a coherent, effective, and unified national security policy (Benedetti 1978). Following 18 months of debate, the US Congress passed the 1947 National Security Act. The Act created the leading institutions of US national security system, including a unified National Military Establishment, National Security Council (NSC), CIA, and National Security Resource Board (NSRB). All these agencies – with the exception of the NSRB – became important parts of the national security state apparatus (Bacevich 2007). The primary task of these institutions was to evaluate the new security threats facing the US after 1945 and ensure that the country was in a permanent state of war preparedness so that it could respond at any given time during the Cold War (Grondin 2004). Thus, the 1947 Act played a key role in creating the US national security state in the post-war era.

In addition, the post-war hearings on the 1941 Pearl Harbour surprise attack by Japan helped to shape US policymakers strategic thinking on the need to modernize America's conventional military forces. Furthermore, two significant events took place in 1949: the Soviet Union became a nuclear power after the successful testing of an atomic bomb, which neutralized the nuclear capability of the US, and Mao Zedong's Communists won the civil war against Nationalist forces in China. These events served to further bolster the idea of a clear and present danger facing the US in the post-war period. The US leadership believed that the Soviets might go to war at any time; therefore, the US had to deal with the Soviet Union as a permanent enemy (Raskin and Hartman 1988).

Admiral Leahy, the then Joint Chief of Staff, pointed out that "experience in the recent [Second World] war demonstrated conclusively that the defence of a nation, if it is to be effective, must begin beyond its frontier" (Leffler 1984). And it should be noted that the Soviet Union played a role in legitimizing the national security state narrative of the US after 1945. The Soviets acted in such a way that the US public was persuaded that the Soviet Union was a real threat to world peace. For instance, the Soviet Union occupied Eastern Europe and tried to expand to other parts of the world. On 24 June 1948, the Soviet Union cut off rail and road access to West Berlin through East Berlin in the Soviet occupation zone of eastern Germany to force "the Western allies" (France, Britain, and the US) out of Berlin altogether. However, the US and Britain countered the Berlin blockade with an airlift and delivered foods, fuel, and other necessary goods to West Berlin. According to an estimate, about 2.3 million tons of food, fuel, and other goods were supplied through the airlift (Kruzel 2008). The Berlin blockade was perceived in Washington as a unilateral Soviet attempt to use force to change the territorial status quo in Europe at the expense of Western interests (Barnet 1985). In addition, religious practices were banned by the Soviet Union in the sphere of their influence, and this worried the people around the world. Thus, the Soviet Union was viewed as a threat not only to US national security but to the international peace of the whole world.

Thus, the American national security state was born in extremely challenging security circumstances by the perceived threat of the Soviet Union at the beginning of the Cold War. Fundamentally, the US national security state was based on anti-communism to protect America's national and global interests. This new security approach revised and transformed the US' relationship with the outside world. For instance, the US played a pivotal role in countering the Soviet threat at the global level and contained its expansion around the world. So the national security state repudiated US isolationism and promoted its sustained engagement in the world.

The advent of the US national security state marked a radical departure from the tradition of semi-isolationism in US foreign policy to one sustained international engagement. The national security state was an institutional expression of America's new determination to maintain a position of permanent war preparedness in its Cold War with the Soviet Union, an arrangement in which certain institutions and ideas combine together in a way in which the state organizes itself for permanent military preparedness. After its creation during the early post-war era, governments in Washington have largely focussed on military strength to counter any external threat. Military expenditure was seen as a key indicator of US foreign policy during the Cold War. Moreover, the US developed both nuclear weapons and sophisticated delivery systems to counter the apparent Soviet threat. Under the auspices of the national security state, the US leadership tended to pursue military solutions to foreign and security policy problems, as it was easy to convince people about the military dangers that were both real and imagined (Ullman 1983).

In this context, the US military, as an institution, gathered privileges and exercised greater control in US foreign and security policies due to its possession of nuclear weapons and participation in covert operations. Throughout the Cold War, the administrations in Washington had overwhelmingly emphasized nuclear deterrence and allocated billions of dollars to build strong nuclear arms to counter Soviet aggression. In 1953, President Eisenhower had reaffirmed America's containment and deterrence strategy by elevating the importance of nuclear weapons (Donohue 2011). As a result, the US had achieved a nuclear superiority that would have enabled it to launch massive nuclear attacks on the Soviet Union to destroy its war-making capability. However, the acquisition of nuclear weapons by the American military apparatus had further strengthened the role of the military in strategic decision making within the national security state (Raskin 1976).

According to some estimates, the US spent a minimum of $5.5 trillion on its nuclear weapons programme from 1940 to 1996 (Schwartz 1998). Despite massive budget allocations for nuclear development, there was no accountability by the policymakers, and their actions were justified by saying it was necessary to maintain secrecy due to national security interests (Gurtov 1982). Consequently, the military not only extended its power with the addition of powerful nuclear arsenals under their control but also escaped civilian oversight of the nuclear programme.

Similarly, the military's covert operations were another major aspect of the US Cold War strategy to protect American interests worldwide and counter the challenge posed by the Soviet Union and its allies (Goodman 2000). Like the nuclear programme, the culture of secrecy in covert operations empowered the US military and also justified its dominant role in strategic decision making in US foreign and security policies (Baesler 2018). The House and Senate intelligence committee authorized the covert operations but there were many ways in which their authority was either restricted or shifted to the Armed Services Committee in case of special operations mission (Kibbe 2014).

Furthermore, the US government allocated massive resources and funding for the CIA's covert operations during the Cold War. As a matter of national security, the intelligence budget has always been kept secret within the defence budget. The Armed Services Committees have ultimate control over the budgetary allocations for covert wars (Kibbe 2014, 220–221). In 2011, the CIA Director Leon Panetta, who was formally in charge of the covert operations, said: "I have to tell you that the real commander was Admiral McRaven because he was on site, and he was actually in charge of the military operation that went in and got bin Laden" (PBS News Hour, May 2011). Thus, the covert operations were also in control of the military during and after the Cold War era. In essence, within a national security state, the military's possession of nuclear weapons and its covert wars provided them with an opportunity to act independently and escape the civilian oversight during and after the Cold War era.

The military-industrial complex: the hub of the national security state

The military-industrial complex is defined as "a coalition of powerful groups and bodies that share economic, institutional or political interests intensifying defence expenditure" (Mintz 1985). According to Aspaturian, "every country that maintains a military bureaucracy and defence industries will effectively sustain a military industrial complex. This occurs simply because representatives of the military bureaucracy and the defence industry naturally seek to maximize their joint interests" (Mintz 1985, 624–625). Thus, the heavy US focus on military spending during the Cold War created what became known as "military-industrial complex," consisting of the military establishment, the administrative bureaucracy, and private corporations (Moskos 1974). For instance, US military expenditure accounted for 7.4 percent of gross domestic product (GDP) between 1947 and 1990. And it was America's largest commitment to international affairs after the Second World War (Fordham 2007). According to some estimates, the US spent a total of US$6,316 billion on the military, averaging about US$162 billion per year during the Cold War (Higgs 1988). This massive spending on defence had created a huge military and defence industry in the country.

Nonetheless, it created employment opportunities for workers and profit to shareholders. For instance, national security accounted for 70 percent of federal employment and 48 percent of public and private spending on research and development at the beginning of the Cold War (Smith 2015). More specifically, the defence establishment directly accounted for 3.5 million persons, and annual military spending on security was more than the net income of all US corporations (Eisenhower 1961). Also, 100 top defence contractors hired 726 former senior military officials. The contractors also lobbied for the armed services and closely worked with the military establishment (Raymond 1961). This military-industrial complex largely benefited the US political, economic, and military elite, but it had put its burden of costs on ordinary American people after the Second World War (Smith 2015).

It should be added that the term "military-industrial complex" was explicitly identified by US President Eisenhower in his farewell presidential address in January 1961. He warned US citizens about the dangers of the militarization of American society. At the beginning of his speech, he acknowledged the importance of the military for keeping peace intact, but said that it had profound implications for the political, economic, and spiritual aspects of the American way of life. President Eisenhower (1960–1961) stressed the influence the military-industrial complex exercised in "every city, every state house, every office of the federal government, affecting the very structure of our society." Eisenhower (1960–1961) warned that "the government must guard against the acquisition of unwarranted influence, whether sought or unsought, by the military-industrial complex." He further stated that the new national security ideology had not only internationalized US foreign policy but also militarized it. This, Eisenhower believed, would have negative implications for the American people and their relationship with the outside world.

Prior to his farewell speech, President Eisenhower had spoken about the risks of excessive militarism in his speech "Chance for Peace" following the death of Stalin in 1953 (Ledbetter 2011; Smith 2015):

> Every gun that is made, every warship launched, every rocket fired signifies, in the final sense, a theft from those who hunger and are not fed, those who are cold and are not clothed. This world in arms is not spending money alone. It is spending the sweat of its laborers, the genius of its scientists, the hopes of its children … This is not a way of life at all, in any true sense. Under the cloud of threatening war, it is humanity hanging from a cross of iron.

Certainly, the advent of a national security state led to a vastly expanded military establishment in the US. A new class of national security managers emerged who were neither elected government representatives nor bureaucrats. Examples of such people were Charles Bohlen, George F. Kennan, and other experts on the Soviet Union after the formation of the national security state (Hogan 1998). Charles Mills (1956) wrote that "nowhere in America is there as great a 'class consciousness' as among the elite; nowhere is it organized as effectively as among the power elite." This new military establishment was very influential in national security policies. Moreover, the groups who were involved in the arms industry became dominant in the decision making of the state (Smith 2015).

According to Jack Raymond (1961), "the basic characteristic of military indus-trial relations is their philosophical alliance and mutual interests in seeking a large defence establishment, bigger and better weapons and bigger devotion to prob-lems of security." Interestingly, the military-industrial complex had democratic legitimacy under the national security state that had deep foundations in the pref-erences of the American public. In fact, members of Congress used public fear to get support for the military business conglomerates (Smith 2015). In this process, the military became a very powerful actor in foreign policy and strategic deci-sion making during the Cold War. Despite its growing military influence, national security advisors often claimed that the national security ideology was necessary to protect American democracy from the threat of Soviet aggression and would not make the US a "garrison state."

Thus, the perception (and exaggeration) of Soviet and communist threats by certain leaders led to the creation and legitimization of the US national secu-rity state which provided the institutional capacity to act globally. Nonetheless, the establishment of the US national security state revised and transformed Washington's relationship with the external world.

Key features of the US national security state model

The realist theory of international relations largely underpinned the paradigm of the national security state. The realists believe that human nature is self-interested and driven by a lust for power, and that war and conflict are constant features in the international arena (Patman ed. 2006). States are therefore motivated by the same human self-interest irrespective of history and culture. Also, states are involved in a constant struggle for power in the international political system. According to Hans Morgenthau (1945), "Politics is struggle for power over men and whatever is its ultimate aim may be, power is its immediate goal and the modes of acquiring, maintaining and demonstrating it determine the technique of political action."

Classical realists believe that the nation-state is the primary actor in provid-ing security against potential adversaries. Military power is said to play a pivotal role in a state's behaviour in its security and foreign policies (Steel 1997). More importantly, states often view their relations with national security in terms of their military power, available national resources, and geographical location. This military-centred national security approach became the dominant paradigm in the conflict-ridden context of the Cold War and was closely associated with the evo-lution of the national security state.

More specifically, this security approach was built around a "security dilemma" in which relations among the states are often characterized by uncertainty and suspicion. Kenneth Waltz argues, "In anarchy, security is the highest end. Only if survival is assured can states seek such other goals as tranquillity, profit, and power" (Baldwin 1997). In the absence of any central international authority, states have little choice in an anarchic system but to protect their national sov-ereignty and territorial integrity either by enhancing their military capabilities through a "self-help system" or by forming alliances to balance the power of would-be adversary states. If an alliance option is not available, states may have to "bandwagon" with a more powerful state to protect their security interests (Baldwin 1997). Jack Snyder argues that external factors define the operational foreign policy contours of weak states in which they "bandwagon and do not balance" with the strong and great powers (Jack, 1991; in Paliwal 2016). In other words, they make an alliance with a greater power to gain economic and military aid in order to maintain their independence.

The realist approach to national security has six features (Smith 2006):

i. Nation-states are considered the key actor in international politics
ii. The sovereign state had no alternative but to rely on self-help to determine its security in the anarchic international system
iii. International anarchy is the main factor in shaping a state's behaviour
iv. Military power is the primary component of the nation state's ability to protect its national interests
v. States are preoccupied with security, survival, and power
vi. States coexist in a security dilemma, but it is difficult to balance defensive capabilities with not threatening adversaries, as states are unaware of the motivations and intentions of other states

The realist school of thought explains the national security state paradigm in international relations which mainly emphasizes the nation-state, military power, international anarchic system, and security dilemma. It differs from other prominent IR paradigms such as liberalism and social constructivism. For example, the liberals emphasize economic interdependency, cooperation, and international institutions. The liberals also propose "democratic peace theory," which means "democracies were inherently more peaceful than autocratic states." They claim that "democracies rarely go to war or engage in militarized disputes with one another" (Rosato 2003, 585). On the other hand, the constructivists' view is that the "international reality is socially constructed by cognitive structures that give meanings to the material world" (Adler 1997). In the constructivist approach, actors in world politics are dynamic because a state's identity and interests change over time and according to the context (Wendt 1992). Thus, the liberal and constructivist paradigms in international relations do not explain the national security state model which was embedded in US foreign and security policies after 1945.

Within the realist theoretical framework, it was possible to identify a number of key features that characterized the American model of the national security state. These were as follow (Ali and Patman 2019):

• A principal defining feature of the national security state is that military power is perceived as the primary instrument of the state for maintaining its national security interests. Because the military guarantees the security of the state against its enemies, it holds a privileged institutional role within that society in general. According to Jack Nelson-Pallmeyer (1992), the military, in a national security state, exerts significant influence over political, economic, and security affairs.

- A second major feature of a national security state is that political democracy and democratic elections are viewed in a qualified fashion. While national security states often maintain an appearance of democracy, ultimate power is said to rest with the military or within a broader national security apparatus.
- A third characteristic of a national security state is that the military and related institutional sectors possess substantial political and economic power. If a state has the goal of being militarily prepared for war on a continuous basis, the military and other security institutions will be able to command a sizeable share of a nation's resources on a long-term basis. At the same time, industries and companies producing arms and other military materials disproportionately benefit from the prominent role of the military. This powerful conjunction of interests has been termed a military-industrial complex.
- A fourth feature of a national security state is its constant preoccupation with enemies or potential enemies. The task of defending the state against such enemies provides a legitimizing device for what is a distorting factor in the economy and a major source of national identity and purpose.
- A fifth characteristic of a national security state is that it can restrict public debate and limit popular participation through secrecy or intimidation. By invoking the imperative of national security, the military and other security agencies can justify secrecy, determine the parameters of "patriotic" debate, and largely control the flow of information made available on security questions to the general public.

The national security state and the post-Cold War era

The Cold War formally ended in 1990 and the Soviet Union, an adversary of the US for more than four decades, disintegrated in December 1991. These developments were seen as a triumph for the US national security state against the Soviet Union, and the US became the sole superpower in the world. Governments in Washington, both Republican and Democratic, believed that the national security state helped the US "win" the Cold War. Consequently, the US retained its national security state model during the post-Cold War era. According to Anthony Lake, the National Security Advisor in the Clinton administration, "now the US's enemies are extreme nationalists and tribalists, terrorists, organized criminals, coup plotters, rogue states, and all those who would return newly free societies to the intolerant ways of the past" (Steel 1997, 3). Nevertheless, the Clinton administration decided, when passing Presidential Decision Directive (PDD) 25 in May 1994, that the US would only participate in UN peacekeeping missions if they were in its national interests (PDD/NSC 25, 1994). This meant that the US would not intervene in conflicts and civil wars within such states when it was not in its national interest to do so.

The 9/11 terrorist attacks in 2001 somewhat modified this state-centric national security approach. But by declaring a "war on terror," the Bush administration lent impetus to the idea that would be a military solution to the challenge of transnational terrorist groups like Al-Qaeda. In the aftermath of 9/11, the Bush administration expanded the parameters of the national security state and substantially increased military expenditure. Moreover, the security policies adopted during the Cold War were largely intact and continued in the "global war on terror" (Patman 2015). For example, the US invaded Afghanistan in October 2001 to topple the Taliban regime. In 2003, the US also overthrew Saddam Hussein's autocratic regime in Iraq after its invasion. Thus, the Cold War national security state was adapted and developed during Bush's war on terror.

But the 9/11 terrorist attacks also exposed the limitations of this state-centric national security approach. President Bush believed that the US must militarily pre-empt any potential threat to the US homeland and de-emphasized the use of diplomacy in the struggle against Al-Qaeda. In this vein, both academics and practitioners believed that the invasion of Iraq was a huge mistake for the US, due to its strategic, diplomatic, and economic costs (Patman 2009). The major problem with the national security state was that the "global war on terror" was always more than a military battle and required a multifaceted approach to counter terrorist groups on both ideological and political fronts. More specifically, the "war on terror" involved winning hearts and minds through tackling grievances and discrediting terrorists and their prescriptions for such problems (Patman ed. 2006).

After campaigning against President Bush's national security approach, President Obama attempted to change the direction of this policy after taking office in Washington. He tried to redefine US exceptionalism and showed more enthusiasm for multilateral security initiatives. Subsequently, the US leadership emphasized the resolution of different international and local conflicts through diplomacy means. According to Professor Robert G. Patman (2015),

> The Obama administration largely jettisoned the "war on terror" rhetoric, withdrew all US combat troops from Iraq, attempted a more even-handed stance on the Israeli-Palestinian conflict, escalated the ideological battle against Islamic terrorism, intensified the war against al-Qaeda and the Taliban in their strongholds of Afghanistan and Pakistan, pledged to reinvigorate diplomacy, ruled out US military intervention in the Syrian civil war, and sought, where possible, to negotiate directly with longstanding adversaries like Iran, North Korea, Cuba or Venezuela.

Although the Obama administration attempted to change the modus operandi of the US national security state, it is still intact, as the US-led a limited military operation against the autocratic regime of Muammar-al-Gaddafi in Libya in March 2011, with the support of international coalition (Cooper 2011). President Obama also authorized the US special operations forces deployment in Syria to complement his air campaign against the Islamic State of Iraq and Syria (ISIS) in October 2015. Moreover, the US has intensified its campaign against the ISIS and other terrorist groups in North and West Africa as well as in Afghanistan and

Pakistan. In fact, at the end of Obama's presidency, the US military was involved in more countries than when he took his office in January 2009 (Delman 2016). Thus, the US national security state is still in place despite the US leadership's periodic efforts to change its national security policies.

It is important to note that states adopt a national security orientation because of a variety of factors, including the international security environment, geostrategic location, internal politics, and economic capabilities. Some states pursue more autonomous strategies, and others may be constrained by key societal interest groups, legislators, and the public. It also depends on the available national resources, as some states have abundant economic means, while others may have limited resources. Some states largely rely on internal balancing by military modernization, and others look towards alliances and collective security (Ripsman and Paul 2005). For instance, in terms of power projection, a global power will maintain at least a global outreach such as the US and Russia, whereas a regional power such as India and Turkey will typically confine its efforts to its neighbourhood (Steel 1997, 2). Thus, states draw their perimeters on the bases of their power and circumstances.

While the US national security state model may have been a poor fit for some developing countries, it is fair to say that this approach has a certain utility in the context of analyzing Pakistan's state behaviour and its foreign and security policies during and after the Cold War. From the time of its establishment as an independent state in 1947, Pakistan perceived an external security threat from neighbouring India. Consequently, Pakistan largely adopted the national security state model, because of both evident local and regional threats and a permissive Cold War security environment which enabled Pakistani military elite to link their own security concerns with those global concerns associated with the American perception of the Soviet threat (see details in Chapter 2).

Nonetheless, Pakistan encompassed many of the key features of the US national security state but there were also significant points of departure. Like the US in the early post-1945 period, Pakistan put itself on a permanent war footing against an external threat from India immediately after its inception in 1947 and allocated a lion share of the government expenditure from the national treasury. However, the US military remained under civilian control in principle whereas the Pakistani military elite acted more independently. Pakistan's experience of national security state was shaped by the country's strategic alliance with the US during the Cold War. However, Pakistan's national security state approach exhibited distinctive features of its own development based on the dominating role of the military elite right at its inception and the parochial economic interest of armed institutes (See Chapter 2).

Note

1 This section is published in my co-authored article: Ali, A. and Patman, R. G. (2019) "The Evolution of the National Security State in Pakistan: 1947–1989," *Democracy and Security* 15:4, 2–4.

References

Adler, E. 1997. "Seizing the Middle Ground: Constructivism in World Politics." *European Journal of International Relations* 3 (3): 319–363.

Ali, A. and Patman, R. G. 2019. "The Evolution of the National Security State in Pakistan: 1947–1989." *Democracy and Security* 15 (4): 301–327.

Bacevich, A. 2007. *The Long War: A New History of U.S. National Security Policy Since World War II.* Columbia University Press.

Baesler, P. J. 2018. "Truth and National Security in the American Cold War Book." *Clearer than Truth: The Polygraph and the American Cold War.* University of Massachusetts Press.

Baldwin, D. A. 1997. "The Concept of Security." *Review of International Studies* 23 (1): 5–26.

Barnet, R. 1985. "The Ideology of the National Security State." *The Massachusetts Review* 26 (4): 483–500.

Benedetti, C. 1978. "The American Peace Movement and the National Security State, 1941–1971." *World Affairs* 141 (2): 118–129.

Berkowitz, M. and Bock, P. G. 1965. *American National Security.* Free Press.

Cooper, H. 2011. "Obama Cites Limits of U.S. Role in Libya." *The New York Times,* March 28, 2011, Retrieved on December 3, 2018, https://www.nytimes.com/2011/03/29/world/africa/29prexy.html.

Cox, M. and Stokes, D., eds. 2008. *US Foreign Policy.* Oxford University Press.

Donohue, K. L. 2011. "The Limits of National Security." *American Criminal Review* 48 (4): 1573–1756.

Delman, E. 2016. "Obama Promised to End America's Wars—Has He?" *The Atlantic,* March 30. Retrieved on November 22, 2018, http://www.theatlantic.com/international/archive/2016/03/obama-doctrine-wars-numbers/474531/.

Eisenhower, D. 1960–61. "Farewell Radio and Television Address to American People." *Public Papers of the Presidents of the United States: Dwight D. Eisenhower, 1960-61* (Washington: GPO): 1035–1040.

Fordham, B. 2007. "The Evolution of Republican and Democratic Positions on Cold War Military Spending a Historical Puzzle." *Social Science History* 31 (4): 603–636.

Goodman, A. M. 2000. "Espionage and Covert Action." In *National Insecurity: U.S. Intelligence after the Cold War*, edited by Craig Eisendrath. Temple University Press.

Grondin, D. 2004. "(Re)Writing the National Security State." *Centre for United States Studies*, Occasional paper no. 12: 1–29.

Gurtov, M. 1982. "The National Security State and Soviet-American Relations." *The Journal of East Asian Affairs* 2 (2): 207–233.

Hermann, C. F. 1977. "Are the Dimensions and Implications of National Security Changing?" *Quarterly Report of Mershon Center*, The Ohio State University 3 (1): 17–19.

Higgs, R. 1988. "U.S. Military Spending in the Cold War Era: Opportunity Costs, Foreign Crises, and Domestic Constraints." *Cato Institute*, Policy Analysis no. 114: 1–14.

Hogan, M. 1998. *A Cross of Iron: Harry S. Truman and the Origins of the National Security State, 1945–1954.* Cambridge University Press.

Jack, S. 1991. *Myth of Empire: Domestic Politics and International Ambition.* Cornell University Press.

Kennan, G. 1947. "The Sources of Soviet Conduct Source." *Foreign Affairs* 25 (4): 566–582.

"Kennan and Containment, 1947." N.D. *The Office of the Historian*. Retrieved on 07 June 2016, https://history.state.gov/milestones/1945-1952/kennan.

Kibbe, D. J. 2014. "The Military, the CIA, and America's Shadow Wars."In *Mission Creep: The Militarization of US Foreign Policy*, edited by Adams Gordon and Murray Shoon. Georgetown University Press.

Kruzel, J. 2008. "Berlin Airlift Dispensed Food, Delivered Blow to Communism." *US Department of Defence*, Retrieved: November 22, 2018, http://archive.defense.gov/news/newsarticle.aspx?id=49878.

Ledbetter, J. 2011. *Unwarranted Influence: Dwight D. Eisenhower and the Military-Industrial Complex*. Yale University Press.

Leffler, M. P. 1984. "The American Conception of National Security and the Beginnings of the Cold War, 1945–48." *The American Historical Review* 89 (3): 346–381.

Leffler, M. P. 1990. "National Security." *The Journal of American History* 77 (1): 143–152.

Lehrer, J. Interview with Leon Panetta. "CIA Chief Panetta: Obama Made 'Gutsy' Decision on Bin Laden Raid." *PBS News Hour*, May 3, 2011. Retrieved from https://www.pbs.org/newshour/show/cia-chief-panetta-obama-made-gutsy-decision-on-bin-laden-raid.

Lippmann, W. 1943. *U. S. Foreign Policy*. The Atlantic Monthly Press.

Lucas, S. and Mistry, K. 2009. "Illusions of Coherence: George F. Kennan, U.S. Strategy and Political Warfare in the Early Cold War, 1946–1950." *Diplomatic History* 33 (1): 39–66.

Mills, C. W. 1956. *The Power Elite*. Oxford University Press.

Mintz, A. 1985. "The Military-Industrial Complex." *Journal of Conflict Resolution* 29 (4): 623–639.

Morgenthau, H. J. 1945. "The Evil of Politics and the Ethics of Evil." *Ethics* 56 (1): 1–18.

Moskos, C. 1974. "The Concept of the Military-Industrial Complex: Radical Critique or Liberal Bogey?" *Social Problems* 21 (4): 498–512.

Nelson-Pallmeyer, J. 1992. *Brave New World Order: Must We Pledge Allegiance?* Orbis Books.

Paliwal, A. 2016. "Afghanistan's India–Pakistan Dilemma: Advocacy Coalitions in Weak States." *Cambridge Review of International Affairs* 29 (2): 465–491.

Patman, R. G. ed. 2006. *Globalization and Conflict: National Security in a 'New' Strategic Era*. Routledge.

Patman, R. G. 2009. "Out of Sync: Bush's Expanded National Security State and the War on Terror." *International Politics* 46 (2/3): 210–233.

Patman, R. G. 2015. "Historical Analogies, Globalization, and America's Great Power Rivalry in the Ukraine." *Centre for International Peace and Security Studies*, Working paper no. 45: 1–23.

"Presidential Decision Directive/NSC-25." May 3, 1994. Retrieved on June 29 2016, https://www.documentcloud.org/documents/1392654-footnote-124-pdd-25.html.

Raskin, M. 1976. "Democracy versus the National Security State." *Law and Contemporary Problems* 40 (3): 189–220.

Raskin, M. and Hartman, C. 1988. *Winning America: Ideas and Leadership for the 1990s Political Science*. South End Press.

Raymond, J. 1961. "The Military-Industrial Complex: An Analysis." *New York Times*, January 22.

"Revelations from the Russian Archives: The Soviet Union and the United States." N.D. *Library of Congress*. Retrieved from https://www.loc.gov/exhibits/archives/sovi.html.

Ripsman, N. M. and Paul, T. V. 2005. "Globalization and the National Security State: A Framework for Analysis Source." *International Studies Review* 7 (2): 199–227.

Rosato, S. 2003. "The Flawed Logic of Democratic Peace Theory." *American Political Science Review* 97 (4): 585–602.

Schwartz, I. S. 1998. "The Hidden Cost of Our Nuclear Arsenal: Overview of Project Findings." June 30, 1998, Brooking Institute. Retrieved from https://www.brookings.edu/the-hidden-costs-of-our-nuclear-arsenal-overview-of-project-findings/.

Smith, D. 2015. "From the Military-Industrial Complex to the National Security State." *Australian Journal of Political Science* 50 (3): 576–590.

Smith, S. 2006. "The Concept of Security in a Globalizing World." Chapter 2 in Patman, R. G. (ed.) *Globalization and Conflict: National Security in a 'New' Strategic Era.* Routledge.

Steel, R. 1997. "A New Realism." *World Policy Journal* 14 (2): 1–9.

Stuart, D. T. 2000. *Organizing for National Security.* Strategic Studies Institute.

Ullman, R. 1983. "Redefining Security." *International Security* 8 (1): 129–153.

Walker, W. 2009. *National Security and Core Values in American History.* Cambridge University Press.

Watson, C. 2002. *U.S. National Security: A Reference Handbook.* ABC-CLIO, United States.

Wendt, A. 1992. "Anarchy is What States Make of It: The Social Construction of Power Politics." *International Organization* 46 (2): 391–425.

Wolfers, A. 1952. "National Security as an Ambiguous Symbol." *Political Science Quarterly* 67 (4): 481–502.

Yergin, D. 1977. *Shattered Peace: The Origins of the Cold War and the National Security State.* Houghton Mifflin Company.

2 The evolution of Pakistan's national security state during the Cold War era

Pakistan's national security orientation after independence[1]

Soon after its independence in 1947, Pakistan perceived external threats to its national sovereignty and territorial integrity from neighbouring countries, especially India. The Indian leadership was apparently convinced that the creation of Pakistan was temporary and it would eventually be reintegrated into a United India. This means the Indian leadership's unwillingness to accept Pakistan as an independent state remained a major constraint in reconciliation between the two countries (Burke 1973). Actually the Indian leadership believed that Pakistan was based on a flawed ideology of the "two nation theory"[2] and that Pakistan's political leadership was ill-equipped to deal with the emerging situation after partition in 1947. For example, Vallabhbhai Patel, India's first minister of Home Affairs and deputy prime minister, emphasized that "Pakistan was not viable and would soon collapse" (Mansergh 1966, 16). So Indian decision-makers tended to view the creation of Pakistan as a temporary development to facilitate the end of British colonial rule in India. According to this perspective, Pakistan would eventually be reintegrated into a greater India that Hindu nationalists called "Akhand Bharat-(re)unified India" (Jaffrelot 2016).

This continued rhetoric to undo Pakistan created the perception of insecurity which had played a major role in Pakistan's foreign and security policymaking since its independence in 1947. Consequently, Pakistani leadership perceived it as a real threat to their national sovereignty and territorial integrity immediately after its inception. General Ayub Khan, the first native commander-in-chief (C-in-C)[3] appointed in 1951, and the martial law administrator after his military coup in 1958, considered in 1948 that "India's attitude continued to be one of unmitigated hostility. Her aim was to cripple us at birth" (Jaffrelot 2016, 2). At the same time, there was no denying that Pakistan was not in any real position to counterbalance the relative preponderance of Indian power in South Asia. In the circumstances, the Pakistani leadership tried to normalize its relations with India and proposed a mutual security arrangement for regional security. In an interview, Muhammad Ali Jinnah stated (Ayaz 2010, 250):

Personally I have no doubt in my mind that our own paramount interests demand that the dominion of Pakistan and the dominion of India should coordinate for the purpose of playing their part in international affairs and the developments that may take place and also it is of vital importance to Pakistan and India as independent sovereign states to collaborate in a friendly way jointly to defend their frontiers both on land and sea against any aggression.

However, India apparently declined such proposals based on the mutual security of the two parties in the immediate period after 1947.

Further, a number of disputes strained relations between the two countries, such as conflicting territorial claims, problems regarding the distribution of assets of British India, refugee issues, and serious tension regarding water-sharing of the trans-boundary rivers (Rizvi 1983). As a result, Pakistan feared India would undo the partition after its inception.

In addition, the Kashmir conflict has continued to be a major source of hostility between the two states since independence. Both countries have been obsessed with Kashmir being an integral part of their respective homelands. On one side, Pakistan believed that Kashmir was part of the unfinished agenda of the 1947 partition and it should be part of Pakistan as it is predominantly a Muslim state. Pakistan has propagated the perception that the Kashmir uprising has been an indigenous freedom movement against occupying Indian security forces. On the other side, India emphasized that Kashmir is very much part of secular India and the partition was completed in 1947. More importantly, Pakistan continued to emphasize that Kashmiris should be given the right to self-determination under the supervision of UN administrators, while "India asserts its right to sovereignty and territorial integrity" (Vaish 2011). Since independence, both countries have blamed each other for the unrest in Kashmir. Pakistan accused the Indian military of involvement in human rights violations and of allowing them to continue with impunity, while India has blamed Pakistan for supporting the armed uprising and outlawed militant groups in Kashmir.

In August 1953, Pakistan and India agreed that the Kashmir conflict should be resolved through a plebiscite under UN supervision. However, it did not take place, due to mutual distrust and hostility between the two countries. Pakistan has engaged in various strategies such as diplomacy as well as conventional and proxy war to wrest Kashmir from India. For instance, Pakistan fought two large-scale wars with India in 1948 and 1965, during the Cold War era, and the small-scale Kargil War in 1999, to try to gain control of Kashmir (Paul 2005). However, Pakistan and India failed to find a military solution to the conflict despite huge military deployments in the disputed territory, particularly by India. The civilian leadership in both countries have promoted at various times the idea of peace talks, but such efforts have failed (see Chapter 4). Thus, the Kashmir conflict has remained unresolved and has been a major source of tension in the international arena.

Afghanistan was a second external threat to Pakistan after its inception in 1947. The Afghan government was reluctant to accept Pakistan as an independent state due to Kabul's historical territorial claims over the western part of Pakistan along the Durand Line. Afghanistan strongly protested against the inclusion of ethnic Pashtun-Baloch areas within Pakistan without the provision of an option of the right to self-determination for its inhabitants. In July 1949, the Afghan government organized a *Loya Jirga* (grand assembly) in Kabul. The Jirga unilaterally passed a resolution that all the treaties, conventions, and agreements between the British government of India and Afghanistan were no longer valid and had no legal standing (Global Security report, Retrieved: 7 September 2016). Afghanistan refused to accept the "Durand Line"[4] as an international border due to its historical territorial claims. Subsequently, Afghanistan voted against Pakistan's admission to the UN in 1947. So Pakistan's western border has also remained unofficial since 1947 and the situation worsened when the movement of Pashtunistan started in the 1950s with the support of some of the Afghan leaders. The objective of the movement was to seek at least the "right to self-determination" or "autonomy" for the Pashtuns living in the north-western region of Pakistan (Jaffrelot 2016). Thus, the border disputes remain a major strain on the bilateral relationship between Pakistan and Afghanistan. However, the threat from Afghanistan remained minimal until 1979. While India's foreign policy apparently sought to isolate and challenge Pakistan's territorial integrity, the Pakistani leadership was mainly worried that India would collude with Afghanistan to destabilize the country on its western border. According to this scenario, Pakistan would face the prospect of war on both its eastern and western borders.

Geographically, Pakistan was divided at independence into two constituent parts – West Pakistan, which comprises present Pakistan, and East Pakistan, which became an independent Bangladesh in 1971. West Pakistan was encircled by India in the south-east, by Afghanistan and Iran in the west, and by the Arabian Sea in the south. Also, Pakistan shared borders with China in the north-east, while the Wakhan Corridor, a long and narrow strip of Afghan territory in the north, separates Pakistan from Tajikistan (a former Soviet republic). Thus, Pakistan was situated in an important geostrategic part of Central South Asia where the territories of the Soviet Union, China, and India converged. Moreover, East Pakistan was surrounded by India on three sides and was physically separated by thousands of miles from West Pakistan (Rizvi 1983; Jalal 1990). Consequently, the presence of hostile India and the superpowers have raised security concerns for Pakistan as the latter have a direct and indirect interest in the Indian subcontinent and its politics (Rizvi 1983). Like other relatively small states, Pakistan found itself in a potentially threatening security environment after its independence.

In this context, the profile of the Pakistani military increased right from the very beginning due to the external threat, especially from India. Subsequently, the Pakistani military devised a strategy of "liberating" Kashmir. Initially, a prominent Muslim League leader Mian Iftikharuddin approached the Pakistani army and asked for unofficial assistance to support the accession of Kashmir to Pakistan. Colonel Akbar Khan, director of weapons and equipment in the Pakistan army, devised a plan of "armed revolt inside Kashmir" in which unofficial assistance would be provided to Kashmiri rebels without any direct participation by

Pakistani forces in the ensuing rebellion. Colonel Khan discussed the strategy with the Pakistani leadership, including Prime Minister Liaqat Ali Khan, and gained their approval. This strategic initiative was divided into two phases: in the first phase, the state government in Kashmir would be destabilized by fuelling unrest in the Poonch area where Maharaja Hari Singh, the ruler of Kashmir state, was unpopular. In the second phase, tribal *Lashkar* (militia) would launch attacks on Kashmir from the Pakistani side of the boundary. The Pakistani army would then provide military aid to the tribal militia. As a consequence, Colonel Khan diverted thousands of rifles and ammunition from the Punjab police to the militia (Kapur 2016). It was hoped the Kashmiris would announce the accession of Kashmir to Pakistan after a successful rebellion by the tribal militia against state authorities in the disputed region.

The first phases of the Pakistani strategy to "liberate" Kashmir went largely according to plan. In October 1947, the tribal militia attacked Kashmir from the northern side and captured Muzaffarabad, the capital of Pakistan-administered Kashmir. The militia occupied the northern part of Kashmir and advanced towards Srinagar, the summer capital of Indian-administered Kashmir. The tribal incursion alarmed Maharaja Hari Singh who requested Indian intervention after losing control of the northern parts of the state. India said they would give support on condition that Kashmir acceded to India. Moreover, the Indian leadership insisted that the Kashmiri people should also ratify the accession through a plebiscite. On 26 October 1947, the maharaja accepted India's conditions and signed the instrument of accession to India. Thereafter, India sent its troops to fight against the tribal militia aligned with Pakistan (Kapur 2016; Krishna 1991). This development led to the first war between India and Pakistan. The Indian military successfully stopped the expansion of the militia in Kashmir. On 1 January 1948, India referred Kashmir to the UN on the advice of Lord Mountbatten, the last British Viceroy of India and briefly its first post-independence governor general. The conflict ended with a UN-mandated ceasefire on 1 January 1949. Under the terms of the agreement, a "Ceasefire Line" (CFL) was drawn, dividing Kashmir into two parts: Pakistan-administered Kashmir and Indian-administered Kashmir. In particular, the CFL was the military control line between Pakistani and Indian security forces in the princely Kashmir state. It was subsequently renamed the "Line of Control" (LoC) under the Shimla agreement in 1972 (Ganguly 2016). In the first Kashmir war, India occupied two-thirds of the disputed territory and Pakistan was clearly defeated during its first war with India (Gates and Roy 2011). Since then, the issue of Kashmir has been the primary factor straining the bilateral relationship between the two neighbouring countries.

After the first India-Pakistan war in 1947, Pakistan found itself in a very vulnerable situation and feared that India would undo Pakistan. The major problem was that Pakistan had a very weak intelligence system and its military was largely unable to respond effectively to immediate security challenges. In this connection, much of the military personnel that had joined the new national Pakistani army came from different units of the former British military. According to General Ayub Khan, the army consisted of a mixture of untrained, half-trained, and highly trained military personnel. Consequently, Pakistan had to regroup and restructure the entire army after its independence. Furthermore, India refused to transfer Pakistan's share of military armaments, equipment, and stores that were allocated to it under the terms of the partition deal by the British before leaving India. Under the agreement, India agreed to transfer 33 percent of British India's military resources and 17.5 percent of its financial resources to Pakistan. With respect to Pakistan's allotted share of military equipment, India supplied around 23,000 out of 100,000 tons of ordnance, and that arrived both late and incomplete (Kapur 2016). Thus, the Pakistani military was not properly equipped and organized to deal with early national security challenges after partition.

In 1950–1951, India again threatened Pakistan twice with invasion as it moved its military closer to the Pakistani border areas. More importantly, Pakistan does not have a first line of defence along its eastern border as its densely populated cities Sialkot and Lahore are situated very close to the Wahgah border. Pakistan was almost defenceless at this time and in no position to counter the military threat of India (S. A. Husain 1979). According to Shuja Nawaz (Skype interview by author, 14 February 2018),

> India was always a real threat to Pakistan particularly in the early years because not only did India stop the transfer of resources but also assisted the Maharaja of Kashmir in making his mind to accede to India by sending troops. India also at one point cut off Pakistan's water resources as a mean of coercing them. So India used coercive diplomacy as well as military power to threaten the country. This fear of Indian aggression coloured Pakistani security thinking from the very beginning till today.

In this situation, General Ayub Khan also tried to address all of the outstanding disputes with India, including Kashmir. In 1956, he proposed a strategic plan for the joint defence of the subcontinent in the event of communist aggression in the wake of China's takeover in Tibet. However, the Indian prime minister, Nehru, did not appear to take the proposal seriously and was reluctant to resolve the issue of Kashmir (Lerski 1974). Since then, the Pakistani military establishment tended to see India as a permanent threat to the nation's security. According to Brigadier Muhammad Saad (interview by author, Islamabad, 14 November 2017), "country's threat assessments are made not on enemy's intent but its capability. Intentions can be changed overnight but not capabilities. India was quite capable of damaging Pakistan right after its independence in 1947." As a result, Pakistan adopted a confrontationist foreign policy towards India instead of accommodating it. More importantly, military competition with India became the priority of the subsequent governments of Pakistan after its establishment as an independent state. General Ayub Khan (1967) explained the strategic priority in his memoirs:

> Our aim must be to make India realize that it is not worth her while to maintain a hostile attitude towards us. India's military strength would always be greater than ours. Our aim should be to build up a military deterrent force

with adequate offensive and defensive power; enough, at least, to neutralize the Indian army. India can concentrate her forces against us without warning. We must, therefore, have a standing army to take the field at moment's notice. In our circumstances a territorial army has hardly any place; it would take too much time to mobilize and train such army.

From the standpoint of the Pakistani civil and military leadership, the young country required an assertive federal government, a strong defence posture, high military expenditure, and a monolithic nationalism for state survival. This led to the creation of a national security state in which the military became the dominant force in the country's foreign and security policymaking. The national security state was largely based on antagonism towards India over the Kashmir conflict and the external threat to its national sovereignty and territorial integrity. During General Ayub's regime, it was considered necessary to have a strong centralized government at the federal level, with a pro-Western foreign policy to get military aid and financial assistance (Rizvi 2000; Ahmad 2011).

In this fashion, the military establishment of an independent Pakistan facilitated the emergence of a national security state, a development largely based on hostility towards India. Nonetheless, many thought that the threat from India was exaggerated and that the military elites used it to justify sustaining and maintaining large armed forces in the country. According to Khalid Rahman (interview by author, Islamabad, 21 November 2017), "the military was ambitious and exaggerated the external threats from India to protect its institutional interest. Subsequently, the military used the security threat for its institutional interest." Professor Muhammad Islam (interview by author, Islamabad, 22 November 2017), confirmed that "the military had growing interests in politics and they needed to justify their dominant role in the policy making that led to the rise of national security state." Consequently, the Pakistani military, with the support of the ISI and civil bureaucracy, increasingly assumed a leadership role within the Pakistani state that led to militarization during the Cold War.

The militarization of Pakistan: the evolution of Pakistan's national security state[5]

Pakistan inherited its institutional structure in the field of security from the British colonial authorities at the time of the partition of India in 1947. A large number of British-trained civil and military officers continued to hold key positions in the Pakistani setup. More importantly, Pakistan's military largely retained the institutional structure bequeathed by Britain at the time of independence. However, the British structure was designed for imperial rule in India and to fight in Britain's wars overseas. Until 1973, Pakistan largely continued with the same military structure (Hafeez 2012). In many ways, the internal and external security environment of Pakistan helped to facilitate the military's dominance of state affairs.

Internally, the institutions that existed before Pakistan was created were the army and civil bureaucracy. Pakistan had to build other state institutions from scratch in order to maintain its independence (Senator Mushahid Hussain Syed, interview by author, Islamabad, 8 December 2017). The Pakistan Muslim League was unable to transform itself into a strong political party and its central leadership had no political constituency of their own in the newly formed country, as they migrated from India. Moreover, the local politicians were not interested in federal politics at the national level. Following the death of Muhammad Ali Jinnah in 1948, and Liaqat Ali Khan in 1951, the political leadership of the country was further weakened, and since then, Pakistan experienced a prolonged spell of political instability after 1947 (Blom 2011). The country saw seven prime ministers and four governor generals during the first decade of independence, a critical time for state building in any new country. The Pakistani leadership failed to formulate a constitution or hold elections during the first nine years of independence. Interestingly, however, there was stability in the military sphere, with no change in the command of armed forces after General Ayub Khan became the first native C-in-C of the newly born country in January 1951 (Rizvi 2000).

The national security state doctrine began in the 1950s under the leadership of General Ayub Khan. The military leadership exploited the political instability in the first decade of Pakistan's independence by forging a strong military establishment that dominated policymaking in the country (Malik 2008). General Ayub established himself as the prominent statesman within the Pakistani political system, filling the political vacuum following the death of the prominent political leaders. Taking on the mantle of the politician, he addressed a gathering of ex-military servicemen and announced the establishment of a cloth factory for them in Punjab province. He also tried to resolve issues relating to military servicemen's salaries and allowances. As General Ayub came from the KP province, which was one of the smaller provinces in the country, he was careful to cultivate links with the Punjab province, a key political constituency and also a prime location for military recruitment (Jalal 1990). Thus, Ayub assumed the mantle of a prominent political actor, with the support of the military, in the key Punjab province.

It is important to note that the military obtained first-hand experience of civil administration in March 1953 when the Pakistani government imposed martial law in Lahore, the capital of Punjab province, after anti-Ahmadiyya[6] riots in the city. The protesters demanded the removal of Foreign Minister Zafarullah Khan, who belonged to the minority Ahmadiyya sect of Islam. On 6 March 1953, Major General Muhammad Azam Khan was appointed martial law administrator to extend the writ of the central state and improve law and order. The army successfully managed the situation in a relatively short period of time and handed back control of Lahore to the civil administration in mid-May 1953. As a result of martial law, Lahore appeared to be much calmer and safer (Rizvi 2000). Professor Hasan Askari Rizvi (2000, 78–79) identified three major implications of the Lahore martial law experience for Pakistan's civil-military relations:

First, the weaknesses and deficiencies of the political institutions and leaders were exposed that they could not satisfactorily perform their primary duty of political and administrative management. Second, it gave the military first-hand experience of civilian affairs and the machinations of the political leaders that some political leaders were involved with smugglers, hoarders and other criminal elements. Third, it created a strong impression in the public mind that the military could cope with a difficult situation even when the political leaders failed, thereby giving a boost to the Army's reputation as a task-oriented and efficient entity with a helpful disposition towards the people.

Thus, the success of the martial law administration in Lahore provided the military with a certain degree of legitimacy to interfere in politics. Since then, the military has consistently become involved in Pakistani politics, blurring the boundary between civilian and military spheres of interest.

The civilian bureaucracy increasingly aligned itself with the military establishment after witnessing the military's growing role in the state's affairs. Also, the bureaucracy often assumed some of the roles of politicians, but they lacked political legitimacy and popular appeal to run the country (Paul 2014). In April 1953, the civil bureaucracy, with the support of the Pakistani military, removed Prime Minister Khawaja Nazimuddin from his office. The major reason for the removal was the deteriorating economic situation (Sayeed 1954). Governor General Malik Ghulam Muhammad summoned Nazimuddin and ordered him to resign. Nazimuddin refused to do so and challenged the decision. However, the governor general dismissed Nazimuddin from his office using his discretionary power under section 10 of the 1935 Government of India Act (Sayeed 1955). The removal of the prime minister marked the beginning of a soft form of martial law administration in Pakistan. According to Iskandar Mirza, the cabinet member and later governor general, the military took key government positions and confined the former prime minister to house arrest after his removal. This demonstrated that the military in Pakistani was ready to assume the task of governing the country. It was left to the governor general to approve the military establishment's coup plan and formally implement the removal of the sitting prime minister (Jalal 1990; Saddiqa 2007). After the soft coup, Muhammad Ali Bogra, a career civil bureaucrat with no political base, was appointed prime minister in April 1953. Bogra formed a new cabinet known as the "ministry of talents." General Ayub was appointed as the defence minister and was allowed to continue as a C-in-C as well (Ahmed 2004). As such, the military had assumed power under the leadership of General Ayub without formal acknowledgement of this.

On 7 October 1958, Governor General Iskandar Mirza, in coordination with General Ayub Khan, removed the constitutional government and imposed martial law. Mirza accused the politicians of being too incompetent to deal with the challenges of political instability and economic crisis in the country. Mirza continued as president with absolute power and banned all political activity in the country. He established military courts under General Ayub to put corrupt politicians on trial. However, Mirza was unable to effectively run state affairs without the presence of the powerful military chief, General Ayub Khan. Ultimately, General

Ayub took over the martial law administration on 28 October 1958, and exiled Mirza to London (Malik 2008; Rizvi 2000). Since then, the military became the dominant actor in the political sphere of state affairs.

Interestingly, the military coup was widely accepted in Pakistan. Many Pakistanis believed that General Ayub would bring stability and order to a much-troubled country. General Ayub removed the civil bureaucrats who opposed his regime. For example, about 1,300 civilian officers were removed or side-lined by General Ayub after martial law administration was imposed. The judiciary extended the martial law administration in 1958 and this further served to legitimize the role of the military in state affairs (Aziz 2008). Thereafter, the judiciary provided a legal cover for the military's unconstitutional acts during the Cold War and beyond. In this process, the military established itself as the saviour of the country and there has been no opposition to the military's interference in state politics.

In a bid to legitimize his rule, General Ayub initiated so-called political reforms and lifted martial law in 1962. Nonetheless, he believed that "parliamentary democracy does not suit the genius of the people of Pakistan" (Salim 2014). He was in favour of the presidential form of government in which it was easy for the military to take control of the state's affairs. General Ayub framed his own constitution and introduced a "controlled democracy" in which the president held most of the power (Siddiqa 2007). On the face of it, General Ayub distanced the military from political power, but key positions in the government were given to his hand-picked politicians. Essentially, the policies of martial administration were largely continued, with the military and civilian bureaucracy remaining as significant partners in the country's policymaking. General Ayub remained the C-in-C of the military with absolute power to take decisions about war and peace without consulting parliament (Cohen 2004). In short, General Ayub introduced a presidential form of leadership that concentrated power in his own hands and heralded a guided or controlled democracy in which the military played a central role. Since then, a "controlled form of democracy" has become the main characteristic of Pakistan's national security state in which the political leadership are blamed for their wrongdoings but are used to present a democratic face to the outside world.

Externally, Pakistan was struggling to compete with India, which dominated the region due to its large population, economy, and military power. Moreover, India was trying to acquire further military power through domestic weapons production and external purchasing of arms from the Soviet Union (Chari 1979). The main objective was to present India as the predominant military power in the South Asia region, and that the region should be treated purely as an Indian sphere of influence (Rais 1991). However, Pakistan opposed Indian hegemony in the South Asian region from the very beginning after its independence. Prime Minister Liaquat Ali Khan in his public speech in October 1948 declared that "the defence of the state is our foremost consideration. We will not grudge any amount on the defence of our country" (Singh and Baily 2013). However, the Pakistani economy was too weak to build such a large military power. In 1947, the country had no significant industrial base and almost no known natural resources, though it was relatively well endowed with agricultural resources (Bose 1983). Therefore, Pakistan looked to external security balancing to help its weak military and provide economic support in order to protect itself from external threats. The options for external sources were limited as the European states were already affected by the Second World War and were looking towards the US for the reconstruction of their war-torn economies. Like other countries, Pakistan requested US$2 billion financial assistance from the US for its defence procurement and economic progress. However, the US refused to give financial support and even to sell arms to Pakistan, as they were unsure of its long-term survival (Jalal 1990).

However, the Pakistani leadership did not lose its hope of making an alliance with the US to get military aid and financial assistance. This was because the Pakistani leadership was convinced that the country could become a key ally of the US due to its geostrategic position in the region. Actually, a "power vacuum" existed in the Indian subcontinent after the end of the British colonial regime. Pakistan was confident that they could fill this vacuum by aligning with the US to contain Soviet expansion in the region (R. Khan, 1985). Hence, Pakistan was looking to gain a bigger role by making an alliance with the Western bloc at the commencement of the Cold War.

Two significant events took place in 1949–1950 that led the US to change its foreign policy towards Asia: China fell into the hands of the Communist regime in 1949 and North Korea invaded South Korea in 1950. The US leadership was worried that it might lose the Cold War in Asia. Subsequently, the US was looking for a regional alliance with "free nations" in order to contain Soviet expansion. For this, the US needed military bases and support around the world. Therefore, the US announced the extension of the Marshal Plan to Asia because of its success in Western Europe. Under the Marshal Plan, the US provided economic assistance, military aid, and a security umbrella to its allies in Europe (R. Khan, 1985). Thus, the US was looking for new allies in Asia to contain the expansion of Soviet and Chinese communism.

In this situation, the Cold War provided a welcome opportunity for Pakistan to form an alliance with the US, as Washington was looking for an ally in South Asia to help contain perceived Soviet expansion. The US was very interested in making an alliance with India, due to its bigger regional power, with which the extension of communism could be contained. Therefore, the US officially invited Indian Prime Minister Nehru to visit the US, whereas they did not invite the prime minister of Pakistan. Nehru visited the US in October 1949. However, he refused to make an alliance with the US and preferred to remain neutral (Alavi 1998). Nehru clearly outlined India's foreign policy in his statement that "We have no intentions to commit ourselves to anybody at any time. India wants no part of that war" (Soherwordi 2010). Subsequently, the US entered formal negotiations with the Pakistani leadership in 1953 to establish military bases in the country in exchange for financial and military aid. The US secretary of state, John Foster Dulles, visited Pakistan to explore ways of developing bilateral relations. It was followed by a visit of the vice-president, Richard Nixon, to accelerate an alliance with Pakistan to contain the Soviet Union and China. In February 1954, President Dwight Eisenhower announced that the US would provide military assistance to Pakistan in order to strengthen the defensive capabilities of its allies in the Middle East (Spain 1954). Initially, the US provided a modest package of military aid that quickly rose to a figure of around US$500 million annually by 1955 (see Table 2.1). Pakistan, therefore, managed to establish a military alliance with the US that helped boost and restructure its military capabilities following its independence.

After aligning with the US, Pakistan signed the "Mutual Defense Assistance Agreement" with the US in May 1954. Additionally, Pakistan signed Western-sponsored military pacts, including the Southeast Asia Treaty Organization (SEATO) in 1954 and the Baghdad Pact in 1955, renamed the Central Treaty Organization (CENTO) in 1958. Pakistan was the only Asian country to be part of both the Baghdad Pact and the SEATO alliance (A. Khan 1967). In March 1956, the SEATO member countries recognized that "the sovereignty of Pakistan extends up to the Durand Line, the international boundary between Pakistan and Afghanistan" (Lerski 1974). Like Turkey and Iran, Pakistan signed a bilateral agreement of cooperation with the US in 1959 that endorsed the defensive purposes of the CENTO agreement. As a result, Pakistan became the closest associate of the US in Asia and was called the "most-allied ally" of the US in Asia (A. Khan 1967). Thus, Pakistan jumped on the bandwagon with the US to protect its national security interests.

General Ayub played a major role in formulating the alliance with the US and used his personal contacts in Washington to get military aid rather than simply working through formal channels to the US Military Advisory Group (Farooq 2016). In a candid explanation of these arrangements, General Ayub (1967, 117) said "the membership of the pacts were dictated solely by the requirement of

Table 2.1 US aid to Pakistan, 1951–1959 (USD in million)

Year	Economic Aid	Military Aid
1951	0.798	0
1952	78.796	0
1953	298.581	0
1954	630.394	0
1955	595.2	439.484
1956	1,007.821	1,190.4361
1957	721.803	856.835
1958	674.785	864.584
1959	1,031.458	400.487
Total	**5039.636**	**3,751.83**
Total US Aid:	**8,791.46**	

Source: US overseas Loans and Grants (Green book) available at https:// eads.usaid.gov/gbk/. In Asif, M. and Muhammad, A. (2017). "Image of USA in Urban Pakistan: An Empirical Assessment." *A Research Journal of South Asian Studies* 32 (2): 539–555.

our security." Following the military aid in the mid-1950s from the US which strengthened the Pakistan military as well as aided first to General Ayub Khan's importance as the defence minister and then as the military head of state. Thus, General Ayub enhanced his credentials as a statesman after forming military alliances with the US and other Western powers that helped Pakistan to significantly enhance its military capabilities. In this process, the Pakistani military became the dominant actor in foreign and security policymaking that became another key characteristic of Pakistan's national security state. Nonetheless, this created structural problems for future civilian governments during and after the Cold War era.

Additionally, Pakistan often tried to include the question of Indian aggression in the bilateral treaties with the US. However, the US was only concerned with Soviet expansion and avoided including the Indian threat in their bilateral agreements. Therefore, the Pakistan-US relationship passed through different phases throughout the Cold War. However, the geopolitical realities and strategic compulsion always joined them together despite the limited natural alliance between the two countries (Mazhar and Goraya 2012). In other words, the relationship was short term, and Pakistan allied with the US because of the Cold War. Simply put, the Pakistan-US relationship developed first in the context of the commencement of the Cold War and then, later, under the imperatives of Soviet intervention in Afghanistan in 1979 (see below section: The advent of ISI as a key player: the Afghan War in the 1980s).

In this context, the US agenda in relation to Pakistan was global in scope and was part of the effort to contain the expansion of the Soviet Union, whereas the Pakistani agenda in relations with Washington was essentially local and designed to help counter Indian dominance in its region. Even though, reluctantly, Pakistan provided military bases to the US in KP and Balochistan provinces in exchange for military aid and economic assistance. This helped the US to observe and monitor Soviet activities. On 5 May 1960, the famous U-2 spy plane, which was shot down by the Soviets, flew from Badaber air base in Peshawar, the provincial capital of KP province. Subsequently, the Soviet Union warned Pakistan and other regional allies of the US, including Iran, Iraq, and Turkey, to stop using their territory against them or be ready for its consequences (Iqbal and Khalid 2011).

US military and economic aid assisted Pakistan to restructure and organize its military in order to meet the new security challenges. The US aid was the principal instrument of their strategy in South Asia. Pakistan received US$8.7 billion aid up to 1959 (Asif 2017):

Furthermore, the US provided a substantial number of modern aircraft and military equipment to Pakistan, which modernized the armed forces. Besides this, the US assisted in the construction of airfields and other military installations in the country. Many military officers were trained in the US, which helped Pakistan establish training centres and programmes in Pakistan. Consequently, the country was able to enhance its defence capabilities and to prepare a deterrent force that was capable of neutralizing Indian military power with adequate defensive and offensive power. This led to Indian protests against the US military aid to

Pakistan. In a Commonwealth conference, Indian Premier Nehru said that the Pakistan-US pacts brought the Cold War to South Asia and disturbed its peace, as well as the balance between India and Pakistan (Jabeen and Mazhar 2011). Nevertheless, the alliance between the US and Pakistan continued.

According to Professor Hans J. Morgenthau (1965):

> The alliance between the US and Pakistan is one of many contemporary instances of an alliance serving complementary interests. For the US it serves the primary purpose of expanding the scope of the policy of containment; for Pakistan it serves primarily the purpose of increasing her political, military, and economic potential vis-a-vis her neighbours.

Thus, the alliance was satisfactory for both countries, as Pakistan provided military bases to the US to contain the spread of communism while Pakistan received defence and financial support from the US, which was necessary for its confrontation with India. However, this meant that Pakistan became largely dependent upon external financing for meeting its military requirements – a situation that has persisted to this day.

Besides the alliance with the US, Pakistan also established very friendly relations with Communist China and supported liberation movements in different Asian and African countries such as Algeria and Palestine. According to Senator Mushahid Hussain Syed (interview by author, Islamabad, 8 December 2017),

> Pakistan's foreign policy had two dimensions that need to be understood: despite aligning with America, we [Pakistan] were considered an adversary of the Soviet Union but not China; and we continued to support liberation movements of Muslim countries in different parts of the world, particularly Algeria, Tunisia, Eritrea and Palestine. In fact, Pakistan was the one country to offer its passports to liberation leader of Algeria and Tunisia who used to travel on its passport.

After the 1962 Indo-China War, Pakistan and China formed an official bilateral relationship and exchanged high-level official visits. According to Zulfikar Ali Bhutto, the foreign minister and future prime minister of Pakistan, "We will not barter or bargain Chinese friendship away for anything" (Soherwordi 2010, 30). Due to Pakistan's hostility towards India, China became a more natural and long-term strategic partner of Pakistan against India in South Asia. In March 1963, both countries successfully resolved all their territorial issues and reached mutual agreements on the border line, and even swapped some territory in the northern areas of Pakistan, despite Indian resentment (Rizvi 1993). China gave around 750 square miles of territory to Pakistan which had been under Chinese control, and this ended territorial disputes between the two countries. Pakistan reversed its policy on Chinese admission to the UN, and in return, China supported Pakistan's claim over Kashmir. China also agreed to provide economic assistance with a US$60 million long-term, interest-free loan to Pakistan (Lerski 1974). Since then, Islamabad has continued to have good relations with China.

It is important to note that the Pakistani military exploited both the internal and external security environments to get the lion's share from the national treasury. For instance, Pakistan has often spent enormous amounts of its fiscal and foreign exchange resources on national defence. During 1947–1988, Pakistan's defence expenditure ranged from about 34 percent to 73 percent of total federal government expenditure, averaging 50.5 percent (Rizvi 1983). The details are given in Table 2.2.

Interestingly, the military justified their defence expenditure on the grounds of Pakistan's strategic vulnerability and by presenting itself as the sole guarantor of the country. The country's parliament backed high defence spending, and there was little questioning of it in cabinet meetings prior to the imposition of the martial law administration in 1958. Since Pakistan's inception, successive governments have discouraged debate on security matters, and the media, to a large degree, has passively supported the government's emphasis on a strong defence force (Rizvi 2000). In this process, the political leadership set the precedent that the defence budget would not be discussed in parliament, which became another feature of Pakistan's national security state. Thereafter, the civilian leadership has failed to exercise oversight over military expenditure since independence. As a result, the military's control over the political system has enabled it to create the means and resources to establish financial autonomy.

Pakistan's military-industrial complex

Since 1954, the Pakistani military has used its political and administrative autonomy to establish its own commercial and welfare enterprises in the country. The military has become directly involved in various commercial ventures, from building roads to housing projects and from cement factories to private banks. Also, there has been both horizontal and vertical growth in its businesses. Over time, they extended their outreach to include private educational institutions, research think tanks, and hospitals, as well as internal policing in major cities, catching electricity thieves and fighting against corruption in the country (Siddiqa 2007). This led to the Pakistani military-industrial complex which provides the means and resources to the Pakistani military to act independently.

The military set up four welfare foundations in the beginning: the Fauji Foundation (FF) for inter-services personnel; the Army Welfare Trust (AWT) for army personnel; the Shaheen Foundation (SF) for air force personnel; and the Bahria Foundation (BF) for navy personnel (Blom 2011). Over a period, such foundations transformed into large business conglomerates. According to some estimates, they run more than 700 companies and hold at least a 10 percent share of the country's private-sector assets. Moreover, these foundations have 96 enterprises, of which only 9 are publically listed for accountability. Thus, most of the enterprises run under the foundations have avoided public accountability and have been exempted from tax under Pakistani law as they have been proclaimed to be welfare organizations (see detail in next sections). In addition to this, the military extended its business into public-sector organizations such as the

Table 2.2 Defence expenditure, 1947–1988 (PKR in million)

Year	Defence Expenditure	Total Expenditure	Defence Expenditure as % of Total Expenditure
1947–48	153.8	236	65.16
1948–49	461.5	647	71.32
1949–50	625.4	856	73.06
1950–51	649.9	1,266.2	51.32
1951–52	779.1	1,442.3	54.01
1952–53	783.4	1,320.1	59.34
1953–54	653.2	1,108.7	58.91
1954–55	635.1	1,172.6	54.16
1955–56	917.7	1,433.4	64.02
1956–57	800.9	1,330.7	60.18
1957–58	854.2	1,521.8	56.13
1958–59	9,996.6	1,956.5	50.93
1959–60	601,043.5	1,846.5	56.51
1960–61	611,112.4	1,894.2	58.72
1961–62	621,108.6	1,986.8	55.79
1962–63	63,954.3	1,795.3	53.15
1963–64	641,156.5	2,337.2	49.48
1964–65	651,262.3	2,736.2	46.13
1965–66	662,855.0	4,498.1	63.47
1966–67	672,293.5	3,765.5	60.09
1967–68	682,186.5	4,077.1	53.62
1968–69	92,426.8	4,371.0	55.52
1969–70	702,749.1	5,109.4	53.80
1970–71	713,201.5	5,751.3	55.66
1971–72	3,725.5	6,303.8	59.09
1972–73	4,439.6	7,480.7	59.34
1973–74	4,948.6	11,724.6	42.02
1974–75	6,914.2	16,139.6	42.83
1975–76	8,103.4	17,613.5	46.00
1976–77	8,120.6	18,161.5	44.71
1977–78	9,674.5	22,781.9	42.46
1978–79	10,167.6	29,851.8	34.06
1979–80	12,654.8	34,845.1	36.31
1980–81 (revised)	15,283.9	39,592.5	38.06
1981–82 (revised)	19,592.9	38,090.0	51.43
1982–83 (revised)	22,095.3	46,910.0	47.01
1983–84	26,798	68,949	38.86
1984–85	31,866	90,074	35.37
1985–86	35,606	100,043	35.59
1986–87	41,335	111,856	36.95
1987–88	47,015	136,151	34.53

Average annual percentage of defence expenditure: 50.51

Source: Compiled from Pakistan Economic Survey, an annual publication of the Government of Pakistan; In Rizvi, H. A. (1983) "Pakistan's Defence Policy" *Pakistan Horizon*, 36:1, 55–56.

National Logistics Corporation (NLC), in charge of transportation; the Frontier Works Organisation (FWO), involved in construction businesses; and the Special Communications Organization (SCO), working in telecommunication networks.

The four subsidiaries FF, AWT, SF, and BF were registered as charitable organizations under the 1889 Charitable Endowments Act. The FF was founded in 1954 and is now one of the largest business conglomerates in Pakistan, with a declared net worth of US$1,304 million and net assets of US$4,211 million (Fauji Foundation, n.d.). The FF is largely involved in various business ventures, from cement to gas production and from cereals to sugar mills. Throughout Pakistan, the FF also runs 100 schools, 11 hospitals, 60 mobile clinics, an artificial limb centre, and a nursing school. The FF was exempted from tax until 1970 as it counted as a welfare organization. However, they claim that currently they are one of the country's major taxpayers (Fauji Foundation, n.d.).

The AWT is another subsidiary of the Pakistani military, established in 1971. The primary objective was to give employment and provide a profit-making opportunity to ex-servicemen as they were facing resources crunch due to the 1960s US arms embargo and the subsequent 1965 and 1971 wars. Like the FF, the AWF was exempted from tax, this time until 1993 (Siddiqa 2007). It has also developed leading business ventures in various areas such as agriculture, manufacturing, sugar, lubricants, real estate, insurance, aviation, gas stations, and private security solutions (AWF, n.d.).

The SF was established in 1977. Like AWT and FF, its objective was the welfare of ex-servicemen of the air force through industrial and commercial enterprises. The SF provides services in various sectors, including education, engineering, health, construction works, housing, advertising, and many other relevant services. The foundation has more than 3,000 employees, of which 700 are ex-Pakistan Air Force personnel (see Appendix 4).

The BF was created in 1982. It has excelled in a diverse range of roles in the commercial, developmental, and industrial sectors, such as maritime works organization, education, commercial businesses, and real estate. The foundation runs about 80 schools and colleges throughout Pakistan. It owns four prestigious residential complexes, having an area of about 486,000 square feet of office space at Karachi and one complex in Gwadar, a newly established coastal area in Balochistan province. Moreover, it has over 7,500 employees working in different parts of the country (Bahria Foundation, n.d.).

The primary objective of these foundations was ostensibly the welfare of the ex-servicemen. However, the evolution of the subsidiaries showed that the core motive was to create economic opportunity for the military to gain economic self-sufficiency as it developed large business conglomerates. In the beginning, they penetrated into the "captive market" in which consumers and customers were from their own military institutions. For example, they sold their plots to military personnel in the real estate sector. In the second stage, they targeted private consumers and clients through their own firms and societies. Moreover, they developed their own independent chains of businesses under the umbrella of the four foundations. For example, military agricultural products are processed and marketed by military-run subsidiaries, while the military-run Askari Bank handled their transactions (Blom 2011).

In addition to this, the setting up of commercial industries has not only provided employment opportunities for ex-servicemen but it has also largely extended the military's influence beyond welfare into the political sphere of the country. For instance, the Pakistani military has presented itself in such a way that not only does it protect national borders but it also engages in the development of the country. According to David R. Mares (2010, 386–387), "the military institution itself is intimately involved in leading the political system and its goals are to transform the country's political and economic institutions." The commercial and business ventures of the Pakistani military flourished during 1954–1969, especially under General Ayub Khan's military regime. According to Ejaz Husain (interview by author, Islamabad, 14 November 2017), "the main rationality behind intervention in politics was to capture political power and advance its institutional power which allowed the military to protect its economic interests." This meant the military was creating an image as a saviour of the country in order to extend its economic empire in the country. Ayesha Saddiqa (2007) noted that "Pakistan['s] military business case often reflects an overlapping of institutional self-interests and [an] anarchic paradigm, where senior generals used their institutional authority and military mechanism for personal predatory appropriation." Thus, the military established its own business empire to protect its institutional and individual interests.

In addition to these subsidiaries, General Zia entrenched the military's role in the economic sphere of the country. The military initiated large infrastructure, transportation, and communication projects by establishing various institutions such as NLC, FWO, and the SCO. General Zia started new industrial projects under the above welfare foundation so there was sectoral growth as well (Siddiqa 2007). The NLC engaged in infrastructure projects such as the construction of roads, bridges, and wheat storage facilities. The NLC had 1,689 vehicles, making it one of the largest public-sector transport fleets in Asia. The company is attached to the department of the Ministry of Planning and Development, but basic control of the organization lies with the army. The operational control of the organization is under the army's Quartermaster General, and it is staffed by 7,279 people, of whom 2,549 are serving military personnel. The rest are retired officers and civilians who are mainly involved in clerical positions (Siddiqa 2007, 134–135). In 2013, the NLC's freight service financial turnover was PKR 3,554.00 million, and it generated PKR 5 billion on average in 2003–2013 (NLC, n.d.). The NLC also charged US$235 per the North Atlantic Treaty Organization (NATO) container for handling, scanning, and toll charges on its Afghan supply route in Pakistan after the US invasion in Afghanistan in 2001 (Rana 2012). Such business ventures allowed the military to maintain its financial autonomy, further entrenching the national security state.

The FWO is the second major commercial venture of the Pakistani military, established in 1966. It has remained the major contractor for constructing roads and collecting tolls in the country. It comes under the Ministry of Defence (MoD) and is largely controlled by the Pakistani military. Since the mid-1990s, the FWO has grown as one of the primary contractors for public-sector road construction in the country. The SCO was originally established in 1976 to handle a telecommunication network project in Pakistani-administered Kashmir and Gilgit Baltistan. Working under the Ministry of Information Technology, the SCO is a public-sector organization headed by a serving military officer. The organization was revitalized towards the end of the 1990s and given the task of expanding the telecommunication network in the abovementioned administered areas (Siddiqa 2007). Media reports said that the SCO demanded full autonomy to operate as a commercial entity and expand its services across the country, something the government feared would undermine the private telecommunications sector, risking millions of dollars of foreign investment by cellular companies (Shahid 2017).

Additionally, the military established small- and medium-sized cooperatives and businesses such as cinemas, bakeries, poultry farms, and other related commercial enterprises. The military often justified their business ventures by claiming that they were better organized and their staff better trained as compared with those administered by civilians. Consequently, the military-run commercial institutions performed efficiently. Nonetheless, it is important to note that the military often used security concerns to win the bidding for government contracts. In case the government gives the project to the best bidder, the military often raises the issue of the security threat to such projects. The military argues that civilian contractors cannot guarantee the security of such projects. Subsequently, they exploit security concerns and gain most of the contracts at very low costs (Siddiqa 2007). In this process, the Pakistani military established a parallel economy through their military-run business ventures.

In many countries such as China, Indonesia, Turkey, Algeria, and Myanmar, the military has been deeply involved in different commercial businesses. The Pakistani case is unique in the sense that it has flourished over a long period, both in terms of setting up new commercial organizations as well as in the sectoral expansion of the Pakistani military foundations which allow it to move into lucrative sectors such as agro-based industries, fertilizer production, and the oil and gas sectors (Blom 2011). As a result, the Pakistani military-industrial complex has gone beyond the welfare of ex-servicemen into the economic sphere of the country. Thus, the military-industrial complex became another feature of Pakistan's national security state.

In addition to this, the military provides compensation to its personnel in order to meet its manning goals such as force size, composition, and wartime capability (Asch and Warner 1994). After its inception in 1947, the military developed a mechanism in which the armed forces enjoy perks and privileges. For example, the government allotted agricultural land as a reward to members of the armed forces on the basis of their ranks and performances in the military as well as different other schemes (*Express Tribune*, Pakistan, 26 January 2017). Pakistan is an agricultural country where land is the most valuable resource. Land was transferred to the military for operational purposes such as containment, border areas, and training grounds. Some land was allocated to the foundations for farms and real estate businesses. Moreover, the government distributes land as rewards to retired military personnel (Blom 2011). In June 1982, the military launched a housing scheme to provide low-cost houses for retired officers, paid for in easy instalments. The first housing project was completed in early 1984 (Rizvi 2003). Subsequently, the military extended its services in different housing schemes and developed its own real estate empire in the country. Under the housing schemes, the military occupied a massive proportion of land in key locations in major cities in Pakistan. For example, the cantonment board holds about 35 percent of prime land in Karachi. There is hardly any debate over the land allocated to military cantonments and housing schemes in the country. The legal status of the lands occupied by the military is hotly contested by the provincial bureaucracies, however (Blom 2011).

The military gives various military awards such as *Hilal-e-Juraat, Sitira-e-Juraat*, and *Tamgha-e-Juraat*, and their recipients received 50 acres, 25 acres, and 12.5 acres of land respectively. According to Professor Hasan Askari, around 300,000 acres of agricultural land were allotted to military personnel in the Sindh province during the Ayub regime, while they received about 450,000 acres of land in the Punjab province between 1977 and 1985 (*Express Tribune*, Pakistan, 26 January 2017). Moreover, General Zia exempted senior military officials from paying customs duty on luxury cars. During 1977–1997, 27 army officers, 10 navy officers, and 6 air force officers took advantage of this facility (Rizvi 2003). In this process, the military established itself as an elite class in the country.

The Pakistani military adopted a strategy of incorporating its military officers into various civilian institutions during General Ayub Khan's regime. Many retired military officers were appointed to key positions in government and semi-government corporations or autonomous bodies. Military officers were also inducted into the civilian elite civil services. Since then, military men have held prominent positions in the civilian institutions. General Zia institutionalized the induction of military officers into civilian organizations. For instance, General Zia allocated a 10 percent minimum quota for the military in civilian jobs, in all government and semi-government services, and appointed military officers as governors of the four provinces (Blom 2011; Rizvi 2003). Since then, this military induction has continued in civilian institutions under both civilian and military regimes. Additionally, many retired military personnel of the rank of captain or colonel were appointed to the police, the civilian-run Federal Investigation Agency (FIA), and the Intelligence Bureau (IB) after retirement (Rizvi 2003). Interestingly, 18 out of the 42 ambassadors posted overseas were from the military in 1982. Moreover, the military attaché, who is usually a serving military officer in the embassy, is more powerful than the ambassador. The induction of military personnel into civilian administration guaranteed the military's autonomy from the civilian bureaucracy and ensured that they were not aligned with political parties. More specifically, the retired personnel remained loyal to their mother institutions. Above all, they protect their commercial and institutional interests in the civilian organizations, as we will see in Chapter 6.

Fall of Dhaka in 1971: the impact on Pakistan's national security approach

General Ayub Khan became widely unpopular, due to his economic policies that largely favoured the military-industrial complex and crony capitalism. Moreover, the leftist politicians accused him of exploiting workers and suppressing the rights of minority ethnic groups, including Sindhis, Balochs, Pashtuns, and Urdu speakers (Mohajirs). Moreover, Bengalis (in East Pakistan), the largest ethnic group, were convinced that the power structure had ignored their political aspirations and socio-economic development. The Awami League, a major political party in East Pakistan, also accused General Ayub of leaving East Pakistan open to attack during the 1965 war against India (*Dawn*, Pakistan, 31 August 2014). Consequently, General Ayub became very unpopular, and countrywide protests were started against his authoritarian regime.

In March 1969, General Ayub resigned following countrywide protests and a growing rift between West and East Pakistan. He handed over power to General Yahya Khan. Prior to becoming the second martial law administrator, General Ayub appointed General Yahya as a major general, and he led an infantry division during the 1965 war (Paracha 2017). In June 1966, he was promoted to C-in-C of the Pakistan Army. After taking office, General Yahya promised to hold elections and restore a parliamentary system in the country. Elections were held in 1970, and the Awami League won the majority of seats, forming a government at federal level. However, General Yahya was reluctant to facilitate a full transfer of power to East Pakistan under parliamentary rule because the Awami League had promised decentralization and provincial autonomy in their election campaign and in Sheikh Mujib's six point, and it was feared that this would undermine the national security state.

In this context, the Awami League launched a mass movement for the political autonomy of East Pakistan. The Pakistani military reacted with a crackdown against the protesters in East Pakistan. This, in turn, led to a bloody civil war between *Mukti Bahini* (the Bengali resistance movement) and the Pakistani security forces that continued for two years. Over 10 million refugees fled to India during the civil war. In November 1971, the Indian military intervened in the conflict to support the resistance movement, and that led to the third full-scale war between Pakistan and India. The war ended after 93,000 Pakistani troops surrendered to India, resulting in the humiliation and defeat of the Pakistani nation (Paul 2014). East Pakistan separated from West Pakistan and became Bangladesh on 16 December 1971. The creation of Bangladesh was both a political and military victory for India and consolidated its dominance in the South Asian region (Ayoob 1976). After the fall of Dhaka, the Pakistani leadership realized that strong centralized government is mandatory for the survival of the country which became another characteristic of the national security state.

After the loss of East Pakistan, however, there was a window of opportunity for the political leadership in West Pakistan to assert some control over the state. It was the first time in the history of Pakistan that military dominance was apparently undermined (Aziz 2008). The military allowed Z. A. Bhutto of the Pakistan Peoples Party (PPP) to form his government in (West) Pakistan. Actually, the military leadership may have calculated they needed some form of civilian rule to avoid harsh criticism for their humiliating defeat in East Pakistan. The new civilian leadership under Bhutto drafted the 1973 constitution. Under this constitution, the civilian government tried to subordinate the military by defining its role as a more defence-oriented one, to protect the country's territorial boundaries. In particular, Article 245 of the 1973 constitution of Pakistan clarified that "the military [are] required to defend Pakistan against external aggression, threat of war, and [are] subject to law, [and must] act in aid of civil power when called upon to do so." It was first time in the history of Pakistan that the role of the military was formally defined in constitutional terms.

However, Bhutto was unable to reconfigure the Pakistani national security state and establish full civilian control. In structural terms, the national security state was deeply embedded within Pakistani society, and Bhutto had to contend with that constraint in policymaking. Under Bhutto's leadership, Pakistan continued with a centralized form of government, intense rivalry with India, and military modernization through external alliances to counterbalance Indian military power (Haqqani 2005; Siddiqa 2007). Bhutto also felt obliged to seek favour with Pakistan's military leadership by not making the Hamoodur Rahman Commission Report[7] public after the separation of East Pakistan. He publicly emphasized the role of the military in disaster relief programmes, and it was under Bhutto's leadership that the military gradually recovered from the loss of prestige following the humiliating defeat in the 1971 war (Haqqani 2005).

After formulating the 1973 constitution, Bhutto also established an "intelligence reforms commission" to carry out an in-depth study of the intelligence organization and its possible shortcomings. On the recommendation of the commission, Bhutto established the ISI's political wing through an executive order in 1975. This recommendation gave legitimacy to the role of the ISI in internal political affairs. In fact, the ISI had been involved in monitoring internal political matters since the 1950s (Rizvi 2000). The primary objectives of the political wing of the ISI were to monitor activities of communists, the minority Ahmadi and Shia sects, cabinet ministers, opposition parties, and members of his own party in both the national and provincial assemblies. Under Bhutto, the ISI's political wing also got involved in vote rigging, bribing politicians, forming and breaking coalitions, and intimidating some opposition parties and leaders (Sirrs 2016). The establishment of the ISI's political wing would arguably prove to be the biggest political blunder by Bhutto, and one which had long-term consequences for the Pakistani state and society, particularly for civilian governments.

On the external front after 1971 debacle, Pakistan avoided direct hostility with India and adopted various other foreign policy initiatives to counter Indian dominance in the 1970s. For example, the country emphasized proactive bilateral relationships with all small South Asian countries. Pakistan tried to play a more active role in regional organizations and forums including the South Asian Association for Regional Cooperation (SAARC), the Organization of Islamic

Cooperation (OIC), and the Regional Cooperation for Development organization (Malik 1994). As a result, Pakistan was able to maintain a credible regional deterrence against India in order to escape a subordinate role in South Asia and prevent further external aggression from India.

In addition, Pakistan also realized that nuclear deterrence was essential in order to avoid such incidents of external aggression in future after the 1971 war. Bhutto had proposed the making of a nuclear bomb when he was the foreign minister in General Ayub Khan's cabinet. Bhutto argued for nuclear deterrence both in cabinet meetings as well as in public. In response to India's developing a nuclear programme in 1965, Bhutto famously said that "If India builds the bomb, we will eat grass and leaves for a thousand years, even go hungry, but we will get one of our own" (Bangash 2015). Z. A. Bhutto (1969) stated in his book:

> Pakistan's security and territorial integrity are more important than economic development ... All wars of our age have become total wars; all European strategy is based on the concept of total war; and it will have to be assumed that a war waged against Pakistan is capable of becoming a total war. It would be dangerous to plan for less and our plans should, therefore, include the nuclear deterrent ... our problem in its essence, is how to obtain such a weapon in time before the crisis begins.

Furthermore, General Ayub Khan also showed his concerns over the Indian nuclear programme during the visit of Glenn Seaborg, chairman of the United States Atomic Energy Commission, to Pakistan in January 1967. Ayub Khan said that "If India was to acquire atomic military capability, we shall have to follow suit and it will just ruin us both" (Baxter ed. 2007, 49; in Hoodbhoy and Mian 2014). It would take a huge strategic effort for a developing country like Pakistan to build its own nuclear programme.

In the wake of the 1971 war, Bhutto found an opportunity to launch Pakistan's nuclear programme. After taking office as prime minister, Bhutto called upon senior scientists and gave them the task of starting a nuclear programme. Pakistan took the official position that "the Pakistan nuclear programme was entirely for peaceful uses" (Hoodbhoy and Mian 2014). The threat from India was the justification for building a nuclear arsenal which would prevent events like those of 1971 in future. From then on, building the nuclear bomb became a major part of Pakistan's national security thinking. General Zia advanced and upgraded the country's nuclear weapon programme by exploiting the opportunity of the Soviet invasion of Afghanistan. More specifically, both the civilian and military regimes worked on building the nuclear capability after Bhutto started the nuclear programme. Nonetheless, the nuclear weapons programme had further strengthened the role of the military in strategic decision making within the national security state.

In addition, Pakistan established the Heavy Industries in Taxila (HIT) in September 1971 and the Pakistan Aeronautical Complex at Kamra the following year. The primary objective was to upgrade, rebuild, and modernize its military capabilities. The HIT has manufactured sophisticated weapons, including tanks, guns, and armoured personnel carriers. These facilities have also produced F-6s, the Mushshak and K-8 Karakoram trainer aircraft, radar and avionics equipment, and recently produced the JF-17 aircraft in collaboration with China (Mirza *et al.* 2015). These measures demonstrated that Pakistan did not accept Indian dominance in the region and that the national security state was still paramount, despite civilians being in power under the leadership of Bhutto.

General Zia's dictatorial regime, Islamization, and Pakistan's military-centric national security approach

Despite Bhutto continuing with the national security state, the Pakistani military establishment did not tolerate civilian rule for very long. In July 1977, General Zia, the then Chief of Army Staff (COAS), dismissed the Bhutto government and inaugurated another period of martial law rule. General Zia became Pakistan's new leader and also retained his position as a Chief of Army Staff. Thereafter, the military introduced the "Revival of the Constitution Order," a move that helped to create the NSC. The NSC was said to have an advisory role in recommending declarations of a state of emergency, security affairs, and other matters of national and strategic importance. General Zia was, however, unable to implement the NSC, which was brought in eventually by General Musharraf in 2004 (Siddiqa 2007). Thus, the primary objective of General Zia's coup was to re-establish the supremacy of the military in the country and reverse the reforms introduced in the 1973 constitution. According to Muhammad Waseem (1989), a prominent Pakistani scholar:

> The 1977 military coup was not a reactive militarism to correct the political situation or bring back order, and must be seen against the egalitarian reforms of Bhutto government and the institutional stresses which [the] military had to endure under the previous government and the way it was ensconced back into the seat of power with a mission to undo most of its predecessor's leftist policies.

Since then, any civilian government in Pakistan which has tried to reassert control over the military faces the direct prospect of losing power through a military coup or less directly by having its powers curbed by a civil bureaucracy and judiciary aligned with the military.

General Zia's coup was not well received in Pakistan or internationally, but the Soviet invasion of Afghanistan in December 1979 provided an opportunity for General Zia's military regime to end its period of global isolation. General Zia was able to reinvigorate Pakistan's alliance with the US and became once again a frontline state in the international struggle against the Soviet occupation in Afghanistan during the Cold War. The Reagan administration announced two substantial military aid packages for Islamabad during the 1980s, worth US$3.2 billion and US$4.2 billion (Kronstadt 2004; Siddiqa 2007). The details of the US aid are given in Table 2.3.

Table 2.3 US aid to Pakistan, 1980–1989 (USD in million)

Year	Economic Aid	Military Aid
1980	143.015	0.000
1981	170.89	0.000
1982	412.313	5.622
1983	551.101	7.331
1984	1,103.76	7.934
1985	1,204.299	7.481
1986	1,248.954	7.940
1987	1,181.043	14.189
1988	1,361.096	53.511
1989	981.408	2.076
Total	**8,357.879**	**106.08**
Total US Aid:	**8,463.96**	

Source: US overseas Loans and Grants (Green book) available at https://eads.usaid.gov/gbk/., In Asif, M. and Muhammad, A. (2017). "Image of USA in Urban Pakistan: An Empirical Assessment." *A Research Journal of South Asian Studies* 32 (2): 539 – 555.

In addition to this, the US also provided F-16 aircraft to the Pakistani military, though Washington did not provide the Airborne Warning and Control Systems requested by Pakistan. US military and financial aid significantly strengthened the position of the Pakistani military (Siddiqa 2007). In return, Pakistan provided a transit route for weapons supplies to the Afghan resistance movement (mujahideen) and hosted training camps for the mujahideen fighting the Soviet presence in Afghanistan (Malik 1994). The Soviet invasion of Afghanistan marked a new stage in the Cold War and led to a new convergence of interests between General Zia's martial law administration in Pakistan and the Reagan administration in the US. Both states were determined to defeat the Soviet forces in Afghanistan through the mujahideen.

In a bid to enhance the legitimacy of his regime, General Zia held local body elections in all the four provinces in 1979–1980. The elections were non-party based to keep out the influential political parties from the election process. In particular, General Zia combined political centralization through his martial law administration and decentralization from the provincial to the local level through local body government (Cheema *et al.* 2005). Moreover, General Zia held a controversial presidential referendum in 1984, which was heavily rigged, and General Zia was somewhat predictably confirmed as Pakistan's new president (Zahid 2011). Like General Ayub Khan, General Zia introduced a controlled form of democracy in the country. In 1985, further non-party elections were held in which Muhammad Khan Junejo became the prime minister. Junejo was General Zia's hand-picked man to extend military rule in the country. Junejo passed a notorious eighth amendment to the constitution. Under the terms of this amendment, power was concentrated in General Zia's presidential office, an arrangement which remained in place until 1997. Under the eighth amendment of the 1973 Constitution of Pakistan Act, 1985:

The President shall dissolve the National Assembly if so advised by the Prime Minister and the National Assembly shall, unless sooner dissolved, stand dissolved at the expiration of forty-eight hours after the Prime Minister has so advised, (2) Notwithstanding anything contained in clause (2) of article 48, the President may also dissolve the National Assembly at his discretion, where, in his opinion ... a situation has arisen in which the Government of the Federation cannot be carried on in accordance with the provisions of the constitution and an appeal to the electorate is necessary.

General Zia's military regime, therefore, institutionalized the power of the president to dismiss the prime minister, parliament, cabinet, and other civilian institutions if that was deemed necessary. Since then, successive presidents have used this discretionary power to dismiss elected governments with the support of the military.

Furthermore, General Zia institutionalized religion in the Pakistani state and society. Nonetheless, it is important to note that Pakistan originated with a single religious identity to have a separate homeland for the Muslims of British India. Therefore, Pakistan denies any other identity that supersedes their religious identity (Akhtar 2009). Both the military and civilian leadership exploited this religious identity to protect their strategic interests and political goals in order to gain control over the Pakistani state and society. Prime Minister Zulfikar Ali Bhutto came into power with a socialist manifesto in December 1971, but he used religious slogans such as Islamic socialism and economics in order to gain power. After taking office, Bhutto declared Ahmadis, a subsect of Muslims, as non-Muslim in order to appease the religious clergy whereas Pakistan played a key role in establishing the Organization of Islamic Conference (OIC) during his regime and started special relations with Muslim countries (Haqqani 2004). Nevertheless, the Bhutto regime provided a foundation to General Zia military regime who took further steps towards Islamization.

General Zia established a legal and educational system based on Sharia laws. He established thousands of religious seminaries and introduced jihadist radical literature in public school syllabus. It is important to note that such curriculums were designed and developed in the University of Nebraska at the US to encourage jihad against the Soviet Union. About US$13 million worth of textbooks based on such a syllabus were distributed in public schools, religious seminaries, and refugees camps in Pakistan and Afghanistan (Ashraf 2009). As a consequent, religious schools mushroomed during General Zia's regime from an estimated 900 religious seminaries to about 8,000 registered and 25,000 unregistered seminaries at the end (Murphy and Malik 2009; Ali 2011). Such seminaries provided a conducive environment to spread religious radicalization, extremism, and sectarian violence and served as a key channel for providing logistic resources and manpower to Afghan mujahideen against the Soviets forces in Afghanistan.

In addition, the Islamization process was further institutionalized in the armed forces by adding Islamic syllabus of new recruits, and religiously conservative officers were promoted in higher ranks. For this purpose, a close alliance was established between the mullahs (orthodox religious scholars) as religiously con-servative scholars from Deobandi and Jamaat-e-Islami (JI) groups were appointed in the military to work with the armed forces (T. Hussain 2009). In this process of Islamization, Pakistan became the epicentre of religious extremism and global jihadi groups who played a key role in defeating 114,000 strong Soviet forces in Afghanistan with support of the US and its allied countries (Murphy and Malik 2009; Ali 2011). This led to the foundation for an extremist religious infrastruc-ture that served Pakistan's strategic interests during the Afghan war. Thereafter, Pakistan emphasized on proxy war to balance a hegemonic India and protect its strategic interests. Nonetheless, proxy wars have become a dangerous phenom-enon in the post-Cold war era when such militant groups began searching for new targets within and beyond the region. In fact, some of the militant groups turned against the Pakistani state (see in Chapter 5).

The advent of ISI as a key player: the Afghan War in the 1980s[8]

Prior to the formation of the ISI, the IB was the only Pakistani intelligence agency that operated after the country's independence. However, the IB's per-formance was generally regarded as very poor during the first Indo-Pakistan war over Kashmir in October 1947. The Pakistani leadership realized that a strong intelligence system, along with a capable military, was vital to counter external threats after independence. As a consequence, the ISI was established in 1948 (Chengappa 2000). It is a semi-military organization and reports to the prime minister or the military chief during periods of military rule. The director general (DG) of the ISI is normally a serving army officer, either a lieutenant general or a major general, appointed by the COAS. Most of the ISI's officers are serving army personnel who are on secondment. However, a small number of ISI cadres are recruited from among civilians as well. Initially, the ISI's primary job was to focus on India and collect other related foreign intelligence (Cohen 2004).

The ISI comprises two branches: the Joint Intelligence Bureau (JIB) and the Joint Counter Intelligence Bureau (JCIB). The JIB's primary function was to col-lect information on military geography, ports, airports, beaches, communications, economics, logistics, and various scientific and technical subjects. On the other hand, the JCIB operated within the military services by supervising counter-intel-ligence operations. However, the JCIB has only handled cases in which personnel of at least two services were involved (Sirrs 2016). The ISI has also formed close relations with other military services, such as the Special Service Group (SSG) of the Pakistani military.

The ISI got a bigger role in the bloody civil war in East Pakistan in 1971. The federal government became convinced that Bengali IB officers could not be trusted in operations against the *Mukti Bahini* insurgency in East Pakistan. Consequently, the military government assigned a primary role to the ISI to deal with the insur-gency. The ISI's major problem was a limited understanding of the Bengali language and culture. They recruited heavily from the Urdu-speaking Bihari com-munity in East Pakistan and relied mainly on Islamist groups, particularly JI to counter the insurgency (Haqqani 2005; Sirrs 2016). Interestingly, the alliance between the ISI and JI was strengthened during the civil war in East Pakistan. Stephen Cohen (2004), a historian and expert on South Asia, pointed out: "This began a long and sordid history of the Pakistani state and its intelligence services using Islamist radicals to terrorize regime opponents, ethnic separatists, the moderate politicians, and, where necessary, radical Islamists." Thereafter, this alliance between the ISI and JI became a prominent feature in Pakistan's national security state. In fact, an unholy alliance was established between the religious class and the ISI which has been involved in the manipulation of political parties, extremist groups, and the Islamists. More specifically, the ISI used Islamist militants as a foreign policy tool to achieve their strategic interests in South Asia during and after the Cold War era and far-right groups to deter anti-military groups and individuals. Nonetheless, asymmetric warfare to balance a hegemonic India and far-right groups to counter anti-military voices became another key feather of Pakistan's national security state.

The ISI emerged as a more effective actor on the external front by demonstrating that it could provide solid information about India's armed forces and its operational planning in the 1971 war. However, the ISI was unable to accurately gauge the anger and frustration of the Bengali resistance movement, and public support for it in East Pakistan, or foresee the formation of the *Mukti Bahini* insurgency in India. In East Pakistan, the ISI was often viewed as a brutal force suppressing the local Bengali population. Despite the ISI's failure in 1971, the experience was a turning point in the transformation of the ISI into a prominent organization in both internal and external matters of the state.

In 1979, the Soviet Union's invasion of Afghanistan created major security concerns for Pakistan owing to the fact that Islamabad shared a long, porous border with Afghanistan. Consequently, the external threat from Afghanistan became more apparent following the Soviet invasion. This was because Afghanistan's political instability and insecurity would have caused possible fallout in its provinces bordering Afghanistan, including KP, Balochistan, and former Federally Administered Tribal Areas (FATA),[9] due to the ethnic affiliations shared on both sides of the border. Afghanistan had been used as a buffer state between the Soviet Union and South Asia but could no longer serve this role with the direct presence of Soviet forces in Afghanistan. It was feared that the Soviet forces might also interfere in the western part of Pakistan to reach the deep Arabian Sea in Balochistan province that could play a key role in the Soviet Union's expansionist designs (Rizvi 1988). As a result, Pakistan became more security-oriented after the Soviet occupation of Afghanistan.

In this situation, General Zia asked the ISI's leadership to prepare a detailed report about the nature of the Soviet threat to Pakistan. General Akhtar, the then DG ISI, reported that the Soviets could invade Pakistan to have access to warm waters in the Arabian Sea through the Balochistan province of the country. At the same time, General Akhtar noted, the Soviets could also join hands with India to undermine Pakistan. As an outcome, General Akhtar recommended neutralizing the perceived Soviet threat by backing the Afghan mujahideen in a proxy war with Moscow. General Zia accepted the ISI's proposal to step up support for the resistance movement in Afghanistan. However, the main concern was to avoid negative fallout from the Afghan jihad on the internal security situation in Pakistan (Riedel 2014). It was believed in Islamabad that the war should be fought within Afghanistan and should not be allowed to spill over into Pakistan.

But the ISI required external support to fight the war in Afghanistan. The ISI asked the Saudi government to provide financial assistance to the Afghan resistance movement. Saudi's financial support was key as it would not only make a real difference to the capabilities of the mujahideen, but also signify the backing of a significant Muslim country. The Saudi state not only provided economic aid to the ISI for the Afghan jihad but also encouraged its citizens to give financial aid and volunteer to join the Afghan mujahideen (Riedel 2014). The US also entered into the Afghan proxy war against the Soviet Union two years later. According to General Asad Durrani (interview by author, Rawalpindi, 22 November 2017),

> The US did bandwagon into Pakistan when we were fighting the Soviet Union. Two years later, the US came and found out that the Afghan mujahideen with [the] help of Pakistan were doing not too badly. So it was not the America but Pakistan and Afghan mujahideen who fought against the Soviet Union.

After the US joined the Afghan war, the ISI closely worked with Washington to stiffen resistance to the Soviet occupying forces in Afghanistan. Many ISI officers were sent to the US for training with US Delta Forces, an elite special services branch of the US Army. This training was designed to develop skills connected to insurgency, infiltrations, and covert operations. The trainees were also taught to handle explosives, master various weapons, and engage paramilitary operations (Datta 2014). Such training played an important role in the professional development of the ISI as an intelligence institution. Together with the CIA, the ISI carried out the world's biggest covert operation against the Soviet forces in Afghanistan during the 1980s. The two agencies recruited many Afghans from their refugee camps in Peshawar. Meanwhile, the ISI was directly in charge of financing and arming the Afghan mujahideen to fight a guerrilla war in Afghanistan. According to various estimates, the ISI distributed covert aid worth more than US$2 billion to resistance groups. The ISI also received a roughly equal amount of aid from Saudi Arabia and other Gulf countries (Haqqani 2005; Datta 2014). A prominent Pakistani journalist, Ahmad Rashid (2008), noted:

> General Zia did not allow the CIA or any other foreign intelligence agency to aid the mujahideen directly, enter Afghanistan, or plan the mujahideen's battles and strategy. That became the prerogative of the ISI, which, with its newfound wealth and American patronage, had become a state within a state, employing thousands of officers in order to run what was now also Pakistan's Afghan war.

Thus, the mujahideen mainly relied on Pakistan for financial and military aid during the Afghan war, with most aid going to those resistance groups that followed the Pakistani government's approach to the Afghan war. The mujahideen groups that received this aid included the *Hezb-e-Islami* party of Hekmatyar, the *Hezb-e-Islami* of Yunus Khalis, the *Ittihad-e-Islami* of the Saudi proxy, Sayyaf, and the *Jamiat-e-Islami* led by Rabbani. Pakistan's frontline position during the Afghan conflict served to professionalize the ISI and gave it new regional leverage over the warring resistance factions in Afghanistan. For example, the ISI used its position to deny military and financial aid to groups such as those of Ahmed Shah Massoud and Abdul Haq that acted independently (Sirrs 2016).

In addition, ISI personnel fought alongside the mujahideen in Afghanistan against the Soviet Union. General Akhtar planned these operations and sent dozens of ISI undercover teams inside Afghanistan to fight alongside Afghan mujahideen against the formidable Soviet forces. The ISI officers did not wear military uniforms and carried no sources of identification that could link them to the ISI and provoke direct retaliation from the Soviet Union. In this process, Pakistan's ISI emerged as a key player during the Soviet occupation of Afghanistan. The size of the agency increased significantly during the 1980s. The ISI's staff was estimated to be around 2,000 in 1978, but grew to 40,000 strong, with a budget of billions of dollars at its disposal (Riedel 2014). As one Pakistani journalist observed (in Sirrs 2016):

> The ISI is powerful, ubiquitous and has functioned with so much authority from the central government that it almost became a state within a state. It is not only responsible for intelligence gathering, but also acts as a determinant of Pakistan's foreign policy and a vehicle for its implementation.

So Pakistan fought the proxy war in the form of a jihad funded by the CIA against the Soviet Union. Subsequently, the proxy war became another characteristic of Pakistan's national security state. Against this context, Senator Mushahid Hussain Syed said (interview by author, Islamabad, 8 December 2017).

> Pakistan went too far ahead in the so called jihad and the reason was General Zia felt it was helping in the conservation and perpetuation of his regime. But this damaged Pakistan as the state was spawning a culture of Kalashnikovs. So we [Pakistan] made a mistake we go all out and this has serious implication for Pakistan state and society.

Thus, Pakistan's proxy wars have severe consequences on the Pakistani state and society which we will see in Chapter 6.

Meanwhile, General Zia utilized the ISI's political wing to monitor domestic politics and influence political parties on sectarian and political lines. The primary objective was to weaken or prevent opposition to military rule in Pakistan. In this connection, the prime minister, Muhammad Khan Junejo, was removed from his office by General Zia with the support from the ISI. Junejo's interest in rejuvenating civilian rule in Pakistan had created serious tensions between him and General Zia (Datta 2014). The removal of Prime Minister Junejo set down a clear red line that the military would not tolerate any government officials that wanted to civilianize power in the country.

In February 1989, the Soviet Union finally withdrew its forces from Afghanistan. However, the US did not have an exit plan for Afghanistan. And the US left Pakistan alone to deal with around 22,000 well-trained guerrilla fighters with radical Islamist leanings that no longer had a battle to fight against foreign occupiers. Pakistan also did not have a programme to reintegrate the mujahideen into mainstream society (Dr Khuram Iqbal, interview by author, Islamabad, 8 November 2017). However, the ISI began to divert this ready-made force of guerrillas to Kashmir to intensify the armed uprising there, following the rigged elections of the late 1980s (Murphy and Malik 2009).

In the space of a nine-year involvement in the Afghan war, the Pakistani military in general and the ISI in particular had further increased the weight and influence of the national security state in Pakistan. A military-centred national security infrastructure had been established, which emphasized the pivotal role of the nation's military in countering the apparent external threat from India. Within the framework of Pakistan's national security state, the interests and concerns of institutions like the Pakistan army and the ISI were given priority from the outset over civilian political institutions. This institutional imbalance created structural problems in the running of the Pakistani state. For instance, the military directly ruled the country for about 24 years between 1947 and 1988. For much of the Cold War era, a tacit alignment between the public bureaucracy and the military was cemented at the expense of the civilian political leadership in Pakistan. The parliamentary system of government was diluted by a number of military dictators into more of a guided democracy, which became the norm. It proved relatively easy for military leaders to manipulate the political system to favour the military establishment in Pakistan. Thus, the military leadership played a decisive role in shaping foreign and security policies as well as domestic politics. Alongside the military, the ISI also played a pivotal role in determining Pakistan's national security policy, especially during the Afghan war.

An assessment of Pakistan's Cold War national security state[10]

As has been shown, Pakistan's national security state was shaped by the experience of working closely with the US and owed a great deal to its existence to the Cold War security environment. Nonetheless, Pakistan had developed distinctive features of its own national security state. Having considered the evolution and development of Pakistan's national security between 1947 and 1988, it is possible to identify some of its key features:

- The first characteristic of Pakistan's national security state was its obsession with antagonism towards India since independence in 1947. The Pakistani military leadership considered India to be a permanent enemy for the foreseeable future in their neighbourhood. So the country was deemed to require a strong military and permanent military preparedness to protect its sovereignty and territorial integrity. Rivalry with India played a major role in the formulation of the country's foreign and security policy. The Pakistani military used the prospect of an external threat from India to justify its dominant role in the country.

- A second defining feature of Pakistan's national security state was that the country required a "hybrid democracy" in which the military held the upper hand in the policymaking of the country. The military leadership maintained a facade of democracy but kept out the civilian leadership from key strategic decision making in the country. The military leadership believed that Western democracy does not suit developing countries like Pakistan. They maintained that the civilian political leadership was too weak to deal with external and domestic security threats confronted by the state.
- A third characteristic of Pakistan's national security state was that the state prioritized military interests over nation-building after independence. Pakistani governments continued to allocate a major portion of its fiscal and foreign exchange resources to the military which left limited resources for the socio-economic development of the country.
- A fourth feature of Pakistan's national security state was the repeated claim that the country needed a strong centralized government. The Pakistani national security state opposed decentralizing power in the country by allowing more autonomy to the provinces.
- A fifth characteristic of Pakistan's national security state was that Pakistan depended on asymmetric warfare to balance a hegemonic India and protect its strategic interests. The Pakistani military embraced religious groups as a politico-military strategy which would increase its prestige and position in the country. More specifically, the Islamists were used as foreign policy tools to achieve this strategic objective in South Asia. Nonetheless, the culture of secrecy in covert operations empowered the Pakistani military and also justified its dominant role in strategic decision making in the country's foreign and security policies.
- A sixth feature of the Pakistani national security state was that the military establishment restricted public debate over defence spending in the national parliament and actively resisted any unilateral cuts to the defence budget by the civilian leadership. Furthermore, the military did not permit civilian authorities to play a role in the governance of their institutional affairs such as nominating promotions within military ranks.
- Finally, Pakistan's national security state not only facilitated and protected the military's commercial interests but also ensured a functional dominance over the civilian leadership in the running of state affairs. That led to the emergence of a hyper-military-industrial complex in which the Pakistani military exercised overall economic and political control of the state.

In light of the above characteristics, it can be said Pakistan complied many of the key features of the US national security state but there were also significant points of departure as well. Like the US, Pakistan's national security state was born out of difficult security circumstances where there were perceived external security threats from neighbouring India, which was significantly larger in terms of territory, population, economy, and military power. Pakistan also put itself on a perpetual war against India after 1947 and allocated a massive defence expenditure from the national treasury. Moreover, the Pakistani military elite possess substantial political and economic power in key strategic decision making in the country. Unlike the US national security state, the Pakistani military had the consistent capacity to act in a much more autonomous fashion and did not allow civilian authorities to interfere in its institutional governance. Also, the Pakistani military elite has used the imperative of national security by projecting itself as indispensable for the very survival of the country. Furthermore, the Pakistani military directly ran various business corporations and intervened in the political sphere of state affairs to produce what could be termed a hyper-military-industrial complex. Nonetheless, the Pakistani military elite largely relied on the proxy militant groups to protect its regional strategic interests.

Within the national security state framework, the Pakistani military elite presented a range of obstacles to political parties or leaders that wanted to change the policy imperatives of Pakistan's national security state. First, the military would not tolerate any civilian government that sought to influence the running of foreign and security policies of the country, especially in issues relating to India and Afghanistan. Second, the military would not tolerate civilian control over military affairs, in particular, civilian oversight of spending on the military. Third, the military would only accept a "hybrid democracy" in the country. Finally, the military would not permit any effort to decentralize power in Pakistan by allowing more autonomy to the provinces. In short, any political party or leader during and after the Cold War, which seriously attempted to challenge the direction of Pakistan's national security state or tried to undermine the military's institutional interests, were effectively countered by a military-led coalition of interests comprising the armed forces, the intelligence agencies, civil bureaucracy, and the judiciary. The Pakistani military effectively used these obstacles to maintain its dominance in state affairs in the post-Cold War era.

Notes

1 This section is published in my co-authored article: Ali, A. and Patman, R. G. (2019) "The Evolution of the National Security State in Pakistan: 1947–1989," *Democracy and Security* 15:4, 5–8.

2 The ideology that religion is the main factor in defining the nationality of Indian Muslims was used by Muhammad Ali Jinnah. He said that Muslims are a nation by any definition of a nation. Hindu and Muslims belong to two religions, philosophies, social customs, and literature. This theory supported the proposal that Muslims and Hindus should be dealt as two separate nations during partition of India.

3 General Frank Messervy and General Douglas Gracey were the first two non-native C-in-Cs of the Pakistani armed forces, who served between 1947 and 1951.

4 The Durand Line is a frontier boundary between Afghanistan and Pakistan. It was established after the 1893 memorandum of understanding (MoU) between Mortimer Durand of British India and Afghan Amir Abdur Rahman Khan.
5 This section is published in my co-authored article: Ali, A. and Patman, R. G. (2019) "The Evolution of the National Security State in Pakistan: 1947-1989," *Democracy and Security* 15:4, 8–17.
6 The Ahmadiyya sect identifies itself as Muslims. The Ahmadiyya community takes its name from its founder Mirza Ghulam Ahmad, who was born in 1835 and was regarded by his followers as the messiah and a prophet. However, it is regarded by orthodox Muslims as heretical because it does not believe that Mohammed was the final prophet sent to guide mankind, as majority Muslims believe is laid out in the Quran.
7 The Hamoodur Rahman Commission, also known as the War Enquiry Commission, was a judicial inquiry commission that was set up in December 1971. The commission investigated the involvement of Pakistan's political–military leadership in East Pakistan from 1947 to 1971. Chief Justice Hamoodur Rahman chaired the commission. The report was made public 29 years later and has raised many questions over the strategic ambiguity and character of the military leadership.
8 This section is published in my co-authored article: Ali, A. and Patman, R. G. (2019) "The Evolution of the National Security State in Pakistan: 1947-1989," *Democracy and Security* 15:4, 17–20.
9 FATA was a semi-autonomous, federally administered tribal region in north-western Pakistan. However, it was merged with KP province in May 2018. FATA will be referred to as "former FATA" henceforth in this book.
10 This section is published in my co-authored article: Ali, A. and Patman, R. G. (2019) "The Evolution of the National Security State in Pakistan: 1947-1989," *Democracy and Security* 15:4, 2–4, 20–22.

References

"A Culture of Excellence – A Tradition of Trust." *Army Welfare Trust* official site. Retrieved from http://www.awt.com.pk/home.
Ahmad, R. 2010. "The Situation in Pakistan." *Asian Affairs* 41 (3): 367–380.
Ahmed, S. 2004. *Bangladesh: Past and Present*. S.B. Nangia, A.P.H. Publishing Corporation.
Akhtar, A. S. 2009. "Moving beyond Islamic." In *The Islamization of Pakistan, 1979–2009*. Viewpoints Special Edition, Middle East Institute.
Alavi, H. 1998. "Pakistan-US Military Alliance." *Economic and Political Weekly* 33 (25): 1551–1557.
Ali, A. 2011. "Pakistan - Ideological and Socioeconomic Perspectives" *Journal of Strategic Studies, Islamabad* 31 (1): 91–106.
Appendix 3: List of Interviewees.
Appendix 4: AWT List of Companies.
Asch, B. J. and Warner, J. T. 1994. *A Policy Analysis of Alternative Military Retirement Systems*. Rand Corporation.
Asif, M. 2017. "Image of USA in Urban Pakistan: An Empirical Assessment." *A Research Journal of South Asian Studies* 32 (2): 539–555.
Ashraf, N. 2009. "The Islamization of Pakistan's Educational System: 1979–1989." In *The Islamization of Pakistan, 1979–2009*. Viewpoints Special Edition, Middle East Institute.
Ayaz, B. 2010. *What's Wrong with Pakistan?* Hay House, Inc.

Ayoob, M. 1976. "Long-Term Trends in India-Pakistan Relations." *India International Centre Quarterly* 3 (4): 253–265.

Aziz, M. 2008. *Military Control in Pakistan: A Parallel State*. Routledge.

Bangash, Y. K. 2015. "Eating grass." *Express Tribune*, Pakistan, January 24, 2015. Retrieved on November 25, 2018, http://tribune.com.pk/story/826538/eating-grass/.

Baxter, C. ed. 2007. *Diaries of Field Marshal Mohammad Ayub Khan 1966–1972*. Oxford University Press.

Bhutto, Z. A. 1969. *Myth of Independence*. Oxford University Press.

Blom, E. 2011. *Pakistan: Coercion and Capital in an Insecurity State*. IRSEM, Paris Papers.

Bose, S. R. 1983. "The Pakistan Economy since Independence (1947–70)." In *The Cambridge Economic History of India*, edited by Dharma Kumar and Meghnad Desai. Cambridge University Press.

Burke, S. M. 1973. *Pakistan's Foreign Policy: An Historical Analysis*. Oxford University Press.

Chari, P. R. 1979. "Indo-Soviet Military Cooperation: A Review." *Asian Survey* 19 (3): 230–244.

Cheema, A., Khawaja, I. A. and Qadir, A. 2005. "Decentralization in Pakistan: Context, Content and Causes." *KSG Faculty Research*, Faculty Research working papers Series: RWP05-034 , 1–43.

Chengappa, B. M. 2000. "The ISI Role in Pakistan's Politics." *Strategic Analysis* 23 (11): 1857–1878.

Cohen, S. P. 2004. *The Idea of Pakistan*. Brooking Institute Press.

Datta, S. K. 2014. *Inside ISI the Story and Involvement of the ISI in Afghan Jihad, Taliban, Al-Qaeda, 9/11, Osama Bin Laden, 26/11 and the Future of Al-Qaeda*. Vij Books India Pvt Ltd.

"Exit Stage Left: The Movement against Ayub Khan," Dawn, Pakistan, August 31, 2014. Retrieved on April 27, 2018, https://www.dawn.com/news/1128832.

Farooq, N. T. 2016. *US-Pakistan Relations: Pakistan's Strategic Choices in the 1990s*. Routledge.

"Freight Services." Retrieved from *NLC official* site: http://www.nlc.com.pk/strategic-uni ts/freight-services.

Jaffrelot, C. 2016. *Pakistan at the Crossroads: Domestic Dynamics and External Pressures*. Columbia University Press.

Jabeen, M. and Mazhar, M. S. 2011. "Security Game: SEATO and CENTO as Instrument of Economic and Military Assistance to Encircle Pakistan." *Pakistan Economic and Social Review* 49 (1): 109–132.

Jalal, A. 1990. *The State of Martial Role: The Origins of Pakistan's Political Economy of Defence*. Cambridge University Press.

Ganguly, S. 2016. *Deadly Impasse: Kashmir and Indo-Pakistani Relations at the Dawn of a New Century*. Cambridge University Press.

Gates, S. and Roy, K. 2011. *Conventional Warfare in South Asia, 1947 to the Present*. Routledge.

Hafeez, N. 2012. "Evolution of National Security Structures in Pakistan." *Journal of Strategic Studies, Islamabad* 32 (2/3): 151–171.

Haqqani, H. 2004. "The Role of Islam in Pakistan's Future." *The Washington Quarterly* 28 (1): 83–96.

Haqqani, H. 2005. *Pakistan: Between Mosque and Military*. Carnegie Endowment for International Peace.

Hoodbhoy, P. and Mian, Z. 2014. "Nuclear Fears, Hopes and Realities in Pakistan." *International Affairs* 90 (5): 1125–1142.

Husain, S. A. 1979. "Politics of Alliance and Aid: A Case Study of Pakistan (1954–1966)." *Pakistan Horizon* 32 (1–2): 11–46.

Hussain, T. 2009. "Post-1979 Pakistan: What Went Wrong?" In *The Islamization of Pakistan, 1979–2009*. Viewpoints Special Edition, Middle East Institute.

Iqbal, M. and Khalid, S. 2011. "Pakistan's Relations with the United States during Ayub Khan's Period." *A Journal of Pakistan Studies* 3 (1): 13–24.

Kapur, P. S. 2016. *Jihad as Grand Strategy: Islamist Militancy, National Security, and the Pakistani State*. Oxford University Press.

Khan, A. 1967. *Friends not Masters: A Political Autobiography*. Oxford University Press.

Khan, R. A. 1985. "Pakistan-United States Relations: An Appraisal." *American Studies International* 23 (1): 83–102.

Krishna, V. R. 1991. *Prepare or Perish: A Study of National Security*. Lancer.

Kronstadt, K. A. 2004. "Pakistan's Domestic Political Developments." CRS Report for Congress.

"Land Allotment: 'Some Elements' Trying to Defame Ex-army Chief." Express Tribune, Pakistan, January 26, 2017. Retrieved on May 21, 2018, https://tribune.com.pk/story/1 307143/land-allotment-elements-trying-defame-ex-army-chief/.

Lerski, G. J. 1974. "The Foreign Policy of Ayub Khan." *Asian Affairs: An American Review* 1 (4): 255–273.

Malik, I. H. 1994. "Pakistan's National Security and Regional Issues: Politics of Mutualities with the Muslim World." *Asian Survey* 34 (12): 1077–1092.

Malik, I. H. 2008. *The History of Pakistan*. Greenwood.

Mansergh, N. 1966. "The Partition of India in Retrospect." *International Journal*, 21 (1): 1–19.

Mares, D. R. 2010. "The National Security State." In *A Companion to Latin American History*, edited by Thomas H. Holloway. Wiley Blackwell Companions to World History.

Mazhar, M. S. and Goraya, N. S. 2012. "An Analytical Study of Pak-US Relations: Post Osama (2011–2012)." *South Asian Studies* 27 (1): 77–87.

Mirza, M. N. Jaspal, Z. N and Malik, A. I. , 2015. "Military Spending and Economic Growth in Pakistan." *Margalla papers*,Islamabad no. 19: 151–184.

Morgenthau, H. J. 1965. "Alliance in Theory and Practice." In *American Defense Policy* edited by Associates in Political Science, US Air Force Academy, Baltimore: John Hopkins Press.

Murphy, E. and Malik, A. R. 2009. "Pakistan Jihad: The Making of Religious Terrorism." *IPRI*, Islamabad 9 (2): 17–31.

"Overview Bahria Foundation." Retrieved from its official site: http://www.bahriafoundati on.com/About-Us.html.

"Overview of Education and Training and Health Service." Fauji Foundation. Retrieved from http://www.fauji.org.pk/fauji/investors/financial-highlights.

"Pashtunistan − 1947–1955." *Global Security* report. Retrieved on September 7, 2016, http://www.globalsecurity.org/military/world/war/pashtunistan-1947.htm.

Paracha, N. F. 2017. "Smokers' Corner: Who Was Yahya Khan?" *Dawn, Pakistan*, March 18, 2017. Retrieved on April 27, 2018, https://www.dawn.com/news/1321359.

Paul, T. V. 2005. *The India-Pakistan Conflict: An Enduring Rivalry*. Cambridge University Press.

Paul, T. V. 2014. *The Warrior State: Pakistan in the Contemporary World*. Oxford University Press.

Rais, R. B. 1991. "Pakistan in the Regional and Global Power Structure." *Asian Survey* 31 (4): 378–392.

Rana, S. "Rs 35 Billion Budget Approved for National Logistic Cell." *Express Tribune*, Pakistan, August 14, 2012. Retrieved from https://tribune.com.pk/story/421706/rs35 -billion-budget-approved-for-national-logistics-cell/.

Rashid, A. 2008. *Descent into Chaos: The U.S. and the Disaster in Pakistan, Afghanistan, and Central Asia*. Penguin Press.

Riedel, B. 2014. *What We Won: America's Secret War in Afghanistan, 1979–89*. Brookings Institution Press.

Rizvi, H. A. 1983. "Pakistan's Defence Policy." *Pakistan Horizon* 36 (1): 32–56.

Rizvi, H. A. 1988. "Pakistan-U.S. Security Relations: Pakistani Perceptions of Key Issues." In *Pakistan-U.S. Relations: Social Political and Economic Factors*, edited by Noor A. Husain and Leo E. Rose. University of California.

Rizvi, H. A. 1993. *Pakistan and the Geostrategic Environment: A Study of Foreign Policy*. Palgrave Macmillan.

Rizvi, H. A. 2000. *Military State and Society in Pakistan*. Palgrave Macmillan.

Rizvi, H. A. 2003. *Military, State and Society in Pakistan*. Palgrave Macmillan.

Salim, I. 2014. "A General's Views." *Dawn, Pakistan*, December 13, 2014. Retrieved on September 21, 2018, https://www.dawn.com/news/1150491.

Sayeed, K. 1954. "Federalism and Pakistan." *Asian Survey* 23 (9): 139–143.

Sayeed, K. 1955. "The Governor-General of Pakistan." *Pakistan Horizon* 8 (2): 330–339.

Siddiqa, A. 2007. *Military Inc. Inside Pakistan's Military Economy*. Pluto Press.

Singh, C. and Baily, M. 2013. "Praetorian Democracy, Illiberal but Enduring: Pakistan as Exemplar." *Southeast Review of Asian Studies* 35: 103–126.

Sirrs, O. L. 2016. *Pakistan's InterServices Intelligence Directorate: Covert Action and Internal Operations*. Routledge.

Shahid, J. 2017. "Military-Run SCO Denied Permission to Operate across Country." *Dawn*, Pakistan, August 18, 2017. Retrieved on November 23, 2018, https://www.dawn .com/news/1352296.

Soherwordi, S. H. S. 2010. "US Foreign Policy Shift towards Pakistan between 1965 & 1971 Pak-India Wars." *South Asian Studies* 25 (1): 21–37.

Spain, J. W. 1954. "Military Assistance for Pakistan." *American Political Science Review* 48 (3): 738–751.

The Constitution of Pakistan (Eighth Amendment) Act, 1985 (Act No. XVIII of 1985), http://www.wipo.int/edocs/lexdocs/laws/en/pk/pk116en.pdf.

Vaish, V. 2011. "Negotiating the India-Pakistan Conflict in Relation to Kashmir." *International Journal on World Peace* 28 (3): 53–80.

Waseem, M. 1989. *Politics and the State in Pakistan*. NIHCR Publication.

Zahid, M. A. 2011. "Dictatorship in Pakistan: A Study of the Zia Era (1977–88)." *Pakistan Journal of History and Culture* 32 (1): 1–27.

3 Pakistan's military-centred national security approach and the post-Cold War era

The security situation in South Asia in the post-Cold War era

Despite a rapidly changing global security environment, there were limited changes in the regional security environment of South Asia, following the end of the Cold War. The dispute between Pakistan and India has continued, and is deeply rooted in historical dynamics. This hostility had been only marginally influenced by the global rivalry between the US and the Soviet Union during the Cold War (Rais 1991). This was unlike other conflicts such as Cambodia, Kosovo, El Salvador, and Afghanistan, where the superpowers were involved either militarily or used their proxies to advance their national interests. There was no direct involvement of the superpowers in the Kashmir conflict between Pakistan and India. The role of the superpowers was limited to the diplomatic support of their Cold War allies at the international level. For instance, the Soviet Union supported India's position on the Kashmir dispute due to Pakistan's participation in pro-West military alliances during the Cold War (Kreisberg 1985). On the other hand, Islamabad sought to gain US support to resolve the issue of Kashmir through a plebiscite by putting pressure on India (Husain 1979). Moreover, Islamabad was successful in gaining military and economic aid to counter Indian military power in the region (Rais 1991). That aside, the Kashmir dispute remained largely unaffected by either hostility or cooperation between the two global superpowers.

Nonetheless, there was a significant decline in interstate conflicts such as Kashmir after the end of the Cold War. The UN intervened in 47 conflicts that occurred during 1988–2007, of which only 3 were interstate conflicts. These interstate conflicts were the 1990 Iraqi invasion of Kuwait, the 1994 Libya-Chad border dispute, and in 1998–2000, the Ethiopia-Eritrea border dispute (Yilmaz 2007). Some observers believed that the new global dynamics would force India and Pakistan to resolve their outstanding disputes, especially with respect to Kashmir. However, the military confrontation over the issue of Kashmir continued between the two countries after the Cold War. In Kashmir, the tension over the LoC brought both countries close to another war in 1990. Both countries moved their troops closer to the border areas. Moreover, the political leadership on both sides often issued hawkish statements about each other. On 13 March 1990, Prime Minister Benazir Bhutto visited Pakistan-administrated Kashmir and warned India that "Pakistan was embarking on a 1,000-year war to wrest Kashmir from India" (Cheema 2015, 57; Dwivedi 2013). In response to the threat of a 1,000-year war, Indian Prime Minister Vishwanath Pratap Singh said that "Our message to Pakistan is that you cannot get away with taking Kashmir without a war. They will have to pay a very heavy price and we have the capability to inflict heavy losses" (Hagerty 1995–1996, 99). Thus, the Indo-Pakistan regional confrontation continued between the two arch-rivals, despite the changing global security environment.

In addition to this, Pakistan had opposed what it saw as Indian hegemonic designs on South Asia since its independence in 1947. India's regional and global aspiration to become a superpower became more apparent after the end of the Cold War. India tried to fill the vacuum left after the reduced presence of the superpowers from the region. India continued to gain military power through external arms purchasing and domestic arms production. Consequently, India's quest for the accumulation of military power shaped regional security in its favour (Rais 1991). India also began an economic liberalization policy in the early 1990s that led to rapid economic growth and trade expansion in the last two decades (Jabeen 2010). By 2017, India's economy was eight times larger than Pakistan's, with a GDP of US$2.1 trillion (Gray 2017). The Indian government was able to allocate extra resources for military modernization and upgrading. Indian military spending in 2017 was seven times higher than Pakistan, and this has widened the military gap to such an extent that Pakistan would be unable to fight a conventional war with India (Prasad 2017). So India not only moved further ahead of Pakistan economically but militarily, which shaped regional security in its favour.

The economic transformation of India has created new strategic challenges for Pakistan in the post-Cold War era. Sustained economic growth has given India an opportunity to establish itself as a greater power in the region as well as in the world. More importantly, India has presented itself as the main contender for a permanent position in the UN Security Council (Jabeen 2010). As a result, it has become very difficult for Islamabad to resist the Indian hegemony in the region, which is based on its large population, economy, and military power (Memon 1994). Thus, the situation shifted further in favour of India's becoming the hegemonic power in South Asia in the post-Cold War era.

Additionally, Afghanistan's stability remained an important factor for regional security in South Asia. After their withdrawal from Afghanistan, the Soviet forces left massive amounts of arms and ammunition in the country, while external support continued to the Afghan warring groups. The Afghan government, led by the People's Democratic Party of Afghanistan (PDPA), was defeated by the warring factions in April 1992 and an interim government of the mujahedeen was established in Kabul (Byrd 2012). However, the mujahedeen failed to bring peace to war-torn Afghanistan due to infighting among the warring groups. This led to a civil war between Hezb-i-Islami led by Hekmatyar, with the support of Pakistan, and Ahmed Shah Massoud's Jamiat-i-Islami, to take control of Kabul. In 1994, the Afghan Taliban, who were mainly madrasah students, emerged under the leadership of Mullah Omer and gradually took control of major parts of Afghanistan. The Afghan Taliban captured Kabul in 1996, which ended the civil war (Collins 2011).

The Afghan civil war had serious security consequences for the South Asian region, especially Pakistan. The flow of Afghan refugees to Pakistan continued in the post-Cold War era. By 1990, about 3.2 million registered refugees were living in Pakistan, as well as an estimated 500,000 unregistered refugees. The influx of Afghan refugees continued in Pakistan throughout the civil war. About 74,000 refugees arrived in 1994 and then 50,000 refugees more in 1996 after the Taliban took over Kabul (Appendix 8). However, it was difficult for Pakistan to accommodate further refugees, due to its weak economy. As a result, Afghanistan remained an economic and security concern for Pakistan despite the withdrawal of Soviet forces.

After the breakup of the Soviet Union, a new radical Islam emerged which became a greater threat to regional security in South Asia. Nonetheless, many Islamist groups and commanders gathered in Afghanistan after the Taliban established its emirates in the mid-1990s (Howenstein 2009). Osama bin Ladin, the founder and chief of Al-Qaeda, returned to eastern Afghanistan in 1996. Bin Ladin formed a close relationship with the Afghan Taliban and provided financial support to the Taliban Emirate of Afghanistan. He also tried to unify different former warlords and commanders under the umbrella of Al-Qaeda (McNally and Weinbaum 2016). In addition, many former mujahedeen, including both Arabs and non-Arabs, returned to Afghanistan under the Taliban regime in Kabul. They had restarted their training camps on the Afghan side of the border with Pakistan. Thus, Afghanistan became a safe haven for international mujahedeen and a major security threat to the world, especially after the 9/11 terrorist attacks. More importantly, it had major security consequences for Pakistan due to the 2,430 km-long porous border with Afghanistan.

As explained in Chapter 2, Pakistan had received external support from the US during the Cold War to contain Soviet expansion in the region. This external support had enabled Pakistan to achieve some level of military parity with India. However, US global interests and priorities changed after the end of the Cold War. The major concerns for America were issues such as nuclear non-proliferation, democracy, human rights, terrorism, and drug trafficking. In fact, the US Congress became very critical of Pakistan's nuclear programme and expressed its reservations about Islamabad's desire to develop nuclear weapons after the Soviet forces left Afghanistan (Mahmood 1997). In October 1990, President Bush senior declared that "he could no longer give the annual presidential certification that Pakistan 'does not possess' a nuclear explosive device, as required by the 1985 Pressler non-proliferation amendment" (Wirsing 2010). Consequently, the US had no longer the same strategic interests in supporting Pakistan in terms of military and economic aid after the collapse of the Soviet Union.

In this context, the US believed that Pakistan had installed a nuclear device at the Kahuta nuclear enrichment plant. However, Islamabad rejected such allegations and gave assurances that its nuclear programme was for peaceful purposes only. Despite such assurances, the US imposed sanctions in October 1990 for pursuing a nuclear enrichment programme. The US reduced Pakistan's economic and military aid under the rules of the Pressler Amendment. The details of the reduction in US aid are given in Table (Asif 2017).

Islamabad was unhappy with the Pressler Amendment because it was country-specific and it was only applied to Pakistan's nuclear programme. Islamabad called this amendment discriminatory as it did not cover the more advanced Indian nuclear programme. However, the US said that the Indian nuclear programme was indigenous, so it fell outside the scope of the US legislation. The Pakistan-US relationship further deteriorated due to US sanctions over Pakistan's development of the M-II missile system in collaboration with China. The sanctions were imposed on both China and Pakistan in August 1993 when it was reported that China had transferred missile technology to Pakistan for building the M-II missile system in 1992. The US said that China had violated its commitment to the Missile Technology Control Regime programme (Mahmood 1997). Thus, American military and economic aid was almost halted which played a greater role in balancing Indian military power during the Cold War. So it appeared as if Pakistan was being abandoned by the US after the end of the Cold War.

Furthermore, India diversified its foreign and security policy in the changing global security environment and redefined its relations with the US during the 1990s. Being an emerging regional power, India was a more natural strategic ally for the US to counter China's rise and to maintain a balance of power in Asia. Consequently, India gradually increased its ties with the US that provided the foundation for a strategic partnership between the two countries during the 2000s (Shakoor 1997). Condoleezza Rice (2000), national security adviser to

Table 3.1 US aid to Pakistan, 1990–2000 (USD in million)

Year	Economic Aid	Military Aid
1990	953.627	2.051
1991	451.256	0.000
1992	29.426	0.000
1993	75.385	0.000
1994	74.231	0.000
1995	24.287	0.000
1996	26.433	0.000
1997	59.886	0.000
1998	38.389	0.000
1999	106.741	2.893
2000	30.829	1.434
Total	**1,870.49**	**6.378**
Total US aid	**1,876.868**	

Source: US overseas Loans and Grants (Green book) available at https://eads.usaid.gov/gbk/. In Asif, M. and Muhammad, A. (2017). "Image of USA in Urban Pakistan: An Empirical Assessment." *A Research Journal of South Asian Studies* 32 (2): 539–555.

the second Bush administration, explained that "the United States should pay closer attention to India's role in the regional balance ... India is an element in China's calculation and it should be in America's too." The improving US-India relationship has had severe consequences for Pakistan. During the Cold War, the US took account of Pakistan's concerns while dealing with India. However, India successfully ruled out the Pakistan factor in its relations with the US. India also tried to improve and strengthen its relationship with Russia, China, and other regional countries, leaving limited room for manoeuvre for Pakistan in the changing global security environment (Travis 1994). As a result, Pakistan was struggling to counterbalance a resurgent Indian regional power in the post-Cold War world.

In this context, the security situation in South Asia essentially remained the same for Pakistan despite the changing global security environment. Similar to the Cold War era, Islamabad has continued to confront major external security threats from its neighbouring countries, especially India. Consequently, Islamabad has continued with the military-centred national security approach it had adopted during the Cold War. Nonetheless, Pakistan was disadvantaged due to the loss of the strategic position it had occupied during the Cold War era. Therefore, Pakistan needed to have a new comprehensive national security approach that took account of the new geographic realities. For example, India maintained its relationship with Russia in the post-Cold War era, but also developed its relations with the US at the same time. Similarly, Pakistan needed to establish relations with Russia after the collapse of the Soviet Union and maintain its strong relations with the West at the same time (Senator Mushahid Hussain, interview by author, Islamabad, 8 December 2017). Nonetheless, a strong government was required to form such a comprehensive strategy in dealing with emerging security challenges in the changing post-Cold War security environment.

Against this backdrop, the new global security environment offered some opportunities for Pakistan to regain its position in international politics. For instance, the major US concerns were anti-liberal, nationalistic, Islamic revisionist states, and fundamentalism. Islamabad had the potential to mediate between the US and anti-liberal and Islamic revisionist states in Muslim countries such as Iran, Libya, and Sudan (Travis 1994). Also, Pakistan was a key member of the OIC, in which it could have provided a moderating role. The emergence of Muslim states in Central Asia after the Cold War opened new economic and strategic opportunities for Pakistan. Due to their geographical proximity and cultural affinity, the new Central Asian Muslim states wanted to strengthen their relationship with Pakistan. More importantly, the landlocked Central Asian states could access Pakistan's deep seaport in Karachi and Gwadar (Memon 1994). Nonetheless, Islamabad reached out to China and strengthened their relations by solving their territorial disputes. Other than its policy towards China, Pakistan continued with its military-first national security approach and did not take the available opportunities to change its policies at the end of the Cold War.

Domestic politics and the extension of Pakistan's national security state

"Quasi-democracy"[1] returned to Pakistan after the death of General Zia in an airplane crash in August 1988. Ghulam Ishaq Khan, the then senate chairman and the most powerful bureaucrat, succeeded as an interim president in August 1988 as stipulated in the 1973 constitution. Interim President G. I. Khan called for a parliamentary general election to be held in November 1988 (Wynbrandt 2008). The PPP led by Benazir Bhutto won the election and became the largest political party in the parliament. It appeared at the time that this second democratic transition had opened a window of opportunity for democratic progress in the country after 11 years of authoritarian rule by General Zia. Nonetheless, the military only agreed to accept Bhutto as a prime minister on condition that she did not interfere in the foreign and security affairs of the state. According to Bidanda M. Chengappa (2000),

> Bhutto was compelled to adhere to certain conditions of the military leadership in order to assume office. These conditions included: (a) to continue the late General Zia's Afghan policy (b) allow General Mirza Aslam Beg and Lt General Hamid Gul to continue in their appointments as Chief of Army Staff and Director General ISI respectively (c) not to depress the defence budget (d) not to initiate any accountability proceedings against army personnel.

Thus, the government would be transferred to Bhutto on the condition that she maintains Pakistan's national security state policies. In November 1988, General Aslam Beg, the then COAS, informed the Joint Chiefs of Staff Committee that "Bhutto agreed with him that there would be no change in the Afghan policy, defence policy or nuclear programme, as well as no meddling in the administrative set-up of the civil service and no harassment of General Zia's family" (Nawaz 2009). This meant that Bhutto was "in office but out of power" as she agreed to continue General Zia's Cold War foreign and security policies under the national security state. The military had already set out that they would take all the key strategic decisions related to foreign and security policies. Moreover, Bhutto retained Sahabzada Yaqub Ali Khan as foreign minister. Sahabzada Yaqub had served as foreign minister under General Zia's regime. So Bhutto agreed to continue with the military-centric national security state policies before taking office.

Against this context, Bhutto pledged to continue General Zia's foreign policy so that the military transfer the government to her. Bhutto was convinced that she could be able to change the policy directions once the power transferred to her. After taking her office, Bhutto wanted to make strategic changes in Pakistan's foreign policy towards India and Afghanistan. In her first address to the nation, Bhutto criticized General Zia's regime and emphasized the reassessment of Pakistan's foreign and security policies, especially towards Afghanistan and India. She said (in Jain 1988):

Zia's narrow-based foreign policy had created an unnecessary environment of security threat for the country. I hoped for stronger links with the United States, better relations with Soviet Union once its pull out from Afghanistan was completed, maintenance of traditional ties with China, consolidation of friendship with the Muslim countries, and understanding with India.

For this purpose, Bhutto wanted to visit India to normalize the two countries' relationships, but the military strongly opposed her visit (Aziz 2008; Jones 2002). Moreover, Bhutto thought that the Kashmir conflict could be resolved through a diplomatic and political process. She was convinced that it had become almost impossible for Pakistan to defeat India militarily in Kashmir. She also rejected the idea of using Afghan mujahedeen in the Kashmir insurgency. Benazir Bhutto (2008, 406–407) explained in her autobiography: "the security establishment needed to understand that the Soviet forces were defeated by US stinger missiles, international finances, diplomacy and politics, not just by proxy war by the jihadists." Any such strategy would bring embarrassment to the country, she further explained. Therefore made it clear to the military elite that her government did not support a war with India (Bhutto 2008).

On the Afghanistan front, there was a serious difference between Bhutto and the military establishment. The ISI wanted to form an Afghan Interim Government (AIG) comprising the major warring factions. It was General Zia's idea to install an AIG in Kabul after the Soviet withdrawal from Afghanistan. In fact, Zia was reluctant to sign the "1988 Geneva Accord" unless it included a proper withdrawal plan for Afghanistan by installing an AIG comprising all the mujahedeen groups. The Pakistani military was convinced that Kabul under the mujahedeen would be largely anti-India due to India being a non-Muslim state. Therefore, in February 1989, the ISI formed the AIG in Peshawar, comprising seven major mujahedeen factions who had resisted the Soviet forces. Actually, the ISI's view was that Islamabad would recognize the AIG that would replace the communist government of the PDPA in Kabul. After Pakistani recognition, other countries would follow suit. However, Bhutto insisted that Islamabad needed to explore a peaceful and orderly transfer of power in Afghanistan. Therefore, she was against recognizing the AIG, arguing that the resistance parties did not have a foothold within Afghanistan. Subsequently, the AIG was not recognized internationally either (Duranni 2013).

Despite government opposition, the ISI continued to support the AIG, who were convinced they could take control of Afghanistan in months as they had already defeated the mighty Soviet forces. Bhutto mentioned in her autobiography (2008, 400–401) that the intelligence chief persuaded her by saying: "Prime Minister, will you deny your men and the Afghan mujahedeen the right to march victoriously into Kabul and pray in the Masjid together after all the sacrifices they have made?" Bhutto was assured by intelligence officials that Kabul would be under mujahedeen rule within a few days. Ironically, the ISI also requested the prime minister to give permission to send Pakistani soldiers to fight alongside the AIG to capture Kabul. Bhutto explained further in her book (2008):

The ISI General told me, Prime Minister, the Afghans are ready to sign an agreement for confederation between Pakistan and Afghanistan. They will call on us as part of the confederation treaty to overthrow the communist order. There will be no borders between us. I rejected the idea of a confederation with Afghanistan. This will give the Indians an excuse to intervene in Afghanistan. And without American, Saudi and Iranian support it will land us in bigger trouble. But the AIG wants a confederation and it can be signed tomorrow, my generals said. "I cannot do it," I replied. I pointed out that the repercussions for Pakistan would be enormous. Expansionist designs on our part would frighten the rest of the world into destabilising us.

However, Kabul did not fall in weeks or even months into the hands of the mujahedeen. In fact, the mujahedeen (AIG) failed to occupy Kabul with support of the ISI.

Installing an AIG in Afghanistan by the Pakistani military elite illustrates a major flaw in Pakistan's policy towards Afghanistan within the national security state. For example, the ISI was making a mistake by favouring different warring groups and attempting to interfere in the internal affairs of Afghanistan by establishing the AIG. According to former Pakistani Interior Minister Aftab Ahmad Sherpao (interview by author, Islamabad, 27 November 2017):

There is fault in Pakistan's policy towards Afghanistan[:] why we should be saying we want a friendly government in Afghanistan which is an independent country. The Afghan people have the right to choose their own leaders and we cannot impose a leadership on them. We must strive for a good neighbourly relationship with Afghanistan but not friendly government which is intruding in their internal domain.

Moreover, Pakistan needed to reach out to all the ethnic groups in Afghanistan, since relying only on ethnic Pashtuns would not serve its interests. Shuja Nawaz (Skype interview by author, 14 February 2018), a prominent political analyst, pointed out that:

Pakistan needs to stop looking [at] Afghanistan as [a] purely Pashtun issue. Afghanistan is the country of many nations including Turkman, Hazara, Uzbek, Tajik and so on. So you cannot see it purely [as] a Pashtun issue. On this point, Pakistan must need to think and change its policy towards Afghanistan.

In this situation, Bhutto's view was that political leadership should control foreign and security policy. In order to bring the powerful ISI under civilian control, Bhutto nominated the ISI chief without prior consultation with the COAS (Aziz 2008). Bhutto removed the ISI chief, General Hamid Gul, from his post in June 1989 and appointed General Shamsur Rahman Kallu, a retired military general (Yousaf and Adkin 1992). However, General Beg transferred the key records and files relating to political intelligence from the ISI headquarters to the General Headquarters (GHQ) in order to counter the civilian move to install General Kallu. Earlier in 1989, Bhutto also sacked retired Brigadier Imtiaz from the ISI and closed its political division. She also appointed retired Major Masood Sharif, a close friend of her husband, Asif Zardari, as the director of IB (Chengappa 2000). This led to serious differences between the government and the military establishment as she had agreed to continue Zia's Cold War policy but was clearly not doing so.

As a result, the civil-military tension created political instability in the country. The military elite were not ready to accept civilian involvement in foreign policy and civilian interference in their institutional affairs. In November 1989, the Pakistani military tried to remove the PPP from the government through a no-confidence vote in parliament. For this, the ISI gave the task to a retired ISI officer under the code name "Midnight Jackal" of persuading parliamentarians to initiate a vote of no-confidence in the national assembly (Fruman 2011). However, this plot to remove Bhutto from office failed as she received a tape recording revealing how her government would be toppled. Despite this failure, the military continued to oppose the Bhutto government (Yasmeen 1994). On 21 July 1990, the COAS decided in the "corps commander meeting" that Bhutto's government was no longer acceptable (Nawaz 2009). It was also decided to use the eighth amendment of the constitution and the president would dissolve the provincial and national assemblies. The military conveyed this message to the president, who was already gathering a list of issues with the prime minister. Ultimately, President G. I. Khan dismissed Bhutto's government through a presidential order, invoking the eighth amendment and Article 58 (2) (b) of the constitution, alleging corruption, nepotism, and incompetence (Yasmeen 1994). Nevertheless, the major reason for the dismissal of the PPP government was differences between the military establishment and the PPP leadership over issues related to foreign and security policy, as well as the military's institutional autonomy. This confirmed that the military would not tolerate a civilian government that interfered in foreign and security policy adopted under the national security state during the Cold War era.

In addition to this, the military manipulated the general election in order to prevent the PPP from winning. The ISI allegedly distributed around PKR 140 million among anti-PPP groups for their election campaign via the Habib and Mehran banks in Pakistan (*The News*, Pakistan, 25 January 2012). Moreover, the ISI allegedly formed Islami Jamhoori Ittehad (IJI) in September 1988. The IJI was an alliance of right-wing conservative parties including the Pakistan Muslim League, National People's Party, Jamaat-e-Islam, and six other small religious-political parties. Their primary task was to oppose the PPP and other secular political parties.

With the support of the ISI, the IJI won the parliamentary elections in October 1990. Since then, the ISI has manipulated the election process to produce a more "hybrid democracy" which suits their military-centric national security state approach in which the military has the upper hand in the running of state affairs. Nawaz Sharif, who was considered a pro-military leader, became the new prime minister of Pakistan. After taking office, Sharif recognized that the military wanted to keep Afghan, Kashmir, and nuclear policy under their exclusive control within the national security state. So he did not interfere in these matters (Nawaz 2009). Thus, Pakistan continued with its military-first national security state in the post-Cold War era.

However, the problem emerged when Sharif tried to assert himself as the chief executive of the country. For example, Sharif wanted to have a role in the promotion and appointment of the new COAS and other key positions within the military. But President G. I. Khan thought that it was his job to appoint the COAS and make other related appointments. More importantly, Sharif knew that the eighth amendment was the main obstacle to civilian supremacy. Therefore, he tried to convince opposition political parties to remove this amendment from the 1973 constitution. Bhutto acknowledged it as a major problem in civilian supremacy but did not come to his support, due to their mutually hostile politics. It is important to note that a political divide has helped the military elite to establish control over state affairs. In 1993, the prime minister and president were trying to remove each other from their respective offices. Consequently, the Sharif government was dismissed by the president on charges of corruption, mismanagement, and maladministration (Bray 1997). Nonetheless, the major reason was the government's promotion of military generals and constitutional reforms.

Sharif challenged the dismissal of his government in the Supreme Court, which was restored after it declared the dismissal illegal. President G. I. Khan was criticized for overusing his presidential powers. During the case hearing, the Supreme Court questioned the president's interventions in the workings of government and the appointment of the COAS. Despite the court's judgement, the struggle for power continued between the two offices. Ultimately, General Waheed Kakar, the then COAS, intervened and reached a settlement whereby both resigned from their offices and elections were held in 1993 under a caretaker government (Bray 1997). So Sharif was dismissed when he was trying to assert his role as chief executive and revoking the eighth amendment which would have established some form of civilian control in the country. Nonetheless, the division between the prime minister and president provided an opportunity to the military elite to intervene in domestic politics and establish its control in state affairs.

In October 1993, the PPP won the parliamentary elections with 89 seats in the national assembly and formed a coalition government at the federal level. Benazir Bhutto became the prime minister for a second time. In November 1993, Farooq Ahmed Khan Leghari, a young PPP party loyalist and landlord from South Punjab, was elected as a president by the national and provincial assemblies (Wynbrandt 2008). Compared with her first term, Bhutto was more submissive to the military in her second term as prime minister and attempted to maintain a good working relationship with the military. She learned that it was necessary to have a cordial relationship with the military in order to remain in power. For example, Bhutto confided with the military establishment before dealing with the US regarding the nuclear programme. In fact, Bhutto wanted to have a uniform view on Pakistan's relationship with the US and other related matters. More importantly, she adopted a pro-military stance over the Kashmir conflict and Afghanistan (Cheema 2015). As a result, Bhutto accepted the ISI's regional policy to extend its control over Afghanistan and Central Asian countries. Unlike in her first term, it was Bhutto's government that backed and recognized the Afghan Taliban government in 1996 (Wynbrandt 2008). But despite her pro-military stance, Bhutto's government did not prevail for a long period. President Farooq Leghari dismissed the government through a presidential order on charges of corruption in November 1996. Nonetheless, this time the president was from the ruling party. Hence, the military elite were relatively successful in limiting the role of secular political parties, especially Bhutto's PPP, in foreign and security policies in the post-Cold War era.

After the dismissal of Bhutto's government, the parliamentary general elections were held in February 1997. The PMLN won the elections with a clear two-thirds majority and formed a government at the federal and provincial levels. Like Bhutto, Nawaz Sharif became prime minister for the second time as well. Previously, the president had dismissed three elected governments through presidential orders, invoking the eighth amendment, before the completion of their full five-year term (Aziz 2008). After forming the government, the PMLN passed the 13th amendment which repealed the presidential power under Article 58 (2) (b) to dissolve parliament and dismiss the prime minister. Moreover, the prime minister has the authority to appoint the three chiefs of the armed forces and the provincial governors (Appendix 9). Thus, the 13th amendment restored the original power of the prime minister, and the president's role became more a ceremonial one, as stipulated in the constitution. The military establishment was against this legislation as it limited their role in the political sphere of the country with the support of the president.

On the external front, India successfully tested its nuclear weapons on 11 May 1998 and became a nuclear power. The major objective was to counter China and Pakistan's aggressive strategic designs in South Asia. As a result, the balance of power completely shifted in favour of India after it announced it had become a nuclear power. In doing so, India provoked Islamabad to pursue its nuclear weapons development. However, Pakistan would face severe economic consequences if it conducted successful nuclear tests, further weakening an already fragile economy. But after India became a nuclear power, there was huge public pressure on Prime Minister Sharif to conduct nuclear tests at any cost, even if the country would then face severe economic sanctions from the US. So Sharif felt it was left with little option but to respond with its own nuclear tests. On 28 May 1998, Pakistan successfully conducted five nuclear tests in the Chaghi district of Balochistan province. It was followed by one more advanced nuclear test in the Kharan district (Kasuri 2016). By responding with six successful nuclear tests compared to India's five, Pakistan was thus able to deter India by adopting a credible first-use nuclear posture (Saikal 2014). Senator Mushahid Husain Syed (interview by author, Islamabad, 8 December 2017) said that "the nuclear power status was the only positive outcome of Pakistan's national security policies which they adopted during the Cold War era."

Strategically, it was a great achievement for Pakistan that it was able to secure deterrence against its arch-rival India. More importantly, both civilian and military leadership were optimistic that the bomb would resolve most of the country's strategic issues. According to Hoodbhoy and Mian (2014):

> Overwhelmed by the power of the bomb, they saw it as magical; a panacea for solving Pakistan's multiple problems. They told themselves and their people that the bomb would bring national security, allow Pakistan to liberate Kashmir from India, bind the nation together, make its people proud of their country and its leaders, free the country from reliance on aid and loans, and lay the base for the long-frustrated goal of economic development.

Nonetheless, the addition of nuclear weapons in Pakistan's military apparatus has extended further military power in the country. More importantly, the nuclear weapons programme has played a greater role in the survival of the national security state in Pakistan throughout the 1990s. As shown earlier, Pakistan's military wanted to keep key strategic decision making such as nuclear policy under their exclusive control after transferring the government to Benazir Bhutto in August 1988. Subsequently, Bhutto was kept out of the nuclear programme. She mentioned in an interview with Shuja Nawaz that she asked for a briefing on the nuclear programme but did not receive any briefing on it after taking office. In fact, it was the US ambassador to Pakistan, Robert Oakley, who briefed her regarding the Pakistani nuclear programme with what the US knew about it. Prime Minister Nawaz Sharif was considered a pro-military leader who did not interfere in nuclear matters as he knew that the military wanted to keep it in their control (Nawaz 2009). Actually, the military establishment propagated that the civilian leadership was weak and would not hold firm against any international pressure over the nuclear programme and this reflected a continuation with a military-centred national security approach in the post-Cold War era.

Sharif sought to limit the military's role in foreign policymaking. He started the normalization process with India which would improve Pakistan-India relations. In fact, the military often justified their enhanced role in state affairs by arguing that the civilians were weak in dealing with India. Therefore, Sharif understood that normalization with India would reduce the role of the military in the political sphere of the country and establish civilian supremacy. Sharif also attempted to pursue an economic-driven foreign policy that would not only help to revive a weakened economy but also assist in developing a cordial relationship with neighbouring countries. The military establishment was worried that such changes in foreign policy would undermine Pakistan's national security interests.

In October 1998, General Jehangir Karamat once again proposed the idea of an NSC in which both civilian and military leaders would make all the major decisions related to domestic and international issues. Sharif's government rejected the NSC idea as it would provide legal cover for and institutionalize the military's role in the political affairs of the state. Consequently, it would further undermine democratic transition and the role of the civilian leadership in the country. The military tried but failed to achieve its aim. Subsequently, General Karamat resigned as COAS and Sharif appointed General Pervez Musharraf as the new army chief. Musharraf was the most junior in the list of potential heads of the armed forces (Malik 2008). The removal of General Karamat and the selection of General Musharraf reflected Sharif's determination to establish civilian supremacy over the military.

In the late 1990s, there was growing international pressure on Pakistan with respect to its relations with the Afghan Taliban and nuclear programme. The military believed that the government was making strategic changes in foreign and security policy due to international pressure. The US had requested Pakistan to ask the Afghan Taliban to extradite Bin Laden from Afghanistan after the Al-Qaeda attacks on US embassies in East Africa in 1998. However, the military establishment believed that such a demand would worsen its relationship with the Afghan Taliban regime and Islamabad would lose its strategic depth in Afghanistan (Lavoy 2009). Actually, Pakistan had no military depth within Pakistan so they were looking for Afghanistan to provide military depth in case of Indian aggression. The military also feared that Prime Minister Sharif would sign the Nuclear Test Ban Treaty (NTBT) in exchange for the lifting of sanctions on Pakistan, without India pledging to do the same. For instance, Sharif promised before the UN General Assembly to sign the NTBT in September 1999 (Jaffrelot 2015). As a consequence, the military decided to directly intervene in the government before it was too late to protect the interests of national security. General Musharraf carried out a military coup on 12 October 1999 and dismissed the PMLN government (Malik 2008). Thus, the Pakistani military elite used a hybrid model of domestic compulsions and geostrategic global environment as a leading cause of military ascendency in the 1990s.

In addition, the military businesses have continued to show significant growth in education, banking, airline, insurance, real estate, fertilizer, textile, sugar, and so forth during the 1990s. Moreover, the civilian governments have given many infrastructure mega-projects to military-run NLC and FWO (Siddiqa 2007). The primary objective was to appease the military elite and to remain in power. In 1999, the Sharif government awarded the contract for collecting tolls on and maintenance of the Grand Trunk Road (N-5) and Sukkur-Lahore highway to FWO. Despite awarding mega-projects to the military-run corporations, the privatization move by Prime Minister Sharif was opposed by the Pakistan Navy. This meant the military institutional interests have continued to override national economic interests (Chengappa 1999). However, the civilian leadership did not show many concerns over the growing business conglomerate of the military. According to former Finance Minister Sartaj Aziz, "the main challenge for us [the Sharif government] was reducing the military's political strength. Had we begun to curb their financial interests as well, it would have had an immediate reaction from the armed forces" (in Siddiqa 2007). So, the primary objective of the political leadership was to reduce the political strength of the military in state affairs during the 1990s.

Furthermore, the Pakistani military elite kept on appointing senior military officers in civil administration. It was reported that the senior military officers held around 100 key civilian positions during 1992–1993. The civil officers showed resentment over such appointments and filed petitions against it in the High Courts. For example, a petition was filed in the Sindh High Court against the Pakistan Navy Vice Admiral Mansurul Haq, who was appointed as the Pakistan National Shipping Corporation (PNSC) chairman. Moreover, the armed forces were involved in maintaining law and order situation under "aid to civil power." Subsequently, the military personnel engaged in policing which brought them in direct contact with people that often create scope for corruption and misuse of power in a country like Pakistan. So, armed forces were dragged into a role for which they were not trained that severely affected their culture of discipline and professionalism (Chengappa 1999). Since then, the military personnel have remained engaged in maintaining law and order situation in major cities in the country.

Overall, the civilian leadership had attempted during the 1990s to assert civilian control over the national security state. But the military was so embedded in the state structures that it was relatively easy for the military elite to manipulate the internal and external security environment in its favour. Consequently, the Pakistani military successfully defied any civilian government attempt to reform the national security state by running state affairs independently. Furthermore, the military resisted civilian interference in their institutional matters, especially those concerning promotions and transfers of senior military personnel. So Pakistan's national security state prevailed in the country despite a decade of apparent civilian rule during the 1990s.

Musharraf's dictatorial regime and the intensification of Pakistan's state-centric national security approach

After his coup in October 1999, General Pervez Musharraf appointed himself as "Chief Executive," declared a state of emergency, and suspended the 1973 constitution under a "Provisional Constitution Order" (PCO), which ensured that his actions could not be challenged in the courts. Like his predecessor, General Musharraf blamed the political leadership for systemic corruption, a weak economy, and political instability in the country. Moreover, he gave assurances that he would revive genuine democracy, improve the economy, and end corruption. Like General Ayub, Musharraf's coup was accepted by the general public, who considered the civilian government corrupt and incompetent. Most of the liberal-minded people in Pakistan also saw some cause for optimism that General Musharraf's rule might bring stability and order to the country. In January 2001, President Rafiq Tarar was forced to resign from his office by means of a PCO, and General Musharraf succeeded as the new president of the country (Kronstadt 2004).

Internationally, Pakistan was becoming more isolated and its Commonwealth membership was suspended after the coup. In March 2000, US President Clinton was on an official visit to India. At an insistent request from Pakistan's foreign office, Clinton visited Pakistan for just five hours, without, however, meeting General Musharraf. Moreover, further international sanctions were imposed on

Pakistan, and the IMF froze the last instalment of the $US1.56 billion credit allocated in 1997 (Jaffrelot 2004). So Pakistan became more of a diplomatic pariah state after the coup.

Like the earlier military regime, General Musharraf wanted to have a civilian government that worked under the direction of the military. Prior to the elections, he incorporated a "Legal Framework Order" in the constitution which increased presidential power over that of the prime minister. The ISI also planned to rig the polls in advance of the elections in 2002 and formed their own king party (pro-military) known as the Pakistan Muslim League – Quaid-e-Azam Group (PMLQ) (*Dawn*, Pakistan 27 February 2008). Like the IJI, the alliance of six far-right Islamist political parties was formed under the banner of Muttihada Majlis-e-Amal (MMA), including the Jamiat Ulema-e-Pakistan, the Jamiat Ulema-e-Islam-Fazl (JUI-F), the Jamiat Ulema-e-Islam (JUI-S), Jamiat-e-Ahle Hadith, Pakistan Islami Tehrik, and JI (Khan 2014). The ISI was alleged to have secretly supported the MMA to counter mainstream secular political parties and used them as an Islamic card in dealing with the US after 9/11 (Abbas 2004).

The general elections were held in October 2002. The PMLQ won the 2002 election with narrow margin winning 77 seats of the 268 seats at the federal level, followed by the PPP with 63 seats (Appendix 10). After the elections, the ISI allegedly formed a forward block within the opposition PPP to support the PMLQ government. Moreover, many politicians changed their party allegiance after the elections and joined the PMLQ by offering key positions in the subsequent government (Abbas 2004). Thus, the political divide has continued that helped General Musharraf to establish PMLQ led government under his rule. Nevertheless, the MMA won 45 seats in the national assembly and won a majority of seats in the KP and Balochistan provinces. For the first time in Pakistan's history, the Islamists emerged as a major opposition political party and formed provincial governments in these two provinces (Appendix 11). On the other hand, General Musharraf excluded the leadership of the two largest political parties, PPP and PMLN, from contesting the elections.

Like General Ayub Khan, General Musharraf maintained military control over state affairs following elections. The PMLQ passed the 17th constitutional amendment through parliament, with the support of the MMA, in December 2003. The amendment reinstated Article 58 (2) (b) and shifted back power to the president by dismissing parliament and the prime minister. More importantly, Musharraf succeeded in establishing the infamous NSC, which undermined civilian supremacy and which previous military generals had failed to implement. Under the NSC, important powers were transferred back to the military (Adeney 2007; Appendix 5). Thus, the NSC has institutionalized the military's role in the political sphere of the country.

In addition, General Musharraf promulgated the National Accountability Bureau (NAB) ordinance in October 1999. The ordinance was approved by the then President Rafiq Tarar (*Pakistan Today*, 28 April 2011). In the past, such anti-corruption campaigns/reforms have been used for the political victimization of high-profile political figures in Pakistan. In fact, two successive elected governments, those of Bhutto and Sharif, were dismissed on allegations of corruption in 1990 and 1993. On the other hand, the military is exempt from the jurisdiction of the NAB ordinance. According to section four of the NAB ordinance (XVIII of 1999), "the applicability extends to all public servants and citizens other than a person who is a member of any of the armed forces of Pakistan." So the Pakistani military has impunity and is outside the ambit of this ordinance.

The NAB, as an autonomous organization, was established under the administrative control of the military. The apparent objective of the 1999 NAB ordinance was to "eradicate corruption and corrupt practices and hold accountable all those persons accused of such practices and matters." The NAB is provided with extensive powers. Under the NAB ordinance, corruption suspects may be placed in custody for 15 days without charge and may be denied access to counsel prior to charging. Moreover, the offences are non-bailable and the chairman of NAB has special powers to decide whether to release or detain suspects under investigation (NAB – XVIII of 1999). With such discretionary powers, the military establishment has used the NAB ordinance as a tool "to either fix political opponents or make them pliable" (Ahmed 2013); Sareen 2018). For example, General Musharraf utilized it to deal with his political rivals in order to prevent any opposition to his dictatorial regime. Most recently, it was used against the former ruling party PMLN and its leader Nawaz Sharif, who was put in jail for alleged corruption just before the 2018 parliamentary elections (BBC News, 6 July 2018). Thus, the NAB was another sword hanging over the heads of political leaders which the military establishment utilized for the persecution of its opponents among the political leaders and subordinate civil servants (Chene *et al.* 2008). In other words, it is an effective tool for political engineering in order to control state affairs within the national security state.

Besides controlling politicians, the military, with the support of the ISI, has maintained a greater control over the media in Pakistan. In March 2002, General Musharraf promulgated the "Pakistan Electronic Media Regulatory Authority" (PEMRA) and relaxed restrictions on the electronic media (PEMRA, Retrieved: 9 November 2018). Many media houses were established, which led to a vibrant electronic media in the country. While public access to information has increased, the flow of information is largely controlled by the military establishment. The ISI has cultivated many journalists in the media houses directly and indirectly, in order to manage public opinion and counter dissent. On the other hand, the military have opened their own television channels and radio stations to counter dissent. In fact, the media has been used to propagate the positive image that the military is the only guardian institution of the country. More importantly, the media houses blamed civilians for all the wrongdoings in the country. Most of the talk shows have recently become media trials of anti-military establishment political parties, politicians, and civil rights groups.

The Pakistani military established its own media agency, known as the Inter-Services Public Relations (ISPR), in 1949. It is headed by at least a serving major general. General Musharraf has extended the ISPR's capacity in order to control both the electronic and print media (Yusuf 2011). They have been involved in the Pakistani film industry, the theatre, and an extensive radio network. The ISPR have run different campaigns through the media to glorify the military chiefs and denigrate politicians. For example, they have funded films, dramas, and songs to propagate their so-called hyper-patriotic security narrative. According to prominent defence analyst Ayesha Siddiqa (2017), "the ISPR is known for intimidation such as directing television channels regarding their choice of news-programme anchors, and in certain cases, even their choice of guests." In this process, the military has emerged as a major stakeholder in the media as well. There is no credible information on how many media channels the military operates. The late Asma Jahangir, a former senior lawyer and human rights activist, submitted a petition to the Pakistan Supreme Court in 2016 to demand information about television and radio channels run by the military. However, the court simply kept prolonging action on the petition (Malik 2016). With the addition of the above institutions, the Pakistani military elite further consolidated its power and extended itself serving national security state under General Musharraf regime.

Internationally, General Musharraf portrayed himself as pro-Western leader who could defeat Islamic militancy in the region after the 9/11 terror attacks. For this, he promoted his so-called agenda of "enlightened moderation" to counter militancy and extremism in the country. However, he provided a politics space to religious groups by ousting major political parties in order to gain political power. Therefore, the Musharraf rule was not really moderate on Pakistani politics, but he successfully gained international support for his illegitimate dictatorial rule by presenting himself as a liberal Muslim leader, who could work with the US to defeat this menace of terrorism (Adeney 2007). More importantly, he adopted dual policy by supporting the US global war on terror but at the same time provided covert aid to the Afghan Taliban in post-9/11.

Similarly, in the post 9/11 era, one of the major concerns was nuclear terrorism as global terrorist groups have been seeking nuclear weapons. All the nuclear power states were worried about the possibility of losing control over nuclear weapons and its materials. So the state must pay greater attention to securing its nuclear weapons (Mowatt-Larssen 2009). About Pakistan's nuclear programme, the international community has constantly raised their concerns due to the rise of home-grown terrorism and political instability in the country that could lead to the nuclear weapons or materials falling into the hands of terrorists. Consequently, it has provided another justification of a strong military-centric national security state in the country as the Pakistani military establishment maintains control over the nuclear arsenal. Thus, General Musharraf used the extremist threat and nuclear terrorism to buttress their national security state in post-9/11.

However, the year 2007 significantly changed domestic politics and internal security in Pakistan. General Musharraf confronted severe challenges in 2007 to his control of the state and society. A crisis loomed when General Musharraf sacked the chief justice of the Supreme Court in March 2007 and later imposed restrictions on the media. The alienated journalists joined the lawyers' movement which had been started as a protest against the suspension of the chief justice of Pakistan. Subsequently, massive demonstrations were carried out against Musharraf, demanding his resignation from office (Chesser 2007).

In July 2007, General Musharraf also cracked down on the radical clerics of the "red mosque" when unrest reached a level which was difficult to control in the heart of Islamabad. Actually, General Musharraf was trying to present himself as the only Pakistani leader able to counter terrorism in the country. In this way, he thought he would tackle the secular lawyer's movement and other groups who were opposing his rule in the country. Nonetheless, the red mosque operation was a turning point in the militant landscape of Pakistan as it led to a series of suicide attacks against security forces and government officials (Schaffer 2008). It was the worst crisis faced by General Musharraf since his military coup in 1999. In order to control the situation, General Musharraf imposed a state emergency on 3 November 2007. The emergency was condemned nationally and internationally. Despite the state of emergency, terrorist attacks continued and, subsequently, General Musharraf further lost control over the government. Finally, he lifted the emergency on 15 December 2007.

Despite international pressure, General Musharraf's regime continued with its support of proxy militant groups active in Kashmir and Afghanistan. However, these proxy wars have severe adverse consequences for the internal security of Pakistan. Many Kashmiri commanders and outfits joined anti-Pakistani state Taliban militant groups and Al-Qaeda. Moreover, the Afghan Taliban insurgency fuelled militancy in Pakistan (Siddiqa 2011). In December 2007, the Pakistani Taliban groups united under the umbrella of Tehrik-i-Taliban Pakistan (TTP), fighting against the Pakistani security forces. Baitullah Mehsud became the central commander of the TTP who pledged allegiance to Mullah Omer, the then chief of the Afghan Taliban. Furthermore, TTP and the Afghan Taliban maintained both logistical and financial support for each other.

After the unification of various militant groups and the army red mosque operation, TTP became the most lethal militant group in the region. According to the Pak Institute for Peace Studies (PIPS), in 2007, around 3,448 people were killed and 5,353 injured in 1,442 terrorist attacks, mainly conducted by the TTP. The lethality and number of terrorist attacks had increased considerably since 2006, when 907 people died and 1,543 were injured in 657 terrorist attacks (PIPS report January 2008). On top of this, the Taliban insurgency spread from tribal areas to settled areas in KP province. Since then, the TTP has carried out major terrorist attacks on military installations, including the GHQ, the Mehran airbase, and the Pakistani Ordnance Factory Wah Cantt.

Benazir Bhutto returned to Pakistan after eight years of self-imposed exile in October 2007. On her return, Bhutto narrowly escaped in two bomb blasts when she was welcomed by a massive crowd at Karachi, in which 149 people were killed. Despite threats to her life, she continued with her political campaign for 2008 elections. On 27 December 2007, Bhutto was assassinated in a public gathering that forced Musharraf to resign and to hold parliamentary elections in earlier 2008. Prior to her assassination, "Bhutto said a sinister cabal of intelligence officers and presidential aides were plotting to kill her, and that Musharraf should be blamed if anything were to happen to her. PPP has always maintained that line" (*The Guardian*, 31 August 2017). General Musharraf's dictatorial rule continued for nearly eight years in which the military had extended further its control over the state affairs.

The post-Musharraf era: democratization in Pakistan and the national security state

Parliamentary elections were held in February 2008. The PMLQ, pro-Musharraf's political party, lost in all its major constituencies in the country. The PPP and PMLN formed a coalition government at the federal and provincial levels. The PPP's Yousuf Raza Gilani became prime minister. Unlike the previous elections in the 1990s, the 2008 one was relatively free and fair. Due to possible impeachment by the national parliament, General Musharraf resigned from his position as president. Asif Ali Zardari, the PPP's co-chairman, became the new president, which ended the dictatorship of General Musharraf. Thus, the appearance of democracy was returned to Pakistan. But the new government inherited a plethora of problems, including home-grown terrorism, US drone attacks, suicide bombings, a weak economy, targeted killings, the Baloch separatist movements, and a Taliban militancy (Zaidi 2011). Nonetheless, the democratic transition once again provided a window of opportunity for the civilian leadership to establish civilian supremacy in the country.

Like previous political regimes, the PPP government attempted to reform the national security state in order to stop military intervention in the political affairs of the state. In April 2010, the government passed the landmark 18th constitutional amendment. The amendment modified 102 out of a total of 280 articles of the 1973 constitution (Appendix 13). It was the largest constitutional change in the history of Pakistan since the 1973 constitution was implemented. The amendment repealed the problematic Article 58 (2) (b), which provided major powers to the president while making the prime minister more a symbolic chief executive of the state. This article was first promulgated in the eighth amendment by General Zia and then revived in the 17th amendment by General Musharraf (Burki 2010). Thus, in 2010, the discretionary powers of the president were removed. Now the president can only consider and approve those bills and orders that have been passed by the parliament and the senate, or upper house. More importantly, Article 6 of the constitution was strengthened to deter any future military takeovers. Under Article 6, a military coup will be considered an "act of treason," and the Supreme Court and High Court can no longer validate a military coup (Appendix 5). In sum, the legislation restored the parliamentary system in the country, and President Zardari transferred his powers as president back to parliament. Thus, the PPP-led government constitutionally prevented direct military intervention in politics.

In addition to this, the 18th amendment initiated decentralization in the country. It gives more power and autonomy to the provinces. Also, the legislation sought to strengthen the senate, in which each province has an equal number of representatives (Burki 2010). Such decentralization of power could further weaken Pakistan's national security state which is based on a strong centralized government.

The PPP government made considerable further efforts to strengthen the democratization process in the country. It tried to assert control over foreign and security policy. In November 2008, the government formulated a "Parliamentary Committee on National Security" (PCNS) through a joint parliamentary resolution. The primary objective of the PCNS was to carry out "a review of the national security strategy and revisit the methodology of combating terrorism in order to restore peace and stability through an independent foreign policy" (PILDAT report 2013). Traditionally, parliamentary committees and bodies had little say in foreign policymaking, which was often influenced by the military by means of their policy recommendations. However, the PCNS was able to draw strength from public anger over events such as the US raid on Bin Laden's safe house in Abbottabad; the CIA contractor Raymond Davis's killing of two Pakistani intelligence agents; and the deadly attack on the Pakistani checkpoint at Salala by NATO forces on the Pakistan-Afghan border in November 2011. Consequently, the PCNS recommended closing the NATO supply route to Afghanistan as well as the Shamsi airbase which was used by the US for their drone campaign in the region. This compelled the US to look for alternative ground routes to Afghanistan, which was very expensive. It also affected drone operations in the region. The Pakistan-US relationship reached an all-time low and the supply route remained closed between November 2011 and July 2012 (Fair 2015). Eventually, the government overruled the PCNS's recommendations and opened the supply route after the military intervened. However, the PCNS was unable to produce a comprehensive national security policy under the PPP-led government due to differences between the PPP and PMLN (PILDAT report 2013).

Like in the 1990s, the political divide provided an opportunity to the military elite to regain its control over the state affairs. The major issue that divided the two parties was the reinstatement of 60 deposed judges who had been removed by General Musharraf (Asghar 2008). Furthermore, President Zardari imposed "Governor's Rule" and dismissed the PMLN provincial government in Punjab when a court declared former Prime Minister Nawaz Sharif and his brother Shahbaz Sharif ineligible to contest elections. Once again, old hostile power politics revived between the two main political parties. The PMLN moved against the federal government and supported a long march by lawyers for the restoration of the Chief Justice Iftikhar Muhammad Chaudhry who was dismissed by General Musharraf. Sharif called off the march after the government announced the restoration of the chief justice. Consequently, Sharif was praised both nationally and internationally for the restoration of judicial integrity. However, the squabbles between the political parties reignited the debate over whether political parties were competent to run state affairs. General Ashfaq Kayani, the then COAS, had played a major role in resolving the political crisis. More importantly, General Kayani gradually restored the image of the military which had been tarnished under General Musharraf's regime (Akhtar 2009). Thus, hostile party politics provided the opportunity for the military elite to resume its role in the political affairs of the state.

Despite the above political divide and numerous other challenges, the PPP government managed to complete her five-year tenure in parliament. Parliamentary elections were held in May 2013 in which the PMLN got the majority. It was the first time in the history of Pakistan that democratically elected government transferred power to another democratically elected government. Unlike previous civilian governments, the Zardari regime exploited the window of opportunity to establish civilian rule in the country in which they were relatively successful to end martial administration and decentralizing powers and financial resources to the provinces under the 18th constitutional amendments. However, the Pakistani military elite maintained its control over other state institutions such as the judiciary, bureaucracy, and media. Beside the political divide, these institutions have been used by the Pakistani military to undermine the political process in the country (Shah 2014).

In sum, Islamabad has persisted with the military-first national security state approach in the post-Cold War era. The Pakistani military and ISI executed the foreign and security policies and took all the major decisions related to strategic importance in the post-Cold War era. The continuous conflict in Kashmir and Pakistan's participation in the global war on terror provide key cases to make in-depth analyzes of Pakistan's military-first national security state approach in the post-Cold War. More specifically, the primary objective of the two cases is to see the effectiveness of the national security state approach in solving major disputes confronted by Pakistan.

Note

1 Quasi-democracy refers to specific patterns of voting behaviour, election procedures, and institutional malfunctioning that have shaped the years of transition.

References

Abbas, H. 2004. *Pakistan's Drift into Extremism: Allah, then Army, and America's War Terror*. Routledge.

Adeney, K. 2007. "What Comes after Musharraf?" *The Brown Journal of World Affairs* 14 (1): 41–52.

Ahmed, N. 2013. "The Dark Side of Authority: A Critical Analysis of Anti-Corruption Frameworks in Pakistan." *Law, Social Justice & Global Development Journal* 15: 1–18.

Akhtar, N. 2009. "Polarized Politics: The Challenges of Democracy in Pakistan." *International Journal on World Peace* 26 (2): 31–63.

Appendix 3: List of Interviewees.

Appendix 5: The 18th Amendment of Pakistan's Constitution in 2010.

Appendix 8: Timeline of Afghan Displacements into Pakistan 1979–2012.

Appendix 9: The 13th Amendment of Pakistan's Constitution in 1997.

Appendix 10: National Assembly General Election Results in 2002.

Appendix 11: Provincial Assembly General Election Results in 2002.

Appendix-13: The 18th Amendment of Pakistan's Constitution in 2010.

"Application Seeks to Revoke NAB Ordinance 1999." *Pakistan Today*, April 28, 2011. Retrieved on October 25, 2018, https://www.pakistantoday.com.pk/2011/04/28/applic ation-seeks-to-revoke-nab-ordinance-1999/.

"Asghar Khan's ISI Funds Case in SC to Blemish Many." *New South, Pakistan*, January 25, 2012. Retrieved on November 24, 2018, https://www.thenews.com.pk/archive/print /619760-asghar-khan%E2%80%99s-isi-funds-case-in-sc-to-blemish-many.

Asghar, R. 2008. "Judges Will Be Reinstated, Senate Assured." *Dawn, Pakistan*, May 13, 2008. Retrieved on March 23, 2017, https://www.dawn.com/news/302580/judges-will-be-reinstated-senate-assured.

Asif, M. 2017. "Image of USA in Urban Pakistan: An Empirical Assessment." *A Research Journal of South Asian Studies* 32 (2): 539–555.

Aziz, M. 2008. *Military Control in Pakistan: A Parallel State*. Routledge.

BBC. 2018. "Pakistan Ex-PM Nawaz Sharif Given 10-Year Jail Term." *BBC News*, July 6, 2018. Retrieved on October 25, 2018, https://www.bbc.com/news/world-asia-4473 7793.

Bhutto, B. 2008. *Daughter of Destiny: An Autobiography*. Harper Perennial.

Bray, J. 1997. "Pakistan at 50: A State in Decline?" *International Affairs* 73 (2): 315–331.

Burki, S. J. 2010. "The 18th Amendment: Pakistan's Constitution Redesigned." ISAS Working Paper No.: 112.

Byrd, W. 2012. *Lessons from Afghanistan's History for the Current Transition and Beyond*. USIP Special Report.

Cheema, M. J. 2015. "Pakistan – India Conflict with Special Reference to Kashmir." *South Asian Studies* 30 (1): 45–69.

Chene, M., Fagan, C., and Plaza, S. 2008. "Overview of Corruption in Pakistan." *U4 Anti-Corruption Resource Centre*, April 9, 2010. Retrieved from http://www.u4.no/helpdesk /helpdesk/query.cfm?id=174.

Chengappa, B. M. 1999. "Pakistan: Military Role in Civil Administration." *Strategic Analysis* 23 (2): 299–312.

Chengappa, B. M. 2000. "The ISI Role in Pakistan's Politics." *Strategic Analysis* 23 (11): 1857–1878.

Chesser, S. G. 2007. *Pakistan: Significant Recent Events, March 26–June 21, 2007*. CRS Report. Retrieved from https://fas.org/sgp/crs/row/RL34075.pdf.

Collins, J. J. 2011. *Understanding War in Afghanistan*. National Defense University Press.

Dawn . 2007. "Political Management' Done in 2002 Polls: Zamir." *Dawn, Pakistan*, February 27, 2008. Retrieved on September 26, 2020, https://www.dawn.com/news /291168/political-management-done-in-2002-polls-zamir.

Duranni, A. 2013. "Strategic Decision Making in Pakistan." *Journal of Strategic Studies, Islamabad* 33 (3/4): 1–22.

Dwivedi, S. S. 2013. "Exploring Strategies and Implications of an Opportunistic Alliance: A Case Study of Pakistan and China." *Asian Journal of Political Science* 21 (3): 306–327.

Fair, C. C. 2015. "Democracy on the Leash in Pakistan." In *Pakistan's Enduring Challenges*, edited by C. Christine Fair and Sarah J. Watson. University of Pennsylvania Press.

Fruman, S. 2011. *Will the Long March to Democracy in Pakistan Finally Succeed?* USIP Report.

Gray, A. 2017. "The World's 10 Biggest Economies in 2017." *World Economic Forum*, March 9, 2017, Retrieved on November 24, 2018, https://www.weforum.org/agenda /2017/03/worlds-biggest-economies-in-2017.

Hagerty, D. T. 1995–96. "Nuclear Deterrence in South Asia: The 1990 Indo-Pakistani Crisis Author." *International Security* 20 (3): 79–114.

Hoodbhoy, P. and Mian, Z. 2014. "Nuclear Fears, Hopes and Realities in Pakistan." *International Affairs* 90 (5): 1125–1142.

Howenstein, N. 2009. "Review Essay of Ayesha Jalal, Partisans of Allah: Jihad in South Asia and Praveen Swami, India, Pakistan and the Secret Jihad: The Covert War in Kashmir, 1947–2004." *India Review* 8 (4): 446–456.

Husain, S. A. 1979. "Politics of Alliance and Aid: A Case Study of Pakistan (1954–1966)." *Pakistan Horizon* 32 (1–2): 11–46.

Jabeen, M. 2010. "Indian Aspiration of Permanent Membership in the UN Security Council and American Stance." *A Research Journal of South Asian Studies* 25 (2): 237–253.

Jaffrelot, C. 2004. *A History of Pakistan and Its Origins*. Anthem Press.

Jaffrelot, C. 2015. *The Pakistan Paradox: Instability and Resilience*. Oxford University Press.

Jain, B. M. 1988. "Indo-Pakistan Relations under the Rajiv-Benazir leadership." *Journal of Asian Affairs* 1 (2): 58–64.

Jones, O. B. 2002. *Pakistan: Eye of the Storm*. Yale University Press.

Kasuri, K. M. 2016. *Neither a Hawk nor a Dove: An Insider's Account of Pakistan's Foreign Policy*. Viking Penguins.

Khan, J. 2014. "The Rise of Political Islam in Khyber Pakhtunkhwa: The Case of Muttahida Majlis-e-Amal (MMA)." *The Dialogue* 9 (3): 299–312.

Kreisberg, P. H. 1985. "India after Indira." *Foreign Affairs* 63 (4): 873–891.

Kronstadt, K. A. 2004. *Pakistan's Domestic Political Developments*. CRS Report for Congress.

Lavoy, P. R. 2009. *A Symmetric Warfare in South Asia: The Causes and Consequences of the Kargil Conflict*. Cambridge University Press.

Mahmood, T. 1997. "Pakistan's Foreign Policy: Post-Cold War Period." *Pakistan Horizon* 50 (3): 101–124.

Malik, H. 2016. "Supreme Court Seeks Reply from Govt, PEMRA Over 'Illegal' Radio Channels Operated by ISPR." *Express Tribune, Pakistan*, July 20, 2016. Retrieved on July 11, 2018, https://tribune.com.pk/story/1145763/supreme-court-seeks-reply-govt-pemra-illegal-radio-channels-operated-ispr/.

Malik, I. H. 2008. *The History of Pakistan*. Greenwood.

McNally, L. and Weinbaum, M. G. 2016. "A Resilient Al-Qaeda in Afghanistan and Pakistan." *MEI Policy Focus*, no. 3. Retrieved from http://www.mei.edu/sites/default/files/publications/PF18_Weinbaum_AQinAFPAK_web_1.pdf.

Memon, M. 1994. "Reorientation of Pakistan's Foreign Policy after the Cold War." *Pakistan Horizon* 47 (2): 45–61.

Mowatt-Larssen, R. 2009. "Nuclear Security in Pakistan: Reducing the Risks of Nuclear Terrorism." *Belfer Center*, July 1, 2009. Retrieved from https://www.belfercenter.org/publication/nuclear-security-pakistan-reducing-risks-nuclear-terrorism.

"National Accountability Ordinance (XVIII of 1999)." *National Accountability Bureau*, March 26, 2010, http://www.nab.gov.pk/downloads/nao.asp#6-3.

Nawaz, S. 2009. *Crossed Swords: Pakistan, Its Army, and the Wars Within*. Oxford University Press.

Pak Institute for Peace Studies (PIPS). 2007. "PIPS Security Report 2007 Executive Summary." *PIPS, Islamabad*, January 7, 2008. Retrieved from http://www.san-pips.com/download.php?f=psr0003.pdf.

"Pakistan Electronic Media Regulatory Authority (PEMRA)." Retrieved on November 9, 2018 from PEMRA official site: http://www.pemra.gov.pk/.

PILDAT. 2013. *Performance of the Parliamentary Committee on National Security*. Publication No: CMR-076. PILDAT.

Prasad, N. 2017. *Changes in India's Foreign Policy towards Pakistan*. Alpha Edition.

Rais, R. B. 1991. "Pakistan in the Regional and Global Power Structure." *Asian Survey* 31 (4): 378–392.

Rice, C. 2000. "Campaign 2000: Promoting the National Interest." *Foreign Affairs* 79 (1): 45–62.

Saikal, A. 2014. *Zone of Crisis: Afghanistan, Pakistan, Iran and Iraq*. I.B.Tauris.

Sareen, S. 2018. "Why Pakistan's Deep State is Targeting Nawaz Sharif." *ORF, International Affairs*, May 14, 2018. Retrieved on November 24, 2018, https://www.orf online.org/research/why-pakistans-deep-state-is-targeting-nawaz-sharif/.

Schaffer, T. C. 2008. "Pakistan: Transition to What?." *Survival* 50 (1): 9–14.

Shah, A. 2014. "Constraining Consolidation: Military Politics and Democracy in Pakistan (2007–2013)." *Democratization* 21 (6): 1007–1033.

Shakoor, F. 1997. "Recasting Pakistan-India Relations in the Post-Cold War Era." *Pakistan Horizon* 50 (4): 86–87.

Siddiqa, A. 2007. *Military Inc. Inside Pakistan's Military Economy*. Pluto Press.

Siddiqa, A. 2011. "Pakistan's Counterterrorism Strategy: Separating Friends from Enemies." *The Washington Quarterly* 34 (1): 149–162.

Siddiqa, A. 2017. "How the Military in Pakistan Influences the Country's Media." *The Carvan, New Delhi*, April 9, 2017. Retrieved on November 25, 2018 http://www.cara vanmagazine.in/vantage/military-pakistan-influences-countrys-media.

Sune Engel Rasmussen, 2017. "Musharraf Declared Fugitive as Bhutto Murder Trial Ends in Pakistan." *The Guardian*, August 31, Retrieved on December 11, 2018, https://www .theguardian.com/world/2017/aug/31/pakistan-benazir-bhutto-two-jailed.

Travis, T. A. 1994. "Advantages and Disadvantages for Pakistan in the Post-Cold War World." *Pakistan Horizon* 47 (3): 35–53.

Wirsing, R. G. 2010. "Pakistan's Security in the 'New World Order': Going from Bad to Worse?" *Asian Affairs: An American View* 23 (2): 101–126.

Wynbrandt, J. 2008. *A Brief History of Pakistan*. Checkmark Books.

Yasmeen, S. 1994. "Democracy in Pakistan: The Third Dismissal." *Asian Survey* 34 (6): 572–588.

Yilmaz, M. E. 2007. "Intra-state Conflict in the Post-Cold War Era." *International Journal on World Peace* 24 (4): 12.

Yousaf, M. and Adkin, M. 1992. *The Bear Trap: Afghanistan's Untold Story*. Leo Cooper.

Yusuf, H. 2011. "Conspiracy Fever: The US, Pakistan and Its Media." *Survival* 53 (4): 95–118.

Zaidi, S. A. 2011. "Is Pakistan Collapsing?" *Economic and Political Weekly* 46 (25): 16–20.

4 The long shadow of Pakistan's military-centred national security approach

The case of the Kashmir dispute 1989–2001

The Kashmir conflict has been one of the longest unresolved military conflicts in the contemporary world. In January 1949, the first India-Pakistan war over Kashmir conflict ended with a UN-mandated ceasefire under chapter 6 of the UN security council resolution. The resolution recommended the restoration of law and order in Jammu and Kashmir and conducting a free and impartial plebiscite under UN supervision (Appendix 12). Since then, Pakistan continued to emphasize that the Kashmir conflict could be resolved under the supervision of UN administrators. However, a plebiscite over Kashmir never materialized despite many UN security council resolutions (Shankar 2016). As a result, it is generally believed in Pakistan that the Kashmir conflict could not be resolved through diplomatic means due to a lack of actions on the UN resolutions over Kashmir. This narrative served the military institutional interests and provided justification to use proxy militant groups and conduct direct military operations to seize Kashmir from India.

The emergence of the peace process in the 1980s

In the international system, states use both peaceful means and violent acts to resolve their outstanding conflicts. They adopt such strategies to safeguard their national interests, such as political and military concerns, as well as economic interests in the prevailing security environment (Adnan and Fatima 2016). Since its inception in 1947, Pakistan has fought three major wars and one limited war with India to resolve their outstanding issues, but has failed to find any military solution, especially to the Kashmir conflict. Pakistan lost two-thirds of Kashmir to India in the first war between the two countries. In the 1971 war, Pakistan lost to India its eastern part, which became Bangladesh. The Kashmir dispute was the major issue between the two countries and remained at the top of the agenda in bilateral relations until the 1971 war. Afterwards, the Pakistani military realized that they could not defeat the strong Indian military power in order to take control of Kashmir (Kapur 2005). In July 1972, a conference was held in Shimla where both countries pledged to resolve their outstanding issues including Kashmir peacefully. They principally agreed on the following points (Appendix 6):

- A mutual commitment to the peaceful resolution of all issues through direct bilateral approaches.
- To build the foundations of a cooperative relationship with special focus on people-to-people contacts.
- To uphold the inviolability of the "Line of Control" in Jammu and Kashmir, which is the most important confidence-building measure (CBM) between India and Pakistan and the key to a durable peace.

Since then, Pakistan has avoided direct confrontation with India and instead has adopted various other foreign policy initiatives to counter Indian dominance in South Asia. India also showed maximum restraint policy until Pulwama terror attack in February 2019.

In the 1980s, India and Pakistan began talks on various issues, including talks conducted at Siachen, Sir Creek, and the Tulbul-Wullar. In this peace process, there was no compulsion on either side to continue the peace process (Misra 2007). So there was limited progress in the peace talks, especially over the issue of Kashmir during the 1980s. Nonetheless, both sides were optimistic in 1988–1989 that the fresh political leadership of Benazir Bhutto in Pakistan and Rajiv Gandhi in India would be able to find a peaceful political solution to the outstanding issues and would begin a new era of Pakistan-India relations. More specifically, both sides showed political will, which was seen as a crucial factor in the resolution of the issues. Unlike the leadership of General Zia, India trusted the civilian leadership under Bhutto and believed that they could move forward and resolve the issues that had been outstanding since Independence in 1947. However, this India-Pakistan rapprochement was part of General Zia's "cricket diplomacy," which he started during his tenure. Moreover, the peace talks were taken due to international pressure, especially from the US in the context of the Soviet withdrawal from Afghanistan (Ejaz Hussain, interview by author, Islamabad, 14 November 2017).

Indian premier Rajiv Gandhi visited Islamabad to attend the fourth SAARC summit in December 1988. It was the first official visit of an Indian prime minister to Pakistan in 28 years (Burki 1999). The primary objective was to progress and change the stagnating relationship between the two countries. According to an Indian official commenting on Gandhi's visit, "I think you will find that we will move things forward in these two days more than we have in the past eleven years of General Zia" (*Los Angeles Times*, 31 December 1988). Therefore, there were high hopes and optimism that the peace talks would be the dawn of a new era for the relationship between the two countries. After the SAARC summit, Gandhi had a detailed meeting with Bhutto and discussed various issues of bilateral interest. At the meeting, they approved three agreements: non-attack on nuclear facilities on both sides, cultural cooperation, and avoidance of double taxation. India agreed to withdraw its opposition to Pakistan's readmission in the Commonwealth which it had left in protest in 1972 after the Commonwealth's recognition of Bangladesh as an independent state. Pakistan rejoined the Commonwealth in September 1989 (Rizvi 1993). According to media reports (Aziz, *Dawn*, Pakistan, 16 August 2016), "Rajiv Gandhi's visit to Pakistan in 1988 was heralded by Benazir Bhutto as a historic departure from over 40 years of hostility." On the other hand, Gandhi was convinced that the policies of Bhutto would be much better compared to those of General Zia's 11 years of dictatorship (Jain 1988).

Rajiv Gandhi made a very successful visit to China in December 1989. During his visit, India and China agreed to improve and develop neighbourly relations and resolve their territorial disputes peacefully (Ministry of Foreign Affairs of China site, retrieved: 24 June 2017). As a result, the India-China border tension eased after Gandhi's visit. Convinced that bilateral issues could be resolved peacefully, Gandhi made another visit to Pakistan within just six months. The primary objective was to take concrete steps to resolve the outstanding issues with Pakistan. At the meeting, Bhutto and Gandhi approved the accord on Siachen which had earlier been agreed at the defence secretary level meeting, in June 1989. Under the agreement, both countries would redeploy their forces, according to the provisions of the 1972 Shimla agreement. The joint statement issued after the meeting said (Aziz, *Dawn*, Pakistan, 21 August 2016):

> There was agreement by both sides to work towards a comprehensive settlement, based on redeployment of forces to reduce the chances of conflict, avoidance of the use of force and determination of future positions on the ground so as to conform with the Shimla Agreement and to ensure durable peace in the Siachen area. The army authorities on both sides will determine the positions.

The settlement of the Siachen conflict was important for CBM between the two usually hostile countries. In return, it would have provided an opportunity to resolve, through peaceful means, other outstanding disputes, especially Kashmir (Ahmad 2006).

From 1989, several rounds of talks were held to settle the unresolved disputes, but with little success. In May 1989, both countries pledged to take significant steps for countering terrorism, smuggling and cross-border infiltration, and drug trafficking, at the home secretary level meetings (Rizvi 1993). These agreements were key steps towards improving bilateral relations between the two countries. The Indian premier described it as a "breakthrough" in the bilateral relations, while Bhutto thought it could create a "momentum for peace and friendship" between the two countries (Jain 1988). Thus, the civilian leaders were eager to find a peaceful solution to all outstanding disputes and commence a new era of relations based on mutual interest and the welfare of their people.

Nonetheless, both leaders publicly disagreed over the core issue of Kashmir and their nuclear programmes. India publicly complained about Pakistan's involvement in the uprising in Punjab state and Indian-administered Kashmir (Rizvi 1993). Moreover, the Siachen agreement was not implemented due to differences over the redeployment of military forces by India and the ceasefire. In particular, India believed that the redeployment of troops to the positions they had held prior to 1972 could provide a strategic advantage to Pakistan. The Siachen area had been under Indian control since 1984. More specifically, the Indian military feared that China would take advantage of the redeployment in the Siachen area (Syed, *Dawn*, Pakistan, 14 April 2012). Despite disagreement over the core issues, the initiative to start the peace process did signal CBMs, with the intention to reverse the deteriorating relations between the two countries evident at the end of the Cold War.

However, the Kashmir crisis began at the end of 1989 when various groups started demonstrations demanding "right to self-determination" in Indian-administered Kashmir. The issue of Kashmir once again plagued relations between the two countries. India accused the Pakistani military of supporting the uprising in Kashmir, whereas Pakistan said that its support was only moral and diplomatic. Consequently, the Kashmir uprising interrupted the peace initiatives and the attempts to normalize the relations between the two countries.

The Kashmir uprising: interruption of the peace process

In March 1987, a state election was held in Indian-administered Kashmir. The Islamist political parties formed an alliance known as the Muslim United Front (MUF) prior to the election. The MUF comprised 13 parties, led by Kashmir-based Jamat-i-Islami (Mahadevan 2009). Before the election, the Indian intelligence agencies estimated that the MUF would win at least ten seats. The pro-India National Conference (NC) party won 66 of the 75 seats, while the MUF won just 4 seats in the election. The voter turnout was 75 percent, which was the highest ever recorded in Kashmir. Widespread cases of election rigging, irregularities, and mismanagement were reported to have taken place. Many MUF leaders were arrested before the election in Kashmir and on election day, the polling agents of MUF were thrown out of the polling stations during the counting, where they had strong support and "vote-bank." The rigging of state elections further alienated Kashmiri youth from the Indian state, and this closed off avenues for legitimate political activities in the Kashmir valley (Schofield 2010).

In this situation, the MUF felt dissatisfied by the political process in India and opted for an uprising following the election. The MUF called for protests and demonstrations against the Indian administration. Some activists also attempted to target Kashmir Chief Minister Farooq Abdullah on his way to his office in May 1987 (Sattar 2010). There was a series of demonstrations and strikes, and even a small number of attacks on government officials, throughout 1988. People from all walks of life participated in the demonstrations. However, the New Delhi administration did not take notice of the protests. The MUF said that "the manipulation of election results disappointed the Kashmiris. We were trying to change the political framework by democratic and peaceful method[s], but we have failed in this. Therefore, we should take up the gun" (Schofield 2010). Sumit Ganguly (1996), a prominent expert on South Asian politics, explains:

The early decay of political institutions in Kashmir, which the government in New Delhi did little to stem [and in some cases encouraged], and the dramatic pace of political mobilization proved to be a combustible mix, driving Kashmiris to the armed rebellion that they had previously rejected.

According to the former Pakistani Ambassador to India, Ashraf Jahangir Qazi (interview by author, Islamabad, 19 November 2017),

The fundamental issue of Kashmir is not a problem of Pakistani interference, fundamentalism and/or terrorism there, those are developments which [have] taken place as a result of the fundamental problem which is the Indian occupation of Kashmir in defiance of UN resolution over Kashmir, human rights and political rise of the Kashmiri people who are quite obviously not willing to be part of India, particularly in the Kashmir valley.

On Pakistan's involvement in the 1990 Kashmir uprising, the former ISI Chief General Asad Durani (interview by author, Islamabad, 22 November 2017) said that:

The Kashmir uprising caught us by surprise. We did not know what happened and why suddenly there was unrest. Later, we found out that it was mostly the youth, educated but unemployed. They were expressing their dissatisfaction with India and this is essentially the cause of the Kashmir unrest. But it was not because of the Afghan mujahedeen or any other Islamists in the uprising.

The Kashmir conflict was basically an internal uprising against India, but it has provided an opportunity for the Pakistani military elite to use the pro-Pakistani Islamists to gain public support in the Kashmir valley. In the beginning, it appeared to be more a case of an indigenous movement striving for *Azadi* (liberation or independence) from India by engaging in protests and other related political activities. However, it was transformed into an armed uprising for the independence of Kashmir. The frequency of violent attacks increased at the end of 1989, and they had become a regular phenomenon in 1990. India accused Pakistan of sponsoring militancy in Kashmir and said that Pakistan had trained 20,000 militants to increase terrorist activities in Indian-administered Kashmir (Gul 2007). India claimed that the ISI was providing training and weapons to armed militant groups in Kashmir. General Vishwa Nath Sharma, the then Indian army's chief, expressed his concerns (Ganguly and Hagerty 2006, 90):

Terrorist groups backed by Pakistani agencies were able to attack railway stations and vital installations which could affect any military movement on our side. Therefore, there was [a] need for the Indian army to go in there to take care of the communication lines and other bottlenecks so that if there was a military flare-up, we could conveniently move our fighting forces from locations deep in the country to the border areas.

The Pakistani government rejected such accusations and said that it was an indigenous movement for the liberation of Kashmir and they would continue their moral and diplomatic support for it. Nonetheless, Pakistani support for the Kashmiri uprising was more than moral support. According to Shabana Feyyaz (interview by author, Islamabad, 20 November 2017), "moral support to [the] Kashmir cause is one thing, but Pakistan provided men, material and minds as well."

The Kashmir uprising was mainly led by the Jammu and Kashmir Liberation Front (JKLF) and Hizbul Mujahideen (HM or Party of Holy Warriors). The JKLF was the core secessionist movement demanding a sovereign and secular united Kashmir, composed of all parts of Kashmir prior to the partition of 1947 (Anant 2009). The JKLF was an umbrella outfit comprising the Jammu and Kashmir Students' Liberation Front, the People's League, the People's Conference, and Al Jihad. On the other hand, HM sought the unification of Kashmir with Pakistan. HM was the military wing of Kashmir-based JI, and the groups that allied with it included the Muslim Students' Federation, the Allah Tigers, the Islamic Student's League, and the Dukhtaran-e-Milat (Daughters of Islam). Another group, Operation Balakote, sought to form a united front comprising the JKLF and HM for the liberation of Kashmir from Indian occupation. Despite their differences, these groups worked together and supported each other's calls for strikes and demonstrations in 1989 (Tremblay 1995). Nonetheless, these groups apparently lacked a clear agenda for independence and thought that the increase in state violence would justify their struggle of liberation to the international community. This would gain recognition for their movement as fighting for a "just cause" and put pressure on India to abandon the Kashmir valley. However, there was no long-term strategy for the liberation of Kashmir (Schofield 2010).

Later in the 1990s, many groups both local and international joined the Kashmiri insurgency, including *Harkat-ul-Jihad al-Islami* (Islamic Struggle Movement); *Jaish-e-Mohammed* (JeM or Army of Muhammad); *Harkat-ul-Mujahideen* (Movement of Holy Warriors); *Al-Badr* (Full Moon); and *Lashkar-e-Taiba* (LeT or Army of the Righteous) (Snedden 2015). These groups were also pro-Pakistani and wanted the unification of Kashmir with Pakistan.

In 1989, the Kashmir militant groups adopted a fourfold strategy to mobilize the general public in support of the demands of the *Azadi* movement. The strategy consisted of regular strikes; targeting government officials, police informers, and security forces; forcing NC party members to publicly withdrew their affiliation with the party; and boycotting the Lok Sabha (state assembly) election in order to delegitimize the Kashmir state government (Tremblay 1995). The strikes that started across Kashmir in January 1989 continued for the whole year. They involved students, doctors, lawyers, teachers, and other civil society activists.

Furthermore, the separatist groups used violent tactics to neutralize the ruling NC party in Kashmir and ensured no public demonstration took place in support of the ruling party. While daily demonstrations demanding the "right to self-determination" continued in the Kashmir valley, the uprising intensified at the end of 1989 when the number of violent attacks in the valley increased. The militants targeted government officials, security forces, and Hindu pundits in Jammu and

Kashmir. In September 1989, militants killed a prominent Kashmiri politician of the Bharatiya Janata Party (BJP) and in December kidnapped the daughter of the Federal Home Minister Mufti Muhammad Saeed. She was released when the Indian government agreed to release prominent militant commanders in exchange (Sattar 2010). The supporters of NC were also forced to resign from the party and asked to publish their resignations in local newspapers under the title "Declaration of Disassociation." This completely disabled the political and civil administration in the Kashmir valley.

In addition, the separatists started celebrating all events related to Islam and Pakistan's independence. However, they observed complete shutdown strikes when days and/or events related to India were commemorated, such as Republic Day and Independence Day in Kashmir (Tremblay 2009). The "Indian republic day" on 26 January 1990 was observed as a "black day," and it was for the first time the Indian flag was not hoisted (Schofield 2010). In this situation, another election was held in Kashmir in 1989, and it was boycotted by the separatist groups. The voter turnout for the Kashmir state election was a mere 4 percent (Tremblay 2009). It was a victory for the separatist groups, which meant that the government lacked the credibility to run the administration of Kashmir state.

In response to the Kashmir uprising, India appointed Jagmohan Malhotra as Governor of Kashmir for the second time in January 1990. The chief minister, Farooq Abdullah, resigned in protest due to differences with Jagmohan. Farooq Abdullah said that "he could not cooperate with a man who hates the guts of the Muslims" (Schofield 2010). After taking office, Jagmohan had a one-point agenda to restore the state's authority by any means and used a heavy hand against protesters and supporters of separatist organizations. He dissolved the Kashmir state assembly in February 1990, explaining that it was necessary to stop political interference in state affairs. The security forces were given a free hand to crush the demonstration and the armed insurgency that broke out after the sacking of the state assembly (Schofield 2010). Moreover, Jagmohan ordered Lieutenant-General Mohammed Ahmed Zaki, commander of the Indian army's 15 Corps, to ensure the government's writ was upheld in the state at any cost (Swami 2006). Jagmohan (1991, 518–519) pointed out:

> Our first and foremost objective was to assert the authority of the state ... no matter what the costs, no matter what the sacrifices. Our resolve, our will, had to be made clear ... It had ... to be conveyed to all concerned, in no uncertain terms, that ... no soft underbelly of the state would be offered to punch or fool with.

This policy of repression had further alienated the Kashmiri people from New Delhi and militarized the Indian-administered Kashmir state.

In addition, the Indian leadership thought that it was a law and order problem in Kashmir, and it could be controlled with a large police force. Therefore, India deployed a 145,000-strong Central Reserve Police Force in Kashmir. More specifically, India passed the Armed Forces Special Power Act, providing the security forces immunity from prosecution and allowing the armed forces to use lethal force (Sattar 2010). This act gave a free hand to the security forces in Kashmir state. On 21 January 1990, Indian forces shot down unarmed protesters, killing dozens of people in what is known as the "Gaw Kadal massacre." According to Human Rights Watch, at least 35 people were killed in the massacre, but other reports estimated the death toll at around 100 (HRW report 2006). The victims were gathered for a peaceful demonstration against the state government, despite the curfew. The *Telegraph* reported that the marchers had chanted slogans such as "Indian dogs go home," "we want freedom," and "long live Islam" (*Telegraph*, 22 January 1990; Siddique 2010). Consequently, there was a complete breakdown in law and order due to continuous demonstrations and government curfews in the Jammu and Kashmir areas.

In this context, the state and militant groups used extensive violence against their opponents, which severely affected daily life in the Kashmir valley. The security forces targeted the civilian protesters, whereas the militants targeted government officials, members of the security forces, pro-government civilians, and Hindu pundits in the valley (HRW report 1999). For example, a prominent Kashmiri leader, Mirwaiz Maulvi Farooq, was killed by unknown assailants in May 1990. His funeral was attended by around 200,000 Kashmiris in Srinagar (Snedden 2015). Ironically, the Indian forces targeted the funeral procession in which more than 60 people were killed. This reinforced the perception that the Indian state was behind the assassination of Mirwaiz Farooq (Tantry, *Tribune*, India, 21 May 2015). As a consequence of continuous violence, civil disobedience, and subsequent state repression, this completely immobilized the state administration in Kashmir.

It is important to note that the use of force against the protesters was a turning point in the Kashmiri struggle for the "right to self-determination." The brutal force used by the Indian forces provided an opportunity for the separatist and/ or Islamist groups to gain further public support, which transformed anti-India protest into armed militancy (Snedden 2015). Praveen Swami (2006) pointed out that:

> For the first time since 1947 ... Jammu and Kashmir did have a genuine mass constituency for the Islamists, hostile both to the National Conference and to New Delhi. Where earlier phases of the jihad had failed precisely because of the absence of such a constituency ... the conditions now seemed right to make another attempt.

So the reappointment of Jagmohan was yet another grave mistake by the New Delhi central government in its dealings with the internal affairs of Kashmir state.

To assist the security situation in Kashmir, the Indian government formed a committee under Prime Minister Inder Kumar Gujral. The committee noted that "the placid environment of the valley is seriously disturbed and it would be a serious mistake to dismiss it as a periodical outburst or a matter than can be dealt with as a law and order problem" (Wirsing 1993). The situation was out of the control of the state administration and New Delhi decided to change its administration and imposed "Presidential Rule" in Kashmir in July 1990, at the request of the governor of Jammu and Kashmir. Girish Saxena replaced Jagmohan as the new governor in Kashmir, and India deployed regular military forces to restore the writ of the state in the Kashmir valley. The Indian military used tactics such as torture, collective punishments, and enforced disappearances throughout the 1990s (Sattar 2010). More specifically, the security forces were involved in widespread human rights violations in the valley. According to an Amnesty International report in 1992 (in Haqqani 2003):

> Widespread human rights violations in the state since January 1990 have been attributed to the Indian army, and the paramilitary Border Security Force and Central Reserve Police Force ... Cordon-and-search operations are frequently conducted in areas of armed opposition activity ... Torture is reported to be routinely used during these combing operations as well as in army camps, interrogation centers, police stations and prisons. Indiscriminate beatings are common and rape in particular appears to be routine ... In Jammu and Kashmir, rape is practiced as part of a systematic attempt to humiliate and intimidate the local population during counter-insurgency operations.

Thus, the extensive Indian military force also produced a lot of sympathy for Islamist militant groups around the world, especially in Pakistan.

For Pakistan, the outbreak of the Kashmir uprising provided a favourable situation for the Pakistani military elite to extend its national security state policies in the post-Cold War era. According to Professor Stephen P. Cohen (2004, 104–105),

> The prerequisites for people's war seemed to exist in Kashmir: a worthy cause; difficult terrain; a determined, warlike people [the Pakistanis]; a sympathetic local population [the Kashmiris]; the availability of weapons and equipment; and a high degree of leadership and discipline to prevent [the guerrillas] from degenerating into banditry.

So the ISI found an opportunity to take advantage of the deteriorating security situation in the Kashmir valley and used the domestic compulsion of Kashmir jihad instrumentally to protect its institutional interests. Subsequently, they capitalized on the worsening security situation in Kashmir and attempted to transform the spontaneous and decentralized uprising into a full-fledged insurgency against India (Kapur 2005). In fact, the Pakistani military was convinced that it was an opportunity to liberate Kashmir from India after 1971 debacle.

On the one hand, the primary strategy was to engage Indian military manpower and other military resources in internal security affairs. Consequently, it would be more difficult for India to further deploy its military along the border with Pakistan. On the other hand, Pakistan would internationalize the issue of Kashmir by highlighting Indian military atrocities at international forums. This would put political and diplomatic pressure on India to resolve the issue of Kashmir (Kapur 2016). Thus, the Kashmir uprising provided an opportunity for the Pakistani military elite to extend its military-centred national security approach in the post-Cold War era. However, the proxy war undermined the peace process adopted by the political leadership in the late 1980s.

After the 1971 war, the Pakistani military realized that it was difficult to wrest Kashmiri territory from Indian control by military means due to the latter's greater military power. However, this perception changed after the emergence of the indigenous Kashmiri uprising, and the Pakistani military elite thought they could seize Kashmir from India through an armed insurgency (Kapur 2005). The Pakistani military adopted a protracted "proxy war" in Indian-administered Kashmir. Pakistan has relied and continues to rely on proxy wars to protect its strategic interests under the national security state during and after the Cold War. Unlike in the previous wars with India, the Pakistani military decided that they would not fight a conventional war. The militants would have to confront the Indian security forces on their own. However, the Pakistani military would provide all kinds of support, such as assistance in recruitment, financial payments, and publication of their propaganda materials, as well as military backing in time of emergency (Kapur 2016).

The Kashmiri separatists and Islamists were used to fighting a '"proxy war" against the Indian security forces in Kashmir. The ISI provided extensive military aid to the Kashmiri fighters across the LoC in Indian-administered Kashmir (Hashim 1997). Many young Kashmiri militants fled to Pakistan and were trained in camps on the Pakistani side of Kashmir as well as former training facilities in areas bordering Afghanistan, which had been used by the Afghan resistance movement during the Afghan war. With the ISI's support, the JKLF was able to establish around 300 sleeper cells across Kashmir (Cohen 2004; Kapur 2016). The trained militants were sent back to the Indian side of Kashmir to increase attacks on the Indian security forces and government officials.

In addition, the Kashmir uprising began at a very crucial time when the Soviet forces left Afghanistan in February 1989. During the Soviet occupation of Afghanistan, the Pakistani military had conducted a proxy war in the form of a jihad, and this was a very cost-effective strategy to defeat the strong Soviet military forces in Afghanistan. As a consequence, the ISI believed that this was the right strategy to replicate in Kashmir to fight against an overwhelmingly superior Indian military power (Rizvi 2003; Kapur 2005). According to former DG ISI General Asad Durani (interview by author, Islamabad, 22 November 2017), "we will be foolish if we did not support the Kashmir uprising. Yes, we replicate the Afghan resistance in Kashmir only when the uprising started but it was not Pakistani mujahedeen who initiated the Kashmir uprising." In fact, Pakistan had a ready-made force of veteran Afghan mujahedeen following the Soviet withdrawal from Afghanistan. Pakistan was the epicentre of the "Afghan resistance movement," which had been used as a proxy against the Soviet forces in Afghanistan during 1979–1988 (see Chapter 2). After Soviet forces withdrew from Afghanistan, Pakistan was left alone by the US to deal with these militants who were equipped with sophisticated weapons. The ISI allowed Islamist militants to operate in Kashmir, which strengthened the Kashmiri militant groups (Taylor 2004). As a result, violence was escalated in Kashmir, which halted the India-Pakistan rapprochement adopted by Bhutto and Gandhi that radically transformed India-Pakistan relations.

Under Pakistan's national security state, the Pakistani military establishment thought that Kashmir policy was the prerogative of the military, who took the key strategic decisions in the country. Subsequently, Prime Minister Bhutto was kept out of the planning of this strategy to use a "proxy war" in Kashmir. After taking office in 1988, Bhutto called a meeting to discuss the issue of Kashmir, and she was informed by the foreign office and DG military operations General Jahangir Karamat that the military did not favour a military solution to the Kashmir conflict. Nonetheless, the Pakistani military had already started a proxy war in the valley (Nawaz 2009). So the Pakistani military kept Bhutto ignorant about the proxy war in Kashmir. Actually, the military believed that Bhutto could be a security risk due to her past history of anti-military campaigns against General Zia (Chengappa 2000). Furthermore, the culture of secrecy in proxy wars justified the Pakistani military dominant role in Kashmir policy and provided them with an opportunity to escape the civilian oversight.

When the civilian government attempted to change the Kashmir policy, the Pakistani military used religio-political parties and far-right groups to build pressure on the civilian government to support the armed uprising in Kashmir. The pro-military opposition alliance asked the government to take a hard line over the issue of Kashmir against India. Some of the opposition parties called upon the civilian government to pursue a jihad against Indian security forces in Kashmir, while others urged it to go for nuclear war against the external threat from India. Qazi Husain Ahmad, the former chief of Pakistan's JI, called in 1990 for the observing of 5 February as a "Kashmir Solidarity Day" for the success and solidarity with Kashmiri mujahedeen, while the opposition leader, Nawaz Sharif, called for complete strikes across the country in solidarity with the Kashmiris (Shaikh 2012).

Beside opposition pressure, there was also huge public support for the Kashmiri uprising against India. According to a Gallup survey in 1990, about 78 percent of Pakistanis thought that they should support the armed uprising in Kashmir by supplying arms to the separatist militant groups. On the other hand, only 12 percent disagreed with supporting the separatist groups (Tajawar, Gallup Pakistan 2016). Given the strength of public opinion and political pressure, Bhutto was publicly left with little choice but to denounce the human rights violation in Kashmir due to internal political and public pressure. Bhutto highlighted the human rights violation at international forums to increase pressurize on India to resolve the issue of Kashmir (Hagerty 1998). She also said that Pakistan could not distance itself from Kashmir and its people's struggle for the "right to self-determination" (Malik 2008). More importantly, Bhutto declared Kashmir Day on 5 February 1990 as a public holiday for solidarity with the Kashmiris' struggle for independence. Thus, the domestic compulsion of Kashmir jihad was used instrumentally by the Pakistani military elite to undermine the civilian government in the country.

In a nutshell, the Kashmir uprising provided an opportunity for the Pakistani military elite to continue its national security state policies at the end of the Cold War. In fact, the military has used the Kashmir conflict to maintain its functional dominance over the civilian government in the state affair by using far-right religious groups. Nonetheless, it had brought to a standstill the attempts to find a peaceful resolution to the outstanding issues between the two countries. Both countries accused each other of causing the unrest in Kashmir. The Gandhi-Bhutto talks ended without any major breakthrough despite the positive political will on both sides at the end of the 1980s. They pledged many accords, but these did not materialize due to the continuous hostility over Kashmir between the two countries. More importantly, it brought the two countries to the verge of another war.

The India-Pakistan crisis in the 1990s: Pakistan's proxy war in Kashmir

In the wake of the Kashmir uprising, India moved its military forces to the international border in its Rajasthan state in May 1990. The Pakistani military became worried that India would attack the railway line in its Sindh province connecting north and south Pakistan. Moreover, India increased its military forces on the LoC in Kashmir as well. The Pakistani military expected that India might attack and target the militant training camps on the Pakistani side of Kashmir (Ganguly and Hagerty 2006). In view of this situation, General Aslam Beg convened a meeting of the corps commanders to assess the prevailing security situation along the LoC and international border. According to General Beg,

> India had deployed a strike force of up to 100,000 men within fifty miles of the border in Rajasthan. They estimated that the Indian units were deployed in such a way as to halve India's normal mobilisation time to one week.
>
> (Ganguly and Hagerty 2006, 93)

General Beg ordered the military to prepare for any possible retaliation from India and moved its military forces close to the LoC. So the Kashmir conflict escalated the Pakistan-India border tension which brought the two countries near to another war.

Internationally, many feared a possible nuclear war between the two countries. US intelligence reported that "Pakistan had put together at least six and perhaps as many as ten nuclear weapons, and a number of senior analysts were convinced that some of those warheads had been deployed on Pakistan's American-made F-16 fighter planes" (Haresh, *The New Yorker*, 29 March 1993). However, India had a more advanced nuclear programme than Pakistan and was ready to counter any retaliation from outside. Robert Gates, the then US deputy national security adviser, noted that "Pakistan and India seemed to be caught in a cycle that they couldn't break out of. I was convinced that if a war started, it would be nuclear" (Charters *et al.* 1996).

In this situation, the US intervened to de-escalate the border tension between the two countries. The US used "shuttle diplomacy" to convince both states that war would not serve their interests. Gates visited both Pakistan and India. On his visit to Pakistan, Gates met President Ishaq Khan and General Beg. He warned that Pakistan would be on the losing side, and the US would not provide any military aid in the case of war with India. He also put pressure on Pakistan to stop its interference in Indian-administered Kashmir by supporting militant organizations. Similarly, Gates met with the Indian leadership and told them that India must avoid any provocation which might escalate things beyond their control. The US conveyed to both states that war was in neither side's interests. As a result of US efforts, the India-Pakistan tension de-escalated, and the two sides agreed to start a dialogue at foreign secretary level to resolve their outstanding disputes, including Kashmir (Hagerty 1995–1996). The US had played a key role in the Kashmir conflict management by reducing the tension between the two countries.

The 1990 crisis ended without a conventional or nuclear war between the two countries. However, Pakistan continued its proxy war in Kashmir. They were convinced that India would not retaliate, due to its fear of a nuclear war (Cohen and Dasgupta 2010). Initially, the ISI supported JKLF as a core militant organization, providing them with covert military aid in Pakistan-administered Kashmir and the Pakistan-Afghan border areas. The ISI supplied sophisticated weapons to JKLF to target Indian security forces, Hindu pundits, government officials, and institutions in Indian-administered Kashmir (Kapur 2016).

However, there were major differences between the ISI and JKLF at the ideological and strategic levels. In his book, S. Paul Kapur has pointed out four major differences between the JKLF and the Pakistani military establishment. Firstly, the JKLF held a secularist ideology and were fighting for their democratic rights, such as the right to self-determination, rather than the pursuit of religious goals. Nonetheless, the group remained largely secular despite being involved in religiously motivated violence in Kashmir. Secondly, the JKLF was a genuinely nationalist organization and was fighting for an independent Kashmir rather than to join Pakistan. More importantly, the united independent Kashmir they hoped for would include Pakistan-administered Kashmir and its northern areas. Thirdly, the group lacked the operational capabilities to carry out successful attacks. Because the JKLF fighters were not hard-core militants, they were unable to use extensive violence in the Kashmir valley. Finally, the JKLF did not allow the ISI to fully control its organization and acted more independently (Kapur 2016). The ISI was at odds with JKLF's secular ideology and its standing for the independence of a united Kashmir. The ISI put pressure on JKLF to downplay this ideology and its pro-independence stance. In 1993, as a consequence, the ISI stopped military aid to JKLF, but continued its support of other separatist militant groups (Snedden 2015).

In the meantime, the ISI was looking for a Kashmiri militant group that could be politically amenable and serve their strategic interests, particularly in Kashmir but also generally in South Asia. Therefore, the ISI turned to Hizbul Mujahideen as they were considered pro-Pakistan and wanted the unification of Kashmir with Pakistan. As a result, the JKLF was replaced by the HM. The latter had received considerable logistic and financial support from the ISI and remained the most influential group throughout the 1990s. More importantly, there was a significant increase in the number of attacks after HM took over as the leading militant group. For instance, the number of attacks increased from 3,700 in 1991 to more than 5,800 in 1995 (Kapur 2016). However, the main problem with HM was that it was a largely indigenous Kashmiri movement, and its major concerns were the welfare of its people. It was also reluctant to engage in extensive violence in Kashmir where the chances of civilian casualties were high. Moreover, the HM's leaders were willing to compromise with the Indian government in return for personal and collective benefits. The HM commander, Abdul Majid Dar, renounced violence and struck a ceasefire deal with the Indian government in 2000 despite ISI opposition. Dar was a very influential commander and encouraged many separatist groups to resolve their differences with New Delhi. Consequently, Pakistan reduced its support for the HM in the late 1990s (Popovic 2014; Kapur 2016).

In this situation, the Pakistani military changed its strategy of proxy war and recruited non-Kashmiri militants to promote its agenda in Kashmir. The non-Kashmiri militants were not concerned with the consequences of the insurgency on the general public in Kashmir. Also, they would not compromise with India and would use extensive violence in the valley. These non-Kashmiri fighters were veteran Afghan mujahedeen who had fought against Soviet forces. The groups, who recruited foreign fighters, included LeT, JeM, al-Jihad, al Omar, Harkat-ul-Ansar, and the Ikhwanul Muslimeen. The ISI provided extensive military, financial, and logistical support to these groups. In these groups, the LeT doctrine of jihad was closer to the ISI's agenda for Kashmir and South Asia. For instance, the LeT's goal was the separation of Kashmir by means of a long-term jihad against Hindu India. Unlike the other militant groups, the ISI thought the LeT would not compromise with India and would continue its militant struggle against India. As a result, LeT became the Pakistani military's favourite militant group comprising non-Kashmiri veteran mujahedeen who had fought against the Soviet Union in Afghanistan (Kapur 2016). It was believed that the LeT would best serve Islamabad's strategic interests in South Asia and would not retaliate against the Pakistani state.

The Pakistani strategy of a proxy war was very effective, but only in the short term. The ISI was successful in engaging the Indian military in the Kashmir conflict and draining its military resources. For example, the Kashmir militancy imposed a substantial financial cost on India, greater than the combined cost of the three earlier full-scale wars with Pakistan (Hashim 1997). Moreover, excessive use of force by the Indian armed forces resulted in human rights violations in Kashmir. It gave an opportunity for Pakistan to propagate reports of human rights abuses by Indian forces to gain diplomatic support for its Kashmir cause (Hoyt 2003). In May 1993, the OIC voted for sanctions against India due to human rights violations in Kashmir. The British Labour Party also raised the Kashmir issue in the parliament and asked the government to put pressure on India to give Kashmiris their "right to self-determination" under UN supervision (R. Ganguly 1998). Thus, the escalation of violence kept the Kashmir issue to the fore globally in the early 1990s, and Pakistan achieved relative success at the international level. More importantly, the proxy war provided a dominant role to the Pakistani military in key strategic decision making in the post-Cold War era.

In 1996, India changed its counter-insurgency approach to normalize the situation in Kashmir. The Indian military used a heavy hand against the militants, but at the same time tried to win the support of the general public by reducing civilian casualties and human rights violations (Schofield 2010). The military carried out targeted operations based on intelligence gathered from captured militants. It was a very effective tactic which neutralized the militants' operational capabilities and countered their attacks. Consequently, the security situation gradually improved in Kashmir (Dhakal 2014). Prior to reforming its counter-insurgency approach, India began a reconciliation campaign and released many prominent political and militant leaders, including Syed Ali Shah Gilani of JI, Abdul Ghani Lone of the People's Conference, Professor Abdul Ghani Butt of the Muslim Conference, and Mulvi Abbas Ansari of the Liberation Council (Jaleel, *The Indian Express*, 31 August 2015). This meant to create an environment for political reconciliation with rebel groups in order to quit violence and reintegrate into mainstream society.

After their release from jail, they formed the All Parties Hurriyat Conference (APHC) in July 1993, and Mirwaiz Omar Farooq became its chairman. The APHC comprised 26 political, religious, and social groups. It was recognized by separatist groups and Indian armed forces. The primary demand of the APHC was to resolve the Kashmir dispute according to the wishes and aspirations of the people of Kashmir (Jaleel, *The Indian Express*, 31 August 2015). The APHC also provided a political platform for the insurgents. Nonetheless, the APHC disassociated themselves from violence and militancy. Furthermore, India was successful in reaching a ceasefire deal with JKLF, which was the core secessionist group. Yasin Malik, the then-current chief of JKLF, declared an indefinite ceasefire with the Indian government and denounced the violent struggle for Kashmir independence after being released from jail in 1994. As a result, the JKLF adopted the democratic struggle for the liberation of Kashmir (Bose 2005). Moreover, the APHC leader Omar Farooq, in an interview in London in 1995 (Schofield 2010, 201–202), said:

> We want the Kashmiri Pandits to return and we feel that the battle has to be fought on political grounds. We know conflict and relations with Afghanistan. We know that the gun cannot really be the answer to the problem. It introduced the Kashmiri issue at the international level, by bringing it out of cold storage into the limelight, but now it is the job of the political leaders to work for the movement.

This was a political turning point in the Kashmiri struggle for freedom. In 1996, the Pakistani army's assessment was that "Kashmiris were tending to stay away from the insurgency and tending to return to their normal lives" (Zehra 2018, 89). Therefore, an environment was created conducive to the conduction of elections in the Kashmir valley which would provide legitimacy to the Indian administration in the valley. New Delhi would convince the international community that most of the people supported the political process and that there was no demand for the "right to self-determination" in Indian-administered Kashmir (Schofield 2010). In May 1996, a national election was arranged in Kashmir, the first in almost a decade, for which a 35–45 percent voter turnout was reported. The national election was followed by a Kashmir state election in September 1996. Despite an election boycott by the militant groups, voter turnout was about 53 percent, which was not much less than the overall national turnout of 57 percent in India (R. Ganguly 1998). The election was won by the NC, led by Farooq Abdullah, a prominent Kashmiri leader and a close ally of India. It was a great achievement for New Delhi to successfully organize elections in the restive Kashmir valley. However, many voters claimed that the military forced them to cast their votes (Dhakal 2014).

The 1996 elections were considered a new beginning for Kashmir, and New Delhi was very optimistic for peace and stability in the valley. After forming a government in Kashmir, Farooq Abdullah continued the reconciliation process with various separatist groups. Muhammad Yousuf Paarray, a former militant commander, won a seat in the state election and worked closely with the Indian security forces. The induction of Yousuf into the political process had encouraged many militants to surrender and work with the government (Dhakal 2014). Thus, the Indian government was successful in providing some form of legitimacy to the government in Kashmir. This led to further improvement in the security situation after the mid-1990s.

Subsequently, India allowed foreign reporters and dignitaries to visit Kashmir. India claimed that militants trained by Pakistan were involved in human rights violations in the valley. More specifically, the main issue in Kashmir was terrorism from across the border in Pakistan. Over time, India convinced the international community that the main issue was terrorism in the Kashmir valley. In the late 1990s, Pakistan lost diplomatic support over Kashmir at the international level. Moreover, Pakistan's close allies adopted a neutral position over Kashmir. China, Islamabad's most trusted friend, adopted a neutral stance on Kashmir after adopting a policy of rapprochement with India. China was worried about the Muslim uprising in its Xinjiang autonomous region. Former Chinese President Ziang Zemin, during his visit to South Asia in November 1996, advised both Pakistan and India to resolve their issues bilaterally (R. Ganguly 1998). China's stance over Kashmir was a great strategic setback for Pakistan's diplomacy at the global level.

Thus, the proxy war adopted by Pakistan under its military-centric national security approach was unsuccessful in providing the desired results. India was successful in their counter-insurgency approach, and many prominent pro-Pakistani militant commanders denounced violence and struck peace deals with the Indian government. More importantly, Pakistan lost international diplomatic support on the Kashmir issue in the wake of the proxy war. More importantly, the Indian narrative over the Kashmir conflict prevailed, as India successfully connected the Kashmir conflict with the global jihad in the wake of the 9/11 terror attacks (Khuram Iqbal, interview by author, Islamabad, 8 November 2017).

The faltering India-Pakistan peace process in the 1990s

After the end of the 1990 Kashmir crisis, the peace talks were resumed at foreign secretary level due to international pressure, especially from the US. Pakistan started negotiations with India to resolve all outstanding issues, including Kashmir, but at the same time continued with its proxy war. On its part, India was reluctant to include Kashmir on the agenda of peace talks and used brutal military force to suppress the Kashmir uprising in the 1990s (Misra 2007). Despite continued hostility, the civilian leadership on both sides attempted to normalize their relationship through peaceful means. However, the peace process was suspended many times due to lack of political will, mistrust, skirmishes on the LoC, terrorist incidents, and political instability in Pakistan in the post-Cold War era. Four rounds of talks were held between 1990 and 1994 during which many accords were signed. There was a three-year deadlock in the peace process, which resumed in 1997 but was suspended after the Pakistani military intrusion into the Kargil area in Kashmir along the LoC in May 1999 (Gul 2007). The peace dialogues were thus thwarted by the Pakistani military using proxy war strategies which it considered necessary for maintaining national security.

In July 1990, the foreign secretaries of both countries met to discuss various bilateral issues between the two countries. It was a welcome sign that both countries agreed to resolve their outstanding issues peacefully at the end of the Kashmir crisis. Considerable progress was made in the second round of talks held at New Delhi in August 1990. There were two draft agreements relating to the non-violation of each other's airspace within 10 km of the border, and the giving of advance warning of troop movements involving 10,000 troops in specific locations. During the third round of talks, in Islamabad, the two countries also agreed in December 1990 on not to attack each other's nuclear facilities, as discussed in an earlier section (Gul 2007). These were significant initiatives by both countries towards confidence building and the avoidance of military confrontation.

However, the talks did not provide solutions to outstanding issues such as Kashmir. India was reluctant to discuss Kashmir and accused Pakistan of supporting separatist groups in Kashmir and sponsoring terrorism in neighbouring countries. Pakistan denied playing any role in the Kashmir uprising other than to provide moral and diplomatic support to the Kashmiris' struggle for independence. Moreover, Pakistan raised the issue at global forums, which India viewed as a violation of the 1972 Shimla agreement. Moreover, the peace process was thwarted by subsequent terrorist attacks and political violence in India. In December 1992, Hindu extremists demolished the old Babri mosque in Ayodhya in India, and then in March 1993, the Mumbai terrorist attacks took place, in which more than 250 people died. These events aggravated the relationship, increasing suspicion and mistrust between the two countries. Pakistan extended its full cooperation to the investigation of the terror attacks but India suspected its involvement and subsequently tried at a global level to declare Pakistan a terrorist-sponsoring state (Javaid and Kamal 2013). In November 1993, the siege of the Hazratbal shrine in Kashmir further damaged the peace process and reversed the gains made by the peace talks between the two countries. According to the Indian army chief, General Bipin Chandra Joshi, "the ISI was responsible for the siege of Hazaratbal shrine," while the Indian premier Narasimha Rao said that "unless Pakistan stopped [aiding] and abetting militancy against India, there was no possibility to improve relations with Pakistan" (Jain 1988, 107–108). As a result, the possibility of dialogue over Kashmir and cooperation on nuclear matters ended without any breakthrough after such attacks.

In October 1993, Benazir Bhutto, in her second term as prime minister, wanted to renew the peace talks with India; they resumed in January 1994. Paradoxically, Bhutto took a very vocal stance over the issue of Kashmir due to Pakistani military pressure but at the same time sought to normalize Pakistan's relations with India, in response to US pressure. The dialogue ended with a deadlock as India was reluctant to include Kashmir on the agenda whereas Pakistan was not ready to hold peace talks without discussing the Kashmir dispute. India continued to blame Pakistan for the Mumbai terror attack and closed its Mumbai consulate. In response, Pakistan asked India to wind up its consulate in Karachi (Gul 2007). As a result, the peace process was stalled between the two countries for around three years.

Both countries attempted to resume the peace process in 1996. Inder Kumar Gujral, the then Indian prime minister, was a visionary leader, and he thought that relations between the two countries would improve if they started talks on all outstanding issues, including Kashmir (Misra 2007). Moreover, Nawaz Sharif became prime minister of Pakistan for the second time, winning an absolute majority in the parliamentary elections. Unlike previous coalition governments, the Indian leadership thought Sharif had a clear public mandate and would take bold steps to resolve all the outstanding issues. This compelled Gujral to recommence the peace process between the two countries. At the SAARC summit in Male, Sharif met with his Indian counterpart Gujral to discuss issues of bilateral interest in May 1997. The agenda of the peace talks included: "peace and security; the Jammu and Kashmir issue; Siachen; the Wullar Barrage/Tulbul Navigation Project; Sir Creek; terrorism and drug trafficking; economic and commercial cooperation; and the promotion of friendly exchanges in various fields" (Adnan and Fatima 2016). It was a diplomatic victory for Pakistan that Kashmir was on the agenda of these peace talks. The two countries also met at the UN General Assembly session in September 1997. However, both meetings ended without any significant progress being made on the major issues.

It is important to note that the peace process resumed due to internal and external pressure on both Pakistan and India. At the international level, Pakistan was isolated due to its proxy war in Afghanistan and Kashmir. More specifically, the US threatened to list Pakistan as a terrorist-sponsoring state if Pakistan were to continue its proxy wars (Grenier 2015). Moreover, economic growth had declined and there were major cuts in government spending, which were even felt in Pakistan's defence expenditure. Therefore, the domestic and international situation compelled Islamabad to engage in a peace process with India. Consequently, the Pakistani military establishment gave its approval to the civilian leadership to start negotiations with India, but warned them not to compromise over Pakistan's principal stand over Kashmir by providing moral and diplomatic support to the Kashmiris; it felt the conflict should be resolved under a UN resolution. On the other side, India wanted direct dialogue with Pakistan in order to remove the Pakistani factor from India-US relations. In the past, the Pakistani factor was dominant in India-US relations due to Pakistan's alliance with the US. Above all, there was not much international pressure on India to resolve the issue of Kashmir first without discussing other bilateral issues (Shakoor 1997). Hence, the bilateral relations between the two countries formally resumed in 1997.

Three rounds of talks were held in New Delhi and Islamabad to identify issues of bilateral interest. However, each side emphasized for divergent issues on the proposed agenda. For Pakistan, it would be very difficult to move forward with other issues without discussing the question of Kashmir. Sharif clarified in his letter to his Indian counterpart that "without some progress on the core issue of Jammu and Kashmir, it will be difficult to initiate cooperation in economic and cultural fields" (Shakoor 1997, 87). India emphasized a step-by-step approach in bilateral relations to resolve all the outstanding issues, setting the Kashmir issue aside. India was more interested in economic and cultural relations and people-to-people contact. The apparent priority of India was to promote economically driven relations instead of focussing on political disputes. Thus, the two sides had divergent motives for resuming talks. However, they did meet at the UN General Assembly session, where the two leaders agreed to reopen the bus link between New Delhi and Lahore and resume dialogue between the two countries.

In March 1998, Atal Bihari Vajpayee became prime minister of India for the second time. After taking office, Vajpayee realized that some concessions were necessary to resolve all the outstanding issues with Pakistan. Unlike other Indian leaders, he took some very bold steps to avoid confrontation with Islamabad. His vision was that war was not an option for resolving differences between the two countries (Layaslalu 2017). The formal diplomatic engagement resumed when he wrote a letter to Nawaz Sharif in June 1998. The Indian premier reiterated his country's commitment to a peaceful relationship between the two countries. Sharif accepted Vajpayee's invitation to meet at the tenth SAARC summit in Colombo in July 1998. Their meeting concluded without any progress as Islamabad wanted to focus on Kashmir, whereas India was more interested in discussing other bilateral issues of interest (Wheeler 2018). So the first few interactions between the two civilian governments after the resumption of talks produced little progress.

In February 1999, Indian premier Vajpayee visited Lahore to begin yet again a new era of cooperation. Prime Minister Sharif invited both the Pakistani political and military leadership to attend the reception welcoming the Indian premier at the Wagah border crossing near Lahore. However, General Musharraf, the then COAS, and other senior military officials refused to attend the reception. Actually, the Pakistani military was sceptical about Vajpayee's visit to Pakistan as Kashmir was not included in the original draft of the "Lahore Summit." However, it was added on the Pakistani army's insistence (Cohen 2004). Thus, the military leadership undermined Sharif's diplomatic efforts to normalize relations between the two countries by using the Kashmir issue.

Against this backdrop, Vajpayee made a symbolic visit to Minar-i-Pakistan, the nation's monument and birthplace. No Indian premier had ever visited Minar-i-Pakistan prior to Vajpayee, and this was India's reassurance that it had accepted Pakistan's independence and territorial integrity. Senator Mushahid Hussian accompanied Vajpayee to the Pakistan monument. He said (interview by author, Islamabad, 8 December 2017):

> I told to Vajpayee that sir you are going to do a great job. Vajpayee replied that I want to give a message to the people of Pakistan that we accept the national sovereignty and territorial integrity of Pakistan. Nonetheless, I know that there will be a massive criticism on me back home in India.

Despite the backlash, Vajpayee took this step for the peace and stability of the South Asian region. Moreover, he wrote in the visitor book that "India is for a united, stable, and prosperous Pakistan" (Wheeler 2018). Furthermore, the two countries signed the "Lahore Declaration" which stated that all the outstanding disputes between the two states should be settled peacefully (Appendix 7). This created a very good environment for the resolution of outstanding issues between the two countries. The political leadership on both sides showed their intent to solve their bilateral issues, including Kashmir. Like in 1988–1989, there was once again a political willingness on both sides to adopt a moderate stance over Kashmir. Both countries also emphasized people-to-people contact and agreed to explore "back channel diplomacy"[1] on Kashmir (Layaslalu 2017). Thus, the visit of Vajpayee provided the basis for a new beginning to resolve all the outstanding issues, including Kashmir.

For the back-channel diplomacy, Vajpayee appointed R. K. Misra, a prominent Indian journalist and publisher, and Sharif chose Niaz Niak, a retired diplomat. A series of secret talks was started in May 1999. The two men agreed that they would go beyond the official stance of each country. However, the solution should be balanced and acceptable to both India and Pakistan and the people of Kashmir. The talks were held in Delhi. The Indian premier Vajpayee was updated about the rules of the talks, and he gave them the go-ahead, but added that "the solution must be final and not partial." Naik and Misra utilized all the possible available options to resolve the issue of Kashmir. They pledged that the solution should be based on a clearly defined international border, but the question was where would be the border line that was acceptable to all parties. Naik proposed that "India should keep everything south and east of the Chenab River" (Jones 2002). However, Misra was not sure, and he neither accepted nor rejected the proposal. So they decided to stop the talks for the moment and report back to their prime ministers before meeting again. They had made very good progress in settling down the issue of Kashmir. Both the civilian governments were serious about finding a peaceful solution to the Kashmir question. However, these peace initiatives were soon thwarted by a Pakistani military offensive in Kargil. The military leadership under General Musharraf was not happy with the peace process and thought that the civilian leadership had attempted to change the direction of foreign policy under the national security state (Paul 2014).

In this situation, the relations between India and Pakistan were stuck between cooperation and conflict throughout the 1990s. According to Farhan Saddiqi (interview by author, Islamabad, 13 November 2017),

> The relations between India and Pakistan is somewhere between enmity and friendship. It is more a mixture of cooperation and conflict which is both embedded and mixed with each other. They are not sore enemy all the time and have a will to cooperate. But this will to cooperate is always put down or hijacked by consequences which don't want peace between the two states to continue.

For example, Pakistan and India continued their peace talks during the 1990s but at the same time blamed each other for the unrest in Kashmir. Former DG ISI General Asad Duranni (interview by author, Islamabad, 22 November 2017) confirmed that "we [military generals] never believed that India would be an existential threat to Pakistan. Yes, we have old enmity and rivalry but we do understand that. India may have the same feelings as well." Contrary to this, Shabana Feyyaz (interview by author, Islamabad, 20 November 2017) argued that "India remains a threat to Pakistan in the strategic perspectives but it is a matter of debate that whether it is high or low level threat from India." In one issue, it might be a high-level threat but at the same time there might be a low level of threat on another issue. Thus, India and Pakistan need CBMs to work on the issues on which both have agreed to negotiate a resolution. This will help to restore mutual trust and cooperation in the resolution of major conflicts such as Kashmir.

The 1999 Kargil War in Kashmir

A war in Kargil was part of the Pakistani military strategy prior to 1999 but its implementation had been rejected by both political and military leaders on all previous occasions. Initially, it was discussed during General Zia's regime, but Zia rejected the proposal as it risked leading to full-scale war with India. Later it was reconsidered but shut down on the same grounds, and it was reported that the proposal could only be implemented when Pakistan was ready for a full-scale war (Abbas 2004). In July 1996, the then Lieutenant-General Musharraf once again forwarded this proposal to Prime Minister Bhutto, at GHQ, Rawalpindi, in his briefing regarding the military plan to wrest Kashmir from India. He tried to convince Bhutto that Pakistan needed to take action in Kashmir before it became too late. General Musharraf explained to Bhutto that the "time window for the resolution of the Kashmir dispute is short, because with passage of time, the India-Pakistan equation in both military and economic dimensions is going against

Pakistan." He further warned that "the differential is increasing and the window will close" (Paul 2014, 53). After the briefing, Bhutto had a detailed conversation with General Musharraf about the military solution of the Kashmir conflict, which she recounted in her autobiography (2008, 418–419):

> Musharraf concluded the briefing with the words that a ceasefire would be in place and Pakistan would be in control of Srinagar – the capital of Indian-held Kashmir. I asked him, "And what next?" He was surprised by my question and said, "Next we will put the flag of Pakistan on the Srinagar Parliament." "And what next?" I asked the general. "Next you will go to the United Nations and tell them that Srinagar is in Pakistan's control." "And what next?" I pushed on. I could see General Musharraf had not been prepared for this grilling and was getting flustered. He said, "And ... and you will tell them to change the map of the world taking into consideration the new geographical realities." "And do you know what the United Nations will tell me?" I looked General Musharraf straight in the eye, as the army chief sat silently by and the room grew still, and pointedly said, "They will pass a Security Council Resolution condemning us and demanding that we unilaterally withdraw from Srinagar, and we will have got nothing for our efforts but humiliation and isolation." I then abruptly concluded the meeting.

So Bhutto also refused to support the Kargil plan to take military action in Kashmir. Thus, both military and civilian leaders concluded this plan could not serve their strategic objectives to wrest Kashmir from India.

Despite this context, General Musharraf had not given up his plan to launch a military offensive in Kashmir and was looking for an opportunity. Ultimately Musharraf started the Kargil War to occupy the Kargil heights in order to give a strategic advantage to the Pakistani military. Like the 1990 Kashmir crisis, the Kargil military conflict occurred when both civilian governments had adopted a rapprochement policy to normalize their relations, as discussed in a previous section. This meant that General Musharraf opposed the peace process to find a peaceful diplomatic solution to the Kashmir situation.

Kargil is located at a peak on the highway connecting Srinagar and Leh, which had served as a main supply route for the Indian forces deployed on the Siachen Glacier since independence (Wheeler 2018). The Pakistani military still thought that the escalation of violence in Kashmir would compel the Western powers to intervene in the Kashmir dispute, to avoid the possibility of a nuclear war. Consequently, Pakistan would be able to draw international attention to Kashmir in order to resolve the Kashmir conflict. In addition, the intrusion in Kargil would enhance the morale of the Pakistani military and stimulate the fading Kashmiri insurgency as well (Bommakanti 2011). Apparently, the objective was to revive the Kashmir militancy and gain international attention for the issue of Kashmir.

The Kargil War, code-named Koh-e-Paima (Operation KP), had suddenly surfaced in May 1999, following the Nawaz-Vajpayee Lahore Summit in which they agreed to resolve all the outstanding issues, including Kashmir, through peace process (Zehra 2018). About 2,000 regular and irregular forces infiltrated Kargil and captured around 100 sq. km of territory in the Dras-Kargil sector (Bommakanti 2011). The Pakistani military used the paramilitary forces of the Northern Light Infantry, the personnel of which mainly came from the Kashmir region. Thus, the Pakistani military tried to avoid the direct conflict with India that would have occurred had it staged a conventional war in Kashmir. Moreover, Pakistan's leaders publicly denied that their forces were involved in the conflict and said that it was instead carried out by the militants (Kapur 2016).

India responded with a limited war, restrained itself to the LoC, and did not advance into the Pakistani side of Kashmir. On 25 May 1999, the Indian premier approved the use of airpower to dislodge the Pakistani forces who had crossed the LoC. India used air strikes only against Pakistan's new positions on the Kargil heights. At the beginning of the operation, the Indian air force made little impact as it had limited capability to target Pakistani positions on the Kargil heights. Moreover, the Pakistani positions were close to the LoC and the Indian pilots found it difficult to remain inside Indian-controlled air space. The Pakistani forces shot down two Indian helicopters, claiming that both had violated the airspace under Pakistani control along the LoC. Thus, it was difficult for the air force to recapture the heights, and it was impossible for the Indian ground forces to operate in a steep mountainous terrain confronting the Pakistani forces (Jones 2002). Thus, the Indian air campaign was ineffective in targeting Pakistani positions.

India revised its plan and applied a long-term strategy. The Indian air force targeted rearward camps and logistic bases instead of chasing the Pakistani forces' positions on the Kargil. They also deployed French-built Mirage fighter-bombers that had advanced defensive systems and could fly at night. Consequently, the Indian forces were able to cut the supply line of the Pakistani forces. However, it was still difficult for the ground forces to target the Pakistani forces' positions. The Indian army considered different possible options and decided to target the vulnerable positions of the Pakistani forces by using heavy artillery. Finally, they decided that they would target the Pakistani positions at Tololung and Tiger Hill, which were the most vulnerable spots in the Kargil region captured by Pakistani forces. On 3 July 1999, the Indian forces mounted a decisive operation to capture the Tiger Hill. The Indian infantry planned to reach the 16,000-foot peak around midnight and targeted Pakistani position from three sides with heavy artillery fire. India successfully recaptured the Tololung and Tiger Hill points, which was a significant victory for the Indian forces (Jones 2002). India had televised the war to show its commitment to the Kashmiri cause and stimulate widespread nationalistic support (S. Ganguly *et al.* 2003). Moreover, India tried to highlight that Pakistan was behind the destabilization of the Kashmir region.

India executed a well-coordinated plan, covering the military, diplomatic, and political fronts to counter the Pakistani attack. India successfully capitalized on "Pakistan's ill-planned, untimely, and technically illegal move in Kargil." This provided India with an opportunity to launch a diplomatic campaign and sent a clear message to Washington (in Zehra 2018, 194),

Pakistan must vacate Kargil, that Pakistan must not be rewarded for aggression by initiating any bilateral dialogue on Kashmir with Pakistani troops still occupying "Indian territory," and that as a nuclear power India would not be irresponsible and open new fronts by crossing the LOC.

Prime Minister Sharif requested the US to find a way out of the Kargil crisis and bring an end to the war between the two countries and avoid a full-scale war. On 4 July 1999, Sharif met with President Clinton, who persuaded him to withdraw his military forces unconditionally from Kargil. Sharif agreed to an unconditional withdrawal of Pakistani forces from Kargil (Cohen 2004). Subsequently, the US intervened to stop the war between the two countries, and Pakistan withdrew its forces. So the US once again assisted in the reduction of tension between India and Pakistan. According to Zafar Khan (interview by author, Islamabad, 10 November 2017), "the US did help Pakistan in conflict management of the Kashmir dispute but not in its resolution between the two countries."

The Kargil military conflict was the first real war between the two nuclear states in South Asia. However, nuclear weapons were not deployed and remained in their normal non-deployed position (Basrur 2010). Both countries went to war but avoided the use of nuclear weapons. So the minimum level of deterrence was applied during the conflict that avoided a full-scale war. Interestingly, Pakistan used its nuclear capability as a cover to build the pressure of the "stability-instability paradox"[2] on India. Under this paradox, the tension and/or conflict is maintained at a level below that of a full-fledged conventional war between the two nuclear states. For instance, Pakistan provided extensive military aid to the Kashmiri militant groups and used direct offensive force in Kargil that escalated the border tension between the two adversaries. In both cases, Pakistan officially denied its role and said that it was carried out by non-state actors. According to Varun Sahni, "India was unable to respond adequately to Pakistani pressure because it would have had to escalate the confrontation and thus risk war" (Basrur 2010). Consequently, India avoided a full-scale war and Pakistan was able to neutralize the conventional military advantage of India due to the risk of a nuclear war (Basrur 2002). Thus, many analysts argued that the nuclear weapons had deterred a full-scale war between the two countries. However, this strategic balance is changed after the Pulwama terror attack when India launched an air strike inside Pakistan beyond the LoC in Kashmir in February 2019. Consequently, India has created a new strategic space for conventional war below the nuclear threshold. This means that India will not continue its strategic restraint policy against Pakistan in case of any further cross-border attacks (see details Chapter 6).

Despite not developing into a full-scale war, the Kargil War had once again exposed Pakistani military strategic unpreparedness, and ultimately Pakistan requested the US to intervene to end the war. The military went for war in Kargil without considering its consequences as highlighted by Bhutto. More importantly, Pakistan had not learnt from its past mistakes such as the 1948, 1965, and 1971 wars as there was no coordination between the civil-military leadership. The Pakistani military elite initiated the wars and were reluctant to consult with the civilian leadership. Since independence, the military had not trusted the civilian leadership and feared that they might leak information. More specifically, they believed that it is the prerogative of the military to take the key decisions related to strategic importance under its military-centred national security state approach. So Pakistan persisted in the post-Cold War era with a national security state where the military has the dominant role in foreign and security policies.

As a result, the Kargil offensive was counterproductive, and ultimately Pakistan withdrew its forces from Kargil. According to Air Marshal Noor Khan, "We should have known that India will not be bogged down in Kargil and could extend the war to other fronts. We should have also known that the international community would not support such covert operations" (Husain 2003, 48). The Pakistani minister rightly pointed out: "the army had climbed up a pole without considering how it would get down" (Jones 2002). Moreover, the Kargil War was another setback for the Pakistani military strategists who failed to find a military solution to Kashmir within the national security state. Islamabad was unable to gain international support to put pressure on India as had been considered by the military prior to the Kargil War. Prudently, India opted for limited war and did not provide any opportunity to Pakistan to complain that they had violated the territorial boundaries. Despite gaining international attention for Kashmir, Pakistan was considered as an aggressor and an irresponsible state, as predicted by Bhutto in her conversation with General Musharraf (Jones 2002). A RAND Corporation study pointed out that "Pakistan now views Kargil-like operations as an ineffective means of dispute resolution" (Mukherjee 2009, 412). Thus, the Pakistani military tried to find a military solution in the post-Cold War but failed to make territorial gains through military means.

Despite the Kargil misadventure, the military blamed the civilian government for the failure and the withdrawal of its forces. General Asad Durrani said "it was a brilliant operation by the Pakistani military. But we had not set our strategic priorities and failed in the diplomatic and political preparations to back it up" (Jones 2002, 267). However, Sharif claimed during his trial after the military coup in 1999 that he had no advance information about the Kargil War. Sharif said that "this ill-planned and ill-conceived operation was kept so secret that the Prime Minister, some corps commanders and the Chief of Navy and the Air Force were kept in the dark" (Ali, *Dawn*, Pakistan, 13 June 2000; ICG Policy Brief 2006). This was at odds with what General Musharraf said in a television interview that "everyone was on board and it was a political decision to withdraw forces from Kargil. The military job was to capture the territory which we did" (Jones 2002, 103). According to security analysts, the army might have told the prime minister about the operation during usual briefings but would not have shared details of the operations with Sharif, as the military often takes unilateral decisions on issues of strategic importance under the national security state.

Thus, the military took a unilateral decision and did not take the political leadership into its confidence under Pakistan's military-centric national security approach. The Kargil offensive was a misadventure of the Pakistani military elite which caused yet another embarrassment for the country. The military lacked a long-term strategy despite the best tactical advance shown in the surprise attack on the strong Indian military power. For this, the military needed to take the political leadership on board to avoid embarrassment for the country and its institutions. Bhutto had warned General Musharraf that the Kargil War would bring international embarrassment to the country.

In addition to this, the Kargil War also created political instability in the county. Prime Minister Sharif wanted to remove General Musharraf from his position as COAS as he had been the architect of the Kargil misadventure. However, General Musharraf imposed a martial law administration and became the chief executive of the country in October 1999. He removed Sharif from office and subsequently appointed himself as president of Pakistan as explained in Chapter 3.

On the Indian front, the Kargil War had a considerable impact on their strategic thinking with respect to Pakistan. It was considered a betrayal by India of the rapprochement policy adopted by Prime Minister Vajpayee during his visit to Lahore earlier in 1999. Vajpayee said "we shook hands like friends. It's a different matter that we were stabbed in the back" (Basrur 2002). The war further deepened the mistrust between the two countries. Former Indian Foreign Minister Jaswant Singh (2007) noted in his book:

> To those of us who accompanied Prime Minister Vajpayee to Lahore, this [Kargil] was a great betrayal. Pakistan could – in its reckoning I suppose with some justification – seek to explain all this away as revenge for 1971, or for Siachen, or for any Indian action earlier, say in the Neelam Valley, but this kind of discussion could go on forever if pursued in terms of retaliation and revenge for every real or perceived wrong … Jammu and Kashmir is inhabited by human beings. That is the most important fact, yet it is overlooked.

Since the Kargil War, the Indian military has adopted a very hostile stance to relations with Islamabad and often tried to influence the political decisions of India with respect to Pakistan (Mukherjee 2009).

The Kargil episode also showed that the Pakistani military elite were against the civilian role in Kashmir dispute by resolving it through diplomatic channels. The military elite believed that a military solution to Kashmir was the only viable and preferred solution under Pakistan's national security state (Wheeler 2018). Nonetheless, it best served institutional interests of the Pakistani military which would provide a primary role for it in the state's affairs (Jones 2002). The Kashmir conflict was used by the military elite to justify its influence in the political process and undermine the civilian governments throughout the 1990s. In fact, the military would resist any other solution that would have strengthened the role of the civilian leadership (Haqqani 2003). This meant that the military was not ready to give up its role in the political process of the country during the 1990s.

The causal relationship between Pakistan's national security state and the deteriorating security environment during the 1990s

Within Pakistan's national security state, the use of proxy war in the form of jihad severely affected the Kashmiri nationalist movement for independence and weakened Islamabad's diplomatic standing over the Kashmir issue. It had been transformed from an independence movement into an Islamist martyrdom and imposition of the Sharia system. For example, the Islamist armed groups targeted civilian and Kashmiri pundits for collaboration with the Indian government, forced women to wear the veil, demolished cinemas and liquor shops, and revived the sectarian divide in Kashmir (Hoodbhoy, *Dawn*, Pakistan, 20 May 2017). As a result, the Kashmir movement has now become a struggle for imposing "a Taliban kind of sharia system" in the Kashmir valley. Moreover, the involvement of non-Kashmiri mujahedeen increased resentment against the militant groups in the valley. About 65 percent of Kashmiris viewed the presence of foreign militants as having adversely affected the Kashmir cause of independence (Mattoo 2003). This meant that Pakistan lost local support within Kashmir. The Kashmiris thought that Pakistan was not much different from India, who was only interested in their land, not in their welfare. According to opinion polls, two-thirds of the Kashmiri population viewed Pakistan as having played a negative role in Kashmir in the previous ten years. More specifically, about 60 percent of Kashmiris believed that they were better off politically and economically as a part of India, whereas only 6 percent said they would be better off being Pakistani citizens. About 90 percent of the Kashmiri people disapproved of violence in Kashmir and believed that violence could not solve the issue of Kashmir (Mattoo 2003). Thus, the Kashmir insurgency was declining in the late 1990s.

In addition, Pakistan's policy of Afghanistan-style "proxy war" in Kashmir was based on a flawed strategy. This is because the Soviet Union supplied relatively limited military resources to Afghanistan. For example, the Soviet Union did not have the required manpower to hold ground throughout Afghanistan. The Soviet forces were restricted to urban centres and strategically significant areas. In contrast, India had enough military manpower and resources to control Kashmir throughout the 1990s. Moreover, the Afghan mujahedeen was supported by the world's most powerful intelligence agency, the CIA, with the support of ISI (Swami 2006). In Kashmir, Pakistan was alone in fighting the mighty military power of India. It is important to note that Bhutto had already explained to the ISI generals that "the Soviet forces were defeated by US stinger missiles, international finances, diplomacy and politics, not just by proxy war by the jihadists." This meant that the political leadership had a much better understanding of the issues of strategic importance in the country.

Under the military-centric national security approach, Pakistan heavily relied on proxy wars in Kashmir throughout the 1990s. However, Pakistan did not achieve its strategic goals through proxy war. In fact, India used Pakistan's proxy war as a justification to suppress the Kashmiris' genuine uprising for the right to self-determination. More importantly, India still holds the greater part of Kashmir and successfully contested elections since 1996. Moreover, Indian territorial boundaries have remained the same since partition in 1947 (Kapur 2016). So Pakistan failed to solve the Kashmir conflict. In 1999, the Pakistani military made a direct incursion into the Kargil area to take a strategic advantage over the Indian military in Kashmir. Once again, it failed to find a military solution to the issue of Kashmir. Nonetheless, India showed its determination to resist any military intrusion into Kashmir, regardless of cost. Moreover, India has revoked the article 370 of the Indian constitution in August 2019 and declared the Indian-administered Kashmir as Indian union territory (see in Chapter 6).

The Pakistani proxy war adversely affected the cause of the Kashmiri struggle for independence. An estimated 60,000 Kashmiris died as a result of state violence and militant attacks during the 1990s (Timeline Kashmir, retrieved: 19 January 2020). Furthermore, the Kashmiri struggle for freedom is considered Pakistani-sponsored terrorism. The people who were fighting for the nationalist cause of the Kashmir liberation now preferred martyrdom and the fight for Islam. Thus, it has negatively affected the indigenous struggle for freedom in Kashmir.

The proxy war also largely contributed to the internal security threat to Pakistan when the government made a U-turn on Kashmir policy after the 9/11 terrorist attacks. Many militant groups and their commanders turned against the Pakistani state and formed alliances with Al-Qaeda and the Pakistani Taliban. It was generally believed that TTP became the most ruthless organization with the support of Kashmir-based militant groups (see Chapter 6).

In addition, Pakistan's proxy war in Kashmir undermined the political process to resolve the issue of Kashmir. This proxy war best served the institutional interests of the Pakistani military to influence the nation's foreign and security policy with respect to India and Afghanistan. In the process, the political institutions became weaker, and this led to political instability throughout the 1990s. It affected both the internal and external affairs of the state (Taylor 2004). Despite its failure, the military did not let the civilian government find a peaceful political solution. The military did not tolerate the civilian governments when they tried to change the direction of foreign and security policies under the national security state.

Internationally, Pakistan was completely isolated after the Kargil War, and its close allies such as China, Turkey, and Saudi Arabia did not come to its support. The US remained neutral in the Kargil War. On the other hand, India was praised at the global level as the more responsible state for not having violated the LoC. Consequently, Pakistan lost genuine support for Kashmiri independence due to the proxy war in Kashmir.

In sum, the Kashmir case (1989–2001) confirmed that Pakistan's military-first national security state approach failed to resolve the Kashmir conflict in the 1990s. Due to culture of secrecy in proxy wars, the Pakistani military continued to take all the key strategic decisions on the Kashmir conflict and excluded the civilians from decision making throughout this period, despite civilian governments being in office in the 1990s. So the military has virtually maintained its autonomous role in formulating Pakistan's defence and security policies and exploited the Kashmiri internal uprising to protect its institutional interests in the region and within Pakistan itself. The Pakistani civilian leadership showed their political will and vision for peace to resolve the issue of Kashmir through dialogues. However, the military elite sabotaged the political process by proxy wars and then a direct military attack in Kashmir.

Notes

1 A secret, unofficial, or informal channel of communication, as used in politics or diplomacy.
2 The stability-instability paradox is an international relations theory regarding the effect of nuclear weapons and mutually assured destruction. The paradox, explained by Robert Jervis in *The Illogic of American Nuclear Strategy*, holds that "to the extent that the military balance is stable at the level of all-out nuclear war, it will become less stable at lower levels of violence."

References

"IV. The Origins of Impunity: Failure of Accountability in Jammu and Kashmir Since the Start of the Conflict." Human Rights Watch. 2006. Retrieved from https://www.hrw .org/reports/2006/india0906/5.htm.

Abbas, H. 2004. *Pakistan's Drift into Extremism: Allah, then Army, and America's War Terror*. Routledge.

Adnan, M. and Fatima, B. 2016. "Peace Process with India: A Challenge for Pakistan." *A Research Journal of South Asian Studies* 31 (1): 291–303.

Ahmad, I. 2006. "Siachen: A By-Product of the Kashmir Dispute and a Catalyst for Its Resolution Pakistan." *Journal of History & Culture* 27 (2): 87–114.

Ali, R. 2000. "Hundreds of Soldiers Fell in Kargil: Army Kept Government in Dark: Nawaz." *Dawn*, Pakistan, June 13, 2000.

Anant, A. 2009. "Identity and Conflict: Perspectives from the Kashmir Valley." *Strategic Analysis* 33 (5): 760–773.

Appendix 3: List of Interviewees.

Appendix 6: Simla Agreement July 2, 1972.

Appendix 7: Lahore Declaration February, 1999.

Appendix 12: UN Security Council Resolution over Kashmir Conflict.

Aziz, S. 2016. "The 'Dawn of a New Era' that Remained a Dream." *Dawn*, Pakistan, August 21, 2016. Retrieved on November 25, 2018, https://www.dawn.com/news/1278747.

Basrur, R. 2002. "Kargil, Terrorism, and India's Strategic Shift." *India Review* 1 (4): 39–56.

Basrur, R. 2010. "Two Decades of Minimum Deterrence in South Asia: A Comparative Framework." *India Review* 9 (3): 300–318.

"Behind the Kashmir Conflict: Abuse by India Security Forces and Militant Groups Continue." *Human Rights Watch* (HRW) report, 1999. Retrieved from https://www.hrw .org/reports/1999/kashmir/back.htm.

Bhutto, B. 2008. *Daughter of Destiny: An Autobiography*. Harper Perennial.

Bommakanti, K. 2011. "Coercion and Control: Explaining India's Victory at Kargil." *India Review* 10 (3): 283–328.

Bose, S. 2005. *Kashmir: Roots of Conflict, Paths to Peace*. Harvard University Press.

Burki, S. J. 1999. *Pakistan: Fifty Years of Nationhood*. Perseus.

Charters, D., Farson, S. and Hastedt, P.G. (ed). 1996. *Intelligence Analysis and Assessment*. Routledge.

Chengappa, B. M. 2000. "The ISI Role in Pakistan's Politics." *Strategic Analysis* 23 (11): 1857–1878.

Cohen, S. P. 2004. *The Idea of Pakistan*. Brooking Institute Press.

Cohen, S. P. and Dasgupta, S. 2010. "Restraint and Affluence." In *Arming without Aiming: India's Military Modernization*. Brookings Institution Press.

Dhakal, C. D. 2014. *Understanding Counterinsurgency in Democratic Settings: Counterinsurgency Success and Failure in Kashmir and Nepal*. Unpublished thesis, Naval Postgraduate College, Monterey.

Ganguly, R. 1998. "India, Pakistan and the Kashmir Dispute." *Asian Studies Institute & Centre for Strategic Studies*, Working paper no. 6: 1–12.

Ganguly, S. 1996. "Explaining the Kashmir Insurgency: Political Mobilization and Institutional Decay." *International Security* 21 (2): 76–107.

Ganguly, S., Blank, J. and DeVotta, D. 2003. "Introduction." *India Review* 2 (3): 1–13.

Ganguly, S. and Hagerty, D. T. 2006. *Fearful Symmetry: India-Pakistan Crises in the Shadow of Nuclear Weapons*. University of Washington Press.

Grenier, R. L. 2015. *88 Days in Kandahar: A CIA Diary*. Simon & Schuster.

Gul, N. 2007. "Pakistan-India Peace Process 1990–2007: An Appraisal." *Pakistan Horizon* 60 (2): 47–64.

Hagerty, D. T. 1995–96. "Nuclear Deterrence in South Asia: The 1990 Indo-Pakistani Crisis Author." *International Security* 20 (3): 79–114.

Hagerty, D. T. 1998. *The Consequences of Nuclear Proliferation: Lessons from South Asia*. MIT Press.

Haqqani, H. 2003. "Pakistan's Endgame in Kashmir." *Carnegie Endowment for International Peace*. Retrieved on May 24, 2017, http://carnegieendowment.org/2003/07/01/pakistan-s-endgame-in-kashmir-pub-1427.

Haresh, S. M. 1993. "On the Nuclear Edge." *The New Yorker*, March 29, 1993. Retrieved on May 21, 2017, http://www.newyorker.com/magazine/1993/03/29/on-the-nuclear-edge.

Hashim, A. S. 1997. "The Evolution of the Indo-Pakistan Conventional Military Balance in the 1990s." *The Brown Journal of World Affairs* 4 (2): 199–208.

Hoodbhoy, P. 2017. "Kashmir: Hard Choices Only." *Dawn*, Pakistan, May 20, 2017. Retrieved on November 29, 2018, https://www.dawn.com/news/1334180/kashmir-hard-choices-only.

Hoyt, T. 2003. "Politics, Proximity and Paranoia: The Evolution of Kashmir as a Nuclear Flashpoint." *India Review* 2 (3): 117–144.

Husain, H. 2003. "Pakistan's Endgame in Kashmir." *India Review* 2 (3): 34–54.

"Indian Prime Minister Rajiv Gandhi Visited China." *Ministry of Foreign Affairs of China*. Retrieved on June 24, 2017, https://www.fmprc.gov.cn/mfa_eng/ziliao_665539/3602_665543/3604_665547/t18017.shtml.

International Crises Group. 2006. "India, Pakistan and Kashmir: Stabilising a Cold Peace." *International Crisis Group*, Policy Briefing Asia, June 15, 2006.

Jagmohan, M. 1991. *My Frozen Turbulence in Kashmir*. Allied Publishers.

Jain, B. M. 1988. "Indo-Pakistan Relations under the Rajiv-Benazir Leadership." *Journal of Asian Affairs* 1 (2): 58–64.

Jaleel, M. 2015. "Hurriyat: Its History, Role and Relevance." *The Indian Express*, August 31, 2015. Retrieved on November 28, 2018, http://indianexpress.com/article/explained /hurriyat-its-history-role-and-relevance/.

Javaid, U. and Kamal, K. 2013. "The Mumbai Terror '2008' and Its Impact on the IndoPak Relations." *A Research Journal of South Asian Studies* 28 (1): 25–37.

Jones, O. B. 2002. *Pakistan: Eye of the Storm*. Yale University Press.

Kapur, P. S. 2005. "Do Nuclear Weapons Stabilize South Asian Militarized Crises? Evidence from the 1990 Case." *Asian Security* 1 (2): 174–189.

Kapur, P. S. 2016. *Jihad as Grand Strategy: Islamist Militancy, National Security, and the Pakistani State*. Oxford University Press.

Layaslalu, M. 2017. "The First Vajpayee Government: Golden Years of Non-Military Confidence Building Measures between India and Pakistan." *IOSR Journal of Humanities and Social Science* 22 (4): 31–39.

Los Angeles Times. 1988. "New Era for Pakistan, India Seen in Bhutto-Gandhi Talks." *Los Angeles Times*, December 31, 1988. Retrieved on June 26, 2017, http://articles.lati mes.com/1988-12-31/news/mn-759_1_rajiv-gandhi.

Mahadevan, P. 2009. *The Politics of Rebellion in Kashmir*. RIEAS Research Paper No.: 134.

Malik, I. H. 2008. *The History of Pakistan*. Greenwood.

Mattoo, A. 2003. "India's 'Potential' Endgame in Kashmir." *India Review* 2 (3): 14–33.

Misra, A. 2007. "An Audit of the India-Pakistan Peace Process." *Australian Journal of International Affairs* 61 (4): 506–528.

Mukherjee, A. 2009. "A Brand New Day or Back to the Future? The Dynamics of India-Pakistan Relations." *India Review* 8 (4): 404–445.

Nawaz, S. 2009. *Crossed Swords: Pakistan, Its Army, and the Wars Within*. Oxford University Press.

Paul, T. V. 2014. *The Warrior State: Pakistan in the Contemporary World*. Oxford University Press.

Popovic, M. 2014. *Fragile Proxies: The Politics of Control and Defection in State Sponsorship of Rebel Organizations*. Unpublished thesis, Central European University.

Rizvi, H. A. 1993. *Pakistan and the Geostrategic Environment: A Study of Foreign Policy*. Palgrave Macmillan.

Rizvi, H. A. (2003) *Military, State And Society In Pakistan*. Palgrave Macmillan.

Sattar, A. 2010. *Pakistan's Foreign Policy 1947–2009: A Concise History*. Oxford University Press.

Schofield, V. 2010. *Kashmir in Conflict: India, Pakistan and the Unending War*. I.B. Tauris.

Shaikh, F. 2012. *Making Sense of Pakistan*. Oxford University Press.

Shakoor, F. 1997. "Recasting Pakistan-India Relations in the Post-Cold War Era." *Pakistan Horizon* 50 (4): 75–92.

Shankar, M. 2016. "Nehru's Legacy in Kashmir: Why a Plebiscite Never Happened." *India Review* 15 (1): 1–21.

Siddique, Z. 2010. "Kashmir Continues to Suffer Indian Oppression and World Focuses on Nuclear War Scare." *Crescent International*. Retrieved on 27 November 2018, https:// crescent.icit-digital.org/articles/kashmir-continues-to-suffer-indian-oppression-and-wo rld-focuses-on-nuclear-war-scare.

Singh, J. 2007. *In Service of Emergent India: A Call to Honor*. Bloomington: Indiana University Press.

Snedden, C. 2015. *Understanding Kashmir and Kashmiris*. C Hurst & Co Publishers Ltd.

Swami, P. 2006. *India, Pakistan and the Secret Jihad: The Covert War in Kashmir, 1947–2004*. Routledge.

Syed, B. S. 2012. "India Asked to Honour 1989 Accord on Siachen." *Dawn*, Pakistan, April 14, 2012. Retrieved on November 25, 2018, https://www.dawn.com/news/710562.

Tajwar, A. W. 2016. "Changing Public Opinion on Kashmir Issue: Some Trends from Gallup Pakistan History Project Polls Data." *Gallup*, Pakistan. Retrieved from http://gallup.com.pk/wp-content/uploads/2016/01/Weekend-Read-23-Chaning-Public-Opinion-on-Kashmir-Issue-by-Abdullah-Tajwar-Research-Intern-at-Gallup-Pakistan.pdf.

Tantry, I. 2015. "Kashmir Shuts on Moulvi Farooq's Death Anniversary." *Tribune*, India, May 21, 2015. Retrieved on November 27, 2018, http://www.tribuneindia.com/news/jammu-kashmir/community/kashmir-shuts-on-moulvi-farooq-s-death-anniversary/83610.html.

Taylor, M. P. 2004. *Pakistan's Kashmir Policy and Strategy Since 1947*. Unpublished thesis, Naval Postgraduate School, Monterey.

Timeline of History. 2020. "Timeline Kashmir." Timeline of History, August 26, 2020, Retrieved January 19, 2020, https://www.timelines.ws/countries/KASHMIR.HTML.

Tremblay, R. C. 1995. "Kashmir: The Valley's Political Dynamics." *Contemporary South Asia* 4 (1): 79–101.

Tremblay, R. C. 2009. "Kashmir's Secessionist Movement Resurfaces: Ethnic Identity, Community Competition, and the State." *Asian Survey* 49 (6): 924–950.

Wheeler, N. J. 2018. "I Had Gone to Lahore with a Message of Goodwill but in Return We Got Kargil: The Promise and Perils of 'Leaps of Trust' in India-Pakistan Relations 'Leaps of Trust' in India-Pakistan Relations." *India Review* 9 (3): 319–344.

Wirsing, R. G. 1993. "The Kashmir Dispute: Prospects for Conflict Resolution." In *Dilemmas of National Security and Cooperation in India and Pakistan*, edited by Hafeez Malik. Palgrave Macmillan, London.

Zehra, N. 2018. *From Kargil to the Coup: Events that Shook Pakistan*. Sang-e-Meel Publications.

5 Pakistan's strategic considerations and regional stability in South Asia

A case of Pakistan's participation in the global war on terror

The 9/11 terror attacks posed a serious security threat to the US in the post-Cold War era. They had significant implications for US foreign and security policy. On 20 September 2001, President Bush said that "All of this was brought upon us in a single day – and night fell on a different world" (*The Washington Post*). Bush called it an act of war against the US and announced a "global war on terror". He emphasized that the war would continue until the eradication of this evil (Patman 2015; Khan *et al.* 2014). Bush further declared (*The Washington Post*, September 20, 2001):

> We will direct every resource at our command [,] every means of diplomacy, every tool of intelligence, every instrument of law enforcement, every financial influence, and every necessary weapon of war to the destruction and to the defeat of the global terror network … Every nation, in every region, now has a decision to make. Either you are with us, or you are with the terrorists. From this day forward, any nation that continues to harbour or support terrorism will be regarded by the United States as a hostile regime.

Declaring all-out war, the US took responsibility to eliminate the "axis of evil" around the world. This meant that the US would not only take any action against Al-Qaeda and Taliban in Afghanistan but would also continue its war against rogue states such as Iraq, Iran and North Korea (Rogers 2013; Gregory 2007). He emphasized that the "global war on terror" was not against Muslims, and the civilized world knew that "if terror goes unpunished, their own cities, their own citizens may be next" (*The Washington Post*, September 20, 2001).

The US blamed Al-Qaeda for the 9/11 terror attacks and formed a global coalition against terrorism. They fought two bloody wars in Afghanistan and Iraq following the 9/11 attacks. The US invaded Afghanistan in October 2001 when the Afghan Taliban refused to hand over Al-Qaeda leader Osama Bin Laden. The Afghan Taliban government was ousted within three months of the US invasion of Afghanistan. The US was also able to kill and capture many prominent Al-Qaeda operatives with the support of Pakistan in the Pakistan-Afghan border areas and other parts of Pakistan. However, they failed to capture Bin Laden. In 2003, the Bush administration started another war in Iraq to dismantle Saddam

Hussein's dictatorial regime which they claimed had links with Al-Qaeda and possessed weapons of mass destruction (Rogers 2013; Patman 2015). These wars had a significant impact on the Pakistani state and society.

The American war on terror and its new relationship with Pakistan

The 9/11 terror attacks changed the security dynamics of South Asia. Pakistan's support in the global war on terror was key in the fight against Al-Qaeda and other extremist groups in the Pakistan-Afghan border region. The US sought Pakistan's support in the global war on terror due to its geostrategic position; its relations with ethnic Pashtuns; information on the hideouts of foreign militants; and engagement with the Afghan Taliban regime during the 1990s (Fair and Jones 2009; Khan *et al*. 2014). Ahmad Rashid, the writer of the bestselling book *The Taliban*, wrote at the time that "Pakistan's knowledge of the Taliban's military machine, storage facilities, supply lines and leadership hierarchy is total. Pakistan also has the most comprehensive information about the role of foreign militants, their bases and their numbers" (*The Nation*, Pakistan, 20 September 2001). Bob Woodward (2003) in his book also noted that "Pakistan was the linchpin for any strategy to isolate and eventually attack Al-Qaeda and the Taliban." Therefore, for the US, the participation of Pakistan in the global war on terror was key for any success against Al-Qaeda and the Taliban regime in Afghanistan.

After the Soviet withdrawal from Afghanistan in 1989, Pakistan was seeking a friendly government in Afghanistan and tried various Afghan proxies to capture Kabul which would provide them strategic depth in Afghanistan in case of attack from India. Therefore, supporting with the Afghan Taliban became a strategic choice for Pakistan which would keep its rival India out of Afghanistan and provide necessary strategic depth. The Afghan Taliban were dominated by ethnic Pashtuns, the largest ethnic group in Afghanistan. Pakistan has maintained relations with Pashtuns in Afghanistan as a large number of Pashtuns also live in Pakistan on the other side of the Pakistan-Afghan border. Thus, Pakistan had influence on the Afghan Taliban. Given this situation and Pakistan's strategic importance, the US was also suspicious of the role Pakistan's ISI might play in relation to the Afghan Taliban. However, the ISI was the only available option that could possibly provide information on the military facilities of the Afghan Taliban and their hideouts (Rashid 2008). From the Pakistani perspective, it was worried that the US would abandon Afghanistan once the Al-Qaeda threat was eradicated and the Taliban regime collapsed. This was because Pakistan-US relations had fluctuated ever since Pakistan became independent. Similar to the Cold War period, both American and Pakistani analysts thought that this new phase in Pakistan-US relations would prove to be short term and more a "marriage of convenience" (Ali 2015). Thus, there was scepticism on both sides after 9/11 as to how durable the improved relations between the two countries would prove to be.

The US used 'coercive diplomacy' to enlist Pakistan's support in the global war on terror. In the NSC meeting on 11 September 2001, the US Secretary of State

Colin Powell clarified that "the US had to make it clear to Pakistan, Afghanistan and the Arab states that the time to act was now" (The 9/11 Commission Report, 330). The meeting decided that "if Pakistan did not help the United States, it would be at risk of attack" (Rashid 2008; Woodward 2003). Immediately after the attacks, on 13 September 2011, the deputy secretary of state Richard Armitage met with General Ahmad Mahmud, the ISI chief, and Maleeha Lodhi, the Pakistani ambassador to the US. General Mahmud was on an official visit to the US when the 9/11 terror attacks took place. He was stranded in Washington due to the shutdown of all airlines after the attacks. Armitage presented seven American demands (The 9/11 Commission Report, 330):

1. Stop Al-Qaeda operatives at the border and end all logistical support for Bin Laden
2. Give the United States blanket overflight and landing rights for all necessary military and intelligence operations
3. Provide territorial access to US and allied military intelligence and other personnel to conduct operations against Al-Qaeda
4. Provide the United States with intelligence information
5. Continue to publicly condemn the terrorist acts
6. Cut off all shipments of fuel to the Taliban and stop recruits from going to Afghanistan
7. If the evidence implicated bin Laden and Al-Qaeda and the Taliban continued to harbour them, to break relations with the Taliban government.

Armitage explained that these demands were non-negotiable. Ahmad Rashid (2008, 61) reported that "General Mahmud promptly replied that Pakistan would do whatever the Americans asked of it." General Musharraf (2006) in his memoir wrote that the US Secretary of State Colin Powell told him: "You are either with us or against us." Musharraf further said that the Bush administration threatened to bomb Pakistan "back to the stone age if the country did not cooperate in its fight against terrorism." Consequently, Pakistan was left with no other option but to join the global war on terror and became a key frontline state. President Bush appreciated the efforts of Secretary Powell and said that "it was the most important thing Powell did after 9/11, that he singlehandedly got Musharraf on board" (Rashid 2008). Thus, the Bush administration was successful to enlisting Pakistan's support in the global war on terror.

Pakistan's Response to the Global War on Terror

In the wake of the 9/11 terror attacks, the Pakistani military presumed that the US would react with full force. So Pakistan had to make a realistic assessment of the prevailing situation by protecting its national interests before taking any decision. Musharraf (2006, 200) later wrote that "America was sure to react violently, like a wounded bear. If the perpetrator turned out to be Al-Qaeda then that wounded bear would come charging straight toward us." Therefore, Pakistan feared that they would be labelled as a terrorist state, as Islamabad maintained diplomatic relations with the Afghan Taliban government who were harbouring Al-Qaeda in Afghanistan and proxy war in Kashmir.

On 12 September 2001, General Musharraf called a meeting of his generals along with a few prominent civilian cabinet ministers. At this meeting, General Musharraf explained that President Bush had already clarified that the US would punish not just the perpetrators of the attack but also any states that harboured terrorists (*The Washington Post*, September 20, 2001). He asked for other opinions: Abdul Sattar, the then foreign minister, said that "we agreed that we would unequivocally accept all US demands, but then later we would express our private reservations to the US and we would not necessarily agree with all the details" (Graham 2012, 98). Rashid (2008) summarises Pakistan's response towards the US demands in a single line: "First say yes and later say but ..." General Musharraf followed this policy for the next few years. More specifically, the ISI's view was that Pakistan's immediate acceptance of US demands would create sufficient space for it to later modify its policy. In this fashion, the Pakistani military adopted a two-track approach after 9/11. Pakistan would cooperate with the US where their national security interests converged and would avoid cooperation where they diverged.

On 14 September 2001, General Musharraf called another meeting of the corps commanders to discuss the US demands. He insisted that Pakistan could not oppose the US demands and had to cut off its relations with the Afghan Taliban. However, Musharraf was confronted with stiff resistance from his main military comrades, including General Mahmud Ahmad, the then ISI chief; Lieutenant General Mohammed Aziz, the Lahore corps commander; and Lieutenant General Muzaffar Usmani, the deputy chief of army staff. All three generals had played a key role in Pakistan's proxy war in Afghanistan and Kashmir. They were prominent supporters of the Afghan Taliban, Kashmiri militants and Islamic fundamentalist parties. Consequently, the three men objected to the US demands and said Pakistan was getting nothing in return, and would face dangerous consequences by making this strategic shift in its policy towards Afghanistan. It would also give negative signals to the Kashmiri fighters. Nonetheless, General Musharraf used anti-India rhetoric to convince his military commanders, saying India was ready to join the US alliance and that would undermine Pakistan's strategic interest in the region. More importantly, India would persuade the US to declare Pakistan to be a terrorist state. After the anti-India card was played, the three generals dropped their objections. General Musharraf met with Wendy Chamberlain, the US ambassador to Pakistan, late at night on 14 September 2001. He informed her that Pakistan accepted all the demands of the US (Rashid 2008).

On 19 September 2001, in a public address, General Musharraf defended his decision to join the global war on terror and said it was necessary in order to secure Pakistan's strategic interests in the South Asian region. He defended his decision, saying in his address to the Nation (President Musharraf Word Press, 2006):

It's not a question of bravery or cowardice. But bravery without thinking is stupidity. Allah has said that he who has *hikmat* [pragmatic wisdom] has a huge blessing. We have to save our interests. Pakistan comes first, everything else is secondary. Our critical concerns are our sovereignty, second our economy, third our strategic assets [nuclear and missiles], and fourth our Kashmir cause. All four will be harmed if we make the wrong decision.

General Musharraf was convinced that India was ready to give military bases to the US, which would have undermined Pakistan's geo-strategic position. So Pakistan feared India would receive international support for its position over the long-standing Kashmir dispute between the two countries. Also, it would jeopardize Pakistan's nuclear strategic assets that enabled the country to achieve a minimum level of deterrence against India (Musharraf 2006). In his briefing to journalists, General Musharraf said Pakistan would provide only administrative support to the US, and India would be kept out of Afghanistan. But India remained the issue on which the Pakistani and American positions converged the least (Wirsing 2007). Thus, the decision was made to avoid Indian influence in Afghanistan and to have a friendly government in Kabul. In the wake of the 9/11 attacks, the Pakistani military elite once again took the decision to become an ally of the US, this time in the global war on terror, a role similar to that it played during the Cold War. Playing such a role was largely based on an anti-India logic, as it had been in the Cold War. So the decision was based on Pakistan's military-centric national security approach.

In this situation, many analysts said that Pakistan had no other option at that time but to join the US-led global war on terror. However, General Musharraf must have negotiated other options for cooperation. According to former ambassador Humayun Khan (interview by author, Islamabad, November 23, 2017), "it was more a 'knee jerk reaction' by General Musharraf. Prior to joining the coalition, the issues regarding bases of our cooperation and ground roles with the US needed to be identified and agreed to [,] ensuring and protecting Pakistan's national interests." Ambassador Khan further argued that,

> When the US Secretary of State Colin Powel called for cooperation, Musharraf could have given a positive response but should have told him that I am sending my foreign affairs team along with military generals to discuss the bases of our cooperation and prevent any untoward moves by the US.

Khalid Rahman (interview by author, Islamabad, November 21, 2017) added that,

> The terms of cooperation with the US should not be limited only on financial terms in joining US-global war on terror but should have considered the invasion in Afghanistan; the future regime in Afghanistan; American presence in Afghanistan; and involvement of other countries in the region.

Thus, General Musharraf did not negotiate any terms and conditions for the coop-eration with the US. He demanded only that there would be no American armed forces on Pakistani soil and that the US would mediate on the Kashmir issue at the international level (T. Schaffer and C. Schaffer 2011). Nonetheless, this was more a case of lip service by General Musharraf, as the US did use Pakistani soil, while it did not mediate over Kashmir. According to General Asad Durrani (interview by author, Islamabad, November 22, 2017):

> We did not work out our terms of engagement with the US that this is some-thing we will do and this is something we will not. Unconditional support is something which no state ever does. Also, there should have [been conveyed a] message that we are not doing this for money only. So the management of our decision was very bad.

General Musharraf claimed that he had consulted his corps commander, cabinet members and other key stakeholders before taking the decision to join the global war on terror. Many observers believed that General Musharraf took the decision unilaterally and informed the corps commander about his decision at the meeting. In any case, there was no major opposition to his decision, as the leadership of the two major political parties, the PMLN and PPP, had been in exile since the 1999 military coup (Yamin 2015). Musharraf explained that he took the decision to join the US global war on terror for three reasons. First, the Pakistani military was very weak compared to the US and any confrontation with the US would have destroyed its military power. Secondly, the Pakistani economy was weak and the country was in no position to sustain its economy in the face of war with the US. Thirdly, the nation was not sufficiently united to confront a superpower (Musharraf 2006). Thus, Pakistan was in no position to conduct a military con-frontation with the US after the 2001 terrorist attacks.

Strategically, Pakistan's decision to participate in the global war on terror was not an easy one to make. Pakistan had heavily invested in the Afghan Taliban for almost a decade in the 1990s by providing military and financial aid. More specifically, Pakistan nurtured, trained and equipped the Afghan Taliban to ena-ble it to exercise control over the Kabul regime (Tellis 2008). Subsequently, the Afghan Taliban provided strategic support to Pakistan and helped keep India out of Afghanistan. Islamabad was worried that Kabul would fall into the hands of pro-India groups (Heine and Ghosh 2011). It was with great reluctance, therefore, that Pakistan cut its ties with the Afghan Taliban after 9/11.

In this context, there was suspicion of and concern about Pakistan's commit-ment to the global war on terror due to the presence of pro-Taliban elements within the Pakistani military and the ISI. In order to ensure the government's commitment to the war on terror and establish its control over the military, General Musharraf declared that "the Taliban's days are numbered" (Whitaker, *Independent*, UK, October 1, 2001). Moreover, he removed the three generals and other pro-Taliban officers from key positions in the military and the ISI. They were replaced by his loyal, moderate and liberal military generals and officers.

Against this backdrop, the 9/11 terror attacks once again provided an opportunity for the Pakistani military to consolidate its military-first national security approach following the Cold War. It also provided an opportunity for General Musharraf to strengthen his regime with the support of the US (Talbot 2002). The alliance with the US would expand the military's institutional and commercial interests in the country. In November 2001, General Musharraf visited the US to attend a meeting of the UN General Assembly. Musharraf met with President Bush and discussed his concerns about the situation in Afghanistan. Musharraf demanded the delivery of F-16 aircraft that would show the serious commitment of the US to Pakistan. Bush pledged $1 billion in aid to Pakistan and said that "We are not ready to talk about F-16s now, but this is a long friendship" (Rashid 2008). The demand for F-16s was driven by the external threat on the eastern border from India, not the one on the western border where Pakistan fought against Al-Qaeda and the Afghan Taliban. Previously, the US had sold F-16s fighters to Pakistan during 1986–1988 to strengthen its defence against the Soviet Union. However, Al-Qaeda and the Taliban had no airpower, so it was of no use against them (Wirsing 2007).

Like previous military dictators, General Musharraf's strategy was to survive politically. Therefore, he more sought a US commitment to his dictatorial regime in the post-9/11 setting. Prominent Pakistani journalist Ahmad Rashid records that General Musharraf asked President Bush "not to pressure him about democratization, or criticize what he would do politically" (Rashid 2008, 68). So the primary intention of General Musharraf was to legitimise his illegitimate rule in the country with support of the US instead of protecting Pakistan's national interests by avoiding negative fallout of the global war on terror. It is important to note that the US often supported military regimes during and after the Cold War. According to Khuram Iqbal (interview by author, Islamabad, November 8, 2017), "the only source of legitimacy for the military regimes in Pakistan has been the US and western support." Brigadier Muhammad Saad (interview by author, Islamabad, November 14, 2017) said that "both General Zia and General Musharraf wanted a legitimacy and then legitimacy overruled all other options in their relations with superpowers." So Musharraf's intention was to extend his regime with the support of the US as well.

Pakistan's Strategic Considerations and Pakistan-US Relations

While Pakistan and the US formed a new relationship after the 9/11 terror attacks, both countries maintained diverging objectives and interests in their global war on terror. The US required Pakistan's support to dislodge the Afghan Taliban regime and eliminate Al-Qaeda whereas Pakistan supported the US war on terror in order to have a friendly regime in Kabul and prevent Indian influence in Afghanistan. Furthermore, Pakistan would gain US military and economic aid to extend its military-industrial complex. Therefore, Pakistan became a strategic ally of the US, but with diverging objectives and interests that surfaced when India increased its influence in Afghanistan and the US turned its attention towards Iraq.

Due, in part, to its past experience of alliance with the US, Pakistan was worried that the US would end its commitment to Afghanistan once American goals were achieved, as they did when the Soviet Union withdrew from Afghanistan in 1989. More importantly, India, being a bigger regional power, would fill the vacuum once the US left Afghanistan. This would give India the opportunity to increase its influence in Afghanistan. In order to prevent this, Pakistan insisted that the US form a government in Afghanistan that would be friendly to Pakistan. Interestingly, General Musharraf raised the issue of Kashmir with US Secretary of State Colin Powell during his visit to Pakistan in September 2001. Musharraf emphasized that Pakistan-India relations could not be normalized without a resolution over Kashmir. Actually, he was trying to remind the US that Pakistan's support for the war on terror came with a political as well as an economic cost for the US (Wirsing 2003).

General Musharraf claimed that Pakistan had set out five major strategic considerations, including: security from any external threat, especially from India; the revival of Pakistan's economy; protecting strategic assets such as nuclear weapons and missiles and their facilities; Pakistan's support for the Kashmiris' struggle for the right to self-determination; and the formation of a friendly regime in post-Taliban Afghanistan (Khan *et al.* 2014; Wirsing 2003). By joining the global coalition fighting the war on terror, General Musharraf also clarified to the US that Pakistan's armed forces would not participate in any military operations outside their own borders in Afghanistan or Iraq (Wirsing 2003).

Pakistan had been reduced to something of a pariah state under Musharraf until Pakistan joined the alliance in the global war on terror. Pakistan had been isolated after the 1998 nuclear testing; the 1999 Kargil war; and the October 1999 military coup staged by General Musharraf. Pakistan-US relations had also been strained throughout the 1990s. All this changed after 9/11: Pakistan became the frontline state in the US global war on terror, and the Pakistan-US relations were restored. This allowed the Pakistani military elite to reinvigorate its military-first national security state. Subsequently, Pakistan was enabled to continue its military competition with India.

On 7 October 2001, the US started Operation 'Endeavouring Freedom' (OEF) to overthrow the Taliban government and dislodge Al-Qaeda from Afghanistan and the areas bordering Pakistan. Initially, Islamabad played a key role in the operation by ousting the Taliban emirates in Afghanistan and capturing and killing many prominent Al-Qaeda leaders and operatives. Pakistan provided the 'ground line of communications' such as military bases and ports, set up joint surveillance centres, facilitated logistical supply to military forces in Afghanistan, and gathered and shared intelligence (Najam Rafique, interview by author, Islamabad, November 19, 2017). General Musharraf allowed the US military to use four military bases: Pasni, Jacobabad, Shamsi and Dalbandin. Around 1,100 members of the US security forces were stationed in Pakistan belonging to CIA paramilitary teams, Combat Search and Rescue Units, US Special Ops and Red Horse squadrons. Islamabad also permitted 74 basing and staging activities of the US armed forces, such as refuelling, medical evacuation, overflight facilities, and the setting up of surveillance and communication sites for its forces inside Afghanistan (Musharraf 2006). So it was misleading when General Musharraf said that Pakistan would not allow the US forces to land in Pakistan and use its bases. This was clearly not the case.

Furthermore, the Pakistani paramilitary forces launched several military operations in former FATA area that had remained ungoverned since the period of British colonial power in India. In December 2001, Pakistan carried out 'Operation al-Mizan' in the tribal areas to capture Al-Qaeda operatives that had taken shelter in the region (Tellis 2008). The Pakistani military also deployed around 80,000 members of the armed forces to secure the Pakistan-Afghanistan border areas, and provided its support to the US forces in the Torabora area of Afghanistan which was the main hideout of Al-Qaeda and the Taliban (D'Souza 2006). Beside these operations, Pakistan established two quick-reaction forces from the Special Services Group in the Kohat district of the KP province and Wana areas of the South Waziristan district of the former FATA. It helped local military commanders to respond quickly by deploying troops rapidly (Fair and Jones 2009). Thus, Pakistan provided all-out support to the US to defeat Al-Qaeda and depose the Afghan Taliban regime in Kabul. Nonetheless, the operation in tribal areas had very negative consequences in the subsequent years.

In addition to this, the ISI played a prominent role in OEF by capturing many senior Al-Qaeda operatives and foreign fighters at the beginning of the operation. According to media reports, 600 Al-Qaeda operatives were captured, including key commanders such as Abu Zubaydah, Khalid Sheikh Mohammed, Ahmed Ghailani, Amjad Farooqi and Abu Faraj Al-Libbi (Gregory 2007). Ironically, Pakistan retained most of the Afghan and Pakistani militants, and handed over just the Al-Qaeda operatives to the US. Despite such success, they failed to capture or kill Bin Laden (Fair and Jones 2009). OEF was partially successful in overthrowing the Taliban emirates in Afghanistan and capturing key Al-Qaeda operatives.

The US State Department praised Pakistan's efforts in OEF by allowing the US military to use its bases, deploying Pakistani security forces on the Pakistan-Afghan border areas and providing intelligence information to enable the capture of key Al-Qaeda operatives (The White House, March 4, 2006; D'Souza 2006). On 24 June 2003, President Bush met with General Musharraf at Camp David, where he thanked Musharraf for his support in the war on terror. Bush declared that "key Al-Qaeda terrorists had been successfully neutralized thanks to the effective border security measures and law enforcement cooperation throughout (Pakistan), and ... to the leadership of President Musharraf" (Tellis 2008). Pakistan's efforts in the global war on terror were generally appreciated around the world. Hence, India failed to isolate Pakistan internationally by trying to present Pakistan as a terrorist state.

Additionally, the sanctions imposed after the 1998 nuclear tests and the 1999 military coup were lifted, and the US provided significant financial assistance in the form of grants, loans, and debt write-offs. For example, the US rescheduled Pakistan's outstanding US $400 million debt and provided US $1 billion for border control, refugee support and poverty reduction, as President Bush had pledged in his previous meeting with General Musharraf. The international financial institutions also facilitated Pakistan to reschedule its external debt of US $38 billion. The IMF provided an additional US $9 billion in debt relief (Weinbaum and Harder 2008). All this provided much-needed financial support at a time when Pakistan was facing a severe economic crisis.

Pakistan was designated as a "major non-NATO ally" (MNNA) of the US under the 1961 US Foreign Assistance Act. Under MNNA status, Pakistan developed close military-to-military relations with the US, as well as access to certain defence equipment from the US (D'Souza 2006). This was invaluable military aid for Pakistan, allowing it to reduce the imbalance with Indian military power in the region. The US also gave Pakistan a US $5.1 billion arms package in July 2006. The package included 36 F-16 fighters, 29 other jet fighters, armaments, and upgrades for its existing fleet of F-16s. Pakistan was also compensated by the US for the non-delivery of F-16s during the 1990s (D'Souza 2006; Fair and Jones 2009). Furthermore, Pakistan received about US $1.2 billion annually in 'Coalition Support Fund', which was the reimbursement for Pakistan's counter-terrorism operations against Afghan Taliban and its affiliated militant groups in former FATA and other parts of the country (Shah, *The Nation*, Pakistan, July 22, 2019). The military-run NLC also charged US $235 per NATO container for handling, scanning and toll charges on its Afghan supply route in Pakistan after the US invasion in Afghanistan in 2001 (Rana, *The Express Tribune*, Pakistan, August 14, 2012). With US military and economic aid, the Pakistani military was successful to extend its military industrial complex in which the military has protected its institutional and commercial interests.

Like the mid-1950s, practically it was also more of a military-to-military relationship between the two countries. However, the US did not support other strategic objectives in the post-9/11 period which Musharraf described in a speech on 19 September 2001. The US never supported Pakistan's military initiatives in Kashmir and often demanded that the Kashmir dispute be resolved bilaterally (Najam Rafique, interview by author, Islamabad, November 19, 2017).

In the post-9/11 setting, General Musharraf exploited the opportunity to crack down on home-grown terrorist organizations. Nonetheless, it was a selective approach, targeting those militant groups whose interests were opposed to the Pakistani military's perception of the national interest. Those groups which could be utilized for Islamabad's external ambitions vis-à-vis India and Afghanistan were spared. Thus, Pakistan supported the war on terror selectively and tried to protect its proxies which would be used against India and Afghanistan to safeguard its military and/or strategic interests. Pakistan assisted the US to neutralize the threat of Al-Qaeda, but continued with its own proxy war in Afghanistan.

Actually, Pakistan was convinced that the US would increase its strategic relationship with India that would undermine Pakistan's strategic interests in the region. US-India relations had improved during the post-Cold War era and the two countries struck a civil nuclear strategic deal in October 2008 which completely shifted the regional balance in favour of India (Siddiqa 2011). The

Pakistani security establishment perceived that the nuclear deal would disturb the "balance of power" in favour of India in the region. Pakistan asked for an identical nuclear deal earlier in 2006 to meet its growing energy demands, but the US declined. The US also opposed the proposed Pakistan-Iran gas pipeline and refused to concede favourable trade agreements, such as those dealing with textile exports. In this context, the Pakistani security establishment was convinced that the US had shifted its strategic and economic relations in support of India (Weinbaum and Harder 2008). This meant that the US did not take into account Pakistan's economic and security concerns in its relations with India in the post-9/11 period. So Pakistan was worried that the US would assign a larger role to India in Afghanistan, thus undermining Pakistan's strategic interests in the region.

After removing the Afghan Taliban government, the US shifted its focus to Iraq and thought the threat from Al-Qaeda in Afghanistan was over, and the Afghan Taliban was now just a local phenomenon. In 2005, the US reduced the number of its troops in Afghanistan and handed over authority to NATO forces (Paliwal 2016). Both Afghanistan and Pakistan leaders realized that the US commitment to Afghanistan was waning. The ISI made several assumptions: that the Pashtuns had lost their dominance to the anti-Pakistan Northern Alliance in Afghanistan; that the US would abandon Afghanistan altogether after it invaded Iraq; and that the US would abandon Pakistan, as they had done when the Soviets left Afghanistan in 1989 (Rashid, 2012). As a consequence, this would open a way for India to play a greater role in Afghanistan, undermining Pakistan's strategic interests in the region. Brigadier Muhammad Saad (interview by author, Islamabad, November 14, 2017) said:

> Pakistan had made wrong assumptions about the US exit plan that the US would leave Afghanistan by 2010 or at least by 2015. It was a flawed thinking and Pakistan should have planned for worst case scenario that the US is not going to leave. Also, we thought that the Afghan thinks that the Indian interests are supreme and they are sold out to the Indians.

Subsequently, Pakistan relied on the Afghan Taliban, especially the Haqqani Network, to protect its strategic interests in Afghanistan. General Musharraf attempted to ensure that the Afghan Taliban would remain as a Pakistani proxy in Afghanistan. More than a decade later, Musharraf admitted in an interview with Jon Boone (*The Guardian*, February 13, 2015):

> The ISI cultivated the Taliban after 2001 because Karzai's government was dominated by non-Pashtuns, the country's largest ethnic group, and officials who were thought to favour India. Obviously we were looking for some groups to counter this Indian action against Pakistan. That is where the intelligence work comes in. Intelligence being in contact with Taliban groups. Definitely they were in contact, and they should be.

Thus, Pakistan had not given up its proxy war in the form of Islamist jihad which they adopted under the national security state during the Cold War. Musharraf played a double game in Afghanistan as he supported the US-led war on terror to fight against Al-Qaeda and the Taliban, but at the same time supported the Afghan Taliban. As a result, the Afghan Taliban reorganized in 2005 and launched a fresh insurgency in Afghanistan (Siddiqa 2011). Nonetheless, Islamist radicalism has become a dangerous phenomenon in the post- Cold War era. The Afghan Taliban insurgency fuelled Taliban militancy in Pakistan that spread to the country's settled areas in 2007. A dangerous nexus has emerged among Al-Qaeda, TTP and Punjabi-based militant groups in the former FATA. Thereafter, thousands of civilians and hundreds of security personnel died in Taliban-linked terror attacks and subsequent military operations in the country. The militant landscape shifted to the Pakistani side of the border, turning the country into a new battleground for Al-Qaeda and its affiliated militant groups (Hussain 2011). Furthermore, Pakistani society has become largely radicalized in the post-9/11 security environment. This growing radicalization and religious extremism have created existential security threats for Pakistan as the militant landscape shifted to Pakistani side of the border and Taliban established its control in former FATA and extended to settled areas in KP province (See Chapter 6).

Pakistan-Afghanistan Relations vis-à-vis India

Afghanistan has always been key to Pakistan's national security due to its long, porous border that has remained unrecognized by Afghanistan. Throughout the 1990s, Pakistan's relations with Afghanistan were more stable as there was a pro-Pakistan Taliban regime in Afghanistan. However, the Taliban regime was overthrown after 9/11. More importantly, the Northern Alliance (NA) emerged as the major political group and it was widely considered to be anti-Pakistan. The NA comprised non-Pashtun groups in Afghanistan. It was an anti-Taliban alliance and was also known as the United Islamic Front for the Salvation of Afghanistan. The NA had maintained close ties with India, Iran and Russia, all of whom were considered hostile towards Pakistan during the 1990s (Khan, *The News*, Pakistan, January 14, 2001). On 13 November 2001, General Muhammad Fahim of the NA occupied Kabul. This was Pakistan's worst nightmare: to lose a friendly Taliban government in Afghanistan. The headlines in two Pakistani newspapers read: "Pakistan's worst nightmare has come true with Northern Alliance control of Kabul" and "a strategic debacle for the army" (Rashid 2008). In Pakistan, General Fahim was considered an Indian spy, so Islamabad was deeply worried about the fall of Kabul to the NA as it would give an opportunity for India to increase its influence in Afghanistan. Consequently, Pakistan sought to convince the US that ethnic Pashtuns must be taken on board in any future settlement for Afghanistan in the post-9/11 Afghan government (Rashid 2008). Therefore, the 9/11 terrorist attacks once again raised Pakistani security concerns regarding Afghanistan. Since then, Pakistan has been struggling to have a friendly government in Kabul in order to prevent Indian influence in Afghanistan.

In December 2001, the Bonn conference was called upon to form an interim setup in Afghanistan after the overthrow of the Taliban regime. The conference was attended by four prominent groups, including the Peshawar Group, the Rome Group, the Cyprus Group and the United Front. These groups were led by anti-Pakistani leaders. On the other hand, the pro-Pakistani Islamist groups, such as the Haqqani Network, Hizb-e-Islami (Hekmatyar), Hizb-e-Islami (Yunus Khalis) and other Taliban figures, were absent from the conference. So the Pakistani position was very weak at the Bonn conference. The conference was also attended by officials from Pakistan, India, Iran and Russia. The conference appointed Hamid Karzai as an interim President of Afghanistan. The Karzai interim government was dominated by the NA faction (Pant 2010; Paliwal 2016). Therefore, 9/11 provided an opportunity to India to resume its relations with Afghanistan, as it had supported the NA against the Afghan Taliban throughout the 1990s.

Both Pakistan and India were in competition to have a friendly government in Kabul to protect their national interests. Pakistan continued with its past policy of favouring particular groups and General Musharraf did not reach out to non-Pashtun ethnic groups in the post-9/11 setting. In fact, General Musharraf adopted an ambiguous policy towards Afghanistan in order to protect Pakistan's strategic interests. Islamabad maintained its relations with Kabul and supported a democratic Afghan government, at least in principle. In practice, it wanted a weak Afghan government under its influence so as to prevent an Indian presence in Afghanistan. Actually, the Pakistani establishment was convinced it needed to have an alternative option in case the Karzai regime failed to secure Afghanistan, or India increased its influence in the country (Tellis 2008). Islamabad also believed that the US would leave Afghanistan sooner or later and this would create a power vacuum in Afghanistan that India would try to fill. Therefore, the Pakistani security establishment viewed the Afghan Taliban as a means to secure its strategic interests in Afghanistan (Pant 2010). Subsequently, Islamabad attempted to protect its proxies in the former FATA and other areas along the Durand line.

Many Afghan Taliban groups withdrew from the western and eastern provinces of Afghanistan after their defeat at the hands of the NA. Pakistan airlifted many senior Taliban commanders beside Pakistani military and intelligence officers from the Kunduz province of Afghanistan in November 2001 during OEF (Paliwal 2016). Afghan Taliban found shelter with relatives and friends in the former FATA area on the other side of the border. It was easy for the Afghan Taliban to settle along the Pakistan-Afghan border due to their ethnic affiliation with Pashtuns living on the other side of the border. More importantly, Islamabad provided sanctuaries and logistical support to the Afghan Taliban in border areas along the Durand line (Saikal 2010; Pattanaik 2012). Nonetheless, some of the Al-Qaeda operatives were also mixed with locals along with Afghan Taliban in the former FATA region. Thus, Pakistan continued with its proxy war in Afghanistan despite being a frontline state in the global war on terror.

On the Indian side, its Afghan policy appeared to be based on three elements: assisting the Afghan government in rebuilding its economic and political infrastructure; reducing Afghanistan's dependence on Pakistan; and aiding and abetting anti-Pakistan groups in Afghanistan (Rabbani 2011). Unlike Pakistan, India adopted a soft power approach towards Afghanistan. In Kabul, India strived for a strong, centralized democratic government and supported the non-Pashtun groups, especially the NA. Nevertheless, India also tried to reach out to Pashtun ethnic groups as well.

After installing the Karzai government, India restored its former relations with Afghanistan and initiated a high level of engagement in economic, political, capacity rebuilding, and humanitarian and infrastructure development. India has made a huge investment in infrastructure development and provided a significant amount of financial aid to the Afghan government for rebuilding its war-torn country (Paliwal 2016). India provided US $2 billion in economic and military assistance to the Karzai regime, which is the largest amount of regional financial assistance given to Afghanistan. Besides aid, the trade between the two countries has increased many-fold since Karzai took over Kabul in 2001. About 4,000–5,000 Indian workers and security personnel were working on many infrastructure projects in different parts of Afghanistan by 2011 (Hussain 2011). India has successfully completed various infrastructure projects such as highways, dams, schools and the current Afghan parliament. Moreover, India constructed several consulates on the Pakistan-Afghan border, including ones in Kandahar, Jalalabad and Herat (S. Jones 2007). Additionally, the Indian military closely worked with the Afghan national security forces and provided training to the Afghan armed forces and military assistance packages, including armoured check posts, watch-towers and military transport vehicles. India also sent its army officer team to train the Afghan National Army (Wirsing 2007; Pant 2010). All these actions by India increased the security problem for Pakistan on its western border in the wake of the 9/11 terror attacks.

Against this backdrop, Islamabad thought that Indian involvement in Afghanistan would be limited to cooperation in the economic and human development of the war-torn country. New Delhi has extended its relations with Kabul in intelligence sharing, supporting anti-Pakistani elements and on defence-related matters (Shabana Feyyaz, interview by author, Islamabad, November 19, 2017). In particular, India's primary objective has been to reduce the dependency of land-locked Afghanistan on Pakistan. This would also help India by easing Pakistani pressure over Kashmir (Yadav and Barwa 2011). Another major factor for India was its desire to present itself as a superpower in the region. India has the economic and military capacity to take up the responsibilities of a major power in the South Asian region and its periphery (Pant 2010). This meant that India wanted to establish its credentials as a major economic power by providing large-scale aid to Afghanistan. In this process, India successfully established a strategic relationship with Afghanistan, and the Karzai government appeared to be favourably inclined towards India.

Islamabad became more worried about the growing influence of India in Afghanistan. According to Zahid Husain (2011, 10), a prominent Pakistani security analyst, "the expanding Indian presence in Afghanistan is seen by the Pakistani security establishment as a strategic defeat and has compounded Islamabad's fears of being encircled." Therefore, Islamabad showed its serious concerns over the growing Indian role in Afghanistan and its consulates in Afghan border areas. Pakistan accused India and the Afghan intelligence agency, the National Directorate of Security (NDS) of espionage and of stirring up the separatist movement in the Balochistan province (Ahmad and Bhatnagar 2007; Rafique and Anwar 2014). In order to protect its interests, Pakistan allowed the Afghan Taliban, especially the Haqqani Network, to reconnect and reorganize in the border areas in the former FATA and Balochistan regions (Tellis 2008). Despite US pressure, Pakistan was reluctant to take action against the Afghan Taliban and other affiliated militant groups such as the Haqqani Network and LeT in the border region (Milam and Nelson 2013). This demonstrated that Pakistan was not prepared to abandon its strategic interests in Afghanistan.

In this context, the Karzai government accused Pakistan of supporting terrorist activities in Afghanistan. In January 2006, President Karzai said that "a neighbour of Afghanistan has had a hand in the increased number of 10 suicide terrorist attacks since mid-2005" (D'Souza 2006). Although Pakistan denied any role in these terrorist attacks, it lost its strategic depth in Afghanistan. Many commentators argue that this was the consequence of Pakistan's flawed military-centric national security approach, with which it persisted following the end of the Cold War (Jaffrelot 2004). Actually, Pakistan heavily relied on the Afghan Taliban as a proxy to protect its strategic interests in Afghanistan. The Pakistan military believed that these proxies would provide the necessary cover to counterbalance Indian military power in the region.

Many US officials believed that Pakistan's alliance in the global war on terror was a tactical move rather than a strategic shift in its two-decade-old policy of using proxy wars to achieve its strategic objectives. The Afghan Taliban maintained its sanctuaries, training camps, recruiting centres and terrorist financing in Pakistan. While Pakistan was very effective against Al-Qaeda and foreign militants, it did little to counter Afghan Taliban militants (S. Jones 2008; Heine and Ghosh 2011). Many Afghan Taliban leaders were based in Pakistan's various cities, including Quetta, Karachi, Islamabad and Peshawar. As one Pakistani journalist wrote, "the Pakistan government plunges into action when they know they can lay their hands on a foreign militant but they are still reluctant to proceed against the Taliban" (Amir, *The Herald*, Pakistan, April 2006; S. Jones 2008, 60). This meant that Pakistan continued with its national security state approach by using proxy militant groups to protect its strategic interests in Afghanistan and there was no strategic shift in its foreign and security policy in the post-9/11 settings.

In addition to this, the India-Pakistan rivalry had a significant impact on regional stability in South Asia. The two countries blamed each other for the terrorist attacks in Afghanistan and Pakistan. On the one hand, Pakistan blamed India for the unrest in the former FATA area and Baluchistan province. Pakistan said that Indian consulates in Kandahar and Jalalabad were being used as launching pads for a covert intelligence operation along Pakistan's western border area. On the other hand, India accused the ISI of the attack on the Indian embassy in Afghanistan in 2008. Moreover, workers from India were abducted and killed on the Zagranz-Delaram highway in Afghanistan, for which Pakistan was blamed by India. In June 2007, India increased its contingent of the Indo-Tibetan Border Police, sent to Afghanistan to protect their workers in Afghanistan after the attacks. Similarly, Pakistan charged India's premier intelligence agency, RAW, with the killing of Chinese workers in the Gwadar area of Baluchistan province in February 2006 (Wirsing 2007). As a result, Afghanistan became a battlefield for the two South Asian countries. David Miliband, British foreign secretary from 2007 to 2010, noted (Ved 2010):

> Given the scale of the geopolitical challenges in this region—including the long-running tensions between India and Pakistan and the presence of Iran— it can seem that Afghanistan is fated to remain the victim of a zero-sum scramble for power among hostile neighbours. The logic of this position is that Afghanistan will never achieve peace until the region's most intractable problems are solved.

Thus, the India-Pakistan rivalry has created insecurity generally in South Asia, and particularly in Afghanistan. India is using its economic power to increase its influence in Afghanistan, while Pakistan is using its proxies to undermine Indian interests in the country.

Pakistan's Successes and Failures in the Global War on Terror

In a strategic parallel to joining the American-led alliance against Soviet communism in 1954, the Pakistani military decided to join the global war on terror and become a frontline state against terrorism. The military did not consult the major political parties before entering the global war on terror. Musharraf's administration was unable to formulate a comprehensive strategy to protect its short- and long-term interests. Pakistan's policy on the war on terror was ambiguous and contradictory. This policy was self-defeating, as the Pakistan military overtly supported the Kabul regime after 9/11 but at the same time covertly aided the Afghan Taliban. Similarly, Pakistan has taken strict action against anti-Pakistan militant groups while providing covert support to militant groups that focus on Afghanistan and Kashmir (Siddiqa 2011).

Pakistan's support for the global war on terror revived Pakistan-US relations and ended its global isolation. Nonetheless, it was more a military-to-military relationship and had a limited impact on the socioeconomic situation of the country. The US lifted sanctions on Pakistan and provided financial and military aid after 9/11. Pakistan received about US $10.5 billion worth of aid between 2002 and 2007 and rescheduled its annual external debt payment of US $3 billion. Most of the aid was military in nature and was used for military upgrades. For example, Pakistan purchased advanced fighter jets, including F-16s, and the training of Pakistani military and ISI officers by American was resumed after being suspended during the 1990s (Weinbaum and Harder 2008). As a result, the Pakistani military was successful in strengthening its institutional interests after

9/11 (Siddiqa 2011). More specifically, the Pakistani military was successful in buttressing itself – serving national security approach in the post-9/11 setting.

The major drawback of Pakistan's participation in the war on terror was ignoring its implications for the domestic stability of the country. The military regime in Pakistan was more preoccupied with its foreign policy goals, such as gaining US military aid, achieving strategic depth in Afghanistan and avoiding encirclement by India, than it was concerned with fallout of the war, domestic stability and the well-being of the Pakistani people. General Musharraf was also keen to gain international support for his autocratic regime. However, the proxies used by Pakistan against India in Kashmir were turned against the Pakistani state post-9/11. In fact, the TTP and Kashmir-based militant groups joined hands and carried out deadly terrorist attacks across Pakistan, including against military installations such as the Mehran airbase, GHQ, ISI regional offices and Wah Cant (See Chapter 6).

There was also a general perception across the country that Pakistan was fighting the US's war on its own territory. General Musharraf was criticised by both religious and secular political parties for dragging the Afghan war into Pakistan (Weinbaum and Harder 2008; Javaid 2011). According to former Prime Minister Bhutto, General Musharraf supported the war on terror to prolong his dictatorship with the support of the West, especially the US. Bhutto further said that society had been further radicalized during Musharraf's regime and the government had lost the authority of the state in different parts of the country (Bhutto, *The Guardian*, August 23, 2006). Moreover, the actual cost of the war on terror was much greater than expected. According to various estimates, Pakistan suffered a loss of about US $70 billion to its economy and infrastructure during the first 10 years of the war on terror, besides heavy losses in human lives, both military and civilian (Saikal 2014). Thus, the war on terror had a significant negative impact on the country overall.

In addition, the Pakistani military was at the forefront of tackling the new security problem from home-grown terrorism that emerged after 9/11. The army had deployed over 100,000 regular and paramilitary forces to conduct military operations against anti-state militant groups in the former FATA and adjoining areas in KP province. However, the operations were selective, and attempted to protect Pakistan's proxy militant groups. More importantly, the Pakistani armed forces had limited experience of counterinsurgency operations in tribal areas as they were mainly trained for conventional warfare against India. Despite deploying massive armed forces, the military was unable to clear the area of militants and stop cross-border terrorism, though there has been a decline in the number of attacks more recently (Hussain 2011). Moreover, there was massive collateral damage and civilian casualties were very high, which further alienated the local population from the military in the area. Moreover, the Pakistani military had concluded a number of peace accords with militants that had further weakened its position in the tribal areas (Weinbaum and Harder 2008). As a result, the militants had strengthened their control in the northwest of Pakistan, especially in the former FATA areas between 2001 and 2013.

Externally, General Musharraf largely failed to prevent the Indian growing influence in Afghanistan. Subsequently, New Delhi established a strategic partnership with Kabul in 2011. The Karzai regime was much closer to India than Pakistan. Consequently, Afghanistan looked to India more as a country interested in rebuilding its war-torn nation, while Pakistan was seen as spoiler in the country (Ahmad and Bhatnagar 2007). As a result, Pakistan failed to secure its interests in Afghanistan, in particular in preventing an Indian presence in Afghanistan. Being a close ally in the global war on terror, Pakistan was also unable to convince the US to pressure India to resolve the issue of Kashmir.

Like the Kashmir case in the 1990s, it was the Pakistani military elite which executed the foreign and security policies in post-9/11 settings. Since then, the Pakistani military has consolidated its political power and control of the state and society. However, the 9/11 terror attacks created a new kind of security problem that was both internal and external. Externally, Pakistan lost its strategic depth in Afghanistan, in which Islamabad had invested for over three decades since 1979, whereas it is confronted as an internal security threat from home-grown terrorism.

As is suggested by the two case studies undertaken in this book, Islamabad has largely failed to protect its national security interests in the post-Cold War era. Despite its failures, Pakistan has persisted with a military-centred national security state in this period.

References

Ahmad, Z. S. and Bhatnagar, S. 2007. "Pakistan-Afghanistan Relations and the Indian Factor." *Pakistan Horizon* 60 (2): 159–174.

Ali, M. 2015. "The United States-Pakistan Aid Relationship: A Genuine Alliance or a Marriage of Convenience?" *Regional Studies* 33 (2): 3–30.

Amir, I. 2006. "Waziristan: No Man's Land." *The Herald*, Pakistan, April 2006.

Appendix 3: List of Interviewees.

Bhutto, B. 2006. "The Price of Dictatorship." *The Guardian*, August 23, 2006. Retrieved from https://www.theguardian.com/commentisfree/2006/aug/23/comment.pakistan.

DOS cable, State 158711. 2001. "Deputy Secretary Armitage's Meeting with General Mahmud: Actions and Support Expected of Pakistan in Fight against Terrorism." September 14, 2001. Reported in *The 9/11 Commission Report: Final Report of the National Commission on Terrorist Attacks upon the United State*. National Commission on Terrorist Attacks, July 17, 2004.

D'Souza, S. 2006. "US-Pakistan Counter-Terrorism Cooperation: Dynamics and Challenges." *Strategic Analysis* 30 (3): 525–561.

Fair, C. C. and Jones, S. G. 2009. "Pakistan's War Within." *Survival* 51 (6): 161–188.

Graham, T. Jr. 2012. *Unending Crisis: National Security Policy after 9/11*. University of Washington Press.

Gregory, S. 2007. "The ISI and the War on Terrorism." *Studies in Conflict & Terrorism* 30 (12): 1013–1031.

Heine, J. and Ghosh, P. 2011. "The Elephant in the War: India and the Afghan-Pakistan Link." *Canadian Foreign Policy Journal* 17 (1): 50–61.

Hussain, Z. 2011. "Sources of Tension in Afghanistan and Pakistan: A Regional Perspective." *CIDOB*, Policy Research Paper.

Interview with Major Amir by Salim Safi, *Geo News* Jirga Talk Show, August 27, 2017. https://www.youtube.com/watch?v=7pbsAY8E92Y.

Jaffrelot, C. 2004. *A History of Pakistan and Its Origins*. Anthem Press.

Javaid, U. 2011. "War on Terror: Pakistan's Apprehensions." *African Journal of Political Science and International Relations* 5 (3): 125–131.

Jones, S. G. 2007. "Pakistan's Dangerous Game." *Survival* 49 (1): 15–32.

Jones, S. G. 2008. *Counterinsurgency in Afghanistan*. RAND study on counterinsurgency.

Khan, I., Khattak, A. S. and Marwat, M. M. 2014. "Pak US Relations: Allies under Compulsion?" *Journal of Political Studies* 21 (2): 81–90.

Khan, K. 2001. "Kabul Fall is Pak's Strategic Debacle." *The News*, Pakistan, January 14, 2001.

Milam, W. B. and Nelson, M. J. 2013. "Pakistan's Populist Foreign Policy." *Survival* 55 (1): 121–134.

Boone, J. 2015. "Musharraf: Pakistan and India's Backing for 'Proxies' in Afghanistan Must Stop." *The Guardian*, February 13. Retrieved on October 12, 2017, https://ww w.theguardian.com/world/2015/feb/13/pervez-musharraf-pakistan-india-proxies-afgh anistan-ghani-taliban.

Musharraf, P. 2006. *In the Line of Fire: A Memoir*. Simon and Schuster.

Paliwal, A. 2016. "Afghanistan's India–Pakistan Dilemma: Advocacy Coalitions in Weak States." *Cambridge Review of International Affairs* 29 (2): 465–491.

Pant, H. V. 2010. "India in Afghanistan: A Test Case for a Rising Power." *Contemporary South Asia* 18 (2): 133–153.

Patman, R. G. 2015. "The Roots of Strategic Failure: The Somalia Syndrome and Al Qaeda's Path to 9/11." *International Politics* 52 (1): 89–109.

Pattanaik, S. S. 2012. "India's Afghan Policy: Beyond Bilateralism." *Strategic Analysis* 36 (4): 569–583.

"President Bush's Address to a Joint Session of Congress and the Nation." *The Washington Post*, September 20, 2001. Retrieved on September 25, 2017, http://www .washingtonpost.com/wp-srv/nation/specials/attacked/transcripts/bushaddress_0920 01.html.

"President Musharraf Address to the Nation September 19, 2001." *President Musharraf Word Press*, July 13, 2006, Retrieved from https://presidentmusharraf.wordpress.com /2006/07/13/address-19-september-2001/.

Rabbani, A. 2011. "Making Sense of Instability in South Asia." *The Dialogue* 6 (3): 206–223.

Rafique, Z. and Anwar, M. A. 2014. "Insurgency in Afghanistan: Implications for Pakistan's Internal and External Security." *Defense & Security Analysis* 30 (3): 266–282.

Rana, S. 2012. "Rs 35 Billion Budget Approved for National Logistic Cell." *Express Tribune*, Pakistan August 14, 2012. https://tribune.com.pk/story/421706/rs35-billion-b udget-approved-for-national-logistics-cell/.

Rashid, A. 2001. "Pakistan, the Taliban and the U.S.," *The* Nation, Pakistan, September 20, 2001. Retrieved on August 26, 2017, https://www.thenation.com/article/pakistan-ta liban-and-us/.

Rashid, A. 2008. *Descent into Chaos: The U.S. and the Disaster in Pakistan, Afghanistan, and Central Asia*. Penguin Press.

Rashid, A. 2012. *Pakistan on the Brink: The Future of America, Pakistan, and Afghanistan*. Viking.

Rogers, P. 2013. "Lost Cause: Consequences and Implications of the War on Terror." *Critical Studies on Terrorism* 6 (1): 13–28.

Saikal, A. 2010. "Afghanistan and Pakistan: The Question of Pashtun Nationalism?" *Journal of Muslim Minority Affairs* 30 (1): 5–17.

Saikal, A. 2014. *Zone of Crisis: Afghanistan, Pakistan, Iran and Iraq*. I.B. Tauris.

Schaffer, H. B. and Schaffer, T. C. 2011. *How Pakistan Negotiates*. United States Institute of Peace.

Shah, S. 2019. "A Peek into US Aid to Pakistan between 1947, 2019." *The Nation*, Pakistan, July 22, 2019. Retrieved on September 12, 2020, https://www.thenews.com.pk/print/50 1752-a-peek-into-us-aid-to-pakistan-between-1947-2019

Siddiqa, A. 2011. "Pakistan's Counterterrorism Strategy: Separating Friends from Enemies." *The Washington Quarterly* 34 (1): 149–162.

Talbot, I. 2002. "General Pervez Musharraf: Saviour or Destroyer of Pakistan's Democracy?" *Contemporary South Asia* 11 (3): 311–328.

Tellis, A. J. 2008. "Pakistan's Record on Terrorism: Conflicted Goals, Compromised Performance." *The Washington Quarterly* 31 (2): 7–32.

The White House. "Fact Sheet: United States and Pakistan: Long-Term Strategic Partners." *The White House*, March 4, 2006. Retrieved from http://www.whitehouse.gov/news/releases/2006/03/20060304-4.html.

Ved, M. 2010. "Af-Pak and India's Options in Afghanistan." *Strategic Analysis* 34 (5): 683–689.

Weinbaum, M. G. and Harder, J. B. 2008. "Pakistan's Afghan Policies and Their Consequence." *Contemporary South Asia* 16 (1): 25–38.

Whitaker, R. 2001. "Musharraf Says Taliban's Days of Power Numbered." *Independent*, UK, October 1, 2001. Retrieved on November 29, 2018, http://www.independent.co.uk/news/world/asia/musharraf-says-talibans-days-of-power-numbered-9132578.html.

Wirsing, R. G. 2003. "Precarious Partnership: Pakistan's Response to U.S. Security Policies." *Asian Affairs: An American Review* 30 (2): 70–78.

Wirsing, R. G. 2007. "In India's Lengthening Shadow: The U.S.-Pakistan Strategic Alliance and the War in Afghanistan." *Asian Affairs: An American Review* 34 (3): 151–172.

Woodward, B. 2003. *Bush at War*. Simon and Schuster.

Yadav, V. and Barwa, C. 2011. "Relational Control: India's Grand Strategy in Afghanistan and Pakistan." *India Review* 10 (2): 93–125.

Yamin, T. 2015. "Examining Pakistan's Strategic Decision to Support the US War on Terror." *Journal of Strategic Studies, Islamabad* 35 (2): 113–135.

6 Explaining Pakistan's strategic limitations

Structural issues facing Islamabad's national security state

Pakistan adopted a military-centric national security approach to counter external, local, and regional threats to its security during the Cold War period. This approach was successful to some extent as the country was able to achieve a measure of military parity with India during this period. However, the end of the Cold War served to highlight its shortfalls and limitations. This approach has not only failed to achieve its strategic goals but also fuelled chronic internal and external security problems. On the Kashmir front, Pakistan was unable to find a military solution to the Kashmir conflict and its standing over Kashmir weakened at the international level. Moreover, Pakistan lost its position of strategic depth in Afghanistan after the dismissal of the Afghan Taliban regime in Kabul, following the US invasion in 2001.

Insecurity in Pakistan has deepened as a result of the activities of the home-grown militant groups, which the military used as proxies in Kashmir and Afghanistan following the 9/11 terror attacks. In 2013, Pakistan was ranked in the top 10 least secure countries on the Global Peace Index (GPI), ranking 157 out of 163 countries (Appendix 14). The security situation worsened to such an extent that General Ashfaq Kayani, the then COAS, acknowledged in his policy speech at the Kakul Military Academy, on Pakistan's independence day in August 2013, that "no state can afford a parallel system or a militant force. The fight against extremism and terrorism is our own war and we are right in fighting it" (BBC News, Asia, 14 August 2012). This is an important admission by the military leadership that the internal security threat was greater than that of the external threat from India. The political leadership had already pointed out the danger of the internal security threat from home-grown terrorism. Earlier, in June 2009, President Zardari met with EU officials in Brussels, where he acknowledged that "India no longer poses a military threat to Islamabad, and that his people's real enemy is terrorism" (Nelson, *The Telegraph*, South Asia, 24 June 2009).

Under Pakistan's national security state, however, the country continued with its proxy war against India in Afghanistan and Kashmir in the post-Cold War era. Pakistan has been accused of being a state sponsor of terrorism due to its support of various militant groups such as the Haqqani Network and Lashkar-e-Taiba. As a result, Pakistan has eroded much of its international support over Kashmir as well as being blamed for many of the wrongdoings and failures of NATO forces and the Afghan government in Afghanistan. In this process, Islamabad became more diplomatically isolated, and the strategic diplomatic space has shrunk for the country in the post-Cold War era.

In sum, Pakistan has gone from a country whose leaders were more worried about external security threats at the time of independence to one where internal security threats from home-grown terrorism and blowback from Pakistan's covert involvement in external conflicts have compounded its security problems. Furthermore, the development of democracy in Pakistan has been impeded by the military's functional dominance over the civilian leadership in questions of national and international security. At the same time, the military has commanded the lion's share of the Pakistani government's expenditure, which has left relatively fewer financial resources to address chronic socio-economic problems. As a result, Pakistan has touched the lowest points, both on GPI and Human Development Index (HDI), in the post-Cold War era and was compared with least secure countries such as Somalia and Afghanistan.

Pakistan's military-industrial complex

Despite radical changes in the post-Cold War strategic environment, Pakistan has largely persisted with its military-centric national security approach. This approach has not only further entrenched the military establishment in the strategic decision making of the country but it has also spawned a vast apparatus to ensure that the Pakistani military continues to be a dominant voice in the political, economic, and diplomatic direction of the country. In other words, Pakistan's military-industrial complex has not only protected the corporate interests of the Pakistani military, but it has also facilitated the military's political control over the state and society. This military-industrial complex has played a major role in preventing any reform of the military's self-serving national security state. Many politicians have admitted that they were not permitted to discuss military businesses and military expenditure in parliament. According to former national assembly speaker Elahi Buksh Soomro (Siddiqa 2007, 176):

> The Military industrial complex was an area that no government wanted to touch. I tried to draw the attention of President Ishaq Khan to the military's burgeoning economic empire, but was told that the issue was like a 'beehive' that shouldn't be touched. The military is too powerful an agency and we [the politicians] will get stuck [if we press the issue].

Foreign Minister Shah Mehmood Qureshi confessed that "all civilian governments ignored [the] military industrial complex or provided economic opportunities to placate the military" (Siddiqa 2007). Thus, the politicians have largely avoided security issues in order to appease the military establishment. However, such behaviour has created a major structural obstacle to exercising civilian control over national security matters in Pakistan.

The Pakistani parliament has often played more of a client role to the military elite, both in civilian and military regimes. Most of the problems confronting

Pakistan have been related to the country's foreign and security policies, but they have been taken over by the military leadership. In practice, the parliamentarians have been unable to debate and formulate foreign and security policy in the parliament. Moreover, the politicians have failed to address any such real issues in the parliament (Hussain 2011). The military leadership often argued that the politicians are weak and incompetent to deal with security challenges confronted by the state. Professor Moonis Ahmar (interview by author, Islamabad, 9 November 2017) pointed out that "the military has a veto in taking strategic decisions related to national security so how can we expect from these civilian government to perform better[?]" Most of the enquiry commissions such as the Abbottabad Commission Report[1] were not made public due to national security concerns that their findings could demoralize the armed forces. The report of the famous War Enquiry Commission[2] was made public only in 2000, after a delay of 29 years (*Pakistan Today*, 29 April 2017). These commissions were mostly related to the country's security. So the Pakistani national security state is going beyond the commercial interests of the military and is encroaching into the political and diplomatic spheres of state affairs, which has become a hyper-military-industrial complex.

Pakistan's military-industrial complex has also provided the means and resources for the Pakistani military leaders to act independently. No civilian government has been allowed to criticize or even investigate military commercial enterprises as this would mean challenging the military establishment in the country. In fact, the Pakistani military often justified their large businesses on the grounds of so-called national security interests. Prominent Pakistani defence analyst Professor Hasan Askari Rizvi (1998) noted:

> The army acts when it believes its corporate interests are threatened; and it does so by disguising it in a message that says that the nation's survival is at risk. The military's primary consideration is not direct exercise of power, but protection and advancement of its professional and corporate interests. If these interests can be protected, it would prefer to stay on the side-lines.

So the military uses the national security narrative to protect its institutional and corporate interests. According to Air Marshal Tanvir Mahmud Ahmed (Siddiqa 2007, 285):

> The Lebanese Prime Minister was forced to cry before media because of weak defence capability of his country and no such thing would be allowed to happen to Pakistan, living nations used to sacrifice their resources for keeping their armed forces combat ready in peace time. This sacrifice was necessary and was aimed at ensuring capability to meet any external threat in future.

This meant that civilians have had to bear the cost of the military in order to remain secure when faced with the presence of a hostile neighbourhood. Hence, this security narrative of Pakistan's survival helped the military elite to protect its institutional interests and maintained its functional dominance over the civilian leadership in state affairs during and after the Cold War era.

The diarchy system:[3] absence of civilian political control

Within Pakistan's national security state framework, the military has a privileged role that excludes civilian control over state affairs. As we saw in Chapter 2, the military has set a range of obstacles to political parties or leaders who want to change the policy imperatives of Pakistan's national security state. Since independence in 1947, civilian governments have been tolerated for only very brief intervals. There has been a constant struggle for power between politicians and the military establishment in Pakistan, with the military always holding the upper hand due to a vast military-industrial complex nurtured under the umbrella of a national security state.

Over time, the Pakistani military elite have increased their influence over the political system. Despite an elected government being in office, a diarchy system existed in Pakistan after the parliamentary elections of 1988. The military has continued to take all the key decisions which they considered are of strategic importance after the Cold War. Prior to taking her office, Prime Minister Bhutto agreed to accept military dominance of key strategic decision making in the country. The Pakistani military held the key ministries, such as the foreign, interior, and finance ministries, at their disposal in the post-Cold War setting. Also, the military has worked from behind the scenes to manipulate the political process in its favour. This meant Bhutto nominally led the government but did not have much say in defence, finance, security, and foreign policymaking of the country.

In addition, the military has often played off one political party against the other in the post-Cold War era. For instance, the ISI allegedly distributed around PKR 140 million among anti-PPP groups for their election campaigns in 1990 (*The News*, Pakistan, 25 January 2012). As a result, Bhutto lost the 1990 elections. Since then, all the elections in Pakistan have allegedly been rigged by the military establishment and none of the prime ministers has completed the full term of five years. With the frequent change of governments and dismissals of prime ministers, there has been political instability in the country. In most cases, the political crisis has been fabricated by the military elite in order to protect its interests and exercise influence over the political leadership by setting up the direction of government policies in their favour (Singh 2015). Nonetheless, the political crises often led to economic instability in the country.

The military has also exercised a virtual monopoly over the definition of "national interests" in the country. They have often defined their institutional interests within the ambit of national interests within a national security state. For this purpose, they have affectively exploited religious beliefs and hyper-patriotism to protect their institutional interests. After his military coup in October 1999, General Musharraf said in an interview that "anyone who did not support the coup was not a patriotic Pakistani" (Faruqui 2014). The military is considered a "sacred cow" in the country which has branded the civilian as either "with us or against us." Subsequently, it has made it easier for the military establishment to deal with any dissent which they consider a danger to the military-industrial complex (Shah 2014a). Any objective criticism of or disagreement with the military establishment has been regarded as unpatriotic and maligning the military. This means that critics are framed anti-state, working at the behest of an enemy state. In most cases, any objective criticism by individuals or groups has brought reprisals against them through formal as well as informal means (Shurong and Rahman 2017). In January 2017, the security agencies abducted four prominent independent bloggers who were strong critics of the military establishment and its policies. Similarly, the military has threatened journalists who were vocal against their security policies. Hamid Mir, Pakistan's most prominent television anchor, was attacked by unknown gunmen in Karachi in April 2014. Mir highlighted the issue of the military's role in the alleged enforced disappearance of missing persons in Balochistan province. He survived the attack and his employer accused the then director general of ISI of involvement in the attack (HRW report, 10 January 2017). Thus, anyone who disagrees with the military is considered anti-state and may face possible reprisals from the security agencies.

Besides controlling politics, Pakistan's military-industrial complex has also given lucrative jobs and business opportunities in the civilian sector to military personnel after their retirement. As a consequence, civilian institutions have been militarized under both military and civilian regimes. Many retired military officers have been offered high official positions in government and the private sector after their retirement. However, retired officers have neither relevant experience nor qualifications in the designated field. The former PMLN government appointed Lieutenant General Muzammil Hussain as chairman of the Water and Power Development Authority (WAPDA) in August 2016 (*Dawn*, Pakistan, 25 August 2016). In addition, military personnel were inducted directly into civilian posts in the public administration, police, and diplomatic services (Shurong and Rahman 2017). Earlier, in 1998, about 35,000 army personnel were deputed to manage the WAPDA. Many retired brigadiers were appointed to civilian academic institutions, such as Quaid-i-Azam University, Islamabad (Rizvi 2003). Thus, the military has occupied key posts in the civilian sector as well. The military personnel maintain their contacts with the army and intelligence agencies by providing them with regular information about the organization and its activities. Thus, the military has used this recruitment as a tool to control civilian administrations.

The Pakistani military elite also have control over the print and electronic media through PEMRA and ISPR. As with the electronic and print media, the military is trying to manage social media. The ISPR and ISI are using social media networks, employing hundreds of fake accounts. The primary objective is to discredit dissent and keep alive the fear of Indian aggression, and even to spread conspiracy theories. According to media reports, many retired military officers have joined WhatsApp, Twitter, and Facebook groups to promote the military's security narrative in the country. However, Twitter and Facebook have blocked hundreds of such accounts that were involved in creating artificial Twitter trends in favour of military establishment and against anti-military and civil rights groups and descent voices (Jorgic and Pal, Reuters, 2 April 2019). The ISI has adopted a "carrot and stick" approach to journalists and the owners of media houses (Haqqani 2018). The media houses are induced to report Indian involvement in terror attacks inside Pakistan. It has become almost mandatory to highlight issues of military interest such as the Kashmir conflict and hyper-nationalism against India (Chawla 2001). Thus, the military has controlled the flow of information through media by presenting a positive image of the Pakistani military elite.

The functional dominance of the Pakistani military

The Pakistani military plays a disproportionate role and maintains its functional dominance in the affairs of the Pakistani state. In practice, they have played a double role in domestic politics: one as an arbitrator acquiring administrative power and the other as a ruler holding political power (Chengappa 1999). For example, the military has been involved in a wide range of local administrative activities, such as managing essential services, monitoring state-owned schools, infrastructure development, and conducting the census and elections. The military has also established its dominance over the paramilitary forces by appointing its senior officers to these forces. The paramilitary forces include rangers, frontier corps, and frontier constabulary, which in principle come under the interior ministry and provincial governments. The paramilitary forces are mainly involved in border protection and internal security. So the military affiliation with paramilitary forces gave them an extra layer to get involved in maintaining law and order in various parts of the country, including the provincial capitals of Karachi, Peshawar, and Quetta (Shurong and Rahman 2017). The military leadership has justified this role under the "aid to civil power" and custodian of national security. As one major general noted (Shah 2014a):

> A focal point of the Army's role in nation building must be that of a surgeon, who has to make hard decisions on behalf of the patient for saving his life, including amputation if required. Those decisions will bother some who have vested interests, but the condition of the patient warrants such bold actions.

This attitude has helped the military to oversee domestic politics and present itself as the guardian of the country. So, the military elite have a veto under the guise of national security in taking strategic decisions related to national security in the country.

In democratic regimes, there is usually civilian control of intelligence agencies in the country. In Pakistan, the military has a monopoly control of the state intelligence agencies, which collect information on internal and external security issues. The intelligence agencies have monitored dissident political groups and individuals in the country and played a prominent role in the dismissal of three elected governments in the 1990s. The ISI gathers information on internal and security matters, which it shares with the COAS. Furthermore, the COAS presides over the Corps Commanders meeting in which they not only discuss organisational and professional matters, but also actively discuss domestic issues such as law and order and the overall political situation, especially when the government and the opposition are engaged in intense confrontation. The military leadership builds its own consensus on the prevailing internal political and security situation. The top military leadership disseminate the agency's information in their meeting with the prime minister and president. So they are well prepared before the meetings with the civilian leadership, and this gives them an advantage over other state institutions (Rizvi 1998).

The Pakistani military has maintained constitutional and institutional leverage to act with impunity. Article 245 clause 1 of the 1973 constitution defines the functions of the armed forces. It says that "the armed forces of Pakistan, under the direction of the federal government, are subject to defend Pakistan against external aggression or threat of war and act in aid of civil power when called upon to do so." In a democracy, state institutions work under the constitution, and no institution acts above the rule of law. However, the Pakistani military has been operating outside the purview of the civilian law.

In reality, the Pakistani military has set up its own mechanisms to protect its supra-legal status and makes sure that the civilian law does not apply to it. It often protects its personnel from civilian scrutiny and accountability before the courts. For instance, the Public Account Committee (PAC) found a large number of corruption cases in which military officials were involved. In July 2011, the PAC referred this to the NAB, the government's primary anti-corruption agency, established by General Musharraf in November 1999. However, General Kayani, the then COAS, intervened to avoid the military officers having to appear in the civilian courts. Their trials were redirected to the military courts by using the Army Act of 1952. Furthermore, the previous government charged General Musharraf under Article 6 of the constitution for his extra-constitutional step of abrogating the constitution twice. However, the government was unable to bring him into custody; instead, the government ultimately provided him with a safe passage out of the country as a result of intense military pressure. So the military opposed even a retired military general appearing before a civilian court as they thought it would have affected the military's public image as the impeccable guardian of the country (Shah 2014b).

In order to combat terrorism, the government introduced a National Action Plan (NAP), following the terror attacks on the Army Public School (APS) in which about 120 students died. Under the NAP, the government granted more powers to the military to extend its role into civilian governance of counter terrorism (Shurong and Rahman 2017). The military has even extended its military courts to try civilian cases, through amendments to the Army Act of 1952 made by parliament. The 2011 Action in Aid of Civil Power Regulation has empowered the military to detain terror suspects indefinitely during its operations in the northwest KP province, especially in tribal areas. The military and ISI have misused these legal prerogatives, resulting in human rights violations such as enforced disappearances and extra-judicial killings across the country (Shah 2014b). In August 2019, the Pakistan Tehreek-e-Insaf (PTI)-led provincial government extended this regulation in the entire KP province. Previously, it was applied only in militancy-hit areas in former FATA and Provincially Administered Tribal Areas (PATA) area of the KP province (Wasim, *Dawn*, Pakistan, 18 September 2019). Thus, the military has extended further its power within the national security state.

In August 2013, the government reconstituted the Defence Committee of the Cabinet (DCC) into the Cabinet Committee of National Security (CCNS). In the DCC, the services chief could be invited by parliamentarians when required, though their presence was not mandatory. However, the presence of the service chiefs, including the Chairman Joint Chiefs of Staff Committee and Chiefs of Staff of Pakistan Army, Navy and Air Force, at the CCNS's meetings has become permanent. The prime minister officer said:

> The Committee will focus on the national security agenda with the aim to formulate a national security policy that will become the guiding framework for its subsidiary policies – defence policy, foreign policy, internal security policy, and other policies affecting national security.
>
> (Dawn, Pakistan, 22 August 2013)

This provides the military with an opportunity to influence the policymaking in the country as they have control over intelligence and other relevant agencies. According to the prominent Pakistani columnist Muhammad Ziauddin (*Express Tribunes*, Pakistan, 27 August 2013),

> The decision to constitute a CCNS appears to have brought to its logical conclusion, the decades' long venture of the army to arrogate to itself constitutional powers to take over the country any time it thought it fit to do so without having to abrogate the Constitution or suspend it.

So this has provided a legal cover to the powerful military establishment to dominate national security policymaking, which was opposed by the civilian leadership, including the then Prime Minister Sharif in his earlier term.

Furthermore, the military has direct or indirect control over the Ministry of Defence (MoD), Ministry of Foreign Affairs (MoFA), and Ministry of Finance. In order to control these ministries, they have appointed serving and retired military officers to high-ranking positions in these ministries, while the civil bureaucrats have also protected the interests of the military. These military officers have maintained their relations with their predecessor institutions and informed them about their activities. Consequently, the military has controlled and monitored the ministries and their activities.

In this context, the Ministry of Foreign Affairs has worked to protect military interests. For example, the MoFA plays a key role in arms procurement decision making and controls the finances of the defence establishment. However, it has faced tremendous pressure from the military to provide extra funds and has no power to override the military's decisions (Chawla 2001). Similarly, the senate and parliament standing committee on foreign affairs has not made any significant impact on foreign policy. Such committees are lacking any institutional mechanism ensuring civilian scrutiny, while there has been no debate or consultation outside the national security establishment under either military or civilian regimes. The Rand Corporation quoted a foreign secretary's statement about Pakistan's foreign policy decisions: "wherever they are made, they are not made in the foreign office of Pakistan" (Fair *et al.* 2010, 113). Thus, the civil institutions in Pakistan lack control of decision making and serve military institutional interests, which have weakened them.

Thus, the military enjoys exceptional power in the Pakistani state and society. Like politicians, the civil bureaucracy has no authority to question military expenditure. In the prominent ministries such as the MoD and MoFA, the military has either direct control over key positions and/or induct pro-military civil bureaucrats to protect their interests. The MoD is dominated by serving and retired military officials, who occupy key positions. They monitor and control the ministry and work according to the desires of the military establishment (Anwar and Rafique 2012). More specifically, Lieutenant General Nasir Khan Janjua was appointed National Security Adviser (NSA) in October 2015. General Janjua had retired only a week earlier from the army to take up this position. He is the second military official to hold the post after Major General Mehmood Durrani, who served as NSA during the Zardari-led PPP government. His mandate was to oversee the national security of the country and build sustainable policies and mechanisms that aim to achieve a positive, progressive, peaceful, and secure Pakistan (*Pakistan Today*, 19 October 2015). Besides the NSA position, Lieutenant General (retired) Zamir-ul-Hassan Shah was the defence secretary in PMLN-led government, holding the key position in the Ministry of Defence. The military has quotas in the MoFA and has transferred personnel from the military to the ministry.

Additionally, the judiciary had also provided legal cover for extra-constitutional acts by the military. For example, the military used Article 58 (2) (b) to dismiss elected governments in 1990, 1993, and 1996. Subsequently, the judiciary justified such actions by the then president, except in 1992–1993, when Nawaz Sharif was dismissed by the president. The Sharif government was restored after the Supreme Court declared the dismissal of the prime minister as illegal (see Chapter 3).

In April 2010, the PPP-led government passed the 18th amendment of the constitution that was designed to restore the parliamentary system in the country and prevent undue military manipulation of the 1973 constitution by military dictators. The amendment removed the presidential power to dismiss parliament and gave authority to the prime minister to appoint military service chiefs (Shah 2014b). Moreover, the amendment provided for provincial autonomy and more financial resources in the national budget. However, General Qamar Zaman Bajwa, the present COAS, showed reservations about the 18th amendment, saying (Ziauddin, *Dawn*, Pakistan, 22 March 2018):

> It is being seen to have caused an imbalance between the federation and the provinces. The provinces do not have the capacity to shoulder all the

responsibilities that the amendment has transferred to the federating units. It is being seen as more dangerous than Sheikh Mujibur Rehman's six points[4] because following its passage the federation has turned into confederation.

Thus, the Pakistani military has expressed reservations about any acts that undermine their institutional interests. Nonetheless, they have maintained its functional dominance in state affairs.

Pakistan's military-jihadi nexus

The Pakistani military embraced Islamist groups as a politico-military strategy which would increase its prestige and position in the country within Pakistan's military-industrial complex. Therefore, the military mainly relied on militant groups to pursue their strategic interests in Afghanistan and Indian-administered Kashmir in the post-Cold War era. In the post-9/11 security environment, Pakistan has cracked down on militant groups, but it was selective as the Pakistani military distinguished between the militant groups on the grounds of their utility and the perceived threat from them. The ideology of the armed groups determines the perception of the threat that they pose to the Pakistani state (Staniland *et al.* 2018). Furthermore, the military considers the possible blowback as a consequence of ceasing aid and as imposing a crackdown on them. As such, the military looks into their reliability and contribution to their regional strategic interests and internal security within the country (Tankel 2018). As Paul Staniland *et al.* (2018, 4) explain:

> The Pakistani military has truly cracked down only when groups ideologically radicalized against the military and began making unacceptable political demands, rather than in response to outside pressure or a change in core military preferences. Pakistan's military appears entirely comfortable with a fractured monopoly of violence, as long as it functions on the military's political terms.

The anti-state groups such as Tehrik-i-Taliban Pakistan (TTP), Al-Qaeda, and Islamic Movement of Uzbekistan (IMU) were considered hostile and were dealt with according to the perceptions of their uncontrollability. For example, the Pakistani military took strong action against Al-Qaeda after 9/11. Being a US ally, there was also a greater international pressure on Pakistan to crack down on such groups. Subsequently, Pakistan targeted Al-Qaeda and handed over its operatives, along with other anti-Pakistan militants, to the US after the US invasion of Afghanistan in 2001. However, the Pakistani army left alone the Afghan Taliban and Pakistani militants, despite US pressure (Rashid 2008).

As regards the TTP, while it took responsibility for all major terror attacks in Pakistan, not every group within the TTP was considered hostile by the Pakistani military. The TTP is an umbrella group of various factions and ideologies in which some groups prioritize their fight against the Pakistani state, while others are involved in sectarian violence and/or are more focused on Afghanistan and the Kashmir insurgency. For example, the Punjabi Taliban, who were also members of Lashkar-e-Jhangvi (LeJ), Sipah-e-Sahaba Pakistan (SSP), and JeM, have been involved in sectarian violence in Pakistan but at the same time participated in the Kashmir militancy (Tankel 2018). Therefore, the Pakistani military has adopted a selective "carrot and stick approach" against the TTP and its affiliated groups. The military has conducted several military operations against the TTP, but it also signed agreements with them. Nevertheless, these groups benefitted from the government's deals and extended their outreach to their neighbouring areas. In the wake of the Mumbai terror attacks in 2008, the Pakistani military immediately changed its position over militant groups such as the TTP and called them "patriotic" Pakistanis. General Shuja Pasha, the then DG ISI, said that "We have no big issues with the militants in FATA. We have only some misunderstandings with Taliban commanders Baitullah Mehsud and Fazlullah. These misunderstandings could be removed through dialogue" (Roggio, *Long War Journal*, 1 December 2008). In response to the ISI's statement, the Pakistani Taliban offered a ceasefire if the military also stopped their operations against them. Actually, the military was sending a message to the US that Pakistan might leave the war on terror in case of Indian aggression in response to the 2008 Mumbai attacks (Hounshel, Foreign Policy, 30 November 2008). Thus, selective tolerance of militancy has remained a major strategic tool of Pakistan's foreign policy.

More specifically, Pakistan provides tacit support to groups that prioritize fighting against India and Afghanistan. Militant groups such as the Afghan Taliban have not only established their sanctuaries on the Pakistani side of the border but also received military aid from the ISI. Such groups are often considered "freedom fighters or liberation forces" by the Pakistani military for their activities in Afghanistan and Kashmir (Haqqani 2005; Siddiqa 2007). These groups included Lashkar-e-Taiba (LeT), the Afghan Taliban, the Haqqani Network, and local militias such as Hafiz Gul Bahadur and Mulvi Nazir in Waziristan. These groups were largely accommodated in former FATA areas, and the military struck peace deals with them (Staniland *et al*. 2018). Furthermore, the Pakistani security establishment maintained positive relations with these groups so that they were aligned with the government's agenda and coerced the militants involved in anti-state activities. For instance, LeT was provided with resources by the state to bring them into the mainstream and engage them in humanitarian work. Similarly, Pakistan was also trying to bring LeJ into the fold and stop their members engaging in anti-Pakistani activities (Tankel 2018). In this process, former FATA areas became a safe haven for militant groups such as the Haqqani Network, along with local Hafiz Gul Bahadur, Lashkar-i-Islam (Mangal Bagh), and Mulvi Nazir groups. Such groups have been involved in maintaining law and order locally in tribal areas. They are now locally known as "good Taliban" due to the tacit support of the Pakistani military (Staniland *et al*. 2018). Hence, the Pakistani military has protected those groups that could be utilized in Kashmir and Afghanistan, which has become Pakistan's military-jihadi complex.

In addition to this, the military formed an alliance with extreme right religious groups which could be used for political purposes to subdue secular political groups and individuals. During the Afghan war in the 1980s, the Pakistani military elite formed an alliance with far-right groups, which acted like a political wing of the Pakistani military. According to Khalid Aziz (interview by author, Islamabad, 5 December 2017), the former interior secretary of KP province,

> The Pakistan military strongly believed that if religious identity is imposed on Pakistan, they will be mentally ready to face any enemies who might attack Pakistan[,] especially India. Consequently, the religious narrative was propagated as the national identity by [the] military establishment.

Consequently, the far-right groups have become a more natural ally for the military. Such groups have often propagated the military's security narrative among the general public and thus served to protect their institutional interests. The IJI was used by the ISI to destabilize Bhutto's government between 1988 and 1990. Interestingly, the IJI worked almost perfectly as a political wing of the military to discredit the political process in the country. For example, the IJI started protests in favour of the Kashmir uprising in order to pressurize the Bhutto's government to end the peace process with India. They had also accused the government of being soft and accepting Indian hegemony in the region. Railway Minister Sheikh Rasheed Ahmed, then a prominent member of the IJI, said that "You cannot solve such historical and sensitive problems by sitting in the lap of Americans and acting according to their wishes" (Jain 1993). The IJI also used various political slogans which were based on an illegitimate distortion of the historical record, such as "You lost Dhaka, we won Kabul," a reference to the Bengali secessionist movement in 1971 and the Afghan resistance movement of the mujahedeen which had the support of the West (Haqqani 2005). Similarly, the IJI accused Nusrat Bhutto, the widow of Z. A. Bhutto and mother of Benazir Bhutto, of offering control of Pakistan's nuclear programme in Kahuta to the so-called "American Jewish lobby" to gain power in the 1990 election (*Nawa-e-Waqat*, Pakistan, 19 October 1990). This was how the military used the IJI to sway public opinion by branding those in control of the government as traitors to their country. Since then, the military has successfully used the religious card to destabilize civilian governments in order to interfere in the political sphere of the state.

Even more important, the Indian premier Vajpayee visited Lahore in February 1999, to normalize his country's relations with Pakistan during Nawaz Sharif's second term as prime minister. However, the then three service chiefs of the military, COAS General Musharraf, Air Chief Marshal Parvez Mehdi, and Admiral Fasih Bokhari, refused to welcome the Indian premier and said the government should not "welcome an enemy nation in this manner." In fact, they were arguing that the presence of Vajpayee would send the wrong message to the armed forces and lower their morale (Iype, Rediff, 20 February 1999). Moreover, the religious political groups such as JI initiated protests against the Indian premier's visit. Qazi Husain Ahmad, the then head of JI, stayed at the house of a military intelligence officer in order to avoid being arrested ahead of the protests (Haqqani 2005; Siddiqa 2007). Thus, the military used religious political groups to derail the political process, and the Islamists were once again acting like the political wing of the military. Since then, the religious class has acted as the political proxy of the Pakistani military.

In addition, General Musharraf wanted to have a civilian government that worked under his direction. The ISI formed their own king party known as PMLQ and secretly supported the MMA to counter mainstream secular political parties and use the MMA as an Islamic card in dealing with the US after 9/11. In the 2002 elections, the MMA emerged as a major political party and formed pro-vincial governments in KP and Balochistan provinces. So the Islamists emerged as a major opposition political party for the first time in the history of Pakistan. In this process of fostering religious groups and individuals, many hard-core religious leaders such as Maulana Azam Tariq became members of parliament after the 2002 election. After taking over the provincial government, the MMA launched an Islamization campaign in KP province. They called the entertain-ment industry un-Islamic and cracked down on musicians, cinema owners, and cable TV operators. They also initiated the Islamization of the education curricula in schools and declared co-education un-Islamic. They passed a Sharia bill in 2003, bringing the judicial, educational, and economic systems into line with the so-called Islamic interpretation (Abbas 2004). The MMA government laid the grounds for Talibanization in the north-west KP province. All this was done by the MMA government, under the so-called pro-West General Musharraf dictator-ship through his political engineering in the post-9/11 period. Thus, Musharraf's regime not only provided political space to the extremist elements but also has created domestic insecurity.

This fostering of extremist groups has continued with the tacit support of the ISI in the post-Cold War era. In 2011, the Difa-e-Pakistan Council (DPC), or the Defense of Pakistan Council, was formed, which the military has utilized for its institutional interests to pressurize the civilian government to adopt foreign and security policies favourable to the military. The DPC is a coalition of more than 40 politico-religious parties with extremist leaders, retired bureaucrats, and mili-tary officers in its ranks. Ironically, when the civilian government cracked down on such groups, especially on the extremist elements, it was the military who released them on bail. At a national security meeting, a former chief minister of Punjab, Shahbaz Sharif, said that "whenever action has been taken against certain groups by civilian authorities, the security establishment has worked behind the scenes to set the arrested free" (Almeida, *Dawn*, Pakistan, 6 October 2016). So the military had protected its proxy extremist groups when the civilian govern-ment took action against them. However, this often led to political instability in the country.

Like the DPC, the Tehreek-i-Labbaik Pakistan (TLP) and the Milli Muslim League are the new manifestation of this phenomenon, established in 2015 and 2017, respectively. Similarly, these groups are composed of Islamists, veteran jihadists, and members of far-right wing parties. Such alliances have been used to pressurize those secular political parties and other groups who are trying to establish civilian supremacy and transform the national security state that serves the military. Furthermore, such groups have opposed any rapprochement with India and the secularization of Pakistan by civilian governments (Rafiq 2012). For example, the former PMLN government proposed "The Elections Bill 2017" in the parliament in which the Khatm-i-Nabuwwat (finality of Prophet-hood) clause of oath was modified as Ahmadi community in Pakistan does not believe on Khatm-i-Nabuwwat. The TLP staged a 21-day sit-in in Islamabad, and finally the government was forced to restore the Khatm-i-Nabuwwat clause to its original form and removed the law minister on the demand of the protesters. The ISI mediated the talks between government and TLP, and the sit-in ended after the ISI official signed the agreement as "guarantor" (*Dawn*, Pakistan, 25 November 2017). The PMLN government was largely destabilized after the sit-in, and many accused that the ISI was behind it. However, the MoD rejected the allegations that ISI was behind the TLP sit-in (Malik, *Express Tribune*, Pakistan, 27 November 2017). Thus, the religious groups have often acted as an informal political wing of the military establishment and provided the opportunity for the army to indirectly control state affairs by subverting civilian rule.

Economic self-sufficiency: the military means and resources

Pakistan's military-industrial complex has provided the military to have its own financial means and resources. The military has burgeoning economic stakes in a range of businesses that have made it relatively financially autonomous and created a military ruling elite that enjoy benefits such as free education, healthcare, clubs, housing, and recreational facilities. Unlike other state institutions, the Pakistani military has used its institutional influence and power to convert official land into private real estate. It was noted, for example, that some military personnel acquire private and public lands at a very low price and then turn them into housing schemes, making millions in profits (Moreau, Foreign Policy, 12 October 2009). Real estate has become the military's biggest business in Pakistan, with the military controlling over 12 percent of all public land in 2007. The Pakistan military owns about 23 percent of the corporate assets of the country, with a net worth of US $20 billion, of which US $10 billion was in land and the remaining half was in private military assets (Aljazeera, Doha, 17 February 2008; Ilyas, Tahir and Khan 2016). This provides a significant financial capability to maintain the military's institutional autonomy within a national security state. Furthermore, the paramilitary rangers in Sindh province have seized fishing rights to more than 20 lakes, marginalizing hundreds of poor fishermen in the province. Professor Pervez Hoodbhoy pointed out: "all countries have armies, but in Pakistan things are reversed. Here, it is the Army that has a country" (Moreau, Foreign Policy, 12 October 2009). This suggests that the military has become a state within a state in Pakistan.

There has been both horizontal and vertical growth in the military-industrial complex since its establishment in 1954. For example, the military has extended its businesses in the private sector and established hundreds of enterprises under the NLC, FWO, and SCO. At the same time, the military welfare foundation has started various large- and small-scale businesses in various economic sectors across the country. The military has utilized its organizational influence to create economic opportunities and to make the military a key actor in the country's largest conglomerate of financial and industrial corporations. In this vein, General Zia gave all the railway cargo services contracts to the NLC after its formation in 1978 (Rizvi 2003). As a consequence, it has not only undermined existing civilian-run public sector entities, such as the railways, but also prevented the establishment of non-military entities.

The Pakistan military-economic empire has grown under both military and civilian regimes. The civilian governments have awarded contracts to military-run corporations to appease them and to remain in power. For example, the Punjab provincial government awarded many infrastructure mega-projects to the NLC and FWO. In 1999, the Sharif government awarded the contract for collecting tolls on and maintenance of the Grand Trunk Road (N-5) and Sukkur-Lahore highway to FWO. In 2017, the PTI provincial KP government awarded the contracts for five development mega-projects to the NLC directly without open bidding (Writ Petition No. 1367-P/2017).[5] The military has often cited security concerns to help ensure contracts go to military controlled entities. If a civilian government seemed likely to award a contract to non-military bidders, the military could react by raising the possibility of security threats and could subsequently obtain the contract at a very low price. Moreover, there have been widespread financial irregularities in the military-run projects. For example, the FWO has been involved in toll collection at major motorways for about 16 years. In 2014, the National Highway Authority (NHA) in Pakistan accused the FWO of declining in toll collections at motorways, despite an increase in toll charges and the flow of traffic. The federal auditors found "gross violations of accounting, bidding and financial rules not only by the FWO but the NHA as well" (Kiani, *Dawn*, Pakistan, 4 March 2014). In this process, the military was also able to gain a monopoly over government contracts in the transport sector while maintaining its budgetary requirements outside the national budget. Nonetheless, this has led to securitization of the Pakistani economy which is shrinking space for private investors.

As well as military business ventures, both civilian and military-led governments have consistently prioritized military expenditure over development spending. The military has traditionally received the lion's share of the national budget, and the country has continued to devote a massive amount to defence expenditure in the post-Cold War era. The details are given in Table 6.1.

While there has been a constant increase in absolute defence spending since 2008, there has been a significant decline in defence spending as a percentage of total government expenditure. However, this apparent decline in relative spending is misleading. Expenditure on the nuclear programme and missile technology are not reflected in the national budget. The cost of nuclear weapons is estimated to be US$5 billion dollars (Soherwordi 2005). Military pensions

Table 6.1 Pakistani military expenditure, 1993–2017

Year	Military Expenditure (Constant) USD in Million	Defence Expenditure as % of Total Expenditure
1993	5,567.89	25.102
1994	5,407.92	27.396
1995	5,501.41	27.206
1996	5,499.96	24.576
1997	5,266.15	25.037
1998	5,266.10	23.447
1999	5,318.17	23.975
2000	5,329.56	22.423
2001	5,701.40	24.032
2002	6,131.35	22.569
2003	6,551.98	25.414
2004	6,821.26	26.058
2005	7,099.59	24.451
2006	7,217.08	21.365
2007	7,267.28	18.028
2008	6,851.56	15.842
2009	7,060.87	16.940
2010	7,322.29	16.835
2011	7,718.75	16.981
2012	8,185.65	16.090
2013	8,455.40	15.907
2014	8,883.15	17.300
2015	9,649.19	17.962
2016	9,973.77	18.032
2017	10,378.21	16.655

Source: SIPRI Military Expenditure Database, 1993–2017, https://knoema.com/SIPRI2018/sipri-military-expenditure-database-1949-2017?tsId=1008580.

are also excluded from defence spending and have been paid from the civilian budget since 2001. The military received PKR 253,000 million in pensions alone in the 2017–2018 budget, which was more than three times higher than the amount devoted to civilian pensions (Budget in Brief 2018–2019). This means that the military is financing defence spending from the civilian budget. In the budget, the government only announces the overall figures for its defence expenditure and does not provide any details (Siddiqa 2002; Chawla 2001). Khwaja Asif, the then defence minister, asked "Whom [are] we are trying to fool by showing the military pension budget as part of the civilian budget?" (Mason 2016). According to official Pakistani budget documents, defence spending was PKR 720 billion in 2015. However, the Stockholm International Peace Research Institute (SIPRI) reported that Pakistan's defence spending was PKR 1 trillion, 40 percent higher than the official government reports (Singh 2015). So there has been no transparency in government military expenditure in Pakistan. Also, the military received a significant amount of the overall budget, and this has largely contributed to the growth of the military apparatus and its power in the state and society.

Furthermore, Pakistan received a significant amount of military and economic aid in the post-9/11 period. Details are given in Table 6.2.

In the post-Cold War era, the military has continued to oppose any public debate over military spending in the national budget and objected to any unilateral cuts to the defence budget by the civilian leadership. As during the Cold War, political leaders are not allowed to give any public statements about military expenditure in the national budget. Military spending came under discussion for the first time since independence in the PAC meeting in 2008. Furthermore, the MoD, headed by a civilian minister, is responsible for the oversight of military expenditure, allocation, and audits. However, there has been no audit of or accountability for military spending. In practice, the MoD must accept, without any debate, the budgetary allocations demanded by the armed forces. Besides the MoD, the Parliamentary Standing Committee on Defence (PSCD) has been technically empowered to investigate military budgets, administration, and policies. Nevertheless, the military hardly appears at the PSCD meetings and often say that they are unable to explain the budgetary allocations due to secrecy. The military has justified its stance by arguing that public debate over military spending would undermine national security and would leak critical information to an enemy state. The military has even advised the government to streamline public expenditure rather than questioning

Table 6.2 US aid to Pakistan, 2002–2017 (USD millions)

Year	Economic Aid	Military Aid
2002	990	100
2003	384	340
2004	109	395
2005	474	393
2006	660	386
2007	545	400
2008	498	483
2009	770	535
2010	1,930	1,024
2011	1,365	734
2012	1,231	84
2013	819	28
2014	735	290
2015	850	304
2016	505	275
2017	538	20
Total	**12,403**	**5,791**
Total US Aid	**18,194**	

Source: US Overseas Loans and Grants (Green book), https://eads
.usaid.gov/gbk/.

the defence budget (Shah 2014b). Thus, the military exploited the culture of secrecy in the defence budget to have economic self-sufficiency and autonomy.

Since 2008, the defence budget has been presented in the parliament, but civilian politicians have had little input. Senator Farhatullah Babar noted that "the defence budget should preferably be discussed in the PAC meeting prior to its approval by the Parliament." Also, the military welfare organization and its defence housing authority are involved in commercial activities, but are not included in the budget. For example, such corporations earned about US$2.3 million in the financial year 2003–2004 but were not mentioned in the budget (Siddiqa 2007). Under Pakistani law, these foundations are not obliged to open their balance sheets either to the public or to the auditor general (Moreau, Foreign Policy, 12 October 2009).

Under Pakistan's national security state, therefore, the military plays a very exceptional role in state and society. The military is economically self-sufficient, shapes domestic politics, and consequently takes all the key strategic decisions related to foreign and security policy, a pattern which is sustained by what might be called a hyper-military-industrial complex. The military has been acting as the sole guardian of the country by projecting itself as necessary for the very survival of Pakistan. In this process, the military claims first rights over the budget and foreign policy on India and Afghanistan and interferes in parliamentary and political developments within Pakistan (Khalid Aziz, interview by author, Islamabad, 5 December 2017). Former Prime Minister Nawaz Sharif said:

> There used to be [a] "state within a state" but now it's "state above the state" but this is not how the countries survive and run and to become a prosperous and democratic country[;] we have to change this course and sooner [rather than later].
>
> (M. Shah, The News, Pakistan, 11 July 11, 2018)

Thus, the Pakistani military-industrial complex has served the political and commercial interests of the Pakistani military elite but at the cost of increasing internal, external, and regional insecurity threats, creating political instability, and contributing to widespread socio-economic problems.

Linkages between the military-industrial complex and Pakistan's national security shortfalls

Internal security threats

As explained in previous chapters, Pakistan has used "proxy war" as a strategic tool of its foreign policy to protect its so-called national security interests. However, such proxy wars have created severe blowback, not reducing but increasing or creating internal and external security threats. The major consequences were home-grown terrorism and political violence in the country by

Islamist militant, sectarian, and separatist groups. The subsequent military operations against militant groups have caused massive collateral damage and injuries
and uprooted millions of people from their homes, causing them to become internally displaced in the country.

The seeds of extremism in Pakistan were sown well before 9/11. Pakistan's
northern part became the rallying point of the transnational jihadi groups fighting against the Soviets in Afghanistan. The Soviet forces were defeated by the
mujahedeen with covert military aid from the CIA-ISI. Brigadier Muhammad
Saad (interview by author, Islamabad, 14 November 2017) said that,

> With [the] collapse of the Soviet Union, a new radical Islam emerged after the
> breakup of Soviet Union. Groups such as Al-Qaeda and its affiliated groups
> came into being that threatened nation states. This was threat to the West and
> all the nation states emerged after Second World War including Pakistan.
> Subsequently, Afghanistan and Pakistan were in turmoil and central Asia
> was threatened.

So Pakistan had to deal with the new threat of radical Islam in the post-Cold
War era, which became a bigger threat to the country in the post-9/11 security
situation.

In the above context, the victory of the mujahedeen in Afghanistan influenced many radical Islamist groups in Pakistan who thought that they could
achieve their objectives through an armed uprising. In June 1989, Maulana Sufi
Muhammad, a hard-core religious cleric, launched the Tehrik-e-Nifaz-e-Shariat-
e-Muhammadi (TNSM or Movement for the Enforcement of Sharia Law) in the
Malakand division of KP province in the north-west of Pakistan (Malik 2008).
The TNSM demanded the "imposition of Sharia" in the Malakand division even
before the emergence of the Taliban as a political force in Afghanistan in 1994
(Ashok 2007). The TNSM protests forced the government to announce the Sharia
Regulation of 1994. However, Sufi Muhammad was not satisfied with the regula-
tion and staged an armed uprising in Swat district in May 1994. Many government
installations, including Siadu Sharif airport, were occupied by the TNSM in the
Swat district of Malakand. The government launched a successful paramilitary
force operation in Swat to crush the TNSM armed uprising (Ali and Khan 2010).
So the rise of Islamist militancy in Pakistan was a pre-9/11 phenomenon.

Furthermore, the TNSM raised an armed *Lashkar* of 10,000 people to fight
against the US-led NATO forces in Afghanistan following the US invasion of
Afghanistan in 2001. Most of the TNSM personnel were killed in the fight with
the Northern Alliance's forces in Afghanistan. However, Sufi Muhammad and
Fazlullah, the future TTP central leader, returned to Pakistan. They were arrested
by the Pakistani military for illegally crossing into Afghanistan (M. Ali, New
American Foundation, September 2010). Fazlullah was released after 18 months
in prison.

Similarly, Maulana Sami-ul-Haq, the chief of JUI-S, demanded a Sharia-
based Islamic system in the 1990s. He was also the director and chancellor of

the infamous religious seminary known as Darul Uloom Haqqania in the Akora Khattak area of Nowshera city in KP province. It is generally believed that most of the Afghan Taliban studied at the Haqqania seminary, including Mullah Omar, the founder of the Afghan Taliban. The seminary was used as a launching pad for the Taliban movement in Afghanistan, and that is why Sami-ul-Haq proudly called himself the "Father of the Taliban" (I. Ali, 2007).

The rise of the Afghan Taliban influenced many outlawed militant and extremist groups based in Pakistan, who demanded the imposition of the sharia law in the country. For example, sectarian and Kashmiri militant groups such as LeJ, JeM, LeT, and the Kashmir-based Jamati Islami increased their sectarian activities targeting minority religious groups in the country. In the post-Cold War era, most of these groups received a significant supply of weapons, manpower, military training, and funds from Afghanistan. It was difficult to distinguish between sectarian and other jihadi organizations as they were involved in both sectarian and jihadi activities at the same time. For instance, JeM was mainly a jihadi organization but it was also involved in sectarian violence, whereas SSP was a sectarian outfit but fought alongside the Afghan Taliban with the alleged support of the ISI. Therefore, the subsequent governments in the 1990s were unable to take action against these groups despite their involvement in domestic violence (Grare 2007). During the period 1990–1999, 1977 terror related incidents were reported, in which 4,338 were wounded and 2,405 killed (Saeed *et al.* 2014). Thus, the Islamist radicalization in Pakistan was a pre-9/11 phenomenon but it significantly increased post-9/11.

In the post-9/11 setting, Pakistani governments did not seem to learn from their experiences and continued with proxy wars in Kashmir and Afghanistan. General Musharraf joined the war on terror, but his policy was somewhat ambiguous and contradictory. For instance, Islamabad supported the Kabul regime after 9/11 but at the same time aided the Afghan Taliban (Siddiqa 2011). Also, Pakistan did not take proactive measures to stop the infiltration of transnational jihadi groups in border areas between Afghanistan and Pakistan following the US invasion of Afghanistan in 2001. Many members of Al-Qaeda and its affiliated jihadi groups and their leadership shifted to former FATA areas and other parts of Pakistan. The militants were mainly Arabs, Central Asians, Chechens, and Afghan Taliban, along with their families. They have used their past connections in the Afghan war to settle in different parts of Pakistan, especially along the Durand line in tribal areas. Interestingly, Al-Qaeda operatives were escorted by their hosts to safe houses in major cities in the country as well (Rashid 2008). North Waziristan became the centre of the Haqqani Network, along with local militant groups such as Molvi Nazir and Hafiz Gul Bahadur who were mainly targeting NATO and Afghan forces in Afghanistan and their supply routes (Waseem 2011). TTP and their affiliated militant groups established their writ in other parts of the former FATA areas in 2004. In this process, the former FATA and the adjacent areas of the KP province became safe havens for Afghan Taliban and Al-Qaeda and their affiliated militant organizations. They established many sleeper cells across Pakistan, mainly in big cities such as

Karachi, Lahore, Faisalabad, and Rawalpindi (Ashok 2007). Thus, the militant landscape shifted to the Pakistani side of the border, and this created a major security threat to Pakistan when the militant groups started targeting Pakistani government installations.

Meanwhile, in May 2002, Pakistan started half-hearted selective military operations in the former FATA area, but it was too late by then as most of the militant groups had found sanctuaries in tribal areas (Rashid 2008). Also the Pakistani military was trying to protect its proxy militant groups, especially the Afghan Taliban and other local groups which emphasize jihad against NATO forces in Afghanistan. For example, Al-Qaeda and its affiliated groups settled in the former FATA and the adjoining areas in KP province, while the Afghan Taliban and its command structure were located in Quetta, the capital city of Balochistan province, so that they could slip under the radar of US forces, which were chasing Al-Qaeda operatives. Moreover, Pakistan handed over Al-Qaeda and other anti-Pakistan militants to the US but kept the Afghan Taliban in their own custody as mentioned. Moreover, the recently emerged Pashtun Tahafuz (protection) Movement (PTM), from tribal areas in Pakistan, claimed that the military had turned a blind eye to Taliban activities in their areas and let them establish their writ in tribal areas in the post-9/11 period (Dawar, *The Washington Post*, 17 April 2019). This meant that because the Pakistan military leaders tried to protect their proxies, the militant activities shifted to the Pakistani side of the border, which posed a security threat to the country.

In 2004, Taliban militancy gradually spilled over into the Swat district of KP province. After releasing from jail, Mulana Fazullah restarted his militant activities in Swat and the neighbouring districts of KP under the banner of TNSM. Many Punjab-based militant groups such as LeJ, LeT, and JeM patronized in the Malakand division as they had a past connection with Swat-based militant commanders. These groups formed their own training camps following the crackdown on militant organizations by the government in 2002 and then following the earthquake of 2005 which had hit the areas where these militants had training camps and facilities (ICG 2013). Ibni Amin, a prominent Taliban commander, along with other Taliban commanders, was reportedly associated with JeM and Al-Qaeda. Subsequently, the TNSM has strengthened its control over Swat and neighbouring areas (Yusufzai, *The News*, Pakistan, 9 May 2009). As in the former FATA area, the government also completely neglected the TNSM's activities in Swat and responded only when the TNSM organization controlled the whole district. In March 2007, the government arranged the first official meeting with the military to discuss the Swat militancy (Roggio 2007). Therefore, the government either was incompetent to counter the Taliban uprising at the beginning or wanted to patronize their proxy militant groups in the Swat district and adjoining areas in KP province.

Like the military operations in the former FATA area, the Pakistani military began half-hearted military operations in Swat in November 2007. The operations continued until January 2009 without any major success. The military used conventional force that further alienated the local population from the Pakistani military due to massive collateral damage and injury. Ironically, the Taliban FM radio, which was their main source of communication with the local population but could have been jammed, continued to operate throughout this period. More specifically, Mulana Fazlullah, known as radio Mullah, used the FM radio very affectively in terrorizing the society in order to establish its writ in the area. The military failed to shut down the Taliban FM radio station until mid-2009 when the Taliban was dislodged from Swat and adjoining areas in the Malakand division of KP province. After consolidating its power in Swat, the Taliban extended their control to the neighbouring districts of Buner, Shangla, and Dir (Zain 2009). In December 2007, Fazlullah joined the TTP and became the general secretary of TTP central and head of the TTP's Swat chapter. The TTP established their sharia courts and used their infamous police force known as the Shaheen Commandos to control the Swat district despite the presence of the district administration of the Pakistani government (Siddique 2012). As a result, Swat became the second stronghold and safe haven of the militants after the former FATA area. Thus, the Taliban militancy extended to settled areas in the north-west of the country. According to Brigadier Asad Munir (*Express Tribune*, Pakistan, 7 November 2012), "when General Kayani took command of the army, about 19 administrative units of former FATA and KP were completely or partially under the control of Taliban." So Pakistan has almost given up the former FATA area, Swat, and its adjoining areas in the KP province to Taliban and other militant groups in order to protect its proxies.

After 9/11, thus, insecurity in Pakistan has deepened as a result of the activities of the home-grown armed groups across the country. There were about 58 religious political parties and 24 armed jihadi groups in 2001–2002. Many of the militant groups operated independently and have established links with religious political parties. After the Cold War, the ISI began to lose control over these groups, who gradually started to engage in anti-state activities following 9/11. Some groups of Pakistan's military-jihadi complex turned against the state when General Musharraf apparently changed the country's Kashmir policy due to international pressure. In particular, the ISI failed to predict the security threat arising from these armed groups (Abbas 2004). Many Kashmiri commanders and organizations joined anti-state TTP and Al-Qaeda groups. Ilyas Kashmir, a former ISI functionary and Kashmiri militant commander, became a prominent Al-Qaeda operative and ran the infamous operational wing of Al-Qaeda known as the "313 Brigade." Ilyas was behind many high-profile attacks on well-protected military facilities in Pakistan due to his former links with the ISI and Pakistani military (Haqqani 2013).

The TTP became the most lethal group after making alliances with the leaders of Kashmir-based militant groups such as LeJ and JeM and their leaderships. They had attacked military headquarters, several ISI buildings and other government installations across the country. The major high-profile terrorist attacks included the Mehran naval air station in Karachi, the Kamra Air Force base in Wah Cantt, the ISI headquarters in Lahore, the GHQ in Rawalpindi, the Sri Lankan cricket team, the Marriot hotel in Islamabad, and the Pearl Continental hotel in Peshawar (PIPS Security Report 2007). Besides this, the militants targeted political gatherings of anti-Taliban parties or groups or individuals, police stations, transport stations, hotels, educational institutions, banks, hospitals, gas stations, funeral ceremonies, and NATO supply caravans. After deadly assaults on the Sri Lankan cricket team in 2009, no major international cricket team visited Pakistan (Zain 2009). Benazir Bhutto, Bashir Ahmad Bilour, Maulana Hasan Jan, Dr. Muhammad Farooq, Mufti Sarfraz Naeemi, and Haroon Bilour are among the high-profile politicians and religious figures who have been killed in terrorist attacks. The estimated economic cost of terrorism was about US$70 billion during the first ten years of the war on terror (Saikal 2014), in addition to about 81,000 civilian deaths. The total number of casualties between 2004 and 2013 is given in Table 6.3.

Thus, the proxy wars in Kashmir and Afghanistan conducted by the Pakistani military have had significant negative consequences for Pakistan's internal security and have largely destabilized the whole country. The internal security threat became almost an existential one to Pakistan in the post-9/11.

Since 2013, there has been a significant decrease in the number of terror attack due to successful military operation against the militant groups across the country. Nonetheless, the country witnessed another wave of terrorism during the last parliamentary elections in July 2018. On 15 July 2018, more than 150 people were killed and 186 wounded in a suicide attack on a political gathering in the Mastung district of Balochistan province. It was the deadliest terrorist bombing in the country after the APS attack in Peshawar in 2014 (S. A. Shah and Sheerani, *Dawn*, Pakistan, 15 July 2018). Overall, more than 200 people, including three electoral candidates, were killed in various terrorist attacks during the election campaign.

Additionally, religious extremism and radicalization is at its peak, which has led to sectarian violence in the country. The minority religious communities are more insecure than before. After taking office, Prime Minister Imran Khan pointed out in an interview (Ratwatte, Daily FT, 25 August 2018) that:

Table 6.3 Number of fatalities resulting from terrorism, military operations, and drones

Civilians and Combatants	Fatalities
Pakistani civilians	48,504
Journalists	45
Civilians killed by drones	416–951
Pakistani security forces	5,498
Militants	26,862
Total	**81,325–81,860**

Source: *IPPNW, PSR and PGS* 2015 Report: Casualty Figures after 10 Years of the "War on Terror" in Iraq, Afghanistan and Pakistan.

This country has been radicalized. We are more insecure than ever before. There is something like US $80 billion that this country has lost in war; US aid is about US $20 billion. The country is sinking into poverty, into chaos; the state is getting weaker. There is a consensus in Pakistan that there is no military solution therefore we will look for a political solution.

On 31 October 2018, the TLP started protests across Pakistan when the Supreme Court acquitted Asia Bibi after eight years on death row over a case of alleged blasphemy. Following the verdict, "the TLP leaders called for the judges to be killed and for army officers to commit mutiny against the army chief [if he supported the decision]" (*Independent*, UK, 2 November 2018). The TLP protests blocked major cities throughout the country. The government failed to maintain the writ of the state for three days and finally surrendered to the protesters' major demands by illegally putting Asia Bibi on the exit control list and reopening her case in the Supreme Court. Nonetheless, she was set free and left the country in May 2019 (N. Siddiqui, *Dawn*, Pakistan, 8 May 2019).

Ironically, the military always took credit for improving the security situation and stability in the country while placing all the blame on the civilians for insecurity and political instability. Nonetheless, Pakistan has confronted internal security threats arising from the military's flawed foreign and security policy under the military-first national security approach. The military diverts the attention of the public when there are massive security lapses. For example, the undetected US Special Force raid in Abbottabad that killed Bin Laden in May 2011 badly damaged the military's reputation in the eyes of the general public. Even so, the military successfully deflected attention from itself by exploiting anti-US sentiments. The DG ISI blamed the US for carrying out a "sting operation" on an ally. The joint session of parliament and senate showed full confidence in the armed forces and strongly condemned the US for its unilateral actions on Pakistani territory (Fair and Gregory 2012). Hence, the military has maintained its control in state affairs despite a massive security failure in the country. Nonetheless, the militarization in Pakistan has not only created insecurity but it has destroyed the political and socio-economic fabric of the society.

External security threats

As argued previously, the policies of successive Pakistani governments proved to be self-defeating, as the country adopted a dual policy to protect its proxy militant groups and also participate in the US-led global war on terror. This ambivalent policy had negative consequences for Pakistan's relations with the outside world, especially with the US, India, and Afghanistan. Consequently, despite an opportunity to fight a common enemy, Pakistan-US relations failed to mature into a viable long-term relationship following the 9/11 terror attacks. Islamabad was often blamed by US governments for security setbacks in Afghanistan. The Afghan government and society also became very hostile towards Pakistan (Ejaz Hussain, interview by author, Islamabad, 14 November 2017). This has provided

an opportunity to India to restore its old relations and establish a strategic partnership with Kabul, which has become another major security concern for the
Pakistani strategists in the post-Cold War era.

In this context, Pakistan also lost its position of strategic depth in Afghanistan
against India, for which it had invested in various warring factions in that country
since the Soviet invasion of 1979. Moreover, the fall of the Afghan Taliban was
a nightmare for Pakistani strategists who had actively pursued this proxy war
policy in the post-Cold War era. Despite this failure, Pakistani strategists have
continued to protect their proxies, which Pakistan could use for any future settlement in Afghanistan. Because of this strategic depth policy, Kabul has become
very antagonistic towards Pakistan, while India has successfully increased its
cooperation with the Afghan government. With Indian influence in Afghanistan,
Islamabad is now confronted by a potential two-front war with India on both
its eastern and western fronts. Islamabad has blamed India for the instability in
Balochistan province and tribal areas in KP province on the western border with
Afghanistan.

In addition, there was increasing international pressure on Pakistan to give up
their pro-militancy policy in the post-9/11 setting, which Islamabad used to further its strategic interests in places like Kashmir and Afghanistan. At the same
time, any strict actions against proxy militant groups would have severe repercussions for Pakistan. Due to external pressure from the US, General Musharraf
had apparently revised his Kashmir policy and announced that "no organisation will be able to carry out terrorism on the pretext of Kashmir. Whoever
is involved with such acts in the future will be dealt with strongly whether
they come from inside or outside the country" (BBC, South Asia, 12 January
2002). Subsequently, Musharraf announced a crackdown on militant groups and
banned LeJ, JeM, LeT, SSP, TNSM, Sepah-e-Muhammad Pakistan, Tehreek-e-
Jaafria Pakistan, and Tehreek-e-Islami (*Express Tribune*, Pakistan, 24 October
2012). Many prominent leaders of the religious political parties, including Fazl-
ur-Rahman and Qazi Hussain Ahmed, were arrested because of their protests
against the US invasion.

However, the crackdown on militant organizations was just a face-saving exercise by General Musharraf to show the US that Pakistan was sincere in the global
war on terror. Nevertheless, there was internal opposition to General Musharraf's
revised Kashmir policy and his apparent agreement to work at the behest of the
US and other Western countries. On 4 February 2004, General Musharraf clarified
to senior journalists that "Pakistan has two vital national interests: being a nuclear
state and the Kashmir cause" (Daily Khabrain, Islamabad, 6 February 2004; in
Haqqani 2005, 6). This meant that Musharraf was reassuring his military and the
religious groups that he had not abandoned the core policies towards Kashmir
and was only making adjustments in some areas to regain US trust and support
(Haqqani 2005). One can conclude that there was no major strategic change in the
Pakistani policy towards militancy post-9/11. The leaders of such groups were
just asked to keep a low profile until the situation had eased and then they would
be allowed to resume their activities (Jones 2002). Consequently, such outlawed

groups resurfaced when the pressure from the US receded. The militant groups later restarted their activities under new names.

In this context, Pakistan was accused of being a state sponsor of terrorism because of its support for various militant groups. However, Pakistan officially denied any link with such groups. According to Shabana Feyyaz (interview by author, Islamabad, 20 November 2017), "India very skilfully changed the world's opinion of the Kashmir insurgency movement by labelling it as a terrorist activity being masterminded by Pakistan against India." Farhan Saddiqi (interview by author, Islamabad, 13 November 2017) said that "the Indian narrative of presenting Pakistan as a state sponsor of terrorism won despite the country's alliance with the US in the global war on terror. It is the failure of the Pakistani ruling elite."

Pakistan had signed the UN Security Council resolution on anti-terrorist financing (Resolution-1267 of 1999) after becoming the US ally in the global war on terror in 2004. Under the resolution, Pakistan must take strict action against militant groups and individuals such as the Haqqani Network, LeT, and their leaderships. Nonetheless, Pakistan has not taken any action against these groups (Sirrs 2016). Consequently, Pakistan was put on the grey list of the Financial Action Task Force (FATF) on money laundering during 2012–2015. Pakistan was removed from the list when Islamabad took significant measures to counter terrorist financing. However, Islamabad softened its policies once the pressure was reduced. According to the former Pakistani ambassador Hussain Haqqani,

> Pakistan has been able to take one step forward to get relief from international pressure, followed by two steps back once the pressure is off and another step forward, when the pressure resumes. The fundamental change in attitude has not been forthcoming.
>
> (N. Shahid, Asia Times, South Asia, 19 March 19, 2018)

In October 2016, the civilian leadership in the All Parties' Conference (APC)[6] warned the security establishment that Pakistan needed to act against militant groups in order to end Pakistan's international isolation. According to foreign secretary Aizaz Chaudhry, "the principal international demands are for action against Masood Azhar and the Jaish-i-Mohmmad; Hafiz Saeed and the Lashkar-e-Taiba; and the Haqqani network" (Almeida, *Dawn*, Pakistan, 6 October 2016). When this information was reported in *Dawn* news, the military establishment accused the civilian leadership of breaching national security, which led to a rift between them. As a result of military pressure, the government declared "the *Dawn* report is planted and fabricated and a breach of national security." The government dismissed the Information Minister Pervaiz Rashid (*The News*, Pakistan, 11 May 2017). Hence, the civilian leadership was unable to take action against the militant groups but dismissed their own information minister to appease the military.

Despite the Pakistani military's denial, Islamabad was warned by the FATF on many occasions, but the Pakistani authority did not take any significant step to stop terrorist financing. As a result, Islamabad was put once again on the FATF's grey list in March 2018. At the FATF meeting, Pakistan's close allies such as China and Saudi Arabia refused to vote in its favour. This meant that China and Saudi Arabia sent a message to Pakistan to crack down on the militants, as they are confronted by similar threats in their countries (Shahid, *Asia Times*, South Asia, 19 March 2018). Therefore, this policy of proxy war has created significant external pressure on Pakistan and the country has been accused of being a state sponsor of terrorism by the US, the UK, Russia, and India as well as Iran, China, and Saudi Arabia (Sirrs 2016). Thus, the proxy wars under Pakistan's military-jihadi complex have perpetuated insecurity within the country and made the external environment more threatening to its state and society. In reality, Pakistan has become a diplomatic pariah state due to its alleged support for the militant groups in Kashmir and Afghanistan.

In addition, the recent flare-up between India and Pakistan started after a suicide attack on the Indian police force in Pulwama area of Indian-administered Kashmir on 14 February 2019 (Pandya 2019). Pakistan-based JeM claimed responsibility for the attack. India blamed Pakistan for the attack and carried out air strikes on alleged JeM training camp inside Pakistan in which India claimed to have killed many prominent militant commanders. The very next day, Pakistan retaliated and shot down Indian aircraft in its own airspace and captured an Indian pilot. The airstrike has significant strategic consequences for Pakistan as India is gone from its traditional policy of restraint following the 1971 war (Yusuf 2019). Soon Pakistan released the Indian pilot in order to deescalate the tension.

In this context, India's response to Pulwama terror attack demonstrates a new Indian strategic aggressive posture towards Pakistan. India is now demonstrating itself as an assertive power in the South Asian region. India sent a clear message to Pakistan that they will not tolerate any further terror attack by alleged Pakistan-based militant groups on its soil, which they will chase across the border in case of further cross-border attacks. In its official statement, India's foreign ministry said:

> The air-strikes were not against any nation, but against terror. India did not attack its neighbour's military installations whereas Pakistan did so. There can be little doubt that the Balakot airstrikes signal the advent of India as a more active – but still restrained – military actor in world affairs.
>
> (Pandya 2019, 67)

This is a significant blow to the Pakistani strategists who relied on proxy wars and believed that India would not react beyond LoC and its borders due to Pakistan's nuclear weapons capabilities. Previously, Pakistan has successfully used nuclear deterrence to prevent war with India in case of terror attacks. This showed Indian resolve to target inside Pakistan by using the strategic space above terrorism and below nuclear threshold. In fact, India has created a strategic space for conventional war below the nuclear threshold. This means that India will not continue its strategic restraint policy against Pakistan in case of any further cross-border terrorism (Chawla, *IPCS*, 8 March 2019). Thus, the Indian airstrikes questioned the Pakistani narrative of nuclear deterrence and its threshold by targeting inside

Pakistan. More importantly, Pakistan's security has been declined due to its use of proxy war.

Furthermore, India is now using its growing global diplomatic clout and much greater financial strength by isolating Pakistan to impose sanctions and declare as a terror-sponsoring country. US Secretary of State Mike Pompeo said that that "the United States stand[s] with India as it confronts terrorism." Similarly, other US officials supported "India's right to self-defense against cross-border terrorism" (Yusuf 2019). Despite Pakistan's opposition, India was invited as a chief guest in the recent OIC conference of which Pakistan is a founding member state. More importantly, the Kashmir issue was not included in the OIC final declaration held in Abu Dhabi in March 2019. The UN Security Council also condemned the Pulwama attack and named Pakistan-based JeM as the main culprit behind the attack (Pandya 2019). Thus, Pakistan's strategic space has also dwindled due to its proxy wars, and now there has been growing international pressure to change its foreign and security policy.

Regional security in South Asia

Unlike other regions, South Asia has confronted many security challenges such as terrorism, nuclearization, ethnic conflict, Islamic radicalism, abject poverty, growing human rights violations, enforced disappearances, refugee crises, and many other related human security problems in the contemporary world (Soherwordi 2005). India and Pakistan are stuck in the security dilemma in which their continuous hostility has a significant impact on the overall security environment of the South Asian region. Kashmir has remained one of the largest military conflicts between India and Pakistan since 1947, while Afghanistan has remained fragile after four decades of continuous war, in which the two countries are fighting for their respective strategic interests.

In this situation, India and Pakistan have emphasized their respective regional security concerns and objectives, but they have chosen different paths. Islamabad is developing and deploying weapons systems below the nuclear threshold in order to counter India's conventional military capability, whereas New Delhi is building weapons to increase its strategic deterrence capability (Dalton and Tandler 2012). Although India says that its systems are intended to counter Chinese military power, Pakistan feels that they are more aimed at Pakistan than China. Consequently, both states have persisted with military competition that has led to an expensive arms race between the two countries despite chronic socio-economic problems such as abject poverty, illiteracy, and a low level of human development. Pakistan purchased Agosta 90B submarines from France in 1994, worth around US$1 billion. This was a huge amount for a poor country like Pakistan and could have financed "a year of primary school education for the 17 million children now out of school, safe drinking water for all 67 million people lacking this facility at present, and family planning services to an additional nine million couples" (Soherwordi 2005, 41). India spent US$4.5 billion on advanced military equipment, which could have financed "primary education for the 45 million children denied such education, safe drinking water for the 226 million people with no access to such facility, and family planning services for an additional 22 million couples" (Soherwordi 2005, 41). Thus, military competition was prioritized over socio-economic development in the region due to hostile relations.

Afghanistan has been a threat to regional stability in South Asia because India and Pakistan have been competing there for their diverse strategic objectives. Afghanistan has become a battleground for Indian and Pakistani strategists to pursue their security interests in the region (Stobdan 1999). While India is trying to support anti-Pakistan elements in Kabul, Pakistan has continued its support for proxy militant groups such as the Haqqani Network in order to counter Indian influence in Kabul. Consequently, Afghanistan has remained destabilized due to the strategic interests of the regional countries, especially India and Pakistan.

The rise of Islamist radicalism has been a greater threat to regional security in South Asia. With the rise of the Taliban in Afghanistan, many Islamist groups and commanders gathered there in the mid-1990s. Moreover, Kashmir-based militant groups joined hands with TTP and Al-Qaeda, and this has become a very dangerous phenomenon in the post-9/11 period (Howenstein 2009). Nonetheless, Pakistan has continued with its proxy wars in Afghanistan in order to counter Indian influence there, whereas India has continued to support anti-Pakistan groups in Afghanistan. As a consequence, the South Asian region has remained insecure due to cross-border terrorism in Pakistan, Afghanistan, and India. Pakistan accused India and Afghanistan of causing unrest in Balochistan and the former FATA area, whereas India and Afghanistan alleged Pakistan's involvement in terrorist attacks in their countries. The Kashmir uprising in 1990 and subsequent cross-border terrorism in 2001 and then 2008 Mumbai terror attacks brought the two nuclear states to the brink of nuclear war, which would have had devastating security implications for regional and international security (Qumber *et al.* 2018).

Furthermore, the India-Pakistan antagonism prevented South Asia from achieving its true economic potential and regional integration. South Asian Association for Regional Co-operation (SAARC) has remained ineffective and, in fact, South Asia is the least integrated region in the world. Interestingly, bilateral and internal security issues are exempted from the agenda of the SAARC, mainly due to the Pakistan-India rivalry and Indian hegemonic strength in the region. Consequently, SAARC has been unable to address any key issue confronted by the South Asian countries (Bailes 2007). Thus, South Asia has been largely destabilized due to the India-Pakistan enmity, both during and after the Cold War.

Most recently, the India-Pakistan relations deteriorated after India annexed Kashmir by revoking Article 370 of the Indian constitution on 5 August 2019. This article granted special status to Jammu and Kashmir including Ladakh area. Moreover, India also removed Article 35A which allowed the Kashmiri legislature to define permanent residents of the state. This change will provide New Delhi full control over Jammu and Kashmir. With the scrapping of the special status of Kashmir, New Delhi has altered its traditional position over Kashmir since the Shimla accord in 1972. Under this agreement, Pakistan and India need to resolve their outstanding issues including Kashmir bilaterally. Now India will consider the Kashmir conflict purely an internal matter rather than a bilateral dispute between India and Pakistan. Rajnath Singh, Indian defence minister, said that "any future talks with Pakistan will be on Pakistan-administered Kashmir only" (Sharma, South Asian Voices, 19 August 2019).

This annexation of Kashmir has provoked outrage in Pakistan and global worries over a fresh armed conflict between the two nuclear weapons countries. Pakistan responded by downgrading diplomatic relations with its neighbour and calling on international allies to take its side. Prime Minister Imran Khan accused the Modi-led Indian government of promoting a "racist ideology." Imran Khan said that "I fear they may initiate ethnic cleansing in Kashmir to wipe out the local population." The Pakistani senior military official said that "The Pakistan army stands firmly by the Kashmiris in their just struggle … We are prepared and shall go to any extent to fulfil our obligations" (Parker, *The Washington Post*, 13 August 2019). So the Indian decision by revoking Jammu and Kashmir special status has further escalated the security situation in the region. This will provide an opportunity for the militant groups to regain its position in Kashmir.

Furthermore, Pakistan has intensified its diplomatic offensive to gain international support over the Kashmir conflict by initiating outreach to the UN, OIC, China, and the US. Moreover, Pakistan expelled Indian high commissioner in Pakistan and stopped cross-border trade between the two countries. The primary objective was to internationalize the issue of Kashmir. In the recent UN general assembly meeting, Prime Minister Imran Khan warned the world leaders about the risk of the Kashmir conflict between the two nuclear states. Imran Khan said that (Borger and Farooq, *The Guardian*, UK, 26 September 2019):

> My main reason for coming here was to meet world leaders at the UN and speak about this. We are heading for a potential disaster of proportions that no one here realises. It is the only time since the Cuban crisis that two nuclear-armed countries are coming face to face. We did come to face to face in February.

The international community has raised concerns about the situation in Kashmir, with UN Secretary General Antonio Guterres urging "maximum restraint" by all parties. US State Department spokesperson Morgan Ortagus said that "We are concerned about reports of detentions and urge respect for individual rights and discussion with those in affected communities. We call on all parties to maintain peace and stability along the Line of Control" (Parker, *The Washington Post*, 13 August 2019). However, Pakistan wanted international community actions, not restraint. The failure of Pakistan is mainly due to India growing diplomatic outreach and Islamabad's support of proxy militant groups. Nonetheless, the continued hostility between India and Pakistan has further destabilized the region.

Political instability

Backed by Pakistan's military-industrial complex, the military has often intervened in the political sphere of state affairs, which has led to weak civilian institutions, and democracy has remained fragile in Pakistan. From Pakistan's inception in 1947, the military elite have controlled state affairs directly and/or indirectly. The military ruled the country directly for 31 years, while maintaining its control over the civilian government from behind the scenes in the remaining years. The military has played a kingmaker role when not directly in power by nurturing loyal politicians, far-right groups, and political parties and manipulating elections to bring their favoured party into power to protect their institutional interests. So the military has been actively involved in the political engineering of the civilian administration which could protect their institutional interests. However, such military interference has often created political instability in the country.

Within the national security state, the Pakistani military elite have set a precedent to have a controlled form of democracy where the military has the power to take all key decisions of strategic importance. The military opposed any attempt by a civilian government to act independently in affairs of state during and after the Cold War. After Bhutto taking office in 1988, the military did not like her initiative to normalize relations with India and her criticism of the military's pro-militancy strategy in Afghanistan. Moreover, Bhutto, being a liberal politician, had a very good reputation across the world, especially in the Western countries, and, had she succeeded, this would have marked the end of military control over state affairs in Pakistan. Therefore, the military was against her government from the beginning and used the IJI to derail her government. This fostering of extremist far-right groups has continued with the tacit support of the ISI in the post-Cold War era (see earlier section). However, it has largely destabilized the country and undermined the democratic process in the country.

Despite having a parliamentary system in the 1990s, Pakistan was ruled by a troika of the president, prime minister, and COAS. In practice, the prime minister had a very limited role in the troika due to the constitutional amendment introduced by General Zia, whereas the president was holding the most powerful position, exercising discretionary powers under the eighth amendment (Nawaz 2009). With the support and influence of the Pakistani military, presidents dismissed three elected governments in 1990, 1993, and 1996, and then General Musharraf imposed martial law in October 1999. No civilian government completed its full five-year term during the 1990s, a reflection of the political instability in the country. The military remained de facto rulers of the country despite civilian government throughout the 1990s.

In this context, Pakistan was unable to formulate a comprehensive strategy to deal with the changing global security environment in the post-Cold War setting. The civilian government and the military establishment fundamentally disagreed on issues of national interest. The ISI continued with their Cold War policy, adopted by General Zia. Subsequently, the military was keen to continue with its proxy war in Kashmir and Afghanistan, whereas the civilian governments were trying to find diplomatic solutions to the problems in the neighbourhood.

General Musharraf's dictatorial rule ended in 2008 when he resigned from his position as president. As in August 2008, the government was transferred to civilian leadership but the military continued to be the dominant power in state affairs. For example, General Ashfaq Kayani, successor to General Musharraf, projected himself as a pro-democratic general, but he continued to interfere in domestic politics during his prolonged six years as a COAS. According to Kayani (*Newsweek*, Pakistan, 19 December 2008):

> Military interventions are sometimes necessary to maintain Pakistan's stability. Kayani likens coups to temporary bypasses that are created when a bridge collapses on democracy's highway. After the bridge is repaired, then there's no longer any need for the detour.

Kayani remained the de facto ruler and was responsible for Pakistan's nuclear programme, operations against TTP and its affiliated militant groups, and dealing with foreign policy, especially the difficult relationship with India (*Newsweek*, Pakistan, 19 December 2008). So the military maintained its dominance in state affairs from behind the scenes under General Kayani. In other words, Pakistan persisted with its military-centric national security approach after the February elections in 2008 as well.

As with previous civilian governments in the 1990s, the major challenge was to establish a real democracy, where the civilian leadership takes all the key strategic decisions. Subsequently, President Zardari attempted to change the direction of the national security state, but he was largely unable to do so. Zardari successfully passed the 18th amendment in parliament and removed the constitutional means the military had used to interfere in the political sphere of government. However, the military maintained its control over other state institutions such as the judiciary, bureaucracy, and media. These institutions have been used by the military to undermine the political process in the country (Shah 2014b). The civilian government had tried to bring the ISI under the operational, administrative, and financial control of the interior ministry. On 26 July 2008, the prime minister approved "the placement of the Intelligence Bureau and the Inter-Services Intelligence under the administrative, financial and operational control of the Interior Division with immediate effect" (Raza, *Dawn*, Pakistan, 27 July 2008). But the military strongly resisted this decision. General Athar Abbas, the then DG ISPR, said that the civilian government had not taken the defence authorities into its confidence before taking the decision. He explained that "the ISI was a huge organisation and the interior ministry could not have handled its financial, administrative and operational affairs" (*Dawn*, Pakistan, 27 July 2008). Consequently, the government withdrew the notification within less than 24 hours due to enormous pressure from the military.

Furthermore, it is the constitutional prerogative of the prime minister to appoint the COAS and other senior military officers. But the military resisted civilian interference in military promotions and their institutional matters. It is the military which decides the list of candidates for such positions (Shah 2014b). This implies that the civilian government failed to establish its supremacy over the military and intelligence security agencies. As in the 1990s, the military maintained its independence despite civilian rule in the post-9/11 period.

Under Pakistan's military-industrial complex, the military interferes in state affairs in order to protect its commercial and institutional interests. Therefore, the military prefers to have a weak political government which provides justification for their interventions in domestic politics. Nevertheless, this often led to political instability in the country, though it has provided the military with an opportunity to influence the political process in their favour. For instance, PTI started a sit-in against the government in Islamabad over alleged election rigging in 2013. The sit-in continued for about 126 days and created a political crisis in the country. In order to end the political instability, General Raheel Sharif played the role of arbitrator between the government and the opposition PTI to end their sit-in in Islamabad (Sattar, *The News*, Pakistan, 19 May 2018). After General Sharif's intervention, the sit-in ended, and the military took full credit. After that, the PMLN government became very submissive and appeared to have ended its rapprochement with India. Thus, the military leadership used political crises as leverage to protect its military-industrial complex (Fair *et al.* 2010).

In this context, the military favours a hung parliament where the prime minister requires military support to run the state affairs smoothly. Moreover, the divided political leadership were not only intolerant of each other but there was also no consensus to oust the military from power. Prime Minister Sharif knew that the eighth amendment was the main obstacle to civilian supremacy as it provided disproportionate power to the president by allowing him to remove an elected government. Therefore, Sharif tried to create a political consensus with the other political parties to remove the eighth amendment from the 1973 constitution during his first term as a prime minister. Bhutto acknowledged this constitutional issue but did not come to support this move due to political differences with Sharif (Bray 1997). So the military took benefits from the divided political leadership and weak political government, which provided the military with a greater role in the government.

In the recently held parliamentary 2018 elections, the Pakistani military was alleged to have rigged the elections to produce a pro-military civilian government. Prior to the elections, the military establishment was accused of setting the stage for Imran Khan's PTI to win. The military, with the support of the judiciary, initiated corruption cases, mainly against PMLN candidates, putting their leader Nawaz Sharif in jail on 14 July 2018. According to the Islamabad High Court (IHC) Justice Shaukat Aziz Siddiqui (*Dawn*, Pakistan, October 12, 2018),

> The spy agency (ISI) had previously approached IHC Chief Justice Muhammad Anwar Khan Kasi and said: We do not want to let Nawaz Sharif and his daughter (Maryam Nawaz) come out [of prison] until the [July 25] elections. Do not include Shaukat Aziz Siddiqui on the bench [hearing Sharif's appeals].

However, the Supreme Court Chief Justice denied Justice Siddiqui's allegations regarding the ISI. Furthermore, there was a media blackout of the PMLN's political gatherings during the election campaign. The secular political parties, such as the PPP and Awami National Party (ANP), were not allowed to hold public rallies, on the pretext of security threats in different parts of the country. So there was scepticism among electoral observers and political parties about whether a level playing field would be provided for all the political parties in the elections. The widespread allegations of military interference led all the opposition political parties to reject the election results. The opposition parties demanded a commission of enquiry to investigate the alleged pre- and post-poll election rigging (Raza, *Dawn*, Pakistan, 18 August 2018). Thus, the political process was undermined by the Pakistani military through alleged political engineering by rigging the elections in the country.

Economic insecurity

Thanks to the existence of Pakistan's military-industrial complex, the military has prioritized and protected their commercial interests at the cost of economic and social development. In the post-Cold War era, economic growth and social development became very important for stability in the country but military competition with India remained the primary concern of the Pakistani military. In order to achieve military parity with India, economic growth and subsequent socio-economic development were largely ignored. In the country's history, Islamabad has never prioritized economic growth and socio-economic development over defence building (Siddiqa 2002). The country allocated about 60 percent of its government expenditure to defence in the first ten years following independence in 1947 (Shah 2014b). Since then, the military budget has remained top of government spending. There was a 34.68 percent increase in defence spending from US \$2,722 million in 1988 to US \$3,666 million in 1995 (Mirza *et al*. 2015). The military budget was constantly increased under the PMLN-led government between 2013 and 2018. The total defence budget for 2018–2019 was PKR 1,100 billion, with a 19.5 percent increase over the previous financial year (*Dawn*, Pakistan, 28 April 2018). So the defence spending has placed tremendous pressure on the national treasury.

Despite this massive defence budget, the military finance their pension payments from the non-defence budget, leaving very limited financial resources for infrastructure and socio-economic development in the country. In the 2018–2019 budget, there was only PKR 90.8 billion for education, PKR 11.8 billion for health, and PKR 2.3 billion for the social sector (Budget in Brief 2018–2019). According to the former Interior Minister Ahsan Iqbal (*Express Tribune*, Pakistan, 27 July 2017),

> There are two major mistakes that we made … One, Pakistan got too much involved in regional and global geo-political games instead of prioritising economic development. Second, Pakistan did not have sustainable political stability. The biggest casualty of these mistakes was the economy of Pakistan.

In addition, economic growth has become very important for national security in the post-Cold War era. However, Pakistan has been confronted by economic crises throughout most of the post-Cold War period (Hussain 2012). Unlike Pakistan, India started an economic liberalization policy in the early 1990s that led to the rapid economic growth and trade expansion, such that by 2011, India's economy was eight times larger than Pakistan's economy. Consequently, the Indian government has been able to allocate a significant amount of its budgetary resources to military modernization and upgrading. Moreover, India has strengthened its military power through external arms purchasing and domestic production, and this has shaped regional security in its favour (N. Ahmad 2015). Due to its economic growth, India's military spending is about seven times higher than that of Pakistan. India's defence budget was US$53.5 billion in 2017–2018, which is almost the size of Pakistan's total budget in 2018 (*The Economist*, 19 May 2011; Behera 2017). The military gap has increased to such a size that it has become very difficult for Pakistan to contemplate fighting a conventional war with India. To try to narrow the defence budget gap, Pakistan continues to upgrade its military, creating more pressure on the national treasury by cutting the development budget. The Indian economic transformation has thus aggravated the security situation for Pakistan, putting pressure on its budgetary resources and leaving less money for economic growth and socio-economic development.

In the post-9/11 period, Pakistan had to allocate more budgetary resources to conducting military operations against TTP, Al-Qaeda, and its affiliated militant organizations in order to maintain law and order. The military often asks for additional special grants to maintain existing infrastructure and for acquiring new equipment to deal with the emerging security situation in Pakistan (Anwar and Rafique 2012). The government provided PKR 4.5 billion (US$39 million) of extra-budgetary grants to the ISI for "strategic assignments" (Shakil, *Asia Times*, South Asia, 2 May 2018). However, the last civilian government led by PMLN refused to allocate further extra defence grants to the military, which created a rift between the civilian and military leaderships. Subsequently, Nawaz Sharif was removed by the Supreme Court for alleged corruption.

Additionally, the cost of doing business increased due to the uncertain law and order situation in the country. On top of this, there has been often political crisis in the country, creating uncertainty in the market for investors. Many foreign investors refused to visit Pakistan and invest in the country (Shahbaz *et al.* 2013). For example, the investment-to-GDP ratio has fallen from 22.5 percent in 2006–2007 to 13.4 percent in 2010–2011, which has affected the job market (Pakistan Economic Survey 2010–2011). Besides reduction in foreign investment, there was also a significant decline in the pace of the privatization programme, economic activities, import demand, tax collection, and the tourism industry (Cheema 2013). According to government estimates, the total direct and indirect cost incurred amounted to US$67.93 billion during the first ten years after 9/11 (Pakistan Economic Survey 2010–2011). Exports declined from 13 percent of GDP in 2006 to 9.2 percent in 2010 (Anwar and Rafique 2012).

In Pakistan, it is important to note that development spending on the social sector has been lower than some of the poorest African countries, who spend more on education and health than Pakistan does. According to Dr. Farukh Saleem (*The News*, Pakistan, 6 May 2018),

> There are more than a hundred countries in the world which spend more on the health of their citizens than does Pakistan. The US spends $4,271 on health per citizen; Pakistan spends $18. Imagine: Iran spends $128. Even Sri Lanka, Burma and Zambia spend more on health than Pakistan.

Similarly, Pakistan spends less on education and other parts of the social sector compared to the least wealthy developing countries. As a result, most of the rural parts of the country present a gloomy picture reminiscent of the medieval period, with few opportunities to maintain a livelihood. In 2019, Pakistan was ranked 152 out of 189 countries in the HDI (UNDP 2019). Thus, the available resources were not utilized for the benefit of the general public, which resulted in chronic socio-economic problems. Moreover, worsening socio-economic and sociopolitical conditions exacerbate intrastate conflicts (Szayna *et al.* 2017). Poor education standards, lack of economic opportunities, and unequal access to avenues of social and economic mobilization are prevalent and contribute to radicalization among Pakistani citizens (A. Ali 2010). The neglect of socio-economic development has provided conditions conducive to militancy inside the country as well.

In sum, Islamabad has not prioritized economic growth under the national security state. Consequently, Pakistan has often faced economic turmoil, which is linked to Pakistan's foreign and security policies. Like previous governments, the present PTI government is confronted by a severe economic crisis as the country's imports have increased considerably and its foreign exchange reserves have been depleted to just US $10 billion, which is sufficient for less than two months' worth of imports. The country is facing balance of payment challenges with a US $95 billion external debt and a US$ 32.5 billion trade deficit, together with a record current account deficit of US $17.994 billion (5.7 percent of GDP) at the end of the fiscal year 2017–2018 (*Dawn*, Pakistan, 3 August 2018). At present, this is a major challenge for the new government that took charge in August 2018. Consequently, the new government was looking for an IMF bailout package to overcome its economic crisis. In July 2019, the IMF approved a US $6 billion package to Pakistan which is its 13th bailout package from IMF (K. Shahid, *the Diplomat*, Pakistan, 18 July 2019). The PTI government promises to make Pakistan a welfare state, but this cannot materialize without the transformation of the national security state by prioritizing economic growth and socio-economic development.

The dynamics of self-interest and conflict

Pakistan inherited a very strong civil and military bureaucracy from the British colonial empire. Most post-colonial states have evolved in response to the needs and demands of their colonial power and subsequent ruling elites, whereas European states have evolved in response to public domestic needs (Professor

Ijaz Khan, interview by author, Islamabad, 10 November 2017). Similarly, Pakistan was established following the end of British rule in India to protect the interests of the successor state and its elites instead of the general public. Nonetheless, in order to sustain the developed state structure, its large military in particular, required massive financial resources to justify its role after independence. According to the former ambassador Husain Haqqani, "Pakistan was not like other countries that raise an army to deal with threats they face; it had inherited a large army that needed a threat if it was to be maintained" (Haqqani 2014). Subsequently, India was chosen as a possible threat to Pakistan due to its conflict over Kashmir. From Independence in 1947, the military establishment has presented the Kashmir conflict in such a way that India has been seen to pose such a real threat to Pakistan's national security and territorial integrity.

After the end of the Cold War era, the Pakistani civilian leadership was keen to find a diplomatic solution to the historical disputes between India and Pakistan. There were extended rounds of talks at foreign secretary level to resolve all the outstanding issues between the two countries. The civilian leadership on both sides showed optimism at the beginning of a new chapter in their relationship. The Indian premier Rajiv Gandhi visited Pakistan twice in a time span of six months after Bhutto became prime minister in August 1988. However, the Pakistani military started providing military aid to the Kashmiri militant groups that sabotaged the peace process, which ended without any major breakthrough. Pakistan became a nuclear power, gaining nuclear parity with India in May 1998. As a consequence, India could no longer pose an existential threat, real or otherwise, to Pakistan. Soon after both countries became nuclear powers, the Indian premier Vajpayee visited Lahore in February 1999, which promised to be a turning point in Pakistan's relations with India. There was a high degree of optimism again that both countries would resolve their outstanding issues, including Kashmir. However, the peace initiative was broken by the Pakistani military's intrusion into the Kargil area of Kashmir in 1999. According to Christine Fair (2010), "the Kashmir conflict justifies an outsized military budget and its overwhelming role in Pakistani politics. The conflict is central to the army's claim that it is the custodian of the state." Thus, the Kashmir conflict has become a lifeline for the Pakistani military elite, and they want to sustain the status quo over the region.

The Pakistani military not only is the guardian of the country's frontiers but is also the custodian of its ideological frontiers as a Muslim state. In particular, the Pakistani military elite often claimed that the reason Pakistan has not become Syria or Afghanistan is due to its having maintained a strong military. Consequently, the Pakistani military has justified massive defence spending by propagating a security threat to Pakistan. Since its inception in 1947, the military has validated its military upgrades and modernization on the grounds of the threat from growing Indian military power. Ironically, the Pakistani civilian leadership has also highlighted the issue of Kashmir and its importance for the survival of the country. This enables the military to play a significant role in Pakistan's foreign and security policy (Chawla 2001). Thus, the military would like to have a real and/or imaginary threat to sustain its military-industrial complex. This means the military will continue with the status quo and oppose any peace process with India which might lead to normalization of relations between the two countries (Fair *et al.* 2010). In other words, the threat from India has become key to the survival of the Pakistani military establishment.

In addition, the Pakistani military has exploited its geostrategic environment to demonstrate a security threat from neighbouring countries. Pakistan, being a nuclear country, has achieved deterrence against potential adversaries. According to Senator Mushahid Hussain (interview by author, Islamabad, 8 December 2017), "India does not have the capability and/or intention to do the kind of damage they [did] to Pakistan in 1971. It is now more a rivalry and competition after Pakistan developed its nuclear weapons." So India is no more a real threat to Pakistan's national sovereignty and territorial integrity.

The Pakistani military has used far-right political groups and leaders to undermine the political process in the country. Nonetheless, it has created intolerance and extremism in society, which provide the opportunity for the military to control state affairs. Moreover, growing radicalization, extremism, and terrorism have reduced the chances of Pakistan becoming a viable democratic country. The military propagated the idea that the political leadership was too weak and corrupt to deal with external and internal security challenges both during and after the Cold War. As a result, the political leadership became very weak due to the military's frequent ejection of civilian governments, which has created not only political instability but also economic crises in the country. The economic crises are presented in such a way that the weak economy is seen to be due to widespread corruption on the part of the civilian leadership. However, the chronic socio-economic problems are due to prioritizing military expenditure over developmental expenditure.

So the military establishment has successfully used external security threats, economic crises, and political instability as the rationale for their extended powers in state affairs and demands for massive financial resources. According to Stephen Cohen, "A full-blown democracy, in which the armed forces come under firm civilian control, will be impossible until Pakistan's strategic environment alters in such a way that the army retreats from its role as guardian of the state" (Waheed and Abbasi 2013, 210). This means the military will continue to exploit the country's means and resources unless there is a major change in Pakistan's strategic position in the region.

Summing up, the Pakistani military not only resisted internal changes in the military-industrial complex but also to the changing global security environment in the post-Cold War era. The military resisted any attempts by civilian governments to change the direction of the national security state. Despite international pressure, Pakistan continued with its proxy wars in Afghanistan and Kashmir in the post-Cold War era. In order to subdue civilian opposition, the military has opened corruption cases against anti-establishment politicians through the NAB and used the media effectively against them by presenting a negative image to the general public based on mere accusations of corruption.

Consequently, the military often took unilateral decisions over all issues of strategic importance and kept the civilian leadership out of decision making in key issues such as the Kashmir conflict and Afghanistan. In practice, the military thought they were not only better trained and organized but also had a better understanding of the prevailing strategic and security environment in the post-Cold War period (Cohen 2004). The Pakistani military held most of the power that led to a hyper-military-industrial complex, under a national security state that served military interests.

The opportunity costs of Pakistan's national security state: the lost decade of the 1990s

In the post-Cold War era, the continuation of Pakistan's military-centric national security state came at a considerable cost to the democratic and socio-economic development of the country and also undermined its domestic and regional security. The military elite have shown little interest in adapting to a new strategic environment. Nevertheless, the country had alternative options to adjust its foreign and security policies in the new global context of the post-Cold War era.

Towards the end of the Cold War, Pakistan had the option to transform itself into a modern Islamic democratic country. For instance, parliamentary elections were held in August 1988 that gave a window of opportunity for democracy to prevail in the country. In the post-Cold War period, this was an important occasion to uphold democratic institutions which would have brought necessary political stability to the country and sustained its alliance with the US in the changing global security environment (Fair *et al.* 2010). Internationally, the US had linked its aid with democracy and human rights. More importantly, Bhutto was leading the civilian administration and understood the regional and international politics of a changing global security environment after the Cold War. Therefore, she pushed for a peaceful transition in Afghanistan and normalization of relations with India. In 1988–1989, India and Pakistan agreed to form a joint ministerial committee to boost trade and cooperation in science and technology. There was also a consensus to reduce conventional arms and resolve the disputes over the Siachen Glacier. The success of Bhutto would have led to a major shift in Pakistan-India relations after the end of the Cold War. However, this opportunity was lost when the Kashmir uprising started in 1990 and the Pakistani military diverted many Afghan mujahedeen to support the uprising. Likewise, Indian Prime Minister Vajpayee visited Lahore to normalize relations with Pakistan in February 1999. During his visit, Vajpayee reaffirmed his country's support for the sovereignty and territorial integrity of Pakistan. However, the peace initiative was soon thwarted by the Pakistani military offensive in Kargil in 1999.

On the Afghanistan front, Pakistan had also an opportunity to have a peaceful transition after the Soviet forces left the country. During the Afghan war, Pakistan hosted about 3 million Afghan refugees and provided military aid to anti-Soviet mujahedeen. In return, Pakistan could have nurtured the goodwill of the Afghan refugees by supporting a peaceful transition in Kabul and the return of these refugees who had put significant pressure on Pakistan's weak economy. Consequently, the Pakistani political leadership emphasized a diplomatic solution to the Afghan conflict after the Soviet withdrawal. The foreign office and Bhutto insisted on supporting political groups that had roots in the Afghans (Memon 1994). In February 1989, Eduard Shevardnadze, the Soviet foreign minister, visited Pakistan to devise a political plan dealing with the post-Soviet situation in Afghanistan. Shevardnadze discussed the exiting plan with Bhutto which envisaged a peaceful transfer of power in Afghanistan, under which the then Afghan President Dr. Mohammad Najibullah would remain in power for the transition period. Pakistan would return 3 million refugees to Afghanistan (Bhutto 2008). However, the Pakistani military was against this transition in Afghanistan and favoured instead an Afghan interim government in Kabul. Consequently, Pakistan lost the opportunity to have a peaceful transition in Afghanistan, a stable country in its backyard, and a new relationship with Russia after the end of the Cold War.

In addition, the post-Cold War security environment offered some opportunities for Pakistan to bolster its position in international politics. Islamabad was a key US ally during the Cold War and played a major role in the defeat of Soviet forces in Afghanistan. The Pakistani leadership established both official and personal relations with the US Congress and the State Department. The US became the sole superpower after the demise of the Soviet Union. The major US concern was anti-liberal, nationalistic, Islamic revisionist states, and Islamic fundamentalism. Islamabad had the potential to mediate between the US and anti-liberal and Islamic revisionist states in Muslim countries such as Iran, Libya, and Sudan (Travis 1994). Also, Pakistan was a key member of the OIC, in which it could have provided a moderating role. With real democratic transition in 1988, Islamabad could have offered a moderate Islamic democratic model to the new Central Asian states after the collapse of Soviet Union, which would have enhanced its international stature (Memon 1994). In return, Pakistan could have asked the US for support to protect its strategic interests vis-à-vis India and the removal of sanctions under the Pressler Amendment (Travis 1994). So Pakistan had the opportunity to sustain its close alliance with the US and improve its international stature following the Cold War.

More importantly, Pakistan had many options to present itself as a "trading nation" instead of a "warrior nation" by exploiting its strategic position for regional trade and energy connectivity. Economic connectivity would have given an upper hand to Pakistan in neighbouring countries as Afghanistan is a landlocked country which was largely dependent on Pakistan's sea routes and its trade. So Pakistan could have used its economic influence to have a good neighbourly relationship with Afghanistan. Furthermore, the Muslim states in Central Asia opened new economic and strategic opportunities for Pakistan after the collapse of the Soviet Union. Due to its geographical proximity and cultural affinity, Islamabad could have strengthened its relations with Central Asian countries. Islamabad could have become a trade route for energy-rich Central Asia to reach the rest of the world through Pakistan's deep seaports in Karachi and Gwadar (Memon 1994).

Pakistan could have looked for alternative economic opportunities which in return would have not only boosted its weakening economy but also the regional connectivity would have guaranteed the sovereignty of the country due to investment from the other countries. As a result of such changes, the political gravity would have automatically shifted towards Islamabad that could have provided the necessary strategic balance in the region.

Despite numerous opportunities throughout the 1990s, the Pakistani military has not accepted diplomatic solutions to the country's outstanding issues with India and Afghanistan. In the post-Cold War settings, Pakistan had failed to establish a liberal democratic system and exploited its geostrategic position for economic development. The major reason was that Pakistan's national security state was unable to adapt quickly to the changing global security environment in the post-Cold War era. More specifically, this national security state provides a privileged role to the Pakistani military, and any change in this security approach would have downgraded or undermined its privileged role in state affairs.

Notes

1 The Abbottabad Commission Report was to investigate the circumstances surrounding the death of Osama bin Laden in Abbottabad in January 2013.
2 This commission of Inquiry was appointed by the president of Pakistan in December 1971 to inquire into and find out "the circumstances in which the Commander, Eastern command, surrendered and the members of the Armed Forces of Pakistan under his command laid down their arms and a cease-fire was ordered along the borders of West Pakistan and India and along the cease-fire line in the State of Jammu and Kashmir."
3 The diarchy system of double government was introduced by the British through the Government of India Act (1919) for the provinces of British India. Under the act, the departments on the "transferred list" were given to local ministers answerable to the Provincial Council. The "transferred list" included agriculture, local government, health, and education. At the same time, all other areas of government (the "reserved list") remained under the control of the viceroy. The "reserved list" included defence (the military), foreign affairs, and communications. Waseem and Mufti (2009: 24) identify Pakistan as a diarchy "comprising two constellations of interests," state elites (military and bureaucracy), and political elites.
4 Sheikh Mujib's six-point agenda called for a greater autonomy for East Pakistan, which turned into a movement for the independence of Bangladesh.
5 The Peshawar High Court (PHC) cancelled the contracts. The judgement said that "The mode and manner in which the five projects have been granted to National Logistics Cell through direct sourcing is violation of the spirit of Khyber Pakhtunkhwa Public Procurement Regulatory Authority (KAPPRA) Act and its Rules."
6 In Pakistan "APC" are called to find a political consensus on key issues confronted by the country.

References

Abbas, H. 2004. *Pakistan's Drift Into Extremism: Allah, Then Army, and America's War Terror*. Routledge.

Ahmad, N. 2015. "Future of War and Strategy: Indo-Pak Dynamics." *IPRI*, Islamabad 15 (1): 1–20.

Ali, A. 2010. "Militancy and Socioeconomic Problems: A Case Study of Pakistan." *Reflection*, ISSI, No: 4.

Ali, I. "The Father of the Taliban: An Interview with Maulana Sami ul-Haq." *Spotlight on Terror*, May 23, 2007, Retrieved from: https://jamestown.org/interview/the-father-of -the-taliban-an-interview-with-maulana-sami-ul-haq/

Ali, L. A. and Khan, N. I. 2010. "The Rise of Tehreek-e-Nifaz-e-Shariat-e-Mohammadi in Malakand Division, NWFP: A Case Study of the Process of State Inversion." *Pakistan Vision* 11 (1): 98–119.

Ali, M. "The Battle for Swat." *New American Foundation*, September 2010, Retrieved from: http://www.humansecuritygateway.com/documents/NAF-TheBattleForPakistan -DIR.pdf

Almeida, A. "Exclusive: Act Against Militants or Face International Isolation, Civilians Tell Military." *Dawn*, Pakistan, October 6, 2016, Retrieved on May 29, 2018, https:// www.dawn.com/news/1288350.

Anwar, M. A. and Rafique, Z. 2012. "Defense Spending and National Security of Pakistan: A Policy Perspective." *Democracy and Security* 8 (4): 374–399.

Appendix 3: List of Interviewees.

Appendix 14: Pakistan – Global Peace Index 2008–2018.

"Asghar Khan's ISI Funds Case in SC to Blemish Many." *New South*, Pakistan, January 25, 2012, Retrieved on November 24, 2018, https://www.thenews.com.pk/archive/print /619760-asghar-khan%E2%80%99s-isi-funds-case-in-sc-to-blemish-many.

Ashok, A. K. 2007. "The Rise of Pakistani Taliban and the Response of the State." *Strategic Analysis* 31 (5): 699–724.

Bailes, A. J. K. 2007. "Regional Security Cooperation: A Challenge for South (and North-East) Asia." *Strategic Analysis* 31 (4): 665–674.

Behera, L. K. 2017. "India's Defence Budget 2017-18: An Analysis." *IDSA Issue Brief No. 3*, Retrieved from: https://idsa.in/issuebrief/india-defence-budget-2017-18_lkbe hera_030217.

Bhutto, B. 2008. *Daughter of Destiny: An Autobiography.* Harper Perennial.

"Body Count: Casualty Figures after 10 Years of the 'War on Terror.'" *IPPNW, PSR and PGS*, 2015 Report.

Borger, J. and Farooq, A. "Imran Khan Warns UN of Potential Nuclear War in Kashmir." *Guardian*, UK, September 26, 2019, Retrieved on January 9, 2020, https://www.theguard ian.com/world/2019/sep/26/imran-khan-warns-un-of-potential-nuclear-war-in-kashmir.

Bray, J. 1997. "Pakistan at 50: A State in Decline?" *International Affairs* 73 (2): 315–331.

"Budget 2018-19: Govt Slashes PSDP, Raises Defence Spending to Rs1.1 Trillion." *Dawn*, Pakistan, April 28, 2018, Retrieved on May 18, 2018, https://www.dawn.com/news /1404209.

"Budget in Brief 2018-19." *Ministry of Finance*, Pakistan, Retrieved from: http://www.fina nce.gov.pk/budget/Budget_in_Brief_2018_19.pdf.

Chawla, S. 2001. "Pakistan's Military Spending: Socio-Economic Dimensions." *Strategic Analysis* 25 (5): 703–716.

Chawla, S. "Has the Pulwama Crisis Altered Strategic Dimensions?" *IPCS*, March 8, 2019, Retrieved from: http://www.ipcs.org/comm_select.php?articleNo=5565.

Cheema, P. I. 2013. "Security Threats Confronting Pakistan." In Chapter 10 *Security Outlook of the Asia Pacific Countries and Its Implications for the Defense Sector*. NIDS Joint Research Series No.9: National Institute for Defense Studies.

Chengappa, B. M. 1999. "Pakistan: Military Role in Civil Administration." *Strategic Analysis* 23 (2): 299–312.

Claire, Parker, "India's Clampdown on Kashmir Continues. Here's What You Need to Know." *The Washington Post*, August 13, 2019, Retrieved on January 9, 2020, https://www.washingtonpost.com/world/2019/08/05/india-revoked-kashmirs-special-status-heres-what-you-need-know-about-contested-province/.

Cohen, S. P. 2004. *The Idea of Pakistan*. Brooking Institute Press.

"Cost of War on Terror for Pakistan Economy." *Pakistan Economic Survey 2010–11*, Retrieved from: http://www.finance.gov.pk/survey/chapter_11/Special%20Section_1.pdf.

Dalton, T. and Tandler, J 2012. *Understanding the Arms "Race" in South Asia*. Carnegie Endowment for International Peace.

Dawar, M. "Why Pashtuns in Pakistan Are Rising Up." *Washington Post*, April 17, 2019, Retrieved on January 20, 2020, https://www.washingtonpost.com/opinions/2019/04/17/why-pashtuns-pakistan-are-rising-up/.

"Dawn Leaks: Inside Story of PM Nawaz, Army Chief's Meeting." *New South*, Pakistan, May 11 2017, Retrieved on 29 May 2018, https://www.thenews.com.pk/latest/203825-Dawn-Leaks-Inside-story-of-PM-Nawaz-army-chiefs-meeting.

"DCC to Be Reconstituted as Committee on National Security." *Dawn*, Pakistan, August 22, 2013, Retrieved on June 3, 2018, https://www.dawn.com/news/1037613.

Fair, C. C. and Gregory, S. 2012. "A State in Flux: Pakistan in the Context of National and Regional Change." *Contemporary South Asia* 20 (2): 173–178.

Faruqui, A. 2014. "The Army and Democracy: Military Politics in Pakistan." *The RUSI Journal* 159 (6): 75–76.

Grare, F. 2007. "The Evolution of Sectarian Conflicts in Pakistan and the Ever-Changing Face of Islamic Violence, South Asia." *South Asian Studies* 30 (1): 127–143.

Haqqani, H. 2005. *Pakistan: Between Mosque and Military*. Carnegie Endowment for International Peace.

Haqqani, H. "Islamism and the Pakistani State." *Hudson Institute*, August 9, 2013, Retrieved from: https://www.hudson.org/research/9952-islamism-and-the-pakistani-state.

Haqqani, H. "Re-Imagining Pakistan." *Hudson Institute*, October 17, 2014, Retrieved on March 8, 2018, https://www.hudson.org/research/10730-re-imagining-pakistan.

Haqqani, H. 2018. *Reimagining Pakistan: Transforming a Dysfunctional Nuclear State*. HarperCollins India.

Hounshel, L. "Pakistani Official Calls Bhutto's Killer 'Patriotic.'" *Foreign Policy*, November 30, 2008, Retrieved on November 30, 2018, http://foreignpolicy.com/2008/11/30/pakistani-official-calls-bhuttos-killer-patriotic/.

Howenstein, N. 2009. "Review Essay of Ayesha Jalal, Partisans of Allah: Jihad in South Asia and Praveen Swami, India, Pakistan and the Secret Jihad: The Covert War in Kashmir, 1947–2004." *India Review* 8 (4): 446–456.

"How the Islamabad Protests Happened." *Dawn*, Pakistan, November 25, 2017, Retrieved on December 6, 2018, https://www.dawn.com/news/1372800.

Hussain, Z. 2011. "Sources of Tension in Afghanistan and Pakistan: A Regional Perspective."CIDOB Policy Research Paper.

Hussain, Z. 2012. "Defining National Security and Economic Security of Pakistan Post 9/11 Era." *NDU Journal*, 26: 71–92.

Ilyas, M. N., Tahir, S. and Khan, K. A. 2016. "Guns or Butter Empirical Analysis of Budgetary Tradeoffs Between Defense and Welfare Spending in Pakistan." *IASET* 1 (2): 39–56.

"Imran Khan and the IMF: Pakistan's Bailout Dilemma." *Dawn*, Pakistan, August 3, 2018, Retrieved on August 27, 2018, https://www.dawn.com/news/1424700.

Interview with Elahi Bakhsh Soomro by Ayesha Siddiqa, in Siddiqa, A. 2007. *Military Inc. Inside Pakistan's Military Economy*. Pluto Press.

Iqbal, A. "Can Pakistan's Economy Afford Political Instability?" *Express Tribune*, Pakistan, July 27, 2017, Retrieved on May 15, 2018, https://tribune.com.pk/story/1 467291/can-pakistans-economy-afford-political-instability/.

Iype, G. "Pak Military Chiefs Boycott Wagah Welcome." *Rediff*, February 20, 1999, Retrieved on May 15, 2018, http://www.rediff.com/news/1999/feb/20bus2.htm.

Jain, B. M. 1993. "Indo-Pak Relations in the Post-Cold War Period." *Indian Journal of Asian Affairs* 6 (1/2): 103–110.

Jones, O. B. 2002. *Pakistan: Eye of the Storm*. Yale University Press.

Jorgic, D. R. and Pal, A. "Facebook, Twitter Sucked Into India-Pakistan Information War." *Reuters*, April 2, 2019, Retrieved on January 19, 2020, https://www.reuters.com/articl e/us-india-pakistan-socialmedia/facebook-twitter-sucked-into-india-pakistan-informati on-war-idUSKCN1RE18N.

"Kahuta Lelo, Kursi de do." *Nawa-e-Waqat*, Urdu newspaper, Pakistan, October 19, 1990.

Kiani, K. "PAC Unhappy Over Drop in Toll Collection at Motorways." *Dawn*, Pakistan, 4 March 2014, Retrieved on 15 December 2018, https://www.dawn.com/news /1090927.

"List of Banned Organisations in Pakistan." *Express Tribune*, Pakistan, October 24, 2012, Retrieved on May 9, 2018, https://tribune.com.pk/story/456294/list-of-banned-orga nisations-in-pakistan/.

"Lt Gen (r) Nasir Janjua Appointed NSA: Report." *Pakistan Today*, October 19, 2015, Retrieved on May 18, 2018, https://www.pakistantoday.com.pk/2015/10/19/lt-gen-r-na sir-janjua-appointed-nsa-report/.

Malik, H. "Ministry Rejects ISI Role in TLP Sit-In." *Express Tribune*, Pakistan, November 27, 2017, Retrieved on December 6, 2018, https://tribune.com.pk/story/1720284/1-i ntelligence-agency-not-orchestrate-faizabad-sit-ministry-defence-report/.

Malik, I. H. 2008. *The History of Pakistan*. Greenwood.

Mason, S. 2016. *Military Budgets in India and Pakistan: Trajectories, Priorities, and Risks*. Stimson Center.

Memon, M. 1994. "Reorientation of Pakistan's Foreign Policy After the Cold War." *Pakistan Horizon* 47 (2): 45–61.

Mirza, M. N. et al. 2015. "Military Spending and Economic Growth in Pakistan." *Margalla Papers*, Islamabad 19: 151–184.

Moreau, R. "The Military's Long Reach." *Foreign Policy*, October 12, 2009, Retrieved on May 17, 2018, http://foreignpolicy.com/2009/10/12/the-militarys-long-reach/.

Munir, A. "In Defence of General Kayani." *Express Tribune*, Pakistan, November 7, 2012, Retrieved on November 30, 2018, https://tribune.com.pk/story/462231/in-defence-of-general-kayani/.

"Musharraf Declares War on Extremism." *BBC*, South Asia, January 12, 2002, Retrieved on February 7, 2018, http://news.bbc.co.uk/2/hi/south_asia/1756965.stm.

Nawaz, S. 2009. *Crossed Swords: Pakistan, Its Army, and the Wars Within*. Oxford University Press.

Nelson, D. "Pakistan: India No Longer a Military Threat." *Telegraph*, South Asia, June 24, 2009, Retrieved on September 5, 2018, https://www.telegraph.co.uk/news/worldnews/ asia/pakistan/5625759/Pakistan-India-no-longer-a-military-threat.html.

"New Wapda Chairman Takes Charge." *Dawn*, Pakistan, August 25, 2016, Retrieved on June 1, 2018 https://www.dawn.com/news/1279795.

"Pakistan Army Chief Ashfaq Parvez Kayani in Unity Plea." *BBC News*, Asia, August 14, 2012, Retrieved on November 22, 2018, https://www.bbc.com/news/world-us-canada -19254070.

"Pakistan: Bloggers Feared Abducted." *HRW Report*, January 10, 2017, Retrieved on May 23, 2018, https://www.hrw.org/news/2017/01/10/pakistan-bloggers-feared -abducted.

"Pakistan: Countering Militancy in PATA." *International Crisis Group*, Asia Report No: 242, January 15, 2013, Retrieved from: http://www.crisisgroup.org/~/media/Files/asia/ south-asia/pakistan/242-pakistan-countering-militancy-in-pata.pdf.

"Pakistan and India: A Rivalry That Threatens the World." *The Economist*, May 19, 2011, Retrieved on December 6, 2018, https://www.economist.com/node/18712274/all-c omments?page=4.

"Pakistani Army's '$20bn' Business." *Aljazeera*, Doha, February 17, 2008, Retrieved on June 1, 2018, https://www.aljazeera.com/focus/pakistanpowerandpolitics/2007/10/ 2008525184515984128.html.

"Pakistan's Ability to Mitigate Sources of Insecurity." Chapter 3, in Fair, C. C. et al. 2010. *Can the United States Secure an Insecure State?* RAND Corporation.

Pandya, A. 2019. "The Future of Indo-Pak Relations after the Pulwama Attack." *Perspectives on Terrorism* 13 (2): 65–68.

"PIPS Security Report 2007." *PIPS*, Islamabad, January 7, 2008.

Qumber, G. et al. 2018. "Security Dilemma in South Asian Context." *A Research Journal of South Asian Studies* 33 (1): 303–313.

Rafiq, A. 2012. "The Emergence of the Difa-e-Pakistan Islamist Coalition." *Combating Terrorism Centre*. Retrieved from: https://ctc.usma.edu/the-emergence-of-the-difa-e-p akistan-islamist-coalition/.

Rashid, A. 2008. *Descent Into Chaos: The U.S. and the Disaster in Pakistan, Afghanistan, and Central Asia*. Penguin Press.

Ratwatte, M. "Imran Khan's Words: Are They Relevant?" *Daily FT*, August 25, 2018, retrieved on December 1, 2018, http://www.ft.lk/opinion/Imran-Khan-s-words--Are-t hey-relevant-/14-661514.

Raza, I. "Opposition Demands Parliamentary Commission to Probe Polls 'Rigging.'" *Dawn*, Pakistan, August 18, 2018, Retrieved on November 21, 2018, https://www.dawn .com/news/1427715.

Raza, S. I. "ISI, IB Put under Interior Division's Control." *Dawn*, Pakistan, July 27, 2008, Retrieved on May 29, 2018, https://www.dawn.com/news/313676.

Rizvi, H. A. 1998. "Civil-Military Relations in Contemporary Pakistan." *Survival* 40 (2): 96–113.

Rizvi, H. A. 2003. *Military, State and Society In Pakistan*. Palgrave Macmillan.

Roggio, B. "Talibanistan Expands in the NWFP." *The Longwar Journal*, April 3, 2007, Retrieved from: http://www.longwarjournal.org/archives/2007/04/talibanistan_expan ds_2.php.

Roggio, B. "Taliban Are 'Patriots,' Says Pakistani Army Official." *Long War Journal*, December 1, 2008, Retrieved on May 6, 2018, https://www.longwarjournal.org/arch ives/2008/12/taliban_are_patriots.php.

Saeed, L. et al. 2014. "Historical Patterns of Terrorism in Pakistan." *Defense & Security Analysis* 30 (3): 209–229.

Saikal, A. 2014. *Zone of Crisis: Afghanistan, Pakistan, Iran and Iraq*. I. B. Tauris.

Saleem, F. "The Defence Budget." *New South*, Pakistan, May 6, 2018, Retrieved on May 15, 2018, https://www.thenews.com.pk/print/313124-the-defence-budget.

Sarral, S. "The Political Impact of India's Removal of Jammu and Kashmir's Status." *South Asian Voices*, August 19, 2019, Retrieved from: https://southasianvoices.org/understandi ng-the-political-impact-of-indias-removal-of-jammu-kashmirs-special-status/.

Sattar, B. "Trotting Out Traitors." *New South*, Pakistan, May 19, 2018, Retrieved on December 1, 2018, https://www.thenews.com.pk/print/318456-trotting-out-traitors.

Shah, A. 2014a. *The Army and Democracy: Military Politics in Pakistan*. Harvard University Press.

Shah, A. 2014b. "Constraining Consolidation: Military Politics and Democracy in Pakistan (2007–2013)." *Democratization* 21 (6): 1007–1033.

Shah, M. A. "Won't Stop Now Whether I'm Taken to Prison or Gallows, Says Nawaz." *New South*, Pakistan, July 11, 2018, Retrieved on July 12, 2018, https://www.thenews. com.pk/latest/340452-returning-to-pakistan-despite-seeing-prison-cell-in-front-of-me-nawaz-sharif.

Shah, S. A. and Sheerani, H. "PM, Balochistan CM Offer Condolences for Mastung Attack Victims As Death Toll Rises to 149." *Dawn*, Pakistan, July 15, 2018, Retrieved on November 21, 2018.

Shahbaz, M. A. et al. 2013. "Impact of Terrorism on Foreign Direct Investment in Pakistan." *Archives of Business Research* 1 (1): 1–7.

Shahid, K. K. "The IMF Takeover of Pakistan." *The Diplomat*, Pakistan, July 18, 2019, Retrieved January 20, 2020 https://thediplomat.com/2019/07/the-imf-takeover-of-pak istan/.

Shahid, K. N. "Pakistan Is Isolated and Has Fewer Friends in the International Community." *Asia Times*, South Asia, March 19, 2018, Retrieved on November 30, 2018, http://www .atimes.com/article/pakistan-isolated-fewer-friends-international-community/.

Shakil, F. M. "Funds for Defense, Debt and the ISI – And Crumbs for the Masses." *Asia Times*, South Asia, May 2, 2018, Retrieved on May 18, 2018, http://www.atimes.com/ article/funds-for-defense-debt-and-the-isi-and-crumbs-for-the-masses/.

Shurong, Z. and Rahman, S. 2017. "Rethinking Civil-Military Relations in a Pakistan: Some Lessons from Turkey." *Journal of Socialomics* 6 (209): 1–5.

Siddiqa, A. 2002. "Political Economy of National Security." *Economic and Political Weekly* 37 (44/45): 4545–4549.

Siddiqa, A. 2011. "Pakistan's Counterterrorism Strategy: Separating Friends from Enemies." *The Washington Quarterly* 34 (1): 149–162.

Siddique, Q. 2012. "Tehrik-e-Taliban Pakistan an Attempt to Deconstruct the Umbrella Organization and the Reason for Its Growth in Pakistan's North-West." *DIIS Report*, Denmark, Retrieved from: http://www.diis.dk/graphics/Publications/Reports2010/RP 2010-12-Tehrik-e-Taliban_web.pdf.

Siddiqui, N. "Aasia Bibi Leaves Pakistan, 'Safely Reunited' with Family." *Dawn*, Pakistan, May 8, 2019, Retrieved on September 11, 2020, https://www.bbc.com/news/world-asia -48198340.

Singh, P. 2015. "Army: The Be-All or End-All of Pakistan Politics?" *Strategic Analysis* 39 (3): 319–325.

Sirrs, O. L. 2016. *Pakistan's InterServices Intelligence Directorate: Covert Action and Internal Operations*. Routledge.

Soherwordi, H. S. 2005. "Human Security in South Asia: Military Expenditures Dimension of India and Pakistan." *Pakistan Horizon* 58 (1): 35–46.

Staniland, P. et al. 2018. "Politics and Threat Perception: Explaining Pakistani Military Strategy on the North West Frontier." *Security Studies* 27 (4): 535–574.

Stobdan, P. 1999. "Regional Security Issues in Central/South Asia and Potential for Cooperation." *Strategic Analysis* 22 (10): 1561–1576.

Szayna, T. S. et al. 2017. *Conflict Trends and Conflict Drivers An Empirical Assessment of Historical Conflict Patterns and Future Conflict Projections.* RAND Corporation.

Tankel, S. (2018) "Beyond the Double Game: Lessons from Pakistan's Approach to Islamist Militancy." *Journal of Strategic Studies* 41: 4, 562.

"The Fall of a High Court Judge." *Dawn*, Pakistan, October 12, 2018, Retrieved on November 21, 2018, https://www.dawn.com/news/1438545.

"The Incidents, the Inquiry Commissions and Hidden Reports." *Pakistan Today*, April 29, 2017, Retrieved on November 20, 2018, https://www.pakistantoday.com.pk/2017/04/29/the-incidents-the-inquiry-commissions-and-hidden-reports/.

"The Newsweek 50: Gen. Ashfaq Pervez Kayani." *Newsweek*, Pakistan, December 19, 2008, Retrieved on May 29, 2018, http://www.newsweek.com/newsweek-50-gen-ashfaq-parvez-kayani-83043.

"Transcript of General Pervez Musharraf's Briefing for Newspaper Editors." *Daily Khabrain*, Islamabad, February 6, 2004, in Haqqani, H. 2005. *Pakistan: Between Mosque and Military.* Carnegie Endowment for International Peace.

Travis, T. A. 1994. "Advantages and Disadvantages for Pakistan in the Post-Cold War World." *Pakistan Horizon* 47 (3): 35–53.

Waheed, A. W. and Abbasi, J. Y. 2013. "Rethinking Democracy in Pakistan." *Asian Affairs* 44 (2): 202–214.

Waseem, M. 2011. "Patterns of Conflict in Pakistan: Implications for Policy." *The Brookings Institute*, Working Paper No: 5.

Waseem, M. and Mufti, M. 2009. *Religion, Politics and Governance in Pakistan.* Working Paper. University of Birmingham.

Wasim Ahmad. S. "Ordinance Extends Actions in Aid of Civil Power to Entire KP." *Dawn*, Pakistan, September 18, 2019, Retrieved on January 19, 2020, https://www.dawn.com/news/1505809.

"Writ Petition No. 1367-P/2017 with Interim Relief." In *Judgement Sheet*, Peshawar High Court, Peshawar, July 12, 2017, Retrieved from: http://www.peshawarhighcourt.gov.pk/PHCCMS/judgments/Microsoft-Word---WP1367-P-2017-The-Contractors-Associations..VS...Government--Procuring-entity.pdf.

Yusuf, Y. "The Pulwama Crisis: Flirting With War in a Nuclear Environment." *Arms Control*, May 2019, Retrieved on January 3, 2020, https://www.armscontrol.org/act/2019-05/features/pulwama-crisis-flirting-war-nuclear-environment.

Yusufzai, R. "Forces to Go After Swat Taliban Commanders." *The News*, Pakistan, May 9, 2009.

Zaheer, M. "Asia Bibi Isn't the First Victim of Pakistan's Outrageous Blasphemy Laws – Yet the Government Refuses to Take Real Action." *Independent*, UK, November 2, 2018, Retrieved on December 15, 2018, https://www.independent.co.uk/voices/asia-bibi-case-pakistan-christian-blasphemy-released-supreme-court-imran-khan-a8614411.html.

Zain, O. F. 2009. "NWFP and the Scourge of Talibanization." *Pakistan Horizon* 62 (4): 25–37.

Ziauddin, M. "Analysing the 'Bajwa Doctrine.'" *Dawn*, Pakistan, March 22, 2018, Retrieved on May 21, 2018, https://dailytimes.com.pk/217943/analysing-the-bajwa-doctrine/.

Ziuddin, M. "A New-Look NSC?" *The Express Tribunes*, Pakistan, August 27, 2013, Retrieved on July 11, 2017, https://tribune.com.pk/story/595954/a-new-look-nsc/.

"2019 Human Development Index Ranking." *UNDP*, Retrieved from: http://hdr.undp.org/en/content/2019-human-development-index-ranking.

Conclusion

This book has sought to analyze why has Pakistan persisted with a military-centric national security state approach at a time when it has faced intensifying security challenges in the post-Cold War era. The book argues that the mismatch between Pakistan's national security stance and the transformed security environment has been facilitated and sustained by the embedded interests of the country's military-industrial complex. The latter developed after Pakistan's independence in 1947, and by the late 1950s, the military had carved out for itself a privileged and virtually autonomous role in formulating Pakistan's defence and security policies. Unlike its counterpart in the US, Pakistan's military-industrial complex is distinctive in that it developed the capability to be relatively self-sufficient in economic terms and consistently evaded civilian control in the area of national security decision making. Furthermore, the existence of the Pakistani military-industrial complex has limited the scope of any domestic debates on national security and has continued to highlight a poor security situation as the continuing reason for a military-oriented national security state. As a consequence, Pakistan's national security policy has not kept pace with a radically changed post-Cold War security environment, and has played a significant part in contributing to internal insecurity, political instability, and economic turmoil within the country during this period.

In the post-Cold War period, Pakistan's military-centric national security approach has been unable to adapt to the new changing security environment. Subsequently, Pakistan found itself with both internal and external security challenges. For instance, many of the old certainties for Pakistan's national security state have changed or disappeared. In particular, non-state actors became an extremely dangerous phenomenon with the rise of radical Islam. Pakistan has continued with its proxy wars in Kashmir and Afghanistan and tried to use militant groups in those locations as foreign policy tools to protect its strategic interests in South Asia. However, these militant forces have demonstrated little allegiance to the Pakistani state. The proxy wars had severe blowback repercussions for Pakistan's internal security, radicalizing its society and shifting the militant landscape into the country from Afghanistan. In 2013, the security situation reached such a level that Islamabad became more concerned about its internal security than about the external threat from India. Thus, in an effort to ensure security against external threats, Pakistan became more vulnerable than ever before, due to growing religious radicalization and terrorism.

Meanwhile, the Pakistani military has continued to have a functional dominance over the civilian leadership in security matters. The Pakistani military presented a range of obstacles to political parties or leaders who tried to transform the national security state and/or touch their military-industrial complex. Moreover, the military has consolidated its control over state institutions, such as the judiciary, civil bureaucracy, and media, which it has used to regulate the political process in the country to protect military interests (Shah, A. 2014). The military has used highly contentious constitutional articles such as Article 58 (2) (b) and Article 62(1) (f) to dismiss elected governments and prime ministers. Moreover, the president, with the support of the military, used Article 58 (2) (b) to dismiss elected governments in 1990, 1993, and 1996. In July 2017, Prime Minister Nawaz Sharif was disqualified by the Supreme Court for not being "honest" or "truthful" under Article 62(1) (f) of the constitution. It was his third term as prime minister, and he became the sixth elected premier since 2002 to be dismissed before completing his full five-year term (Masood, *The New York Times*, Asia, 28 July 2017). It should be emphasized that the frequent turnover of civilian governments has created political instability in the country and enabled the military to safeguard its dominant role in the making of national security policy.

At the same time, Islamabad has continued to spend disproportionally on the military in the post-Cold War era. In 2017–2018, the military budget was US$11 billion, making it the second-largest item of government spending after debt repayment (Budget in Brief 2018–2019). Furthermore, the military runs more than 50 various business entities, ranging from grocery superstores and real estate to banks and airlines, as reported in the media. According to conservative estimates, the net worth of the military's business empire is more than US$25 billion (Ellis, *Asia Money*, 29 March 2018; *Dawn*, Pakistan, 21 July 2016). So the military has a disproportionate role in the country's economy that has been largely utilized to serve the military's institutional and personal interests. Moreover, the military has occupied many key positions in civilian administrations, such as the security advisor to the prime minister, which is equal to a ministerial-level position. As a result, the military-industrial complex is able to provide sufficient resources for the military to act in a fairly autonomous fashion. Nevertheless, Pakistan's national security state has come at a substantial socio-economic cost to much of the wider society. In 2018, Pakistan was ranked 150 out of 189 countries in the Human Development Index (HDI) (UNDP 2018). The country is designated as the "least developed country," along with countries such as Somalia and Afghanistan.

Pakistan's military-centric national security approach has contributed to regional insecurity in South Asia. Islamabad has largely relied on proxy wars to protect its regional strategic interests, and has provided covert support to the Afghan Taliban and Kashmiri militant groups. The primary objectives were to seize Kashmir from India and to have a client government in Kabul which could serve Pakistan's strategic interests in the region. However, Islamabad failed to find a military solution to the Kashmir conflict and has played a part in making the South Asia region a nuclear flashpoint by failing to establish rapprochement with a resurgent India on a sustained basis. Islamabad also lost its policy of strategic depth following the fall of the Taliban regime in Afghanistan in late 2001. The international reputation of the country has also suffered. Pakistan has been accused of being a country that sponsors terrorism due to its support of Kashmiri and Afghan militant groups. In 2018, Islamabad was once again put on the grey list of the FATF for its suspected support to terrorists for the second time in the 2010s.

Against this backdrop, Pakistan's military has remained more popular than major political parties in the country. This is because the military has used fear of threat (internal and external) and actively involved in public relations to manage public opinion and counter dissent in its favour in order to establish social control in the country. The military has presented their personal and institutional interests within the ambit of national security interests. In post-9/11, the military establishment often justified that Pakistan has not destabilized like Syria or Afghanistan because of having a strong-armed force. Furthermore, the military has been actively involved in disaster relief programmes across the country. More importantly, the military has established a monopoly over the media in order to project its positive image. They have not only cultivated many journalists in media houses but also been running their own television channels and radio stations. In daily current affairs shows, the media often presents the Pakistani military as the only guardian institution of the country, whereas the civilians as being responsible for all the problems such as internal insecurity, political instability, corruption, and economic insecurity. The media houses often telecast the military funded songs, film, and dramas to propagate their positive image in the country. As a result, the military has established public perception that a strong military is necessary if the country has to survive and maintain its integrity.

In sum, Pakistan's military-centric national security approach has been increasingly out of sync with the post-Cold War security environment. It has not only perpetuated long-standing perceptions of a major external threat from India but also contributed to the emergence of blowback in Pakistan from Islamist militants that it has covertly supported. An alternative approach to security, therefore, has to be found if the country is to overcome the crippling security, political, and socio-economic problems that have been created. In the words of the country's founder, Muhammad Ali Jinah:

> Not to forget that the armed forces were the servants of the people and you do not make national policy; it is we, the civilians, who decide these issues and it is your duty to carry out these tasks with which you are entrusted.
>
> (Khan, R. *The Nation*, Pakistan, 22 November 2012)

Implications of this study

The overriding insecurity in Pakistan is the major implication of the country's military-centric national security approach, as it has created internal security threats and has exacerbated the hostility of the external environment. Pakistan used proxy wars as foreign policy tools to protect its strategic interests in the region. However, this led to massive adverse consequences for the country's overall security environment and made Pakistan a diplomatic pariah state. It was the Pakistani military who ran the state's affairs during and after the Cold War era. The military tried to find military solutions to the outstanding issues confronted by the country, but it failed to do so. Therefore, it could be argued that the situation would have been much better if civilians had been in power in Pakistan. Also, Islamabad must seek alternative options to deal with its security challenges. This study recommends Pakistan to adopt an economic-driven foreign policy based on non-interference in other countries' affairs, especially those of neighbouring countries like Afghanistan. This will restore the country's image, both regionally and globally, and will help normalize its relations with neighbouring countries who often accuse Pakistan of being a terror-sponsoring state.

An economic-driven foreign policy has great potential as Pakistan is located at the crossroads of South, Central, and West Asia where China, Central Asia, India, and Afghanistan meet. Afghanistan and the Central Asian states are landlocked countries, and Pakistan could be the shortest sea route for them to the outside world. So Islamabad can take advantage of the country's geographic position to enhance bilateral and multilateral economic and trade ties with surrounding countries. For example, Afghanistan was economically dependent on Pakistan and bilateral trade reached US$2.1 billion in 2013 from US$0.83 billion in 2006, but it was significantly reduced in recent years due to the worsening relations over cross-border terrorism and other related matters (Husain and Elahi 2015). For instance, the number of containers/trucks that used to transport goods into Afghanistan has reduced to 7,000 from a peak of 70,000 (Rahim, *The Diplomate*, Pakistan, 25 May 2008). So instead of using proxy militant groups, Pakistan needs to restore its economic ties with Afghanistan, and this will help to foster a friendly government in Kabul. As a result of economic connectivity, the political gravity will be shifted towards Pakistan that will assist its regional aspiration to become a major regional power in South Asia.

Democracy has not been nurtured in Pakistan, where political leadership has remained weak due to the functional dominance of the military within the national security state. Consequently, civilian institutions are weak and/or dysfunctional and are unable to address the domestic insecurity, economic crisis, and political instability facing the country. The Pakistani military has not allowed the civilian leadership to formulate foreign and security policy, and as a result, they failed to produce a comprehensive strategy to deal with the country's chronic security challenges in the post-Cold War era.

In this context, Pakistan is confronted by structural, economic, and socio-political issues, as well as worsening internal security. Therefore, the country desperately requires substantive democracy where the elected civilian leaders have the opportunity to deal with such intractable problems. Benazir Bhutto in

1988, being a democratically elected prime minister, had a vision and understanding of the regional and international politics of a changing global security environment after the Cold War. Unlike the Pakistani military, Bhutto wanted to transform foreign policy and emphasized normalization with India to open a new chapter in India-Pakistan relations. She also pushed for a peaceful transition of power in Afghanistan when the Soviets announced their withdrawal in 1989. However, the military was keen to continue General Zia's Cold War policies, which had failed to produce a solution to the Kashmir and Afghanistan conflicts.

The Pakistani state's behaviour has been based on a realist theoretical framework of the national security state in which the state has to enhance its own security, emphasizing military power to protect itself from security threats. However, the application of a realist framework to the analysis of Pakistan's security situation has created major conceptual problems. For instance, the security situation in Pakistan is quite different from that of the developed world as the country has a very weak economy with which to sustain substantial military power and to deal with chronic socio-economic problems. Consequently, Pakistan depends on external powers and proxy wars to deal with external threats from neighbouring countries, especially India. In this process, Pakistan has become a client state of the greater power while confronting home-grown terrorism in the post-Cold War era. Thus, in a developing country like Pakistan, the realist security framework misleads decision-makers, who hold on to the belief that the only way to increase security is merely to increase military power. It is important to note that, although the military remains a very crucial component of national security, it is only one of many facets.

References

"50 Commercial Entities Being Run by Armed Forces." *Dawn*, Pakistan, July 21, 2016. Retrieved on August 27, 2018, https://www.dawn.com/news/1272211.

"Budget in Brief 2018-19." Ministry of Finance, Pakistan. Retrieved from http://www.fina nce.gov.pk/budget/Budget%20in%20Brief%202017-18.pdf.

Ellis, E. 2018. "Pakistan: A Quiet Sort of Military Might." *Asia Money*, March 29, 2018. Retrieved on August 30, 2018, https://www.euromoney.com/article/b17jscxn0zgtln/p akistan-a-quiet-sort-of-military-might?copyrightInfo=true.

Husain, I. and Elahi, M. A. 2015. "The Future of Afghanistan-Pakistan Trade Relations." *USIP*, Peace Brief. Retrieved from https://www.usip.org/sites/default/files/PB191-The -Future-of-Afghanistan-Pakistan-Trade-Relations.pdf.

Khan, R. 2012. "Quaid's Visit to Staff College Quetta." *The Nation*, Pakistan, November 22, 2012. Retrieved on January 21, 2020, https://nation.com.pk/22-Nov-2012/quaid-s -visit-to-staff-college-quetta.

Masood, S. 2017. "Nawaz Sharif, Pakistan's Prime Minister, Is Toppled by Corruption Case." *The New York Times*, Asia, July 28, 2017. Retrieved on August 27, 2018, https ://www.nytimes.com/2017/07/28/world/asia/pakistan-prime-minister-nawaz-sharif-re moved.html.

Rahim, S. A. 2008. "Capricious Afghanistan-Pakistan Trade: Who Wins?" *The Diplomate*, Pakistan, May 25, 2008. Retrieved on December 6, 2018, https://thediplomat.com/2018/05/capricious-afghanistan-pakistan-trade-who-wins/.

Shah, A. 2014. "Constraining Consolidation: Military Politics and Democracy in Pakistan (2007–2013)." *Democratization* 21 (6): 1007–1033.

"The 2018 Statistical Update." *UNDP* report. 2018. Retrieved from http://hdr.undp.org/en/2018-updat.

Appendix 1

Pakistan – global peace index

Date	Global Peace Index	Global Peace Ranking
2018	3.079	151
2017	3.058	152
2016	3.145	153
2015	3.049	154
2014	3.107	154
2013	3.106	157
2012	3.000	153
2011	3.070	149
2010	3.153	143
2009	3.087	140
2008	2.886	132

Source: https://countryeconomy.com/demography/global-peace-index/pakistan

Appendix 2
Primary field research questionnaire

1. In your opinion, what were the factors that led to Pakistan's national security state after its independence in 1947? What were the consequences of national security state over the Pakistani state in society?
2. Do you think that has India remained a real threat to Pakistan after the Cold War?
3. On the Kashmir front, in your opinion, did Pakistan achieve its strategic objectives by supporting the internal uprising in Kashmir during the 1990s?
4. Do you think that Pakistan's position on Kashmir strengthened by supporting Kashmir uprising trough a proxy war?
5. In your view, was Pakistan's participation in the global war on terror a right option?
6. Do you think that Pakistan adopted a dual strategy to war on terror as the CIA blamed General Musharraf of playing a double game in the war? If yes, has this strategy worked?
7. Did Pakistan achieve its strategic objectives by participating in the global war on terror?
8. How do you think Pakistan's security policies are likely to evolve in the future? Do you think that Pakistan needs to reform its state-centric national security approach to deal with its current security challenges?
9. Do you think Pakistan's national security policy is working? If not, why not?
10. If Pakistan's national security policy is not working, why has such a policy persisted?

Appendix 3

List of interviewees

No	Name	Designation/ Positions	Affiliation	Place	Date
1	Dr. Khuram Iqbal	Assistant Professor	National Defence University	Islamabad	8 November 2017
2	Dr. Moonis Ahmar	Professor	Karachi University	Islamabad	9 November 2017
2	Dr. Zafar Khan	Assistant Professor	National Defence University	Islamabad	10 November 2017
4	Dr. Shabana Feyyaz	Associate Professor	Quaid-i-Azam University	Islamabad	20 November 2017
5	Dr. Farhan Hanif Siddiqi	Associate Professor	Quaid-i-Azam University	Islamabad	13 November 2017
6	Dr. Syed Rifaat Hussain	HoD/Professor	National University of Sciences and Technology	Islamabad	23 November 2017
7	Dr. Ijaz Khan	Professor (retired)	University of Peshawar	Islamabad	10 November 2017
8	Dr. Muhammad Islam	HOD/Professor	Iqra University	Islamabad	22 November 2017
9	Dr. Ejaz Hussain	Associate Professor	Iqra University	Islamabad	14 November 2017
10	Mr. Najam Rafique	Director Americas/ Programmes Coordinator	The Institute of Strategic Studies, Islamabad	Islamabad	14 November 2017
11	Malik Qasim Mustafa	Senior Research Fellow/Editor	The Institute of Strategic Studies, Islamabad	Islamabad	6 December 2017
12	Dr. Ayesha Siddiqa	Research Associate/ Pakistan Fellow	SOAS, South Asia Institute, UK The Woodrow Wilson Center, Washington, DC	Skype	21 June 2018
13	Dr. Arabinda Acharya	Assistant Professor	National Defense University, Washington, DC	Skype	9 February 2018
14	Dr. Moeed Yusuf	Associate Vice President	Asia Center, the U.S. Institute of Peace, Washington, DC	Skype	2 March 2018

(*Continued*)

(*Continued*)

No	Name	Designation/ Positions	Affiliation	Place	Date
15	Mr. Shuja Nawaz	Distinguished Fellow/ Director	South Asia Center, Atlantic Council	Skype	14 February 2018
16	Mr. Raza Rumi Ahmad	Director	Department of Journalism, Roy H. Park School of Communications	Skype	25 February 2018
17	Amb. Tariq Azizuddin	Former Pakistan's Ambassador to Afghanistan and Turkey	Pakistan's Foreign Affairs	Rawalpindi	17 November 2017
18	Amb. Ashraf Jehangir Qazi	Former Pakistan's Ambassador to China, India, and the US	Pakistan's Foreign Affairs	Islamabad	19 November 2017
19	Dr. Humayun Khan	Chairman; former Pakistan's High Commissioner to Bangladesh, the UK, and India	The Institute of Rural Management and Pakistan's Foreign Affairs	Islamabad	23 November 2017
20	Mr. Khalid Aziz	Chief Secretary/ Civil Service Officer (retired)	Khyber PakhtunKhwa and Federal Governments	Islamabad	5 December 2017
21	Mr. Muhammad Nauman Saeed	Brigadier/Director (retired)	Inter-Services Intelligence (ISI)	Islamabad	12 November 2017
22	Mr. Saad Muhammad	Brigadier/Defence Attache (retired)	Pakistan Army/ Pakistan's Embassy in Kabul	Islamabad	14 November 2017
23	Mr. Muhammad Hassan Miraj	Army Officer/ Writer	Pakistan Army	Rawalpindi	22 November 2017
24	General Mohammad Asad Durrani	Lieutenant General/ Director General (retired)	Pakistan Army/ISI	Rawalpindi	22 November 2017
25	Mr. Mushahid Hussain Syed	Politician/ Journalist/ Senator	Pakistan Muslim League (Nawaz) PMLN Served with both civilian and military regimes on key positions	Islamabad	8 December 2017

(*Continued*)

(*Continued*)

No	Name	Designation/ Positions	Affiliation	Place	Date
26	Mr. Aftab Ahmad Sherpao	Politician; former Chief Minister of the Khyber Pakhtunkhwa and Federal Interior Minister of Pakistan	President Qaumi Watan Party; former Provincial President of PPP	Islamabad	27 November 2017
27	Mr. Khalid Rehman	Director General	Institute of Policy Studies	Islamabad	21 November 2017
28	Amb. Ali Server Naqvi	Executive Director; former Pakistan's Ambassador to the United Nations, London, Paris, and Brussels	CISS and Pakistan's Foreign Affairs	Islamabad	24 November 2017

Appendix 4

AWT list of companies

Year of operation	Company/business unit
1971	Army Welfare Trust
1972	Stud Farm Probyanabad
1984	Askari Sugar Mills Badin
1984	Stud Farm Boyalgunj
1990	Askari Real Estate Unit
1990	Askari Projects (Woolen & Shoes)
1990	Blue Lagoon & Army Welfare Mess
1995	Askari Aviation Pvt Ltd.
1995	Askari General Insurance Company Ltd.
1996	Askari Guards Pvt Ltd.
1996	Mobil Askari Lubricants Pakistan Ltd.
2002	Askari Fuels
2004	Askari Seeds
2009	Askari Enterprises Pvt Ltd.
2011	Lahore Lagoon
2014	Fauji Security Services Pvt Ltd.
2017	MedAsk
2017	AWT Investments
2017	Askari Air Pakistan
2017	Hydro Power Project

Source: www.awt.com.pk/home/history

Appendix 5

The 17th amendment of Pakistan's constitution in 2010

Constitution (Seventeenth Amendment) Act, 2003

A Bill further to amend the Constitution of the Islamic Republic of Pakistan

WHEREAS it is expedient further to amend the Constitution of the Islamic Republic of Pakistan for the purposes hereinafter appearing;

It is hereby enacted as follows:-

1. **Short title and commencement:**

(1) This Act may be called the Constitution (Seventeenth Amendment) Act, 2003
(2) It shall come into force at once.

2. **Amendment of Article 41 of the Constitution:**

In the Constitution of the Islamic Republic of Pakistan, hereinafter referred to as the Constitution, in Article 41,

(1) In clause (7), in paragraph (b), for the full stop at the end, a colon shall be substituted and thereafter the following proviso shall be added, namely;

"Provided that paragraph (d) of clause (1) of Article 63 shall become operative on and from the 31st day of December, 2004.";

and

(2) After clause (7) amended as aforesaid, the following new clauses shall be added, namely:-

"(8) Without prejudice to the provisions of clause (7), any member or members of a House of Majlis-e-Shoora (Parliament) or of a Provincial Assembly, individually or jointly, may, not later than thirty days from the commencement of the Constitution (Seventeenth Amendment) Act, 2003, move a resolution for vote of confidence for further affirmation of the President in office by majority of the members present and voting, by division or any other method as prescribed in the rules made by the Federal Government under clause (9), of the electoral college consisting of members of both Houses of Majlis-e-Shoora (Parliament) and the Provincial Assemblies, in a special session of each House of Majlis-e-Shoora (Parliament) and of each Provincial Assembly summoned for the purpose, and the vote of confidence having been passed, the President, notwithstanding anything contained in the Constitution or judgment of any court, shall be deemed to be elected to hold office for a term of five years under the Constitution, and the same shall not be called in question in any court or forum on any ground whatsoever.

(9) Notwithstanding anything contained in the Constitution or any other law for the time being in force, the proceedings for the vote of confidence referred to in clause (8) shall be regulated and conducted by the Chief Election Commissioner in accordance with such procedure and the votes shall be counted in such manner as may be prescribed by the rules framed by the Federal Government:

Provided that clauses (8) and (9) shall be valid only for the forthcoming vote of confidence for the current term of the President in office."

3. Amendment of Article 58 of the Constitution:

In the Constitution, in Article 58, after clause (2), the following new clause shall be added, namely:-

"(3) The President in case of dissolution of the National Assembly under paragraph (b) of clause (2) shall, within fifteen days of the dissolution, refer the matter to the Supreme Court and the Supreme Court shall decide the reference within thirty days whose decision shall be final."

4. Amendment of Article 112 of the Constitution:

In the Constitution, in Article 112, after clause (2), the following new clause shall be added, namely:-

"(3) The Governor in case of dissolution of the Provisional Assembly under paragraph (b) of clause (2) shall within fifteen days of the dissolution refer the matter to the Supreme Court with the previous approval of the President and the Supreme Court shall decide the reference within thirty days whose decision shall be final."

5. mission of Article 152 A of the Constitution:

In the Constitution, Article 152 A shall be omitted.

6. Substitution of Article 179 of the Constitution:

In the Constitution, for Article 179, the following shall be substituted, namely:

"179. Retiring Age-

A judge of the Supreme Court shall hold office until he attains the age of sixty five years, unless he sooner resigns or is removed from office in accordance with the Constitution."

7. Substitution of Article 195 of the Constitution:

In the Constitution, for Article 195, the following shall be substituted, namely:

"195 Retiring Age-

A judge of the High Court shall hold office until he attains the age of sixty-two years, unless he sooner resigns or is removed from office in accordance with the Constitution."

8. Amendment of Article 243 of the Constitution:

In the Constitution, in Article 243, in clause (3), for the words "in his discretion" the words "in consultation with the Prime Minister" shall be substituted.

9. Amendment of Article 268 of the Constitution:

In the Constitution, in Article 268, in clause (2), for the full stop at the end, a colon shall be substituted and thereafter the following proviso shall be added, namely:

"Provided that the laws mentioned at entries 27 to 30 and entry 35 in the Sixth Schedule shall stand omitted after six years."

10. Substitution of Article 270-AA of the Constitution:

In the Constitution, for Article 270 AA, the following shall be substituted, namely:-

"270-AA- Validation and affirmation of laws etc.

(1) The Proclamation of Emergency of the fourteenth day of October, 1999, all President's Orders, Ordinances, Chief Executive's Orders, including the Provisional Constitution Order No. 1 of 1999, the Oath of Office (Judges) Order, 2000 (No. 1 of 2000), Chief Executive's Order No. 12 of 2002, the amendments made in the Constitution through the Legal Framework Order, 2002 (Chief Executive's Order No. 24 of 2002), the Legal Framework (Amendment) Order, 2002 (Chief Executive's Order No. 29 of 2002), the Legal Framework (Second Amendment) Order, 2002 (Chief Executive's Order No. 32 of 2002) and all other laws made between the twelfth day of October, one thousand nine hundred and ninety-nine and the date on which this Article comes into force (both days inclusive), having been duly made or accordingly affirmed, adopted and declared to have been validly made by the competent authority and notwithstanding anything contained in the Constitution shall not be called in question in any court or forum on any ground whatsoever.

(2) All orders made, proceedings taken, appointments made, including secondments and deputations, and acts done by any authority, or by any person, which were made, taken or done, or purported to have been made, taken or done, between the twelfth day of October, one thousand nine hundred and ninety-nine, and the

date on which this Article comes into force (both days inclusive), in exercise of the powers derived from any Proclamation, President's Orders, Ordinances, Chief Executive's Orders, enactments, including amendments in the Constitution, notifications, rules, orders, bye-laws or in execution of or in compliance with any orders made or sentences passed by any authority in the exercise or purported exercise of powers as aforesaid, shall, notwithstanding any judgment of any court, be deemed to be and always to have been validly made, taken or done and shall not be called in question in any court or forum on any ground whatsoever.

(3) All Proclamations, President's Orders, Ordinances, Chief Executive's Orders, laws, regulations, enactments, including amendments in the Constitution, notification, rules, orders or bye-laws in force immediately before the date on which this Article comes into force shall continue in force, until altered, repealed or amended by the competent authority.

Explanation: In this clause," competent authority "means,-

(a) in respect of President's Orders, Ordinances, Chief Executive's Orders and enactments, including amendments in the Constitution, the appropriate Legislature; and

(b) in respect of notifications, rules, orders and bye-laws, the authority in which the power to make, alter, repeal or amend the same vests under the law.

(4) No suit, prosecution or other legal proceedings, including writ petitions, shall lie in any court or forum against any authority or any persons, for or on account of or in respect of any order made, proceedings taken or act done whether in the exercise or purported exercise of the powers referred to in clause (2) or in execution of or in compliance with orders made or sentences passed in exercise or purported exercise of such powers.

(5) For the purposes of clauses (1), (2) and (4), all orders made, proceedings taken , appointments made, including secondments and deputations, acts done or purporting to be made, taken or done by any authority or person shall be deemed to have been made, taken or done in good faith and for the purpose intended to be served thereby."

Source: National Assembly of Pakistan, www.na.gov.pk/uploads/documents/132 1274383_862.pdf

Appendix 6

Simla Agreement 2 July 1972

The Simla Agreement signed by Prime Minister Indira Gandhi and President Zulfikar Ali Bhutto of Pakistan on 2nd July 1972 was much more than a peace treaty seeking to reverse the consequences of the 1971 war (i.e. to bring about withdrawals of troops and an exchange of PoWs). It was a comprehensive blue print for good neighbourly relations between India and Pakistan. Under the Simla Agreement both countries undertook to abjure conflict and confrontation which had marred relations in the past, and to work towards the establishment of durable peace, friendship and cooperation.

The Simla Agreement contains a set of guiding principles, mutually agreed to by India and Pakistan, which both sides would adhere to while managing relations with each other. These emphasize: respect for each other's territorial integrity and sovereignty; non-interference in each other's internal affairs; respect for each other's unity, political independence; sovereign equality; and abjuring hostile propaganda. The following principles of the Agreement are, however, particularly noteworthy:

- A mutual commitment to the peaceful resolution of all issues through direct bilateral approaches.
- To build the foundations of a cooperative relationship with special focus on people to people contacts.
- To uphold the inviolability of the Line of Control in Jammu and Kashmir, which is the most important CBM between India and Pakistan and a key to durable peace.

India has faithfully observed the Simla Agreement in the conduct of its relations with Pakistan.

Simla Agreement

Agreement on Bilateral Relations Between The Government of India and The Government of Pakistan

1. The Government of India and the Government of Pakistan are resolved that the two countries put an end to the conflict and confrontation that have hitherto marred their relations and work for the promotion of a friendly and harmonious relationship and the establishment of durable peace in the sub-continent, so that both countries may henceforth devote their resources and energies to the pressing talk of advancing the welfare of their peoples.

   In order to achieve this objective, the Government of India and the Government of Pakistan have agreed as follows:-

   - That the principles and purposes of the Charter of the United Nations shall govern the relations between the two countries;
   - That the two countries are resolved to settle their differences by peaceful means through bilateral negotiations or by any other peaceful means mutually agreed upon between them. Pending the final settlement of any of the problems between the two countries, neither side shall unilaterally alter the situation and both shall prevent the organization, assistance or encouragement of any acts detrimental to the maintenance of peaceful and harmonious relations;
   - That the pre-requisite for reconciliation, good neighbourliness and durable peace between them is a commitment by both the countries to peaceful co-existence, respect for each other's territorial integrity and sovereignty and non-interference in each other's internal affairs, on the basis of equality and mutual benefit;
   - That the basic issues and causes of conflict which have bedevilled the relations between the two countries for the last 25 years shall be resolved by peaceful means;
   - That they shall always respect each other's national unity, territorial integrity, political independence and sovereign equality;
   - That in accordance with the Charter of the United Nations they will refrain from the threat or use of force against the territorial integrity or political independence of each other.

2. Both Governments will take all steps within their power to prevent hostile propaganda directed against each other. Both countries will encourage the dissemination of such information as would promote the development of friendly relations between them.

3. In order progressively to restore and normalize relations between the two countries step by step, it was agreed that;
   - Steps shall be taken to resume communications, postal, telegraphic, sea, land including border posts, and air links including overflights.
   - Appropriate steps shall be taken to promote travel facilities for the nationals of the other country.
   - Trade and co-operation in economic and other agreed fields will be resumed as far as possible.
   - Exchange in the fields of science and culture will be promoted.

In this connection delegations from the two countries will meet from time to time to work out the necessary details.

4. In order to initiate the process of the establishment of durable peace, both the Governments agree that:
   - Indian and Pakistani forces shall be withdrawn to their side of the international border.
   - In Jammu and Kashmir, the line of control resulting from the cease-fire of December 17, 1971 shall be respected by both sides without prejudice to the recognized position of either side. Neither side shall seek to alter it unilaterally, irrespective of mutual differences and legal interpretations. Both sides further undertake to refrain from the threat or the use of force in violation of this Line.
   - The withdrawals shall commence upon entry into force of this Agreement and shall be completed within a period of 30 days thereof.
5. This Agreement will be subject to ratification by both countries in accordance with their respective constitutional procedures, and will come into force with effect from the date on which the Instruments of Ratification are exchanged.
6. Both Governments agree that their respective Heads will meet again at a mutually convenient time in the future and that, in the meanwhile, the representatives of the two sides will meet to discuss further the modalities and arrangements for the establishment of durable peace and normalization of relations, including the questions of repatriation of prisoners of war and civilian internees, a final settlement of Jammu and Kashmir and the resumption of diplomatic relations.

Sd/-	Sd/-
(Indira Gandhi)	(Zulfikar Ali Bhutto)
Prime Minister, Republic of India	President, Islamic Republic of Pakistan

Source: Ministry of External Affairs, Government of India, https://mea.gov.in/in-focus-article.htm?19005/Simla+Agreement+July+2+1972

Appendix 7
Lahore Declaration February, 1999

Lahore Declaration February, 1999

The Lahore Declaration Joint Statement |||
Memorandum of Understanding

The following is the text of the Lahore Declaration:

The Prime Ministers of the Republic of India and the Islamic Republic of Pakistan:

Sharing a vision of peace and stability between their countries, and of progress and prosperity for their peoples; Convinced that durable peace and development of harmonious relations and friendly cooperation will serve the vital interests of the peoples of the two countries, enabling them to devote their energies for a better future; Recognising that the nuclear dimension of the security environment of the two countries adds to their responsibility for avoidance of conflict between the two countries;

Committed to the principles and purposes of the Charter of the United Nations, and the universally accepted principles of peaceful co-existence; Reiterating the determination of both countries to implementing the Simla Agreement in letter and spirit; Committed to the objective of universal nuclear disarmament and non-proliferation; Convinced of the importance of mutually agreed confidence building measures for improving the security environment;

Recalling their agreement of 23rd September, 1998, that an environment of peace and security is in the supreme national interest of both sides and that the resolution of all outstanding issues, including Jammu and Kashmir, is essential for this purpose;

Have agreed that their respective Governments:

- shall intensify their efforts to resolve all issues, including the issue of Jammu and Kashmir.
- shall refrain from intervention and interference in each other's internal affairs.
- shall intensify their composite and integrated dialogue process for an early and positive outcome of the agreed bilateral agenda.

- shall take immediate steps for reducing the risk of accidental or unauthorised use of nuclear weapons and discuss concepts and doctrines with a view to elaborating measures for confidence building in the nuclear and conventional fields, aimed at prevention of conflict.
- reaffirm their commitment to the goals and objectives of SAARC and to concert their efforts towards the realisation of the SAARC vision for the year 2000 and beyond with a view to promoting the welfare of the peoples of South Asia and to improve their quality of life through accelerated economic growth, social progress and cultural development.
- reaffirm their condemnation of terrorism in all its forms and manifestations and their determination to combat this menace.
- shall promote and protect all human rights and fundamental freedoms.

Signed at Lahore on the 21st day of February 1999.
Atal Behari Vajpayee – Prime Minister of the Republic of India
Muhammad Nawaz Sharif – Prime Minister of the Islamic Republic of Pakistan

Joint statement:
The following is the text of the Joint Statement issued at the end of the Prime Minister, Mr. A. B. Vajpayee's visit to Lahore:

1. In response to an invitation by the Prime Minister of Pakistan, Mr. Muhammad Nawaz Sharif, the Prime Minister of India, Shri Atal Behari Vajpayee, visited Pakistan from 20-21 February, 1999, on the inaugural run of the Delhi-Lahore bus service.
2. The Prime Minister of Pakistan received the Indian Prime Minister at the Wagah border on 20th February 1999. A banquet in honour of the Indian Prime Minister and his delegation was hosted by the Prime Minister of Pakistan at Lahore Fort, on the same evening. Prime Minister, Atal Behari Vajpayee, visited Minar-e-Pakistan, Mausoleum of Allama Iqabal, Gurudawara Dera Sahib and Samadhi of Maharaja Ranjeet Singh. On 21st February, a civic reception was held in honour of the visiting Prime Minister at the Governor's House.
3. The two leaders held discussions on the entire range of bilateral relations, regional cooperation within SAARC, and issues of international concern. They decided that:
   - The two Foreign Ministers will meet periodically to discuss all issues of mutual concern, including nuclear related issues.
   - The two sides shall undertake consultations on WTO related issues with a view to coordinating their respective positions.
   - The two sides shall determine areas of cooperation in Information Technology, in particular for tackling the problems of Y2K.
   - The two sides will hold consultations with a view to further liberalising the visa and travel regime.

- The two sides shall appoint a two member committee at ministerial level to examine humanitarian issues relating to Civilian detainees and missing POWs.

4. They expressed satisfaction on the commencement of a Bus Service between Lahore and New Delhi, the release of fishermen and civilian detainees and the renewal of contacts in the field of sports.

5. Pursuant to the directive given by the two Prime Ministers, the Foreign Secretaries of Pakistan and India signed a Memorandum of Understanding on 21st February 1999, identifying measures aimed at promoting an environment of peace and security between the two countries.

6. The two Prime Ministers signed the Lahore Declaration embodying their shared vision of peace and stability between their countries and of progress and prosperity for their peoples.

7. Prime Minister, Atal Behari Vajpayee extended an invitation to Prime Minister, Muhammad Nawaz Sharif, to visit India on mutually convenient dates.

8. Prime Minister, Atal Behari Vajpayee, thanked Prime Minister, Muhammad Nawaz Sharif, for the warm welcome and gracious hospitality extended to him and members of his delegation and for the excellent arrangements made for his visit.

Lahore,

February 21, 1999.

Memorandum of Understanding

The following is the text of the Memorandum of Understanding signed by the Foreign Secretary, Mr. K. Raghunath, and the Pakistan Foreign Secretary, Mr. Shamshad Ahmad, in Lahore on Sunday:

The Foreign Secretaries of India and Pakistan:-

Reaffirming the continued commitment of their respective governments to the principles and purposes of the U.N. Charter; Reiterating the determination of both countries to implementing the Shimla Agreement in letter and spirit; Guided by the agreement between their Prime Ministers of 23rd September 1998 that an environment of peace and security is in the supreme national interest of both sides and that resolution of all outstanding issues, including Jammu and Kashmir, is essential for this purpose; Pursuant to the directive given by their respective Prime Ministers in Lahore, to adopt measures for promoting a stable environment of peace, and security between the two countries;

Have on this day, agreed to the following:-

1. The two sides shall engage in bilateral consultations on security concepts, and nuclear doctrines, with a view to developing measures for confidence building in the nuclear and conventional fields, aimed at avoidance of conflict.

2. The two sides undertake to provide each other with advance notification in respect of ballistic missile flight tests, and shall conclude a bilateral agreement in this regard.

3. The two sides are fully committed to undertaking national measures to reducing the risks of accidental or unauthorised use of nuclear weapons under their respective control. The two sides further undertake to notify each, other immediately in the event of any accidental, unauthorised or unexplained incident that could create the risk of a fallout with adverse consequences for both sides, or an outbreak of a nuclear war between the two countries, as well as to adopt measures aimed at diminishing the possibility of such actions, or such incidents being misinterpreted by the other. The two sides shall identify/ establish the appropriate communication mechanism for this purpose.

4. The two sides shall continue to abide by their respective unilateral moratorium on conducting further nuclear test explosions unless either side, in exercise of its national sovereignty decides that extraordinary events have jeopardised its supreme interests.

5. The two sides shall conclude an agreement on prevention of incidents at sea in order to ensure safety of navigation by naval vessels, and aircraft belonging to the two sides.

6. The two sides shall periodically review the implementation of existing Confidence Building Measures (CBMs) and where necessary, set up appropriate consultative mechanisms to monitor and ensure effective implementation of these CBMs.

7. The two sides shall undertake a review of the existing communication links (e.g. between the respective Directors-General, Military Operations) with a view to upgrading and improving these links, and to provide for fail-safe and secure communications.

8. The two sides shall engage in bilateral consultations on security, disarmament and non-proliferation issues within the context of negotiations on these issues in multilateral fora.

    Where required, the technical details of the above measures will be worked out by experts of the two sides in meetings to be held on mutually agreed dates, before mid 1999, with a view to reaching bilateral agreements.

    Done at Lahore on 21st February 1999 in the presence of Prime Minister of India, Mr. Atal Behari Vajpayee, and Prime Minister of Pakistan, Mr. Muhammad Nawaz Sharif.

(K. Raghunath) Foreign Secretary of the Republic of India
(Shamshad Ahmad) Foreign Secretary of the Islamic Republic of Pakistan

Source: Ministry of External Affairs India, https://mea.gov.in/in-focus-article .htm?18997/Lahore+Declaration+February+1999

Appendix 8

Timeline of Afghan displacements into Pakistan 1979–2012

1979: The first major wave of Afghan refugees enters Pakistan following the Soviet invasion. At least one million Afghans are estimated to have reached Pakistan by 1979, with a total of 3.3 million having fled to Pakistan and Iran by 1980.1980: UNHCR sets up its first office in Pakistan in the wake of the refugee influx.

1981–1990: According to official Pakistan government figures, the number of registered refugees reaches two million by 1981, and 3.2 million by 1990, in addition to an estimated 500,000 unregistered refugees. As the influx continues in response to conflict, 334 official camps are established in Khyber Pakhtunkhwa, Baluchistan and Punjab provinces.

1994: Seventy-four thousand refugees arrive in Pakistan following fighting between Hezb-e-Islami and Jamiat-e-Islami, two of the Mujahdeen groups engaged in a struggle for the control of Afghanistan after the 1989 Soviet pull-out.

1996: The capture of the eastern city of Jalalabad and the capital Kabul by the Taliban brings 50,000 refugees to Pakistan's North West Frontier Province (renamed Khyber Pakhtunkhwa in 2010).

1998–1999: The northern Afghan city of Mazar-i-Sharif falls to the Taliban, leading thousands more to flee to Pakistan.

1999: The complete takeover of Afghanistan by the Taliban pushes 30,000 new refugees, mostly ethnic Hazaras who fear discrimination, into Pakistan. Many head to southwestern Balochistan Province.

2001: After 9/11 the US begins attacks on militant targets in Afghanistan, prompting a fresh wave of migration to Pakistan. Around five million Afghans have crossed into Pakistan since 1979.

2002–2007: After the fall of the Taliban, the UNHCR assists 2.7 million Afghans to repatriate to Afghanistan from Pakistan. According to the agency, the 1.5 million who voluntarily went home in 2002 marked the single largest refugee return in the world since 1972. An estimated 1.1 million others return home independently, without UNHCR assistance.

2007–2012: Voluntary returns to Afghanistan decrease dramatically as a result of increased conflict in Afghanistan and a realization that there are few livelihood opportunities.

Sources: UNHCR, Commissionarate Afghan Refugees, KP, Human Rights Commission of Pakistan: Afghan refugees in Pakistan: Push comes to shove, April 2009, Middle East Institute, Herald magazine, Dawn daily, The News International, www.irinnews.org/news/2012/02/27/timeline-afghan-displacements-pakistan

Appendix 9
The 13th amendment of Pakistan's constitution in 1997

The Constitution (Thirteenth Amendment) Act, 1997

Further to amend the Constitution of the Islamic Republic of Pakistan

WHEREAS it is expedient further to amend the Constitution of the Islamic Republic of Pakistan for the purposes hereinafter appearing;

It is hereby enacted as follows:-

1. **Short title and commencement -**
(1) This Act may be called the Constitution (Thirteenth Amendment) Act, 1997.
(2) It shall come in to force at once.

2. **Amendment of Article 58 of the Constitution** - In the Constitution of the Islamic Republic of Pakistan, hereinafter referred to as the Constitution, in Article 58, in clause (2) sub-clause (b) shall be omitted.

3. **Amendment of Article 101 of the Constitution** - In the Constitution, in Article 101, in clause (1) for the words "after consultation with" the words "on the advice of" shall be substituted.

4. **Amendment of Article 112 of the Constitution** - In the Constitution, in Article 112, in clause (2) sub-clause (b) shall be omitted.

5. **Amendment of Article 243 of the Constitution** - In the Constitution, in Article 243, in clause (2) in sub-clause (c) the words "in his discretion" shall be omitted.

STATEMENT AND OBJECTS OF REASONS:

In order to strengthen parliamentary democracy, it has become necessary to restore some of the powers of the Prime Minister which were taken away by the Constitution (Eighth Amendment) Act, 1985.

The Bill seeks further to amend the Constitution of the Islamic Republic of Pakistan to achieve the aforesaid purpose.

Source: National Assembly of Pakistan, Islamabad, www.na.gov.pk/uploads/documents/1324604273_276.pdf

Appendix 10

National assembly general election results in 2002

Political Group	Total
Pakistan Muslim League-Qaid-i-Azam (PML/Q)	77
Pakistan People's Party Parliamentarians (PPPP)	63
Muttahida Majlis-i-Amal (MMA)	45
Pakistan Muslim League (Nawaz)	14
National Democratic Alliance (NA)	13
Mohajir Quami Movement (MQM)	13
Pakistan Muslim League (Functional)	4
Pakistan Muslim League (Junejo)	2
Pakistan People's Party (Sherpao)	2
Pakistan Muslim League (Zia-ul-Huq)	1
Independents	29
Others	9
Comments:	
There are 60 others seats reserved for women and 10 seats for non-Muslim minorities.	
Distribution of seats according to sex:	
Men:	268
Women:	74
Percent of women:	21.64

Source: http://archive.ipu.org/parline-e/reports/arc/2241_02.htm

Appendix 11

Provincial assembly general election results in 2002

	PPPP	PMLQ	PMLN	MMA	NA	MQM	ANP	INDP	OTHR	Total	Out of
Punjab	60	127	37	6	12			39	6	287	297
Sindh	50	10		13	12	28		5	12	130	130
NWFP	8	8	5	48			8	12	10	99	99
Balochistan	2	8		14	3			7	14	48	51

Note: The above acronyms are the major political parties in Pakistan except INDP which stands for independents.

Sources: www.heraldelections.com; www.satp.org/
satporgtp/countries/pakistan/database/nationalassembly_results.htm

Appendix 12

UN security council resolution over Kashmir conflict in April 1948

47 (1948). Resolution of 21 April 1948

[S/726]

The Security Council,

Having considered the complaint of the Government of India concerning the dispute over the State of Jammu and Kashmir,

Having heard the representative of India in support of that complaint and the reply and counter complaints of the representative of Pakistan,

Being strongly of the opinion that the early restoration of peace and order in Jammu and Kashmir is essential and that India and Pakistan should do their utmost to bring about a cessation of all fighting,

Noting with satisfaction that both India and Pakistan desire that the question of the accession of Jammu and Kashmir to India or Pakistan should be decided through the democratic method of a free and impartial plebiscite,

Considering that the continuation of the dispute is likely to endanger international peace and security,

Reaffirms its resolution 38 (1948) of 17 January 1948;

Resolves that the membership of the Commission established by its resolution 39 (1948) of 20 January 1948 shall be increased to five and shall include, in addition to the membership mentioned in that resolution, representatives of ... and ..., and that if the membership of the Commission has not been completed within ten days from the date of the adoption of this resolution the President of the Council may designate such other Member or Members of the United Nations as are required to complete the membership of five;

Instructs the Commission to proceed at once to the Indian subcontinent and there place its good offices and mediation at the disposal of the Governments of India and Pakistan with a view to facilitating the taking of the necessary measures, both with respect to the restoration of peace and order and to the holding of a plebiscite, by the two Governments, acting in co-operation with one another and with the Commission, and further instructs the Commission to keep the Council informed of the action taken under the resolution; and, to this end,

Recommends to the Governments of India and Pakistan the following measures as those which in the opinion of the Council are appropriate to bring about a cessation of the fighting and to create proper conditions for a free and impartial plebiscite to decide whether the State of Jammu and Kashmir is to accede to India or Pakistan:

A. Restoration of peace and order

1. The Government of Pakistan should undertake to use its best endeavours:
   (a)   To secure the withdrawal from the State of Jammu and Kashmir of tribesmen and Pakistani nationals not normally resident therein who have entered the State for the purpose of fighting, and to prevent any intrusion into the State of such elements and any furnishing of material aid to those fighting in the State;
   (b)   To make known to all concerned that the measures indicated in this and the following paragraphs provide full freedom to all subjects of the State, regardless of creed, caste, or party, to express their views and to vote on the question of the accession of the State, and that therefore they should co-operate in the maintenance of peace and order.
2. The Government of India should:
   (a)   When it is established to the satisfaction of the Commission set up in accordance with the Council's resolution 39 (1948) that the tribesmen are withdrawing and that arrangements for the cessation of the fighting have become effective, put into operation in consultation with the Commission a plan for withdrawing their own forces from Jammu and Kashmir and reducing them progressively to the minimum strength required for the support of the civil power in the maintenance of law and order;
   (b)   Make known that the withdrawal is taking place in stages and announce the completion of each stage;
   (c)   When the Indian forces have been reduced to the minimum strength mentioned in (a) above, arrange in consultation with the Commission for the stationing of the remaining forces to be carried out in accordance with the following principles:
       (i)   That the presence of troops should not afford any intimidation or appearance of intimidation to the inhabitants of the State;
       (ii)   That as small a number as possible should be retained in forward areas;
       (iii) That any reserve of troops which may be included in the total strength should be located within their present base area.

3. The Government of India should agree that until such time as the Plebiscite Administration referred to below finds it necessary to exercise the powers of direction and supervision over the State forces and police provided for in paragraph 8, they will be held in areas to be agreed upon with the Plebiscite Administrator.

4. After the plan referred to in paragraph 2 (a) above has been put into operation, personnel recruited locally in each district should so far as possible be utilized for the re-establishment and maintenance of law and order with due regard to protection of minorities, subject to such additional requirements as may be specified by the Plebiscite Administration referred to in paragraph 7.

5. If these local forces should be found to be inadequate, the Commission, subject to the agreement of both the Government of India and the Government of Pakistan, should arrange for the use of such forces of either Dominion as it deems effective for the purpose of pacification.

B. Plebiscite

6. The Government of India should undertake to ensure that the Government of the State invite the major political groups to designate responsible representatives to share equitably and fully in the conduct of the administration at the ministerial level while the plebiscite is being prepared and carried out.

7. The Government of India should undertake that there will be established in Jammu and Kashmir a Plebiscite Administration to hold a plebiscite as soon as possible on the question of the accession of the State to India or Pakistan.

8. The Government of India should undertake that there will be delegated by the State to the Plebiscite Administration such powers as the latter considers necessary for holding a fair and impartial plebiscite including, for that purpose only, the direction and supervision of the State forces and police.

9. The Government of India should, at the request of the Plebiscite Administration, make available from the Indian forces such assistance as the Plebiscite Administration may require for the performance of its functions.

10. (a) The Government of India should agree that a nominee of the Secretary-General of the United Nations will be appointed to be the Plebiscite Administrator.

    (b) The Plebiscite Administrator, acting as an officer of the State of Jammu and Kashmir, should have authority to nominate his assistants and other subordinates and to draft regulations governing the plebiscite. Such nominees should be formally appointed and such draft regulations should be formally promulgated by the State of Jammu and Kashmir.

    (c)   The Government of India should undertake that the Government of Jammu and Kashmir will appoint fully qualified persons nominated by the Plebiscite Administrator to act as special magistrates within the State judicial system to hear cases which in the opinion of the Plebiscite Administrator have a serious bearing on the preparation for and the conduct of a free and impartial plebiscite.

    (d)   The terms of service of the Administrator should form the subject of a separate negotiation between the Secretary-General of the United Nations and the Government of India. The Administrator should fix the terms of service for his assistants and subordinates.

    (e)   The Administrator should have the right to communicate directly with the Government of the State and with the Commission of the Security Council and, through the Commission, with the Security Council, with the Governments of India and Pakistan and with their representatives with the Commission. It would be his duty to bring to the notice of any or all of the foregoing (as he in his discretion may decide) any circumstances arising which may tend, in his opinion, to interfere with the freedom of the plebiscite.

11. The Government of India should undertake to prevent, and to give full support to the Administrator and his staff in preventing, any threat, coercion or intimidation, bribery or other undue influence on the voters in the plebiscite, and the Government of India should publicly announce and should cause the Government of the State to announce this undertaking as an international obligation binding on all public authorities and officials in Jammu and Kashmir.

12. The Government of India should themselves and through the Government of the State declare and make known that all subjects of the State of Jammu and Kashmir, regardless of creed, caste or party, will be safe and free in expressing their views and in voting on the question of the accession of the State and that there will be freedom of the press, speech and assembly and freedom of travel in the State, including freedom of lawful entry and exit.

13. The Government of India should use and should ensure that the Government of the State also use their best endeavours to effect the withdrawal from the State of all Indian nationals other than those who are normally resident therein or who on or since 15 August 1947 have entered it for a lawful purpose.

14. The Government of India should ensure that the Government of the State releases all political prisoners and take all possible steps so that:

    (a)   All citizens of the State who have left it on account of disturbances are invited, and are free, to return to their homes and to exercise their rights as such citizens;

    (b)   There is no victimization;

    (c)   Minorities in all parts of the State are accorded adequate protection.

15. The Commission of the Security Council should at the end of the plebiscite certify to the Council whether the plebiscite has or has not been really free and impartial.

C. General provisions

16. The Governments of India and Pakistan should each be invited to nominate a representative to be attached to the Commission for such assistance as it may require in the performance of its task.
17. The Commission should establish in Jammu and Kashmir such observers as it may require of any of the proceedings in pursuance of the measures indicated in the foregoing paragraphs.
18. The Security Council Commission should carry out the tasks assigned to it herein.

Adopted at the 286th meeting.

Note: The draft resolution was voted on paragraph by paragraph. No vote was taken on the text as a whole.

Source: http://unscr.com/en/resolutions/47

Appendix 13

Extracts from the 18th amendment of Pakistan's constitution in 2010 related to Pakistan's national security state

The Constitution (Eighteenth Amendment) Act, 2010

ACT NO. X of 2010

(April 19, 2010)

An Act further to amend the Constitution of the Islamic Republic of Pakistan

WHEREAS it is expedient further to amend the Constitution of the Islamic Republic of Pakistan for the purposes hereinafter appearing;

AND WHEREAS the people of Pakistan have relentlessly struggled for democracy and for attaining the ideals of a Federal, Islamic, democratic, parliamentary and modern progressive welfare State, wherein the rights of the citizens are secured and the Provinces have equitable share in the Federation;

AND WHEREAS it is necessary that the Legal Framework Order, 2002, as amended by the Chief Executive's Order No. 29 and the Chief Executive's Order No. 32 of 2002, be declared as having been made without lawful authority and of no legal effect, and the Constitution (Seventeenth Amendment) Act, 2003 (Act No. III of 2003), be repealed and the Constitution further amended to achieve the aforesaid objectives;

It is hereby enacted as follows:

1. **Short title and commencement.**—(1) This Act may be called the Constitution (Eighteenth Amendment) Act, 2010.

   (2) It shall come into force at once, save as otherwise provided in this Act.

2. **Repeal, etc.- Subject to Article 264 and the provisions of the Constitution (Eighteenth Amendment) Act, 2010.**
   (a) the Legal Framework Order, 2002 (Chief Executive's Order No. 24 of 2002), the Legal Framework (Amendment) Order, 2002 (Chief Executive's Order No. 29 of 2002) and the Legal Framework (Second

Amendment) Order, 2002 (Chief Executive's Order No. 32 of 2002), are hereby declared to have been made without lawful authority and of no legal effect and, therefore, shall stand repealed; and

(b) the Constitution (Seventeenth Amendment) Act, 2003 (Act No. III of 2003), is hereby repealed.

3. **Amendment of Article 1 of the Constitution.**—In the Constitution of the Islamic Republic of Pakistan, hereinafter referred to as the Constitution, in Article 1, in clause (2), in paragraph (a), for the word "Baluchistan" the word "Balochistan," for the words "North West Frontier" the words "Khyber Pakhtunkhwa," and for the word "Sind" the word "Sindh," shall be substituted.

4. **Amendment of Article 6 of the Constitution.**- In the Constitution, in Article 6, —

(i) for clause (1), the following shall be substituted, namely: —

"(1) Any person who abrogates or subverts or suspends or holds in abeyance, or attempts or conspires to abrogate or subvert or suspend or hold in abeyance, the Constitution by use of force or show of force or by any other unconstitutional means shall be guilty of high treason."

(ii) in clause (2), after the word "abetting" the word "or collaborating" shall be inserted; and

(iii) after clause (2) amended as aforesaid, the following new clause shall be inserted, namely:

"(2A) An act of high treason mentioned in clause (1) or clause (2) shall not be validated by any court including the Supreme Court and a High Court."

5. **Insertion of new Article in the Constitution.**—In the Constitution, after Article 10, the following new Article shall be inserted, namely:—

"10A. Right to fair trial.—For the determination of his civil rights and obligations or in any criminal charge against him a person shall be entitled to a fair trial and due process."

6. **Substitution of Article 17 of the Constitution.**—In the Constitution, for Article 17, the following shall be substituted, namely:–

"17. Freedom of association. (1) Every citizen shall have the right to form associations or unions, subject to any reasonable restrictions imposed by law in the interest of sovereignty or integrity of Pakistan, public order or morality.

(2) Every citizen, not being in the service of Pakistan, shall have the right to form or be a member of a political party, subject to any reasonable restrictions imposed by law in the interest of the sovereignty or integrity of Pakistan and such law shall provide that where the Federal Government declares that any political party has been formed or is operating in a manner prejudicial to the sovereignty or integrity of Pakistan, the Federal Government shall, within

fifteen days of such declaration, refer the matter to the Supreme Court whose decision on such reference shall be final.

(3) Every political party shall account for the source of its funds in accordance with law."

7. **Insertion of new Article in the Constitution.**—In the Constitution, after Article 19, the following new Article shall be inserted, namely: —

"19A. Right to information.—Every citizen shall have the right to have access to information in all matters of public importance subject to regulation and reasonable restrictions imposed by law."

8. **Amendment of Article 25 of the Constitution.**—In the Constitution, in Article 25, in clause (2), the word "alone" occurring at the end shall be omitted

9. **Insertion of new Article in the Constitution.**—In the Constitution, after Article 25, the following new Article shall be inserted, namely:

"25A. Right to education.—The State shall provide free and compulsory education to all children of the age of five to sixteen years in such manner as may be determined by law."

10. **Amendment of Article 27 of the Constitution.**—In the Constitution, in Article 27, in clause (1), in the second proviso, for the full stop at the end a colon shall be substituted and thereafter the following proviso shall be inserted, namely: —

"Provided also that under-representation of any class or area in the service of Pakistan may be redressed in such manner as may be determined by an Act of Majlis-e-Shoora (Parliament)."

11. **Amendment of Article 29 of the Constitution.**—In the Constitution, in Article 29, in clause (3), for the word "the National Assembly" occurring for the first time the words and brackets, "each House of Majlis-e-Shoora (Parliament)" shall be substituted and after the word "National Assembly" occurring for the second time the words "and the Senate" shall be inserted.

12. **Amendment of Article 38 of the Constitution.**—In the Constitution, in Article 38, —
    (i) in paragraph (e), the word "and" at the end shall be omitted;
    (ii) in paragraph (f), for the full stop at the end a semicolon and the word ";and" shall be added and after paragraph (f) amended as aforesaid, the following new paragraph shall be added, namely: —

"(g) ensure that the shares of the Provinces in all Federal services, including autonomous bodies and corporations established by, or under the control of, the Federal Government, shall be secured and any omission in the allocation of the shares of the Provinces in the past shall be rectified."

13. **Amendment of Article 41 of the Constitution.**—In the Constitution, in Article 41,–
    (i) in clause (3), the words, brackets and figure "to be elected after the term specified in clause (7)" shall be omitted; and
    (ii) clauses (7), (8) and (9) shall be omitted.

14. **Substitution of Article 46 of the Constitution.**—In the Constitution, for Article 46, the following shall be substituted namely:

    "46. President to be kept informed.- The Prime Minister shall keep the President informed on all matters of internal and foreign policy and on all legislative proposals the Federal Government intends to bring before Majlis-e-Shoora (Parliament)."

15. **Amendment of Article 48 of the Constitution.**- In the Constitution, in Article 48,—
    (i) In clause (1), —
        (a) after the word "act" the words "on and" shall be inserted; and
        (b) in the proviso, after the word "that" the words "within fifteen days" shall be inserted and after the word "shall" the commas and words ",within ten days," shall be inserted; and
    (ii) for clause (5) the following shall be substituted, namely: —

    "(5) Where the President dissolves the National Assembly, notwithstanding anything contained in clause (1), he shall, —
        (a) appoint a date, not later than ninety days from the date of the dissolution, for the holding of a general election to the Assembly; and
        (b) appoint a care-taker Cabinet."
    (iii) for clause (6) the following shall be substituted, namely: —

    "(6). If at any time the Prime Minister considers it necessary to hold a referendum on any matter of national importance, he may refer the matter to a joint sitting of the Majlis-e-Shoora (Parliament) and if it is approved in a joint sitting, the Prime Minister may cause such matter to be referred to a referendum in the form of a question that is capable of being answered .by either 'Yes' or 'No.'"

16. **Substitution of Article of the Constitution.**—In the Constitution, for Article 58, the following shall be substituted, namely:—

    "58. Dissolution of the National Assembly.—(1) The President shall dissolve the National Assembly if so advised by the Prime Minister; and the National Assembly shall, unless sooner dissolved, stand dissolved at the expiration of forty-eight hours after the Prime Minister has so advised.

    Explanation.- Reference in this Article to 'Prime Minister' shall not be construed to include reference to a Prime Minister against whom a notice of a resolution for a vote of no-confidence has been given in the National

Assembly but has not been voted upon or against whom such a resolution has been passed or who is continuing in office after his resignation or after the dissolution of the National Assembly.

(2) Notwithstanding anything contained in clause (2) of Article 48, the President may also dissolve the National Assembly in his discretion where, a vote of no-confidence having been passed against the Prime Minister, no other member of the National Assembly commands the confidence of the majority of the members of the National Assembly in accordance with the provisions of the Constitution, as ascertained in a session of the National Assembly summoned for the purpose."

90. Substitution of Article 243 in the Constitution.—In the Constitution, for Article 243, the following shall be substituted, namely:—

"243. Command of Armed Forces.—(1) The Federal Government shall have control and command of the Armed Forces.

(2) Without prejudice to the generality of the foregoing provision, the Supreme Command of the Armed Forces shall vest in the President.
(3) The President shall subject to law, have power —
   (a) to raise and maintain the Military, Naval and Air Forces of Pakistan; and the Reserves of such Forces; and
   (b) to grant Commissions in such Forces.
(4) The President shall, on advice of the Prime Minister, appoint —
   (c) the Chairman, Joint Chiefs of Staff Committee;
   (d) the Chief of the Army Staff;
   (e) the Chief of the Naval Staff; and
   (f) the Chief of the Air Staff,

and shall also determine their salaries and allowances."

Source: National Assembly of Pakistan, www.na.gov.pk/uploads/documents/130 2138356_934.pdf

Index

For Product Safety Concerns and Information please contact our EU
representative GPSR@taylorandfrancis.com
Taylor & Francis Verlag GmbH, Kaufingerstraße 24, 80331 München, Germany

www.ingramcontent.com/pod-product-compliance
Lightning Source LLC
Chambersburg PA
CBHW071601110726
47908CB00007B/2195